THE

She-Hulk

DIARIES

THE

She-Hulk

DIARIES

MARTA ACOSTA

HYPERION

NEW YORK

marvel.com

TM & © 2013 Marvel and Subs.

Library of Congress Cataloging-in-Publication Data

Acosta, Marta.
    The she-hulk diaries / Marta Acosta. — First edition.
        pages   cm
    ISBN 978-1-4013-1101-8
  1. Women heroes—Fiction. 2. Superheroes—Fiction. I. Title.
    PS3601.C67S54   2013
    813'.6—dc23

                                 2012042184

Book design by Judith Stagnitto Abbate / Abbate Design

FIRST EDITION

10   9   8   7   6   5   4   3   2   1

SUSTAINABLE FORESTRY INITIATIVE   Certified Sourcing   www.sfiprogram.org   SFI-00993

THIS LABEL APPLIES TO TEXT STOCK

We try to produce the most beautiful books possible, and we are also
extremely concerned about the impact of our manufacturing process
on the forests of the world and the environment as a whole.
Accordingly, we've made sure that all of the paper we use has been
certified as coming from forests that are managed, to ensure the
protection of the people and wildlife dependent upon them.

THE

She-Hulk

DIARIES

OPENING STATEMENT

JANUARY 1

The problem with New Year's Resolutions is that you're expected to make tectonic lifestyle changes immediately after the holidays, when your brain is as lumpy and dried out as a slice of fruitcake that someone shoved under the sofa. When I advise a client who is in a state of physical/mental/emotional exhaustion, I always say, "Take time to decide your priorities. Write down your goals so that you can stay on target and identify problems."

That's why I'm starting this year by keeping a record of my own activities. I'll make a special effort to accurately transcribe conversations so they won't get jumbled in my head when I replay them over and over. I wish life was like being in court: because I can drill someone under oath and have the stenographer keep a record.

Ruth gave me this journal when I stopped by the Avengers Mansion to sign several hundred Christmas cards with "oxox, She-Hulk, aka Shulky" in her childish loopy script. Ruth reminds me of a summer camp counselor, but in a good way, with her khaki pleated pants and pastel polo shirts. I love her carrot-top curls and bright blue eyes that are always open in OMG! amazement.

"She-Hulk was supposed to do this herself," I said. "These are for *her* VIP pals, not mine."

"Here's something for you, Jen!" Ruth handed me this journal with the cute stripey kitten hanging from a branch on the cover.

I assumed she'd grabbed it from the LAST MINUTE GIFTS! display, but Ruth said, "I know things haven't been easy for you lately, what with all the conflict with the others . . ."

"I don't take it personally," I said. "She-Hulk's not as responsible as they are, so it's natural that they'd get tired of her antics."

Ruth reached over and patted my hand. "She's so OMG! rambunctious and exciting. I don't worry about her, and I was a little worried about you, but I'm sure this year will be totally awesome if you *keep hanging in there!*"

I thanked her and was already intending to re-gift this journal, when Ruth added, "You know the reason I like cats so much? Besides their amazing fluffiness! It's because they have an internal gyroscope — no matter how far they fall, they figure out a way to land on their feet, just like you!"

I informed Ruth that I didn't even have a job, and she was good enough to point out that I'd lost several positions in the past, always managing to go on to better ones. She's right. I'm not going to let the dark winter weather get me down. I'm going to be like that fluffy kitten and be brave enough to take ~~an honest~~ a ruthless assessment of my life so that I can improve it:

CURRENT STATUS: No job, no boyfriend, no permanent place to live, no car, and most of my clothes are held together with staples and duct tape. Bank account almost wiped out. Many of my former associates have expressed a desire that I never darken their doorways again for legal and financial reasons.

She-Hulk ~~got us~~ got us kicked out of the Avengers Mansion. People keep posting videos online of her New Year's Eve shenanigans: twirling flaming telephone poles in Times Square, climbing the Empire State Building while dangling Anderson Cooper, dancing wildly at parties, and commandeering a motorcycle cop's ride to do wheelies across the Brooklyn Bridge.

POSITIVES: Excellent health. Don't smoke, floss daily, exercise and train regularly. Allowed to store weapons collection at the Mansion. Allowed access to Mansion's fleet of vehicles. I have the use of fantastic corporate loft with a private elevator that goes directly from my foyer to a secret subbasement entrance.

I think the private elevator is worth bonus positive points — since I'm the one who has to sneak back home in shredded clothes and clean up the trail of wreckage that Shulky leaves in her wake.

That is why I've made a decision that's as huge as She-Hulk's ginormous inflated ego. I'm not relying on her anymore to live my life. Okay, I've made this New Year's Resolution ~~once occasionally~~ frequently before. I am a bright and accomplished woman — so why do I always slip up and revert to being a six-foot-seven, jade-green party girl/superhero? Even the other superheroes don't want to deal with her anymore, not that she cares.

If that happened to me, I would totally care. My reputation means everything to me.

After considerable deliberation, I've decided that my problem is that I try to adhere to life-altering resolutions *too* soon. Marathoners train for months and carbo load before the actual race. Medical students practice on cadavers before operating on a patient. Attorneys draft outlines before drawing up a suit. So doesn't it make absolutely perfect sense to allow myself a warm-up period before challenging myself with extremely difficult goals? Yes!

Instead of New Year's Resolutions, I am setting Valentine's Day Resolutions. Now I have an entire month and a half to prepare for them.

I have narrowed down my list to these important goals.

VALENTINE'S DAY RESOLUTIONS

I, Jennifer Susan Walters, being of sound mind ~~and body bodies~~ *whatever* do promise to try to achieve the following life-improving objectives beginning February 14:

1. Stop hanging around the loft playing online games (take sabbatical from Skyrim, BF3, Massive Threat, etc.) and get a new job as myself: apply to my five top dream legal firms. Update CV. Replenish business wardrobe with clothes that can survive hulking out.

2. Meet an actual human man and establish an actual relationship. He should: (a) be employed, (b) have a sense of humor, (c) like me no matter how I look that day, (d) not be attempting to rule the galaxy, and (e) be considerate (e.g., remember to put the toilet seat down). Cancel account with Smingles.com because they match me with smorons. ~~Stop~~ ~~Severely restrict~~ Moderate cyber-stalking and crank calling exes.

3. Have a *real* date on Valentine's Day: flowers, lingerie, the whole deal. Going out for burgers with my cousin again DOES NOT COUNT.

4. Seek balance in work environment and social life. Have fun *and* learn how to speak up for myself without doing anything that will get me fired. Participate in more activities and get more culture: buy membership to Met, go to opera, ballet, and theater. Join a book club?

5. Stretch outside my comfort zone. Don't automatically reject opportunities to do something new and different especially if there's a chance to meet friends/boyfriend.

I'm totally psyched to take control of my life and I'm determined that my new year will be the best one yet!

JANUARY 2

Bought tickets to see *Wicked* again, so I'm off to a great start culturewise! If people can get over initial ookiness to green skin, they'd realize that most green ~~people~~ sentient beings have wonderful qualities. Case in point: Kermit the Frog.

JANUARY 3

Took my last remaining good suit to the dry cleaner. They said they can fix the ripped seams. Then I went to the bookstore, where bleary holiday survivors hovered around the self-help section, all of us hoping to go from good to great.

I skimmed through several books and there seemed to be a surfeit of banal encouragements and/or magical thinking. I thought everyone knew by now that magical thinking only works if you actually possess magical powers. Even Dr. Doom prefers to use gadgetry to achieve his nefarious ends because Murphy's Law always applies where magic is concerned. That's why I advise my clients, "Although casting an enchantment or invocation seems like a shortcut, I strongly recommend that you avoid magic because it has deeply regrettable blowback consequences."

Then I had brainstorm #2.

Doesn't it make sense for me to follow my own expert advice instead of taking advice from a stranger who probably made up his credentials? Yes! I was excitedly thinking about the brilliant guidance I could give myself when I received a high-priority message.

Text from Dahlia: Meet me @ Laundromat STAT!! Bring
Korean tacos & raspberry Joocey Jooce!

I bought kitten-hanging-from-a-branch supplies (calendar, notebooks, pencil case, pencils) and slogged out into the frigid sludgy day. I followed Dahlia's link to a nearby food truck, got two plates of food, and extra Sriracha, kimchee, and lime wedges.

Even though I walked by three Joocey Jooces on my way to Delancey Street, they all had lines out the door. I'll never understand New Yorkers: people were shivering on the sidewalk to buy cold fruit smoothies.

The blast of heat from the Laundromat thawed me out. Dahlia was ignoring the "Do not sit on folding table!" sign and wearing a black mini-skirt, spiderweb stockings, platform boots, and a gray security guard jacket. Her short spiky hair was electric blue today and so were her contacts, making her look like an anime character.

As I approached her, I heard a nasty yipping from the Juicy Couture bag on the floor.

"Hey, Dahl, what's the emergency?"

"I'm critically hungry. Where's my drink?"

"I wasn't going to wait in line at Joocey Jooce. Or like they say here, *on* line. That doesn't even make sense." Naturally, the tacos were cold, but still tasty. After I'd eaten one, I said, "Okay, why are we here?"

"Rodney did a revenge piss on the comforter after I took him to the groomer, and the big machine at the salon is broken. Rodney doesn't even look that bad. See for yourself."

The small dog growled at the sound of his name.

"I'm not sticking my hand in that bag. He bit me the last time."

She scrunched her face. Girls as petite and pretty as Dahlia can scrunch their faces and still look cute. If I scrunch my face, I look like I'm suffering from irritable bowel syndrome. "Don't be such a sissy, Jen. He's got itty-bitty little teeth. They don't hurt that much."

"I am *not* a sissy. Azzan says I'm his most fearless student. But it's not as if I can body slam that glorified rat when he attacks."

"Is Azzan your sex therapist? Do you body slam him?" She slapped her palms together and pulled them away while making a horrid sucking sound.

"Hardy-har-har. I body slam him because he's my Krav Maga coach. You're sick."

"I'm normal, and you are a perplexing blend of kick-ass chick and honor-roll nerd. How was your Christmas?"

"Beyond dismal. My dad's condo is so motel-generic and grim that I kept looking around for chalk outlines of bodies. It was smoggy, and my cousin and I sat by the pool and drank lukewarm eggnog from a carton."

"How is Bruce? The last time I saw him, he looked seething in a very intriguing way, like he was about to erupt, but maybe trying to teach science to teenagers has that effect."

"He's always had anger issues," I said, so she wouldn't get any ideas about him. "It's hard to tell with Bruce, because he's not exactly 'peppy' — one of my mom's favorite words — but he seemed as morose as I felt."

"No wonder — Lost Angeles! Smell-A! Hell-A," Dahlia sneered. "My years there were a nightmare of enduring bleached blond hair-tossing and 'Hi, I'm Wendy!' Grown men wear shorts all year round. Ugh."

"You're a terrible snob for a girl from El Paso. You met *me* at UCLA."

"Being your roomie and clubbing in West Hollywood were the only things that kept me sane. Even then I had to self-medicate."

"Yes, I remember when I had my wisdom teeth removed and you appropriated my Percocet for your alleged psychic pain. How was your Christmas?"

"It was like Sarajevo but with endless football games, tamales, and lumpia. All the ethnic and religious factions sniped at one another. My parents got in a shouting match about the best way to peel a potato, I kid you not. Total spud wars between the moms and pops! That's what happens when you live with someone too long — you look for drama in the minute random shit."

Dahlia had left her radishes on the paper plate so I snagged them. "One, stop being so dour. Two, I like your new hair color, but the turquoise contact lenses make you look like you're trying to mesmerize people. And, three, I came up with a list of personal resolutions that will begin to take effect Valentine's Day."

"Sounds fascinating. Can you elaborate, Counselor?"

I described my plan and my goals, leaving out the She-Hulk details. Dahlia thought they were genius, but she'd also convinced me to wear lederhosen and pigtails once to a dorm Oktoberfest dinner, so she's not the most reliable judge.

She swung her pixie legs and said, "Starting on Valentine's Day seems completely arbitrary. Why not go for the gusto now, and if you slide back, you can start again."

"That never works. I think it's like the Hokey Pokey. You can put your left foot in and your left foot out, but at a certain point you realize you're going in circles and abandon the greater plan of action."

She grinned. "That incisive mind is why you get paid the big bucks — when you actually have a job. Let's move on to a more fascinating topic. Where are you going to find a boyfriend, Jen? Should I go through my client list? I have a top-secret grid that grades every interesting man on an extensive range of talents — from A for abdominals to Z for zexterity."

When I made a face, she said, "Zexterity is zen plus sex plus dexterity — it's for laid-back guys with tantric endurance, but frankly I don't like getting friction blisters on my girly parts."

"After all these years, Dahl, you still enjoy squicking me out. The people who go to your salon are all too trendy. I want someone . . ."

"Dull as a tater tot? Bland and processed as instant mashed?"

"So you're committed to the tuber theme?" She nodded and I said, "I want someone as hot, crisp, and irresistible as excellent *pommes frites*."

"You say that, but you only go out with megalomaniacs or drips."

"Tony Stark isn't a megalomaniac or a drip," I said, even though Tony thrives on the massive attention he gets as Iron Man while most of us prefer to keep our human identities secret.

"Please, Jen. The most important thing I got from my history degree is an ability to recognize the narcissistic personality disorder that is characteristic in dictators. I will concede that he does have fantastic hair."

I agreed that his hair is fantastic, and she quizzed me about how he achieved the look, and I admitted that he woke up with fantastic hair, and she discussed natural wave, texture, and hue, before returning to the previous subject and saying, "You never date anyone interesting and creative."

We watched the comforter spinning around in the industrial dryer and I said, "I have so. Ellis Tesla."

She let out a hoot that set Rodney to barking. "You're calling the one time you had a weekend hookup a date?"

"It may have been a hookup, but we had serious, meaningful talks."

"Naked talks always seem deep. Yeah, Ellis Tesla was ten kinds of hot. Did you ever find out where he went?"

"The last known sighting of Ellis and Fringe Theory was at that concert in Oslo when they proved that they could destroy a tank by precisely targeting pumpkins from a catapult. Ellis was fond of medieval weaponry in general, and catapults in particular. I've visited — okay, snooped around — MIT alumni sites, but no one's telling his real name. I looked for anagrams of Ellis Tesla, but can't find any Leslie Lasts or Teasel Sills. For all I know, Fringe Theory might not even be on Earth anymore."

She patted my arm. "I don't know what it says about a drunken hookup — I mean *meaningful relationship* — when the guy won't even stay on the planet for a second drunken weekend — I mean *significant liaison.*"

I gave her a warning look. "Dahlia, you do know that I can grab you by your peewee ankles, hold you upside down, and then shove you into that dog carrier bag and let Rodney bite you all over until your guts leak out like spaghetti sauce in a colander?"

She grinned. "He wouldn't do that because his doggy brain senses that any other pet-sitter would flush him down the toilet. How come you never talk to other people like that?"

"Because I'm shy."

"Only when it's convenient for you to avoid things you don't want to do. Add this to your list of goals—'Learn to talk to people like I talk to Dahlia'?"

"That might be fun, but I'd never get past the first round in a job interview."

"Well, I do like it when you get a paycheck and can support me in the manner to which I've become accustomed, i.e., food truck lunches." She reached over to look in the bag from the bookstore. "A cat calendar? Is becoming a cat lady one of your resolutions?"

"It's a gift for Ruth. You met her once when we toured the Avengers Mansion, remember?"

"The one who always talks like everything is OMG! AMAZING!"

I nodded. "Yes, she handles all of She-Hulk's admin work, and she's always really nice to me."

"You and your fancy-ass friends at the Mansion. When are you going to introduce me to She-Hulk?"

I have thought long and hard about telling D the truth about Shulky and me, but she's safer not knowing my secrets. "My relationship with her is strictly business. All we talk is contract law. It's as exciting as supermarket potato salad."

D gave me one of her skeptical *huh*s and then made me promise to come to dinner and watch a movie with her. I said yes, even though she only chooses movies based on historically significant hairstyles, like *Shampoo* and *Love Story*.

As part of my wardrobe makeover, I went to Mood Fabrics. I wandered around hoping to spot my imaginary gay boyfriend, Tim Gunn, but no luck.

A supercute clerk was very helpful, and after talking to me for a few minutes, he recommended iron-on tape that he said "looks as good as sewing to most people" and a variety pack of safety pins. He also gave me the name of a designer who specializes in what he called "breakaway costumes." I guess that's a technical term.

Feel as if I've made important inroads in preparation to beginning my resolutions!

JANUARY 5

I called Holden's office at 6:30 a.m. and he answered, "Goodman, Lieber, Kurtzberg, & Holliway. Holden Holliway here."

Holden never answers his own office line, and I was so shocked I blurted, "What are you doing answering the phone and so early?"

"Jennifer, is that you? I haven't left from last night. What are *you* doing calling this early?"

"I was going to leave a message." After an awkward pause, I said, "I'm applying for positions at other firms and I was wondering . . ."

"You were wondering if I'd have a drink with you and we could discuss things."

Holden is a crafty bastard. "Yes, that's *exactly* what I was wondering."

"Will you be coming or will your glamorous jade friend meet me?"

It's a relief to talk to one of the few people who knows both my identities and prefers me. "It will be me. I'd like to try to stay Jennifer more often this year."

"I can't say that I mind. Shulky's a real pistol, but at my age, I prefer a rubber chicken." He named a bar I'd never heard of and said, "Seven p.m. Be there or be square!"

Did that mean that Holden thought *I* was the rubber chicken?

6:00 P.M.

The weather was miserable and cold. I didn't want to go out, especially since there was a *Hoarders* marathon on TV, but I put on a businessy-type pantsuit and yanked on waterproof boots. I was taking a chance because boots are always a problem if I have to shift.

I schlepped to First Street, shivering against the sleet, and arrived at a grimy little dive. I peered in the window to make sure it was the right address and spotted Holden immediately since his snowy hair practically glowed in the murk. I stepped into the dark bar and hung my coat on the rack. There was a distinct pickled smell in the air, but I couldn't tell if it was the ancient wooden floorboards or the patrons.

Holden waved to me and I went back to his booth and slid in across from him. We did the handshake-and-hello thing, and when a brimming martini was set in front of me, he said, "Jennifer, come back to GLKH and work for me."

I'd just taken a sip of the martini, which tasted like paint stripper and Pine-Sol, and I started coughing. When I'd gotten my breath back, I said, "Absence makes the heart et cetera, Holden. I'd like to work at a more normal place for a while, where every case isn't an end-of-the-world-type calamity."

"Come on, Jennifer — I'm going to establish a new specialty branch and you know you loved the excitement."

"It was fun pounding my fist on a table and challenging witnesses, but I'm trying to be more professional and resolve issues without things going ballistic."

"It's nice to have good intentions, Jen," he said, and then his expression grew more somber. "Did you hear the news that the latest clone twins died? It happened this afternoon, and they still had the balloons in their rooms from their second birthday party. Total organ failure."

We were quiet for a minute, and I said, "It's cruel and unethical to keep growing them when they just die."

"We can't ignore the inevitable. Clones will soon be as viable as the robot maid. Per usual, the law is far behind technology. Right now, cyborgs can't even vote or marry."

"You know that I believe in full civil rights for alternative human entities, Holden."

"Yes, but it's good to hear it again," he said. "You look like you've got something on your mind."

The voices at the bar got louder. Two burly men were shouting and shoving each other.

I smiled at Holden and hoped I looked friendly, not panicky. "Actually, I wanted to make sure I could give your name as a reference since I left in such— Well, I understand that the final bill for damages was unexpected. However, I will point out that I won every one of my cases."

"My accounting team already gave me a big binder with the cost/expense breakdown to the penny, but I told them to recycle it. You'll always be a valuable asset in my eyes." A stool was thrown against the mirror over the bar and shattered glass crashed down. Holden glanced at the commotion and said, "They're getting pretty noisy. Jen, do you mind?"

I needed his job reference, so I said, "Of course not, sir." I slipped off my jacket and went to the bar.

One man was holding a beer bottle and the other was waving his hands and saying, "Come on! Come and try, asshole!" Each was drunk, angry, and solidly built.

I cleared my throat and said, "Erm," but they didn't notice. I had to step close to them and speak louder. "Uhm, gentlemen, would you mind keeping it down a bit? It's difficult for others to have a conversation."

One laughed and said, "Oooh, a *conversation!*" and the other one said, "Mind your own business, girlie!"

If he'd said that to She-Hulk, she would have snatched him up and thrown him through the plate-glass window. "I really don't want to interfere with your—" I started, but the bottle-man swung at the come-on man.

I reached out and blocked the swing. One of them shouted, "Bitch!" because they always do, and tried to shove me with one of his germy hands, eww! I deflected the strike with an upward thrust of my forearm, which threw him off his balance. Then I jammed the butt of my palm directly into his solar plexus.

I couldn't enjoy watching him go "uh-uh-uh" and collapse backward because the come-on man screamed, "Whadidya do to my brother?" and charged me like a rhino.

I took a step aside, hooking my foot around his ankle to trip him. As he stumbled, I gave a firm chop to the back of his neck and let gravity do the rest. He landed on top of his brother.

By this time, the bartender had come forward with a Louisville slugger. "I'll take it from here. Thanks, ma'am," he said, and other customers came over to drag the brawlers out into the street.

I took a deep breath and went back to the booth.

"Jen, you're as pale as a ghost!" Holden said.

"He called me ma'am! Holden, am I really a ma'am?"

He had the nerve to laugh, but I knew the truth: once a girl gets her first "ma'am," her chances of ever getting an interesting, sexy, intelligent boyfriend are numbered. Tick-tock, tick-tock, tick-tock!

As if things weren't bad enough, Holden told me that the GLKH partners wanted to know when I planned to move out of the company loft. "I'd let you stay as long as you like, but as the premier firm specializing in superhuman law, our out-of-town and interplanetary guests have plenty of occasions to use a private elevator."

My heart skidded sideways as I thought fondly of the loft's panoramic windows with bulletproof glass, the heated floor, the deep whirlpool bathtub, and the elevator that allowed me to sneak in and out. I thought of the friendly doormen and the proximity to both Dahlia's salon and her longtime pet-sitting condo. "I really appreciate you letting me stay there."

"Frankly, I was hoping you or Shulky or the both of you would come back to GLKH and then we could work the transfer of the property into your signing bonus."

"Holden, I thought you didn't want Shulky working for you."

"Caught me. I don't, but only because she prefers using her muscle even when she could resolve a situation more calmly with her impressive brain. I'd sure like *you* back, though."

"You know I loved working for you, but the cases at GLKH require 24/7 involvement. I want to participate in activities other than intergalactic negotiations. I want to have a life outside of my profession."

"I understand." He patted my hand in that nice grandpa way of his. "There's no rush. Take your time finding another place."

We chatted a while longer, but I couldn't remember anything we talked about because I was FREAKING OUT. There are lots of things I don't like doing (tax returns, walk-of-super-shame barefoot and in shredded clothes after a hulk-out, yearly performance reviews at the Mansion), and moving was right there at the top of the list.

New priority resolution: find a new apartment as soon as I have a job and can pay deposits and rent.

10:30 P.M.

Extremely disturbed by Holden's rubber chicken comment. Also perturbed by being called ma'am. Have I become an old lady rubber chicken? Shulky is annoyed with me trying to analyze this, and she's grousing, which feels like someone is putting up drywall behind my eyes.

INFECTIOUS INVALIDITY

11:45 P.M.

I have one month and nine days until the actual starting date for my resolutions. I picked up my aPhone and sorted through Shulky's Tweets looking for invites. It's not as if I have to get up early tomorrow, since I really don't need to try to find a job just yet.

Fergie wanted to know if She-Hulk wanted to hit a few clubs in the Meat Packing District. Dancing *is* exercise and listening to music *is* a cultural experience, and the Meat Packing District *is* an important historical location.

JANUARY 6, 4:30 P.M.

Still in my pajamas but only because I've been working very hard on my goals. Sent off letters to top five dream firms. Okay, since the whole point of this journal is for me to be honest with myself, let me amend that. I sent letters to the top five law firms that haven't already told me to leave and not let the door hit my ass on the way out. Or to forget we ever met. Or that they can't miss me if I won't go away. There have been a lot of variations.

Did a preliminary search on Craigslist for an apartment, but became distracted by vacation rentals. I've been to outer space, but never to Paris.

What does that say about me? On my ~~date~~ ~~romance~~ hookup with Ellis Tesla, he'd invited me to join the band on their tour of France, and he said dirty things in French with that sexy smutty gravelly voice. *Le sigh.*

It's stupid to moon about a solitary weekend with him just because of the amazing sex and him singing to me and six-feet-five-inches of rock-solid flesh and brown-hazel eyes and conversations that were much too earnest for our brief acquaintance. Well, they were earnest for me, but he's had a million girls and promised them all sorts of things.

I must be doing something wrong romantically, because even Shulky's managed to sustain long-term boyfriends. I've only had sincere relationships that got me exactly nowhere.

I was about to add "Visit Paris" to my Valentine's Day list, but I didn't want to sabotage myself by getting overly ambitious. This way, if I do make it to Paris, I'll score bonus points. Maybe I should assign different goals different weights because finding a fantastic boyfriend will be quantitatively more difficult than finding an apartment, once I have a good job.

Do I want to ask D to help me create a calibrated grid? She's very good at that, but probably not, because she'll trap me in her flowchart, Venn diagram madness. Sometimes I regret ever encouraging her to take a statistics course.

While I wait for a response to job inquiries, I'm watching public television. Instead of squandering time/money going out, I am becoming more cultured, one of my goals, while wearing my pajamas. Three Tenors = triple opera points. And they sing *way* better than Ellis Tesla.

JANUARY 7

VALENTINE'S DAY RESOLUTION
COUNTDOWN: 1 MONTH AND 1 WEEK

Inspired by makeover shows, I went through my closet and pulled out all the clothes I'd never worn and never will wear — jackets with sleeves too short for my long monkey arms, skirts that were too narrow for a round-house kick, and revealing dresses that Dahlia convinced me to buy. She doesn't understand how high-powered attorneys are supposed to dress.

Superheroes have a different dress code, too. Shulky's PVC, Lycra, leather, sequined, and studded ensembles crammed the guest closets. She always dumps her clothes on the floor, expecting me to put away her thigh-high boots, spangled bikini bottoms, and chain-mail bras. One of her halter tops had something gross and sticky on it. I threw it away and scrubbed my hands with hot water and antibacterial soap.

What advice would I give someone whose messy roommate often saved the world? I'd say, "If finding another roommate is not an option, request compensation for your additional household chores." Well, that wouldn't work. "If you have no alternatives, try to see the totality of the relationship and not fixate on individual tasks. Does your roommate provide other services that you are not taking into account?"

Well, Shulky had hung the drapes and she always changed the light-bulbs without complaining. She kills scary spiders in the corners. She only eats out, so she never leaves dirty dishes. Frequently, she brings back bottles of expensive wine, which are useful as hostess gifts, and she always gets passes to movie previews. I didn't feel so irked as I organized her collection of BeDazzled booty shorts.

JANUARY 8

Revised/updated CV so it's ready to go if I get a response to my inquiries. Emailed it to Amy Stewart-Lee for her expert opinion. Ten minutes later Amy called me.

"Jen, it's so impressive! I sometimes forget all your accomplishments."

"People tend to remember the chaos," I said. "Did you find any typos?"

"No, but you might want to focus more on your Supreme Court win and not your extraterrestrial law because most firms want lawyers who'll remain on terra firma. You should remove your martial arts expertise from 'Other Interests.' You don't need to remind anyone of unfortunate courtroom incidents. Not that I blame you one bit. Lord knows, if I had your mad wrestling skills I'd constantly be putting opposing counsel in headlocks."

Amy gave me all the legal gossip from the DA's office, and she said, "Look, I know you've got your online gaming and your real superhuman pals, but the Forestiers, my LARP team — you know what that is, right?"

"Live-action role-playing. I'm actually cutting back on online games. I think I should have more RL interaction."

"What perfect timing! The Forestiers are having weekly meet-ups in preparation for our Mayfest battle games, and a few of our members moved away, so we're recruiting. We're an early Middle Ages team, based on Sherwood Forest legends. It would be great if you could come."

"Er . . ." I was trying to think of a way out.

"Don't *er* me, Jennifer Walters, Esquire! You always *er* before you let loose a scathing opposing argument. This is a way for normal people to enjoy creativity and questing in their lives. Knights and ladies, castles and magic, swords, costumes! We have scenarios and we practice fighting with weapons made of safety-approved materials."

I sighed and then hoped she couldn't hear me over the phone. One of my resolutions was to try new things and meet new people. "I really like Sherwood Forest stories. Okay, send me the information. This is not a setup, is it?"

"You are so weird about guys, in light of your adventurous dating history."

"I'm not adventurous. I met most boyfriends through jobs. Anyway, if it was a setup, that would be *okay*. I'm open to meeting new guys."

"That's a change! Most of our team are in relationships, but there are always drop-ins. I can check for single guys at work."

"None of your defendants, please. Allow me to clarify: I'm open to meeting new guys without a criminal history."

"Picky, picky! We charge so many elite perps, and if the bail is high enough, they're usually in town for a Saturday night date. I wish we could hire you here, but we're still getting claims from the time your client shot off lightning bolts in our conference room."

"That was definitely one of the downsides of working in the superhuman branch of Goodman, Lieber, Kurtzberg, & Holliway. Also, occasionally I got stuck in alternate dimensions."

"I hate when that happens. I'll put you on the Forestiers newsletter list and tell our game master to email you info and schedules."

After we hung up, I checked out the Forestiers' website and forum. I set about creating my own avatar and dubbed her LadyGreene.

AFTERNOON

Dragged myself to mandatory session with Dr. Rene Alvarado. It always strikes me as *not* funny that his brownstone is on West 4th, which was once called Asylum Street. He told me that, hardy har har, at my first session. He'd thought I'd ask for Kleenex and confess that I had some terrible dark secret and then he could write up my case in the *Journal of Superhuman Psychiatric Disorders*.

I sat in one leather chair and he sat in another. He looked like an escapee from a hippie lovefest with his Birkenstocks and wooden prayer bead necklaces. His tight wavy hair was as jet-black as it was in old photos. I wondered if he'd stopped his aging process through magic.

He was drinking a Joocey Jooce, which was so predictable, because he'd buy into their "Play nice!" marketing.

We did that standoff thing, waiting for the other to speak, and I won. Our conversation was the usual "So, Jennifer, I would like you to take this opportunity to discuss anything that's on your mind," and "Thank you, Dr. Alvarado, and please call me *Ms.* Walters," because I know about negotiating.

"*Ms.* Walters, you agreed to these meetings as part of your settlement with the Avengers Mansion Trust in order to work on your rage issues, so you have acknowledged that you have a problem."

"I made no such admission, Dr. Alvarado. She-Hulk has rage issues."

"Yet you choose to manifest as She-Hulk."

"Do we really have to go over this again? She-Hulk is the natural consequence of my exposure to gamma radiation."

"Is she?" He clicked his prayer beads against his teeth, which was really annoying. "There's no definitive proof that gamma radiation *always* exhibits in rage. Did you choose this bestial form because of repressed pain over your mother's murder?"

She-Hulk grumbled within me, but I knew Dr. Alvarado had used "bestial" to provoke a reaction. I didn't say anything, and he finally gave up waiting for me to respond.

"Let's move on, Jennifer."

"Ms. Walters."

"*Ms.* Walters." He gave me that fake, granola-eating, wavy-arm-dancing smile. "Most people look at the New Year as a time to reflect and reassess their lives, as well as make positive changes. Have you made any New Year's Resolutions?"

"No. New Year's Resolutions are designed to fail since they're made at a time when people are exhausted emotionally and physically."

"I see." Teeth-tapping ensued. "Do you plan to continue living exactly as before?"

I gave him my perjury-busting, let-me-rephrase-my-question fake smile. "I am presently seeking a new position at premier law firms. I am also balancing my life by exploring interests in the performing arts and international culinary arts, as well as staying fit with a disciplined exercise regimen."

"What about dating? She-Hulk's had significant relationships, but you haven't really dated anyone since, let's see . . ." he said and looked down at his file as if he didn't already know.

"I've joined a social group expressly for that purpose."

He didn't believe me, but I *had* told Amy that I wouldn't mind meeting men.

"What are your plans for She-Hulk? I mean, aside from her lively party schedule."

"Per usual, She-Hulk will always be available in times of municipal, state, national, planetary, and intergalactic crisis." Fake smile.

"I believe you're in denial about her situation. Hasn't she been asked to step away from those greater issues and resolve problems that are smaller in scope, like overturned vehicles and commuter tie-ups?"

I hated his passive-aggressive technique, and I wasn't going to say that, yes, Shulky had been demoted to a superstrong meter maid. Fake smile. "Shulky is a proud resident of New York and is delighted to be able to assist in matters great and small. Rest assured that she will act without hesitation to protect the inhabitants of this great city, state, nation, and Earth, including you, Dr. Alvarado."

"I was afraid of that."

Then we gave each other bogus smiles until my time was up.

JANUARY 9

Dahlia called and told me to get to the salon stat! She also gave me the location of a Moroccan food truck. I shuffled out in the freezing, drizzling day and got two plates of lamb, spicy merguez, and couscous, and two cups of mint tea.

Before I went into Dahlia's Arrested Youth, I checked out her new window display. She had arranged her collection of Barbies in a disturbing Spanish Inquisition-meets-Catholic schoolgirls tableau. Dr. Alvarado would love to get inside her twisty brain.

She was finishing up with a client, so I went back into the break room and picked up a *Vogue*. I was sipping hot sweet tea and studying an article about accentuating eyes for girls with glasses when she joined me.

"What's the emergency, Dahl?"

"Your hair. I was watching *Charlie's Angels* last night — the classic series not the supposedly ironic movie — and admiring Farrah's hair."

"Kindly don't go there. That hairstyle probably requires a dedicated staff and relentless upkeep."

"The classic Farrah required staff, but I'm going to reinterpret it for you."

"No."

"Yes."

"No."

"Yes, yes, yes, yes!" Dahlia scrambled up on a chair and pointed at me, saying, "I command you to submit to my greater hairstyle authority."

I might as well have argued with Rodney, who was on a pillow in the corner, licking his puny privates. I threw a piece of lamb to him. "I accept your stylistic authority, but I don't want anything high-maintenance. You need to keep it long so I can put it in a ponytail for the gym."

"If you took hula-hoop class with me, you could let your hair and your hips swing free."

I needed a trim anyway, so I let her have her way. I liked being in her salon and watching other clients in the mirrors, although they were all blurry with my glasses off. I told Dahlia, "Remember, I don't want it too short."

She handed me a new *Marie Claire* and said, "Shut up and let me work."

I flipped through the pages and stopped when I saw a feature on ReplaceMax.

Dahlia looked over my shoulder and said, "That ReplaceMax is pretty amazing."

"I'm surprised to see a story about an organ-cloning company in a fashion mag."

"Oh, the beauty community can't wait to use it for cosmetic applications."

"Seriously, Dahl? That seems fraught with problems. First, the company has been accused of falsifying test results to get early approval. Second, ReplaceMax grows organs, not eyebrows. Third, the price would be prohibitive. And fourth, people are claiming that ReplaceMax organs degrade. No one would want that."

She grinned. "A, did you actually say 'fraught'? B, beauty treatments are a natural extension of medical procedures. *Everyone* would want it, including men who want, uh, to be extended naturally. C, no one would care about the cost or if it would kill them. D, dermafillers and other treatments already degrade."

A woman sitting at the next station stared at us, and I sunk down into my seat, but her stylist told her, "Don't pay any attention to them. They're like weird twins who have a secret language."

My haircut? Awesome! So why did I always worry that Dahlia would hack off hunks at the back of my head?

ADVICE TO SELF: All beginning professionals make errors. Establish a relationship with someone who has learned from those errors, and trust in their experience.

4:00 P.M.

My hair is still fantastic, very full with lots of waves and feathery bangs. Since it looked so good, I headed over to Park Avenue to take Ruth the cat calendar. I stopped by a Joocey Jooce to buy a smoothie for her. Even though the shop was crowded, everyone smiled and waited patiently, which seemed strange for New Yorkers. The counter help were smiling and laughing, and their cheerfulness — and my new haircut — put me in a very hopeful mood.

The public spaces on the first floor of the Avengers Mansion were full of tourists per usual, but I was able to walk right through the crowd without anyone turning around. I felt a little like a tourist myself, still thrilled after all this time to be near the greatness of the superhero residents. It seemed impossible that I'd lived here, too, albeit existing inside She-Hulk, who didn't share my respect for the grand mansion. I think she did miss all the big assignments, though. It was as if she'd been on the board of directors and was now relegated to being a janitor.

The impressive curved banister on the stairs and the chandelier looked as if they'd never been demolished. The only trace of Shulky's last escapade was a faint discoloration on the ceiling from smoke damage when she built a bonfire with the antique, sixty-person dining set.

I ducked into a hall and used my bioprint to get access to the staircase. Ruth has moved into a roomy office on the third floor, but she's already covered the walls with photos of her herself and the Avengers. Ruth was on the phone, and she began wildly miming at her own head and mouthing "OMG, your hair!" when I came in. After she hung up, she said it aloud. "OMG, Jen, your hair looks AMAZING."

"Hi, Ruth. I just wanted to tell you that I'm back and to see how things are." I handed her the Joocey Jooce and the cat calendar and listened to five more minutes of OMGs and amazings! I sat in the guest chair, setting off the automassage, which began gently pulsating the tense places on my back. "I want to marry this chair."

"Everyone does." She tacked up the calendar beside another cat calendar on a bulletin board and beamed. "Can I tell you something privately? The Mansion is having a hovercraft derby and the others decided that it was best not to invite Shulky, but I know it would be okay if you came. You shouldn't be shut out because she's been sidelined."

I felt my face tighten, but I smiled. "What's a hovercraft derby?"

"Everyone will have personal hovercraft shoes. They're Mr. Stark's — I mean Tony's, because he told me to call him that — invention. He's such a genius! And I swear he gets better looking every year."

"I'm sure he thinks so, and thanks for inviting me, but I can't make it. Speaking of Tony, is he around?" I tried to sound casual.

NOTE TO SELF: *Stop* looking for excuses to see Tony! It is always the same:

- Five minutes of being dazzled by his brilliance and looks.
- Ten minutes of giving him free legal advice while being dazzled by his brilliance and looks.
- Fifteen minutes in which he argues with my advice because he's such a know-it-all, which immediately diminishes my appreciation of his dazzling brilliance and looks.
- Five minutes of defending my point of view before realizing that it would be easier just to kick his ass.

- Five minutes of him getting turned on by my anger and trying to get his hands under my clothes.
- Two minutes of caustic good-byes.

Ruth said, "No, the Pentagon called him away on a secret mission! It's so exciting. I'm sure he'll solve whatever problem it is." She frowned. "Jennifer, I got your message — are you really going to keep She-Hulk out of action? Won't you miss being superhuman?"

"I'm trying to balance my superhuman and human personas. Shulky doesn't need to be around on a daily basis, especially since the others have always treated her as if she's not in their league, because they're all such serious important crime fighters and she's, well, she's Shulky. I won't miss her partying hardy and waking up god-knows-where with god-knows-whom."

Ruth looked to the right and to the left, and then leaned toward me. "I think Shulky is AMAZING, but she doesn't seem to care that the guys here . . . I totally love them all, but they're going to judge any female as a slut if she's as sexually active as they are."

"She resents that inequity and isn't going to let the double standard restrict her, um, enthusiasm," I said.

"You know what she said to me once? 'Male is not the default gender for superhero.'" Ruth smiled. "I enjoy my more serious conversations with Shulky."

"She likes them, too," I said. "How's the new fan club president working out? Alec?"

"Alex. Amazing! He's all caught up on her social media and I'll forward his log of personal messages." Ruth pursed her mouth. "Jennifer, I hate to ask, but can you sign off on some damage reports? I'd like to clean up all the reimbursements before Shulky sets off a new round of destruction."

"No problem, Ruth."

I was in the right mood to go to the arsenal room in the basement. I looked over my wonderful collection of weapons and decided to check out my Smith & Wesson and do a little target practice. The heft and balance of this revolver always feels so comfortable in my hands, and the patina of the walnut grip becomes richer every year.

When I turned in my gun to the young weapons master, he said, "Planning to hold up a stagecoach with that antique, Ms. Walters?"

"My dad gave it to me for my Sweet Sixteen," I said. "I love New York, but sometimes a girl just wants to be out in a field under the blazing LA sun blasting cans off a fence post."

"She-Hulk always tells me 'bigger is better.'" He gave me a wink. "Well, she would say that, wouldn't she? Of course, she needed serious firepower when she was working with the Avengers on catastrophic situations. You're probably fine with your karate stuff, right?"

"Yes," I said and smiled. Because while all the other superheroes are saving the world, I'm looking for a job and an apartment, and no one is inviting me to the parties either. "Bye."

"Have a nice day, ma'am!"

INVITED ERROR

JANUARY 12

Only one month and two days until my resolutions begin! I'm feeling very optimistic, but not overly optimistic. As I advise my clients, "A negative attitude is an invitation to look at every setback as a failure. A realistic attitude prepares you to handle the vicissitudes that are typical in every business. An optimistic attitude allows you to go beyond the vicissitudes and see the possibilities." I told Dahlia this when she was having problems with the square footage of her salon, and her answer was "Did you actually say 'vicissitudes,' poodle?"

Great things about my neighborhood:

- Dahlia's salon and pet-sitting condo are nearby.
- So many eateries I never have to cook.
- Azzan, one of my all-time fave martial arts instructors, teaches at the gym five minutes away.
- Excellent access to public transit *and* two secret passageways to tunnel system.
- Lots of activity and always something to do.

Negative things about my neighborhood:

- Because Dahlia is nearby, she always expects me to bring her lunch.
- Buying takeout every day is an unnecessary expense, and I should learn to cook.
- Whenever I see Azzan on the street, he criticizes me for not training more.
- So expensive that I'll have to move somewhere else unless I get a job with a huge salary.

Yesterday, while I was on my way home with a bacon cheeseburger, chocolate milkshake, and double fries, I ran directly into Azzan. He looked down at the paper sack and shook his head. Then he gave me a ten-minute lecture on my lack of discipline. His English is not perfect, but his thick black eyebrows are fluent in the international language of disdain.

I did a lot of *ers* and *ums*, but he wasn't interested in excuses, so today I had a private session with him. After two hours of kicks, wrestling moves, and throws, my muscles were limber, and my mind was as clear as my bank account was empty. Maybe I can freelance until I find a job.

As I was toweling off, Azzan squinted at me. He has a very unnerving squint. I'm convinced it's a Mossad interrogation skill.

"Jennifer, why is such a nice girl wants to learn military fighting technique?"

"The streets can be dangerous for a woman."

He gave a derisive snort. "I am thinking that maybe you are not a nice girl."

I tried not to react. "My legal career is on public record. In fact, I'm between jobs right now, so I'll have to scale back on private lessons."

Azzan waggled his hand in a distinctly foreign way. "To bullshit me is an insult, Jennifer, so please do not do this again. If there is money problem, I know peoples who would very much like to employ such a girl as you for a honey trap — the nerdy shy librarian who will take off the glasses and shake the gorgeous hair and beautiful perky ass, and then, after intelligence gathering with kinky sex, can recruit an asset or terminate a target by breaking his neck with her iron-firm thighs."

Gorgeous hair! "Thank you, Azzan, but I plan to continue my legal career."

He shrugged. "The offer is open and I don't judge — except for your diagonal dives and rolls, which need to be tight and fast. Give me fifteen more minutes on the mat."

Afterward I went to Whole Foods and stocked up on fruits, vegetables, chicken, fish, and grains. I could feel Shulky itching inside when I passed by a tequila display, but I resisted. She itched more when she saw a huge guy whose muscled neck was as wide as his head. He smiled my way and I hurried down another aisle. I honestly don't get her taste sometimes.

I got back to my building just as the nice doorman, Claude, was ending his shift. Here is how I got maneuvered into doing free legal work by an old man.

First, Claude looked very happy and said, "Evening, Miss Jennifer. How are you doing?"

"Hi, Claude. I'm good. How's everything today?" [My first mistake; never ask a question without knowing the answer.]

"Everything here is fine, but I just got this letter . . ." He pulled a letter from his jacket pocket, which meant that he'd been prepared to ambush me. "I can't make heads nor tails of it. Am I in trouble? I can't afford to pay more. My niece always took care of the taxes for me, but she's gone and moved away." [He sensed my vulnerability for the poor-poor-pitiful-me tactic.]

The letter was a boilerplate notice from the IRS about a miscalculation, but the numbers were all wonky. [Lured me with unusual problem.]

He smiled again and somehow made his eyes look twinkly. [Helpless and friendly making it hard for me to say no.]

"I'm not a tax specialist, Claude, but it may be a simple fix. Do you have a copy of your filing and any supporting documents?"

He bent over so slowly I could practically hear the *creak-creak-creak* of his bones, and then he hauled a large cardboard file box from under his desk. "Here they are."

Good gawd! I did an *er* here and a *gosh* there, but Claude said, "You're the only one I know who's good at this stuff. I didn't want to ask anyone else here because them other tenants are so important. But you're not like that."

This was basically the rubber chicken all over again. At least he didn't call me ma'am.

I hauled the box to the loft, intending to set it aside since it wasn't a priority. Curiosity got to me though, and within ten minutes I was browsing through the contents. I found unorganized receipts, invoices, bank statements, county assessor notices, and several dozen two-for-one Joocey Jooce coupons.

I started sorting everything into piles on the dining room table. It became apparent that Claude didn't have a simple income tax issue. He had a *hydra monster* of a tax issue. Shulky had had a brutal encounter with Madame Hydra, but even that diabolical mastermind didn't have the terrifying ability to charge compound interest.

Tomorrow I'd tell Claude that he needed to get a specialist. I made file folders for his papers so he wouldn't be charged additional fees for clerical work.

JANUARY 13

I keep thinking about Dahlia's prediction that dangerous cloned organ technology would be used for beauty treatments. Spent the day reading about advances in the field, as well as learning about ReplaceMax complications that go far beyond the usual risks associated with human-to-human transplants. Most of the news is only conjecture, but there are too many reports of organ recipients now on life support.

Legal bloggers are saying that Quintal, Ulrich, Iverson, Ride, and Cooper (QUIRC) are rumored to be moving against ReplaceMax. QUIRC is described as "an elite boutique firm led by eccentric senior partner E. Charles (Quinty) Quintal III, who defected from the prestigious firm his grandfather founded to establish a more 'bohemian' practice. QUIRC specializes in resolving high-profile cases with extremely secretive settlements."

I wrote a letter to E. Charles Quintal III, attached my CV, and sent it off.

JANUARY 16

VALENTINE'S DAY RESOLUTIONS
COUNTDOWN: 30 DAYS

I know that shopping is fun for most women because they can fit in normal clothes and the clothes won't be ripped to shreds by the end of the month. I went to Bloomie's, gritted my teeth, and paid crazy prices for five nearly identical black suits that were too big, so that the sleeves and skirts were long enough.

I took the suits to the Garment District and found the shop that specialized in "breakaway garments."

The designer, who wore a tape measure around her neck, looked me up and down. "Most strippers your age look more chewed up at the edges, if you know what I mean. If you're gonna get implants, tell me so I can leave some give for the plastic."

Grit teeth smile. "It's for a private client who likes me to be stylish."

When I gave her the new suits, she tut-tutted, and said, "These are too good to ruin, hon. You don't want me to cut them up."

"Trust me," I told her. "If they don't have breakaway releases, they'll get ripped off my body and ruined anyway."

She seemed suspicious, so I bought two of the lovely dresses in her showroom. One was a deep scarlet because I plan to have a Real Date on

Valentine's Day. I was going to leave, but she made me try on the suits and then said, "A couple of tucks here and there and you'll look classy even while you're being trashy."

Grit teeth smile.

5:30 P.M.

As Ruth would say, OMG, AMAZING! I got a call from Quintal, Ulrich, Iverson, Ride, and Cooper. QUIRC wants to meet with me ASAP. So glad I picked up my suit from the cleaners. The repairs to the seams are hardly noticeable.

Must call Amy to schedule intense interview prep session.

If things keep going so excellently, I'll have achieved so much, I can add "Visit Paris" to my list of goals!

10:15 P.M.

Excitement is now churning in my guts with nausea. My skin crawls and I feel like I'm going to barf. I want to be judged by what I've done, not how well I can impress people on casual acquaintance, which is not at all. Amy said not to worry, that my CV speaks for itself.

If this fails, I can always take Azzan up on his offer of the international assassin job.

11:45 P.M.

I'm doing sit-ups to burn off my anxiety when my aPhone buzzes. I grab it. "Yes?"

It was the emergency nightline at the Mansion. "Jennifer, we've got a situation and everyone else is at the hovercraft derby. Mr. Stark thought She-Hulk could handle it."

Because I'm the rubber chicken. "Sure, so long as she doesn't have to leave the planet, because I've got a job interview."

"She doesn't even have to leave the state. Someone's built a platform in the Hudson, and it's supporting a giant peashooter, pulling water from the river and firing water spheres at the theater district. The tourists are running scared and wet. Detective Palmieri will meet Shulky at Pier 83."

I was going to ask how water could be formed into spheres that would travel that distance, but now was not the time to get technical. "Shulky will be there stat!"

I pulled off my flannel pajamas and took a breath.

11:50 P.M.

Everyone who shifts experiences something different. With me, there is the initial tingle of expectation that runs through my body. I feel it in my fingertips, on my scalp, and down my spine.

The sensation builds as my body stretches and grows dense with muscle. My skin takes on an intense green hue, and my slight curves swerve into dangerous turns of boobs and ass. And then, *kaboom!*, it's like being in a volcanic eruption and She-Hulk is the volcano, roaring out, as big and bold and badass as she wants to be.

I'm somewhere inside. I can see what she sees and feel what she feels, but I have ~~limited little~~ no control of her behavior.

She grinned at herself in the mirror and shook out her long waves of hair that were the deep shade of green ink. She grabbed a purple pleather bodysuit and silver boots from the closet, then wiggled into them and sighed with pleasure.

In less than a minute, she'd hit the express button in the private elevator, which dropped so fast it was almost like being in free fall.

The elevator opened to the subbasement, which had access to one of the secret tunnels that crisscross Manhattan. Shulky ran because she's faster than a car in city traffic. She was happy to be out, happy to stretch her long legs, happy to be wearing clothes she thought made her look hot. Or as she spells it, hawt.

She slipped out of the tunnel at 42nd Street by the Hudson River Greenway. She kept to the shadows as well as a six-foot-seven jade Amazon could keep to the shadows, and then she burst out under the street lamps.

A crowd had gathered to watch the action, and they shouted, "She-Hulk! She-Hulk's here! Shulky!" and she gave a wave while noticing the silver arc of a water sphere shooting like a meteorite across the sky before plummeting down in the direction of Broadway.

A dozen black-and-whites had red lights flashing at the base of the pier. She scoped out the raft bobbing a hundred yards off in the dark water. Centered on the raft was a contraption with a wheeled turret and mantel that supported a long metal cylinder. The white foam churning around the raft indicated an engine below the surface.

Sergeant Patricia Palmieri, our favorite NYPD superhuman liaison, waved She-Hulk over. "Shulky, glad you made it."

"What's the scoop, Patty?"

"We can't tell if the giant peashooter is remote-controlled or not, since anyone who gets close gets blasted. The main target is the goddamn theater district."

"That's taking the bad reviews of *Spider-Man* a little too far," Shulky snarked. Patty laughed because people think anything Shulky says is hilarious. "Is the ammunition just water?"

"Yes, but you'd have to ask a goddamn physicist how it's been formed into giant cannonballs. The loading interval seems to take at least twenty-five seconds."

"That's long enough for me to get there. Not to worry, Pattycakes."

Another waterball flew through the sky, and She-Hulk sprinted down the pier, her long legs eating up the distance. Then she extended her arms and dived into the river, setting off waves on either side.

Her legs propelled her quickly to the edge of the raft. Her muscles were so dense that when she hauled her 680 pounds up on the raft, it began to tip over. She rolled to the center of the raft, and as it righted itself, the pea-shooting metal cylinder swung right at her head.

She thought she heard a manic giggle as she reached up, grabbed the cylinder, and crushed it as easily as a normal human would crush an aluminum can.

An engine suddenly roared, and the raft rocked violently in the wake of a silver capsule jetting away on the surface of the water.

He'd left too easily.

When a miscreant departed without a struggle, it was usually because his plan was about to go into Phase II, known among the superheroes as the Let's-blow-this-mother-up Phase.

Shulky remained poised on the raft for an instant before she hurled herself off and backflipped into the water. She stretched out, using her massive arms to propel her quickly away from the raft. She took a deep breath then ducked under the surface, going as deep and fast as she could.

She was already under the pier when she felt the shock waves as the raft exploded.

She waited until the shrapnel stopped raining on the river before she rose to the surface. She pulled herself out of the river, shook like a dog, and banged on her ear to get the water out. Sergeant Palmieri was soon by her side saying, "You all right?"

"I will be as soon as my hair dries."

"Did you see the perp?"

"I only heard him. He giggled like a kid, a crazy kid. The peashooter, that's like something a kid would build. Maybe your team will find out more from the wreckage, but it was almost like a prank — except for the explosion. That's attempted murder."

"So you don't think there's superhuman involvement?"

"If I had to guess, I'd say no. Superhuman evildoers are more goal-oriented. This was merely mayhem."

"For all of our sakes, I hope you're right."

She-Hulk looked at the bright lights of the city. "Patty, do you mind sending a copy of your report to the Mansion? Cuz I hear a party calling my name."

JANUARY 17, 3:47 A.M.

Returned home without Shulky sexing up anyone. Which was not easy. She is cutting into my sleeping hours, but at least there won't be any embarrassing videos.

10:00 A.M.

Underestimated Shulky's capacity to be photographed doing something scandalous. Why didn't I notice that she was grinding on that DJ? And why did she think it was so funny to leave a foil three-pack of condoms like a bookmarker in this journal?

She wears me out.

· 4 ·

NOLO CONTENDERE

JANUARY 20

VALENTINE'S DAY RESOLUTION COUNTDOWN: 25 DAYS

When I walked into the conference room at Quintal, Ulrich, Iverson, Ride, & Cooper, a young woman at the table took one look at me and said in a voice as rich and sweet as Tupelo honey, "Oh, brown pinstripes — how quaint!"

Thus it begins. I was prepared for mind games, because top attorneys are as bloodthirsty as sharks, and they'd want to make sure that I was one of them. I'm fierce in the courtroom when my adrenaline surges and when I inhabit the role of legal badass, but now I had to surreptitiously wipe my clammy palms on my skirt before shaking hands.

I recognized Amber Tumbridge from her bio on the QUIRC website, but that small photo didn't convey how perfectly pretty she was — but in a way meant to intimidate. Her glossy golden blond hair fell perfectly below her shoulders, her complexion was perfectly smooth and creamy, her blue-gray eyes were perfectly clear, her lithe body was perfectly toned, her teeth were perfectly pearly, and her suit was a perfect blue-black color.

But her physical beauty was nothing compared to her exquisite voice. I found myself wanting to hear her speak even though everything she said was aggressive. The others in the room faded into the background as Amber took control of the interview. Clearly, she'd been designated to hammer me down.

She managed to mention her Yale Law degree (twice), the *Yale Law Review*, a recent victory in a corporate espionage case, the renovation of her historic brownstone, and her friendship with prominent political families. She did this while playing with a ginormous diamond engagement ring on her delicate finger.

I wouldn't have been surprised if she'd pulled out a tiny tiara and told me that she'd once been crowned America's Most Accomplished Toddler.

Amber gave me more attitude during the Q&A. She called UCLA "a nice public school" and my time with the DA "nice public work." When I mentioned Dad's job, she said, "A county sheriff? How nice that he's a public servant."

I could tell that she thought "public" was synonymous with second-rate. Or third-rate. Amber's lips were smiling, but her eyes were sneering, an expression Dahlia calls smeering. This snideness seemed almost personal, but Amber was that kind of woman.

My roiling emotions caused Shulky to wake inside of me, yearning to get out and grab Amber by her naturally blond hair, swing her until she whirred like helicopter blades, and launch her at the wall. She wanted to hear that delicious voice as a pure scream. I pressed Shulky back down and forced myself to look calm while Amber questioned me repeatedly about my rapid exodus from several firms.

Amber kept studying my CV, but one of the time manipulators at the Mansion had tweaked my history to account for the occasions when Shulky had been off-planet. The TM could also jimmy the continuum so I could take weekends off — or maybe visit Paris!

I'd rehearsed my answers so I sounded reasonably smooth even though my nerves were jittering. "I've worked for a variety of companies in order to build up a range of experience so that I can better handle the complexity of my clients' cases."

Amber didn't say, "What a pile of hooey," but it was in her eyes.

I aced the other questions, throwing in heaps of legal Latin, all *audi alteram partem* this and *ex turpi causa non oritur actio* that, and I was in the home stretch when Amber said, "We at QUIRC will expect partner-track attorneys to surpass two thousand billable hours," and watched to see if I'd react to the insane amount of work required at top-echelon firms. "We're not interested in hiring someone who will decide that spending time with family and friends is more important."

"I would expect no less."

Amber gave me another smeery look. She waved toward the windows with their stunning view of Manhattan, which still look my breath away, especially at times like this, with a new flurry of snow sparkling in the winter light on building ledges and cornices.

She said, "The vast majority of the human population is satisfied with the banalities of an average life. One day blurs into the next, one week is indistinguishable from another. Their existence consists of waiting for the weekend, then waiting for retirement, and then waiting for death."

Well, hell, she almost made me want to throw myself out the window and let buzzards eat my carcass. Or, considering the geography, rats and pigeons, eww.

Quinty Quintal peeked at his gold watch and gave me a wink. Something about him seemed familiar, and not just from his photos.

Amber continued spewing. "Only an exceptional few have the intelligence, skill, and determination to succeed in a place like QUIRC. Do you really believe you're that rarity, Ms. Walters?"

I wished I could give her a Valley Girl *fer sure*, but I said, "My record of successes speaks for itself, Ms. Tumbridge."

She wasn't ready to STFU yet. "We are aware of your friendship with a certain notorious superhuman, but celebrity connections will not factor into our decision."

Shulky kicked me behind my eyeballs, and I said, "The appropriate term for She-Hulk is super*hero*, not the generic super*human*, since her efforts have saved humanity from destruction on numerous occasions. However, I expect no favors because of my outside relationships."

Quinty said, "Ms. Walters, I'm very impressed with your UCLA degree — go Bruins! — and with your LLM from Harvard, a very nice *private* school." He lifted one bushy eyebrow. "I know that your experience at Goodman, Lieber, Kurtzburg, & Holliway prepared you for our grueling schedule. Anyone good enough for Holden Holliway is good enough for me."

He chuckled, and everyone but Amber obediently chuckled along, and then he said, "Ms. Walters, if you're as smart as I think you are, you're aware of our impending action against ReplaceMax Laboratories."

I sat up straight. "Yes, I've heard that you were planning a suit against their organ cloning division."

"I can't reveal details about our plans, but Maxwell Kirsch continues to stand by ReplaceMax's defective products," Quinty said. "If anyone should take ReplaceMax on, the fight will be dirty and brutal."

I felt the thrill that I get when I'm challenged in court. I looked Quinty in the eye and said, "If I worked for QUIRC, sir, and you had a case against ReplaceMax, I'd say, 'Bring it!'" I let that hang there, gazing slowly around the room to let them all know that I was ready to crush any opposition.

Why can't I have that kind of confidence all the time?

Half an hour later, the senior partner was saying, "Call me Quinty," and escorting me to the minimalist lobby. "Ms. Walters, I can't speak for the others, but I'd be delighted to have you onboard."

It wasn't "We want to hire you," but it was encouraging, and I said, "Call me Jennifer."

"Jennifer, after hearing about your reputation, I thought you'd be a battle-scarred warrior, not a soft-spoken young lady. You're quite a catch, you know. Legally, I mean."

Quinty's eyes had a sort of *Mad Men* glint — a far-off expression that men get when they're nostalgic for the days when they could pinch a girl's ass and ask for a martini and a blowjob. I wondered what he'd looked like when he was in his prime.

I didn't have to wonder for long. The elevator pinged, the doors slid open, and a taller, brawnier, younger version of Quinty stepped out. A version that looked *exactly* like Ellis Tesla, down to the scar across his right eyebrow.

Ellis Tesla stepped out of the elevator.

Allow me to repeat: Ellis smoking-hot-rockin'-sex-god-and-star-of-my-most-fevered-fantasies Tesla stepped out of the elevator.

I did a quick assessment to see if I'd been thrown into a parallel dimension, but the clock on the wall didn't show lost time and everyone around us was still speaking English and wearing the same clothes. No one had any extra limbs or was walking on the ceiling.

Ellis Tesla said to Quinty, "I thought I'd have to drag you out of your office."

My brain felt like it had driven off a freshly paved interstate and down a steep embankment when Quinty said, "Hello, Ellis. Meet our newest recruit, Ms. Walters. Ms. Walters, this is Ellis the fourth. My family is not very imaginative with names. Ellis — Dr. Quintal — runs a science school in Jersey. He takes after his mother, who taught physics."

Quinty was E. Charles Quintal III = Ellis Charles Quintal III. So Ellis was teaching science instead of working in the family business.

"Hello, Ms. Walters," Ellis said with a brief smile. He still had that appealing roughness to his voice.

I was FREAKING OUT because I didn't know if he recognized me, and I didn't know if I wanted him to recognize me in a quaint suit. His deep chestnut hair was still thick, and his eyes were still the mutable browns and golds of autumn leaves. His face was still ruggedly handsome, as if he was the ideal genetic offspring of pirates and lumberjacks.

He still had those broad shoulders that a girl could hang on to while he held her by her hips and shoved her up against a wall and made her scream for more.

He wore a navy suit and a pale blue shirt. His one concession to quirkiness was his tie, which had an atomic structure motif.

My throat constricted so tightly that I could barely choke out, "Nice to meet you."

When Ellis shook hands with me, all I could think of was the delicious things he'd done to me with those long, strong fingers. I was SO FREAKED OUT that I felt like unsweatable parts of my body were sweating, like my teeth and my kneecaps.

I tried to keep my voice steady and said, "I haven't actually been hired yet."

"Sure you have. It's just not official." Ellis turned to his father. "Dad, ready for lunch?"

"Give me a minute." Quinty said to me, "Scientists are selfish with their time because they don't bill by the hour," and he left us in the lobby.

Ellis hadn't really focused on me yet and was glancing down the hallway. "Ms. Walters. Are you the Ms. Walters who used to be in the DA's office and at GLKH?"

He could say absolutely anything in that voice, which sounded like he'd been swigging tequila and gravel since preschool, and it would seem like a perverse and irresistible proposition.

"Guilty as charged," I said, trying to sound blasé, and feeling relieved — or was I? — that he didn't remember me. I could start fresh, and he'd see me as a successful professional and not a drunk coed dancing in front of the stage at a concert.

"You've tried some very high-profile cases," he said.

"I wasn't looking for publicity. I was looking for justice." Agh! I sounded dull and pretentious, which wasn't a significant improvement over drunk and slutty.

"Really?"

I couldn't tell if he was being sarcastic. Whatever it was, I felt a bead of sweat slide down my spine, but I wasn't finished proving that I was both tedious and prissy. "It's the duty of those with access to power and privilege to protect and defend the rights of the common man, or woman, or children, those who have no voice . . ."

I wished to heavens that I had no voice, but I could not stop, even though I saw Ellis's smile drop away, and he turned to face me straight on. I kept telling myself, *shut up, shut up, shut up!* but I continued to jabber and at the same time I was thinking about him naked. I was remembering the taste of his mouth and the touch of his hands. I may have glanced down at the front of his pants.

Ellis took a step toward me and said quietly, "Genevieve?"

My brain short-wired. I said "Uh, uh," and then I said it some more.

Ellis gave me a slow smile that made me feel as if my panties had just vaporized. "Those green, green eyes. Ginny, from the party at Caltech. *That* weekend."

Someone shut a door, and the noise knocked me out of my short-circuited loop. I nodded and my voice came out in a whisper. "Jenny, not Ginny. Jennifer Walters."

"No wonder I couldn't find you. I checked USC law school, looking for you."

I was confused because I *knew* I'd given him my phone number. To the best of my recollection. "I went to UCLA, not USC."

He laughed and said, "I was pretty ripped when you told me. But not too ripped to forget . . . that was *some* weekend, wasn't it? I didn't recognize you at first because you weren't dressed." He hesitated so long that in a movie calendar pages would have been flying by, and then he said, "Like this."

He talked like that, all suggestive pauses for me to fill in. He still had something that was more a smirk than a smile, but a fantastic smirk, sexy and confident. I was caught in his gaze and we stood looking at each other for long seconds.

"Your hair was lighter, shorter, and . . ." Agonizing pause. "I didn't expect to see you in this context, here in New York."

"My hair gets lighter with the sun," I said, and suddenly remembered one of Dahlia's early coloring and cutting experiments. "I'm sorry Fringe Theory broke up."

"That happens. Our song still gets airplay on top cult hits shows."

Did "our" mean his *band's* song, or *our* song?

"I've heard," I said. "Do you still, uh, play?"

"Yeah, I play [significant pause] for fun. I like to do things for fun. My work is lots of fun. What about you?"

"Uh, I like fun, too." It was official: I was an idiot.

"So glad to hear that," he said with a lowered voice that made me have the mad thought that he'd grab my hand, drag me into a stairwell, and rip my clothes off. Which probably would not have been appropriate *après*-job-interview behavior.

I realized that he could easily find me online now that he knew my name. And if I got hired by QUIRC, I'd see Ellis when he visited his father. Even if I didn't get hired, he could look me up if he wanted to. "My full name is Jennifer Susan Walters," I said. "Jennifer S. Walters, Esquire."

He dropped his head closer to mine as he asked, "So what kind of things do you do for fun, Jennifer S. Walters, Esquire?"

Out of the vast wasteland that lay between my ears, I heard the faint echo of Dahlia's advice to me once: *Play it cool, but not too cool!* "I'll tell you the next time I see you, and you can tell me more about your music and your teaching. It's really nice running into you, Dr. Ellis C. Quintal, the fourth. Well, I'd better be going." I punched the elevator button.

"Next time then," he said. "Jenny."

He made me so nervous that I punched the down button again.

A female voice said mockingly, "Trying to escape so quickly from QUIRC?"

I looked to see Amber, who'd put on a black wool trench with fur trim. Quinty was escorting her toward us.

"Hello, darling!" she trilled, because she had the sort of voice that trilled like birdsong, as she went to Ellis and kissed him.

At this point, any remaining circuitry in my brain immediately fried. I could practically smell the burning insulation as Amber slipped her arm through Ellis's and told me, "Ms. Walters, I see you've already met my fiancé. Now, don't get any ideas about poaching because he's already turned me down about handling legal matters for his business." I thought she must be saying this to make him feel more important about SAT tutoring, or whatever he did.

Sexy, flirty Ellis Tesla was instantly replaced by a more formal man, who said, "I have a longtime relationship with my attorney."

Quinty looked at me and said, "His college roommate is his lawyer. He knows Ellis's dirty laundry."

Was I part of Ellis's dirty laundry? Did he *still* have my panties? Agh!

"He doesn't have dirty laundry anymore," Amber said with a cool smile. "Like many men, all he needed was a weekly cleaning service to rid him of detritus."

Was Amber talking in code about groupies? Had I been a groupie? Ellis's expression remained impassive.

I didn't trust myself to speak again, so I smiled pathetically. I know it was a pathetic smile because when the elevator arrived and we entered, I could see it reflected on the mirrored door. On the floor below, a large group got in, and they shoved me to the back of the elevator.

The stuffy air and the combination of damp wool, fur, and someone's overpowering aftershave made my nose itch. A lot.

I really, really tried not to sneeze, and I thought I had subdued my urge. Isn't that how it always is — you think you've got something under control, but you don't.

My sneeze was explosive. And not ladylike. And right on the back of Amber's coat. I swiped at it within the confines of the elevator, saying, "Sorry! Sorry!"

Amber looked over her shoulder at me and said coldly, "Leave it. I'll send it to the cleaners." The elevator reached the first floor and the doors opened.

"Please let me pay for the cleaning! Send me the bill," I said, following Ellis, Quinty, and Amber into the marble-floored main lobby.

"That's a very nice offer, Ms. Walters," Amber said and smeered. "But not everyone needs public assistance."

It's generally a bad sign when my skin begins to change colors. This time I felt it going hotly pink.

Quinty let out an exasperated breath and said, "Ellis, Amber, I'll see you two at the restaurant." He gave me a more patient look and added, "Ms. Walters, I look forward to talking to you soon," and he strode away.

Amber slid off her coat to inspect the back of it. Her mouth went down in disgust. "I can donate it to charity."

Ellis said, "Come on, Amber, it's not like Ginny has contagious necrotizing fasciitis." I saw an *oh shit!* expression flash across his face, and he quickly said, "I meant Jenny. I meant Jennifer. It's not like *Jennifer* has the flu."

But it was too late. Amber laser-focused her icy blue eyes at me. "*You're* the Flesh-Eating Bacteria girl?"

"I must be going," I said. "Very nice meeting you, Ms. Tumbridge, Mr. uh, good-bye."

8:30 P.M.

I'm ignoring Dahlia's phone call because I'm in bed with the blanket over my head thinking about everything that happened today and remembering the night I met Ellis.

I'd been a Fringe Theory fan ever since high school, when Bruce had given me a mix of their songs, my favorite being "I Wanna Be Your Frankenstein." ("I'll put you together/my very own creature/I'll lovingly suture/Your limbs and your features.") I went to their site and crushed on the lead singer, Ellis Tesla, the hard-rocking PhD chem student, with his beat-up jeans, vintage nerd T-shirts, and smoldering sardonic stage presence. Brains and brawn, he was my ideal man.

When I heard that the band was touring the West Coast's premier science programs, I begged a Caltech acquaintance to get me into the sold-out show.

The Fringe Theory concert ended with fireworks, a two-story waterslide, and lots and lots of their signature Rocket Fuel shots. I felt like Ellis was singing right to me as I danced in front of the stage in a cami and cutoffs. It was a sultry Pasadena night, and when someone sprayed a hose at the crowd, I let the water rain down on me.

A homemade missile whizzed into a Porta Potty, setting it ablaze. A siren wailed, and a few minutes later, squad cars and fire trucks roared up, eager to shut down the party. When cops rushed the stage, Ellis reached into his pocket, took out something, and threw it in the opposite direction.

In the instant that brilliant flames licked out and smoke billowed, he leapt off the stage, grabbed my hand, and said, "Come on, babe! Run!"

And we ran until we were far from the crowd. We hid in someone's yard, and Ellis pulled me close and said, "You're quite a stretch of a girl, aren't you? I like that."

I was breathing hard from the run and the excitement. I asked, "What was that you threw?"

"Magician's flash paper. Because sometimes I need to divert attention while I steal away with a gorgeous girl."

Then he kissed me, and the warmth and solidity of him made my knees weak. The slip of his tongue into my mouth sent pleasurable currents through my body.

When he said, "I'm staying nearby," I said, "Okay."

I remember a rambling wood-shingled house. We stumbled upstairs, kissing and grabbing at each other.

Then we were in an academic's room, with books, computers, papers. Moments later, we were naked. Being with Ellis Tesla felt like a dream where I was someone other than a dutiful, serious, lonely grad student. I was wild and shameless as we did things I'd fantasized about and things I'd never imagined.

While taking a breather between filthy hot sex, Ellis held me in his arms and said, "I want to write a song for you. Name a subject and I'll write a song about it for you."

I was feeling OMG! amazed that I was with the hawtest geek in the most rockin' geek band of pranksters in the nation. "Really?"

"Anything you want, babe."

I saw a book titled *Flesh-Eating Bacteria: Conquering Necrotizing Fasciitis* on the desk, and I said teasingly, "Write a song about flesh-eating bacteria."

Ellis reached over and grabbed a guitar, keeping me close. He strummed and hummed for a minute or two and then sang:

> *She's consuming me, this long-legged babe*
> *Eyes green as jade, she's making me crave*
> *More and more, though I know her kisses infect*
> *My heart, my soul, my life, I can't protect*
> *Because the girl's unstoppable, like a flesh-eating bacterium,*
> *An erotic juggernaut, she drives me to delirium*
>
> *I can't resist her touch, can't resist her voice*
> *Can't resist the contagion, I got no choice*
> *My skin's on fire, she's all I desire,*
> *So flexible, she's incredible*
> *So cerebral, she's chimerical*
> *My gorgeous flesh-eating bacteria girl.*

We laughed about the song because, really, what could be less romantic than necrotizing fasciitis, but two months later it was at the top of the charts and it stayed there for weeks. There was lots of speculation about the actual identity of the Flesh-Eating Bacteria Girl. I never told anyone.

And now Amber, a member of the QUIRC hiring committee, knows that I was one of her fiancé's groupies. Not just any hapless giggling groupie, but the inspiration for his first big hit. I can say good-bye to that job opportunity. It doesn't seem to matter much, because I'm obsessing about Ellis. I would never have thought a scientific rocker renegade like him would end up with a hammerhead shark in Armani like Amber Tumbridge.

I've kept my secret long enough. Tomorrow I'll tell Dahlia.

Then I realized: this is exactly one of those setbacks that would have stopped me dead in my tracks if I'd made New Year's Resolutions.

I'm not going to let this get me down. Why should I care about a man who couldn't even remember my name or bother to call me? If he's engaged to Amber, he must be a horrible human being. It's time to let go of my teenage daydream and move on to someone who has actual boyfriend potential.

Like a stripey kitten, I'm going to keep hanging in there!

FRESH START

9:50 P.M.

Now that I have Ellis's real name, I was able to find him online. I feel pretty stupid for not locating him before — because *everyone's* heard of Manic Quantum Mechanics Science Camp. Okay, maybe not everyone, but I remember my cousin mentioning it. Why didn't Bruce tell me that Ellis owned the program?

Text to Bruce:	Did you know that Ellis Tesla of Fringe Theory is Ellis Quintal of Manic Quantum Mechanics?
Text from Bruce:	Yes.
Text to Bruce:	Why didn't you tell me?
Text from Bruce:	Can suggest science camps if yr interested. Do you want practical or theoretical?
Text to Bruce:	I was an FT fan. You gave me a mix tape of their songs in high school.
Text from Bruce:	So? You lovd Titanic & I dont send updates on oceanography.
Text to Bruce:	Nevermind.
Text from Bruce:	Already forgotten.

I watched a dozen videos of Ellis and his MQMC team of scientists and engineers leading kids to conduct insane experiments, competing in wild challenges, and even having the president's wife test-drive a rocket car built with recycled materials and fueled with organic compost and carrot juice. He looked amazing in a wife-beater and cargo pants with a tool belt low on his waist.

He was listed as a consultant for the Institute of Ethics for Science & Bioscience, and I found his social networks. Ellis C. Quintal IV is "engaged." Everything else is set to private.

I could ask one of the hackers at the Mansion to find out more, but there could be blowback if they decide to find out why I want to know. Do I really want the other superheroes to know that I'm stalking a ~~old boyfriend romantic interest~~ drunken hookup? No.

11:15 P.M.

I'll never be able to sleep. Checked my aPhone, and Shulky has a message from Trey and Matt. *The Book of Mormon* cast wants to treat her to "borscht and belly dancing" for saving Broadway from the water sphere attack. Shulky loves both borscht and belly dancing.

JANUARY 21

I thought I'd have to wait until the salon closed this evening to talk to Dahlia, but she answered my a.m. call right away or, as she'd say, stat!

I picked up two lattes and met her at Washington Square Dog Park. The day was freezing and she was trying to get Rodney out of his carrier. She'd dressed him in a bulky orange sweater. Every time she took him out, he'd scramble back in.

"What's wrong with him?" I asked. "Dogs are supposed to like running around."

"He hates orange and thinks these dogs are not as chic as the dogs at Tompkins Square. He has a point, but I don't condone his canine elitism."

"I thought dogs don't see colors."

"Rodney does. It's one of his many talents. So how did your interview go and what's your reason for the 911?" We walked around stomping our feet to keep them warm.

"I thought I did okay in the interview, but the only time I'm verbally impressive is in the courtroom, which they know. As for the 911: Ellis Tesla. I saw him yesterday. He's the son of the senior partner at QUIRC."

"OMG! Tell me everything!"

I relayed the facts, which took several minutes because I kept repeating "I was FREAKING OUT!"

Dahlia slugged me on the shoulder and said, "I asked you a kazillion times if you were the Flesh-Eating Bacteria Girl and you said no, *nyet*, *nein*. Why did you lie to me?"

"Maybe Ellis got the idea for the song when he was with me, but if I really was the girl he described, he would have called. Yesterday he said that he'd tried to find me at USC and thought my name was Ginny, but I'd given him my number, so his claim is easily disputed."

"He was on the road, Jen, and, OMG, are you going to try to lure him away from this evil bitch, Amber Hammerhead?"

"No, they're engaged and I respect that commitment. Also, it would be like sticking my hand into a bear trap for a cupcake. I won't get the job now, and I'll never ever see him again."

"You're delusional. This city is like college. We see the same people over and over. He's here. You're here. Your long legs and beautiful eyes are here. Every time he's heard that song, he's thought of you — naked and servicing his every perverse whim! He's got . . ." and here she scrunched her face and calculated. "If he heard the song once a week, and that's on the low side, for six years, then he's had over three hundred sexual fantasies about you!"

"That's simply conjecture!"

"No, it's simply multiplication — on the subject of men, I am an expert witness. How many other songs did he write about you?"

"None."

She sighed dramatically. "What happened to that innocent sweet

Jennifer who stuttered when she tried to tell a fib? Never mind . . . Rodney! What the hell are you eating? Drop it! Drop that!"

Dahlia tried to wrest something that looked like a frozen mouse from Rodney's nasty pointy teeth, and I hoped she'd forgotten the subject, but she finally let the dog eat whatever it was, and then said, " 'Gin and Entropy.' It was about you."

"It was about martinis and depression."

Before I could stop her, she took out her phone, searched for the song and hit *Play*, and Ellis's lusty rough voice cut through the thin winter air.

All I wanted was Gin on a hot summer night
The thermodynamics of two systems acting
And reacting, bodies moving and adapting
All my expectations
Vanished with her in flagrante delectations
Lithe and long and all night long
She was,
Lithe and long and all night long.
All I wanted was Gin,
All I needed was Gin,
Oh, god, give this poor thirsty man his Gin.

I had velocity and parameters
Yet she made me nervous as an amateur
How ironic to have a disorder molecular and atomic
When my world shift was enormous and tectonic
The way she talked and walked and rocked me,
Give me more, give me more, give me more.
All I wanted was Gin
All I needed was Gin
Oh, god, give my disordered system long smooth Gin.

Despite the chill of the day, I felt my temperature rising, and I said, "The lyrics are nonspecific."

Dahlia looked at Rodney and said, "Your Honor, the prosecution would like to treat Ms. Walters as a hostile witness."

Then that damn rat-dog yipped as if he understood.

"Dahl, I didn't only wait for Ellis to call. I called *him*. You know that was excruciating for me, and he never ever called me back. I kept thinking he would, but he never did."

"Maybe there's a good reason."

"Yes, he just wasn't that into me and there were hundreds of hot girls in line." Funny, how old hurts are still painful even when one is a successful, if temporarily unemployed, top-level attorney. "You can't tell anyone! I've already wrecked my chances with QUIRC and I don't need other firms knowing that—"

"That you are an internationally notorious mystery sex goddess? Okay, I will protect your deepest darkest secret!"

Rodney saved me from trying to think of a response. "D, that rodent-thing is pooping on someone's knockoff Vuitton."

JANUARY 22

In order to get Ellis out of my head, which is already crowded by Shulky sprawling all over the place, I decided to participate in something outside my comfort zone. After searching singles meet-ups, I found a *Game of Thrones* marathon party at an establishment called Professor Sam's. I thought I'd meet other bookish battle fans and we could talk about favorite weapons and comment on the authenticity of the broadsword scenes.

I dressed appropriately for a visit to an academic soiree—a navy Shetland wool sweater over a button-down shirt, jeans, ankle boots with Velcro closures. I don't know how Shulky can move in the sky-high heels she adores, but it's true that she can fling a stiletto shoe with the force and accuracy of, well, an actual stiletto.

I should have Googled images for the location, because the address was a bar. Women who complain that there are no men in Manhattan obviously haven't visited a sports bar on a night where everyone gets a free Jell-O shot each time a character is stabbed, beheaded, or cudgeled in a fantasy adventure show.

All the men were friendly. Very friendly. Too friendly. The Jell-O shots may have had something to do with it. They all seemed to know one another and they were all using insider slang, so I slipped away to the ladies' room and ran cold water over my wrists until I had the nerve to go back out.

I found a place by the bar and kept my eyes on the big screen.

A man sidled up to me and said, "How's it going? Your first time here?"

"Mmm, yes. It's very crowded." I turned to look at him. I didn't mind that he was shorter than me. A lot of men are. I didn't mind that he smelled a little minty — I like the smell of mint. I *did* mind that he was wearing a T-shirt with an image of a topless Rogue on it, prominent headlights and all, because she's my friend.

He said, "We're always glad to have more of the lady fans here. We like to have a good time."

I couldn't stop staring at his horrible shirt.

"You like my shirt? I did the graphics myself. Rogue modeled for me." He seemed nervous as he lowered his voice. "She was wearing less than this by the time we were done. She kind of spoils a man, but you're not bad as far as normal human chicks go."

Shulky growled within me, but I shushed her. I grabbed my coat and walked by the too friendly drunken crowd and out the door. As I was wrapping my scarf around my neck, feeling upset about everything, I heard the bar door open and then the dweeb was beside me, crossing his arms tightly on his narrow chest and saying, "I'm sorry! Geez, I'm sorry!"

"Why?" was all I could say.

The little man looked miserable, shivering so much that his teeth rattled. "I signed up for a class on how to pick up girls and this was our first field trip and my assignment was to . . ." He trailed off. "I'm supposed to wear something provocative, but I hate this stupid shirt and we're supposed to like give girls 'negs.' You know, I have to say something negative to bring down a girl's ego and then she'll want to impress me. But it's really mean, right? I feel mean and stupid, and I paid a *lot* of money to feel this way."

"You won't feel anything unless you get out of the cold. What's your name, and do you have a jacket?"

"Nelson Kaspar and my jacket is inside? I don't want to go back in there. Numinous, that's the pickup master who teaches the class?" Nelson was one of those people who speak in questions. "He'll humiliate me if I don't score, okay? I already tried to get my money back and he just insulted me."

I'd heard about the scummy pickup tactic, and I felt for the little guy. "We're going inside and I can get you a refund. You just have to agree to let me represent you."

He said "yes" and "but, but" a few times, and we went back into the loud, warm bar. Now that I knew who I was looking for, I immediately spotted Numinous. He was a tall, bone-thin guy with long bleached white hair, guyliner, and a silver-topped walking stick that he twirled in his skinny ringed fingers. Three women, who looked like actresses hired for a performance, fawned over him.

He leered at me as I came up. "Sorry, nerdette, you'll have to stand in line, although I'll bump you up if you give me a good reason."

"Mr. Numinous, my name is Jennifer S. Walters and I represent Nelson Kaspar, who would like a full refund of his payment for your class."

Numinous sneered. "He got his money's worth, picking you up, didn't he? If you don't mind." He turned from me and said to the by-the-hour talent, "Losers."

I spoke in my firmest courtroom voice. "Mr. Numinous, you are compelling your students to engage in second-degree harassment, which is a violation of New York Penal Code Section 240.26. When my client enrolled in your course, he believed that all activity would be both legal and ethical."

Numinous continued to look the other way, but I could tell he was listening, so I said, "Now, if you do not refund Mr. Kaspar's course fees, I will be forced to pursue legal recourse, including posting a notice in all local print and online publications seeking your students and victims of your students in order to ascertain the full extent of your malfeasance."

"All right!" Numinous squirmed in his chair and hissed, "All right, I'll give the little weasel his money back!" He reached into his pocket and pulled out a checkbook. He snapped his fingers and one of the girls brought out a pen from her clutch. "Kaspar, you could have gotten laid big-time, you could have been a man, but you're too much of a wuss and you had to go running to mommy to take care of you."

"Confident men do not denigrate women," I said. "Cease abusing my client or I shall seek redress."

Norman took the check and gave me a big smile as we were leaving. He had very nice teeth. "Thank you, Jennifer! You were so brave."

"Only about legal things. I hate bullies." We stood out on the cold dark street.

"How did you know that code right off the top of your head?"

I knew it because Shulky has been charged in violation of Section 240.26 ~~once a few times~~ frequently. I said, "I really wanted to watch the show."

"I live near here? That's not a line because, uh, I prefer girls my height. Looking up at you is giving me a neck crick."

My resolution to make new friends hadn't started yet, and I was planning to turn him down, when he said, "I have a bag of Cool Ranch Doritos?"

He seemed sweet once he'd dropped the douche act. "Sure. We can catch the last two hours."

I expected a grubby studio, but Nelson had a terrific space with comfortable leather furniture, dark wood floors, a big-screen TV, and a fireplace that he soon had roaring. I found out that he was a dentist, which explained his great smile. He spent several minutes deliberating on the right wine for Doritos, and finally decided on ale from a new microbrewery.

While we watched the show, we talked about the fight scenes. Well, *I* talked about the fight scenes and he asked questions and then said, "Jen, how come you know so much about sword fighting?"

"When I was a kid, my cousin and I used to battle it out in the fields with sticks. I never stopped. It was always fun."

"I couldn't do anything like that," he said. "I'm not brave?"

"Nelson, most people would be terrified to do your job. I'm sure you could learn the fundamentals of swordsmanship."

"You think so?"

"Absolutely."

I taught him a few basic moves with umbrellas. He was a fast study and listened to instructions. I was nice and cozy as the TV blared, the fire crackled, and Nelson practiced feints and jabs. He threw the awful T-shirt in the flames and we toasted with a second bottle of beer. I told him about the Forestiers, and he said he'd like to go to the next meet-up and asked if there would be any shortish girls there. I told him yes, because Amy Stewart-Lee was shortish, single, and always brushed and flossed after lunch.

I'd gone outside my comfort zone, and after an initial awkwardness, I'd made a new friend, enjoyed delicious salad dressing-flavored chips, and watched an exhilarating show. Nelson complimented my smile, which made those years of braces seem worthwhile, and even gave me pocket-size samples of dental floss!

The entire evening had passed without me fixating on Ellis. With Amber. In their brownstone. Having naked sex while he sang her a love song about sensual consensual mitosis and rhymed it with "Too much Gin gave me emotional cirrhosis."

JURY INSTRUCTIONS

JANUARY 23

After reviewing my Valentine's Day Resolutions, I realized that most are contingent upon getting a job and a boyfriend. Would it have been better to structure them in a diagram with consecutive steps, or would that slow down all progress? I'm beginning to see other bugs in my plan. For example, how can I have a real date for Valentine's Day when Valentine's Day was the official start to my resolutions? Luckily, I have time to amend my goals!

AMENDMENT A: I will assign points to every achievement and work toward 100 cumulative points per week. That way, if I don't get a job ASAP, which I'm giving 500 points because a job is a really big deal, I can compensate with social activities, or by going on a date.

AMENDMENT B: Since my first day of resolutions actually starts a month and a half after New Year's, my Valentine's Day date should be rescheduled as well. My goal is now to have a date of Valentine's Day-type *quality* in the week preceding or after April 1, as April 1 has non-romantic implications.

I credited myself with 50 points for making a new friend. However, friends can be lifelong, so I may bump up the points.

To continue my friendship/social credits, I checked the Forestiers site and saw that I had an email from the game master. He liked the profile I'd created for LadyGreene and gave me helpful tips on selecting skills so that my character wouldn't get killed quickly.

I wrote him a thank-you and congratulated myself for scoring extra life/work balance points.

So I was already feeling as if I'd achieved meaningful accomplishments when my phone rang with the most wonderful, awesome, OMG, amazing news! QUIRC offered me the job! We've got to negotiate the contract, but they hope that once we get through the paperwork I'll be able to sign with them right away. There are still three weeks until Valentine's Day and Goal #1 is accomplished. Five hundred points!

I phoned Dahlia, who said, "That means you'll be seeing Ellis all the time!"

"I hadn't thought of that."

"Liar, liar, pants on fire! You absolutely did. You've probably been fantasizing about his size-proportionate man-handle nonstop."

"I have not!" I was glad she couldn't see my red face.

"Whatever. If you're really not going to make a play for Ellis, then you have to treat every other man you meet as a potential future-love-of-your-life, hereafter to be known as PFLOYL."

"Dahl, I just took a ginormous step toward my Valentine's Day Resolutions. I don't need to rush into finding a potential future love of my life, hereafter to be known as PFLOML."

"Thank you for your attention to detail, but I think you do, because one of your resolutions was a date for V-Day!"

"It was, but I amended it to compensate for the delayed start of my resolutions."

"I am not accepting your justifications for being a dating-chicken. Start looking for your PFLOYL stat! Don't eliminate anyone with the XY chromosome, or is it XX? I'm sending you a big smacking kiss congratulations! We'll celebrate soon."

"Without Rodney."

"Without Rodney and *with* cocktails."

In the interest of full disclosure: I will admit that I have thought about Ellis ~~occasionally~~ ~~frequently~~ nonstop since meeting him again. However, I am fully aware that he is engaged and that any future association will be friendly and appropriate.

I left a message telling Holden my news and offering to take him out for a drink soon.

I called Amy, who was thrilled that I'll be at QUIRC and glad that I had already recruited Nelson as a new Forestier. "I think this is going to be your year, Jen."

"Amy, can I ask you something?"

"Sure."

"Does anyone ever call you ma'am?"

"Only all the time! Take it as a sign of respect for your status. I dated a Texan who used to call me that even in the bedroom. God, how I miss that man," she said.

"Amy, are you seeing anyone?"

"Since last week? No, I'm still New York's most eligible bachelorette, besides you, natch. Okay, I'm sending you info on our next Forestiers meet-up. A stage-fighting director is going to lead the group, so it will be fun. Bring something to use as a weapon."

I thought longingly of She-Hulk's broadsword at the Mansion, but that was too heavy for me to lift. "I'll make something out of cardboard and foam core. See you then, Amy."

2:00 P.M.

Returned from picking up my five new black business suits, which look and fit amazing, fulfilling one of my goals. The Velcro releases and snaps aren't visible, and the clothes are sleek on my body. I practiced stripping out of them until I got my time down to seven seconds. I didn't include panty hose removal because that's hopeless.

I ordered wholesale lots of panty hose in nude, matte sheer, sheer satin, opaque, and patterns for fun. The only good advice Tony Stark ever gave me was "Spare no expense on those incredible legs, baby."

I'm counting the suits and stockings as 75 points, so my score this week is already $500 + 50 + 75 = 625$. It's only sensible to allow myself to carry over extra points since I can't be expected to get a new job every week. If my total goal is 5200 points/year, then I only have to accrue 4575 more points for my resolutions to be a success!

Back to the topic of attire: I really want stylish boots that I can wear to work and wear out. Tony was always talking about how sexy the other girls at the Mansion looked in their boots. I will make stealthy inquiries about modified leather that can expand to fit She-Hulk's big old feet. If I figure that out, I'd give myself 200 points. Or 300 even, because boots are important.

I don't know what category to put Claude in because he's not job-related or cultural, but he is a man and Dahlia would say he qualifies as a romance interest, at least chromosomally.

I went down to talk to my doorman/PFLOML, during his break in the little office behind the lobby. I'd figured out that the crux of his tax problem was nonpayment on a rental property in Queens. I told him that and mentioned that he'd also missed significant deductions.

My PFLOML scratched his head and gave me the following info:

- The building had been his uncle's welding shop.
- The current tenant worked for Joocey Jooce, which explained the coupons.
- Claude was not a Joocey Jooce aficionado because citrus gave him acid reflux, but he did enjoy a warm glass of milk before bed.
- Said tenant was named Adam, might be foreign, didn't have a phone number or a last name, and had done electrical and plumbing upgrades in lieu of rent.
- Adam was a "heck of a nice guy" and "a little funny if you know

what I mean," accompanied by a circular movement of Claude's forefinger near his temple.

- The "heck of a nice guy" had secured the property with guard dogs and a fence topped with concertina wire.
- No lease agreement had been signed.

Trust and generosity are traits I want in a future husband, but I thought Claude was carrying things too far, because he said, "A man is only as good as his word. Adam and me shook and agreed that when he did better, I'd raise the rent to something fair."

I was beginning to doubt that Claude and I had a passionate future together (especially since he told me that he'd just celebrated his fortieth anniversary), but I told him that I would try to resolve the nonpayment of rent.

I tracked down the contact info for Joocey Jooce's CEO and CFO and fired off an email. I was able to draw upon my vast experience with eviction notices to make it sound impressive.

11:45 P.M.

My job celebration dinner was French dip sandwiches with Dahlia at a new gastropub on DeKalb, and we went to the lounge next door for drinks. I didn't comment when Dahlia, who is a vodka drinker, ordered a gin gimlet. Instead, I sipped my basil margarita and talked about QUIRC and apartment hunting.

On her second drink, D said, "You were the big Fringe Theory fan, not me, so I never paid too much attention to their songs. I looked up their discography and found many, many songs with references to gin."

"It's an easy rhyme."

"Especially with sin." Dahlia took out her phone. "What's Tony Stark's phone number?"

"That is a high-security number. I am not authorized to release it."

She glared at me with those scary turquoise contacts, and I caved and told her. "You can't call him! What are you going to say?"

She sucked in her cheeks and after a moment told me, "Eetz ringing. Here is hiz message," and then she pitched her voice higher and said, "Toneeee, zees eez Claudette. You must dream of how we had ze most spendid ooh, la la. I am missing ze, how you say, ze cycle and you are ze papa! Alors, I ham talking to my attorneez today. You weell be zo happy with le famileee, Toneee! Sink of a name. Je adore Hasselhoff. Hasselhoff Stark!"

I was laughing so hard that my margarita went up my nose, which Dahlia thought was hilarious. Finally, I said, "It won't work. He'll never believe it because . . ." But how do you tell someone your genius ex-boyfriend invented microscopic nanobots to retrieve wayward sperm? You don't.

11:30 P.M.

I really didn't want to go all the way out to Queens, but I was feeling protective about my trusting PFLOML. Some unnamed superhero, whose name might rhyme with Baloney Snark, always took advantage of the transportation services offered by our organization even when he already had drivers, aircraft, jetpacks that didn't burn your butt, etc. He used to say, "Take care of the pennies and the multibillions will take care of themselves." People always laughed the same way they do when Shulky jokes. If you're rich or powerful, everyone assumes you're incredibly witty, too.

I don't exploit the system, so I had to take the tedious slow route of a train, a bus, and a long walk. The industrial neighborhood was eerily quiet.

Claude's property was at the end of a block. A chain-link fence surrounded a two-story brick building with an office on one side and an empty parking lot. The building had a roll-down metal gate with a faded sign reading VINCE'S WELDING. Yellowed venetian blinds covered the windows.

A heavy chain and lock secured the gate. I rang the buzzer a few times and waited. No one answered. I rang again and waited. There was one security camera, aimed toward the office door.

I circled the perimeter of the property, casually looking for signs of life and more surveillance equipment. The rear roll-up gate was shut, too, but as I approached, a pack of massive mutts burst out from a dog door and began snarling and lunging at the fence.

Foam drooled from their gaping jaws, and their dark eyes shone in the night. Looking at them reminded me of how I yearned for a real dog—something non-Rodneyish—but pets needed a place with a yard and an owner with regular hours. D couldn't dog-sit for me because Rodney didn't play well with others.

The whole setup seemed peculiar. Why would an employee of a juice company need so much security and such an out-of-the-way location?

I felt that I had done due diligence. Shulky could figure it out another time, so I went home.

JANUARY 24

Woke up and found that Dahlia had sent me a message that said,

> Exhibit #3, OMG! what did you do 2 him?

with a link to Fringe Theory's "The Alchemy of Sin."

> I am a modern man with no superstitions
> Yet Gin dissolved all my inhibitions
> Turned poor metal into something priceless
> Spun me through an emotional crisis
> Cuz I didn't believe in love magic,
> Didn't fall for sleight-of-hand,
> But Gin changed me in ways I can't understand.
> She was my transmutation
> Into some glorious distillation

Of sin and purification.
Gin all night long.

When that song came out, almost a year after my night with Ellis, I had listened to it over and over and over and over, aching with jealous conviction that he was using "Gin" to sing to another girl. Or hundreds of girls. Now I didn't know what to think.

OBJECTION TO
DISCHARGEABILITY

FEBRUARY 6

Today I went to QUIRC to sign my contract. I made a special effort not to look for Ellis in the halls. Because he's engaged and utterly, absolutely, unequivocally unavailable.

QUIRC gave me everything I asked for: the salary, an experienced paralegal, the additional private "meditation" space, the supply of No. 1 Ticonderoga pencils, use of the car service, club memberships, and an allowance for my Krav Maga training.

The office manager, Bailey, showed me to my roomy office with leather, stainless steel, and glass furniture. She said, "I took the liberty of ordering a few paintings to cheer up the room, but you can replace them with whatever you like."

Was I supposed to know anything about art? I should have watched *Sister Wendy at the Norton Simon Museum* instead of the *Big Valley* marathon, but I couldn't resist a show with golden California hills, a gallant lawyer, a leather-clad brawler, and gun-slinging Barbara Stanwyck. I said, "The pictures are really nice, Bailey. Thank you."

She showed me a small refrigerator hidden in a credenza. "We'll keep it stocked for you with your preferred brands. There's always Joocey Jooce, so if you have any favorite flavors, please tell the office manager."

"I didn't know they sold it bottled. I thought it was only available freshly made."

"They bottle a small amount for special clients. Ms. Tumbridge requested it as an efficiency measure when she thought we were spending too much time making smoothie runs." Bailey opened a door on the far wall and said, "Here's your mediation — I mean, *meditation* room."

"I know it was a peculiar request, but I find that I need solitude and quiet time to prepare for court."

"Like an actor's dressing room!" she said, and then added a little shyly, "I saw you in court when you were with GLKH, Ms. Walters, and your performance, well, it's legendary. I hope this will be satisfactory. It was converted from a storage space, but we tried to make it comfortable."

I stepped into a small windowless room with a low-pile rug, an armoire, and a sofa long enough for me to nap on, which is probably what the partners thought I'd be doing here. The armoire could hold several outfits and I could change easily here in an emergency. "Thanks, Bailey. It's perfect."

I got my office passkey, ID badge, and an employee manual. As I was introduced around, I felt a rising panic. Everyone was so sophisticated and fancy, and I was just a girl who'd liked to spend quiet evenings with her dad cleaning guns while her mom made a pan of brownies.

Quinty dropped by my office just as the HR manager was leaving. He sat in the leather-and-chrome chair across from my desk. I tried to very casually check out those features that Ellis had inherited, and I hoped Amber hadn't told him, "Her credentials might not be too shabby, but you do know that she was a trashy little slutty groupie, right? You'll definitely want to disinfect anything she sits on."

Quinty was wearing the same tweed jacket and had a monocle dangling from his pocket. "Have you got everything all sorted out?"

"Yes, sir." I tried not to stare at the monocle.

"I just wanted you to know that it's official. We've got the Replace-Max suit, and I'm putting you on lead."

My heart did a flip. "Thank you, sir! I won't let you down."

"I hope not. In fact, we hired you especially for this case. If you hadn't approached us, we would have gone to you, since Dr. Sven Morigi, our client, greatly admires the work you did at GLKH. He'd like to meet you this week to talk about the case."

"Yes, sir. It's an amazing opportunity for me. What's the catch?"

He raised his bushy white eyebrows. "Hmm?"

"I'm not here for one day, yet I get a case that any of the partners would kill for. There's got to be a catch."

His laugh boomed through the room. "The first one is that Amber expected to be lead, and she won't be happy being second chair. If you make any mistakes, she'll use them against you and she'll be unforgiving."

"I'm glad to have a second who is watching for anything I might miss, because I want the best for our client."

"Good attitude. The second catch is not really your concern. Amber has the appearance of conflict, which is why I agreed to allow a new hire to be first chair." He frowned and then shrugged. "My son, Ellis, is good friends with Maxwell Kirsch, the CEO of ReplaceMax, and he doesn't want us to take this suit. Ellis has always been ruled by his heart, so that's to be expected."

Was he telling me that Ellis was in love with Amber, so don't get any ideas? "I appreciate your caution, sir. It's always best to avoid even the suspicion of compromise."

"Amber and I have met with Dr. Morigi to fully apprise him of the situation," he said. "I know Amber well enough to trust that she won't allow a personal relationship to influence her professional conduct."

Was this code for "because she conceded to letting us hire you even though you're a skanky ho"? Maybe.

Quinty sighed deeply. "No, I would bet my bottom dollar that Amber would never let a human emotion sway her dedication to the big win. If she did, we'd have to eliminate our business relationships with a good portion of the female population."

Quinty winked, and I knew that my skanky ho-ishness was official. "Sir, I just want to say . . ."

He held up his hand and said, "No need. I gather that you and my son met when you were both graduate students. We all have private lives, including me."

I tried to smile, but my muscles might have been making another expression entirely. "Anything else, sir?"

"A few of our witnesses are terminally ill, so we need you to get an expedited trial date. By expedited, I don't mean in a year. We need to try the case *within* the year." He pulled his monocle out of his pocket and swung it by the gold chain. "You're going to tell me that it's impossible."

"No, sir. I'm going to tell you that's improbable, because I don't think anything is impossible. I'll do all I can to schedule a trial date ASAP."

"That's what I hoped to hear. Well, every second counts!"

When I walked through the front door of my building, Claude was waiting for me, ecstatic that he'd received a check by special delivery. "Joocey Jooce paid all the back rent for my tenant!" He clutched my hands, saying, "Thank you, Miss Jennifer, thank you!"

He told me the amount of the check, which was more than what the tenant owed even at the current market rate, let alone the original monthly rate. "They must value your tenant's work to pay so much and so quickly," I said to my solvent PFLOML.

Either things were coming too damn easy for me, or my luck had changed. And I didn't believe in luck. Satisfied with the resolution to his rent problem, I told Claude to contact a tax attorney to take care of the error on his filing.

"But you're my lawyer!"

"Okay, as your lawyer, I strongly advise you to see a tax specialist. I'll give you the name of a friend of mine who'll take good care of you."

"I guess she'll have to do, Miss Jennifer. But you're the best, you know."

It was funny how the appreciation of a doorman meant just as much to me as a big win in court, but it did.

8:00 P.M.

Text to Dahlia:	Does olde English use lots of extra e's?
Text from Dahlia:	Yeesth. Whye?
Text to Dahlia:	I've joined a new LARP teamee. Medieval age. Castles & Knights.
Text from Dahlia:	Yere suche a geekey wenche! I'll helpeth u with youre dressee. Any hawt knights for hawt nites?
Text to Dahlia:	Hope so but suits of armor can be deceiving.

11:40 P.M.

I changed into black sweats and a hoodie and tied my hair back. I love this city at night, even on cold, wet nights. It's so charged with energy, and the millions of lights glow and glitter and shimmer against the darkness. I hit a fast pace, so that by the time anyone noticed me, I was already gone, baby, gone.

In a few minutes, I'd warmed up. I felt strong. Not superhuman strong, but really good anyway, and almost hoping that ninjas would leap out from a doorway and attack so I could throw a few moves at them while shouting "Bam! Kapow!"

After I put in seven miles, I loped over to the Mansion's garage. I sighed as I passed by all the gleaming muscle cars, shiny roadsters, and beefed-up trucks, and chose a beat-up Toyota, which wouldn't attract attention. I checked out the tricked-up features: the car had the standard invisibility shield and a nice hydroplane function, but sadly no sideways rotation or flamethrowers. Because you never know.

When I asked for the key, the guy, whose name really is Guy, said, "Sorry, Ms. Walters, but you need to sign the release to take it out and you aren't permitted to race, do stunts, or to transform in it."

I had no intention of transforming in the car because She-Hulk's head would rip right through the roof like a green jack-in-the-box. "Don't worry. I'm only using it for surveillance. I'll bring it back in one piece."

The attendant cringed back as if he thought I was going to punch him. "I'm really sorry, but I'm just following the rules: no signature, no car."

"Fine." I signed the release, which I had drawn up myself, including provisions and exclusions that might come in handy. As I always advise my clients, "Allowing your legal opponent to set the terms of a contract is like hiring a fox to design the security system for a chicken coop."

I drove to Queens and parked down the street from my PFLOML's warehouse. The building was dark and I hoped no one was in. There was an alley that ran behind the warehouse, and I slipped in beside a stack of pallets and quickly yanked off my sweats. I tucked my glasses into one of my shoes for safety.

I was wearing one of Shulky's favorite black bodysuits beneath, and it sagged at my boobs, hung at my crotch, and pooched at my butt, ugh! But as I transformed, the fabric stretched taut. I felt my body growing large and solid with muscle, my vision sharpening, my blood moving through my arteries as I acquired her incredible strength.

And then I felt the roar of She-Hulk's personality — the bravado, the swag, and sexiness. There was a sharp moment when we coexisted, when I was She-Hulk and She-Hulk was Jennifer Walters, and it always felt amazing, like pure shimmering joy, like utter rightness and balance and perfection, and the universe stopped for that moment.

Then it was gone, and I existed like a shadow within her.

Shulky left my shoes and clothes by the pallets and rambled back to the fence. While I'd never break and enter, she had different rules. She sprung up in an easy standing back flip, clearing the vicious concertina wire just as the guard dogs tore out of the building.

The leader of the pack, which looked like a cross between a Rottwei-ler and a Kodiak bear, went straight for her jugular, as the other dogs cir-cled. Shulky embraced the dog and laughed.

The beast recognized Shulky as an alpha, and in seconds she'd placed him on the ground and was giving him a vigorous tummy rub.

"I'd love to play with you all night, Fido, but there's business to take care of."

She went to the dog door, which wasn't wide enough for her line-backer shoulders, and grabbed on to the corrugated steel edge of the roll-down gate. She pushed, but not so hard as to make the metal crum-ple. The chain mechanism ratcheted loudly as the gate rolled up a few feet, and she dropped to the ground and rolled underneath and into the warehouse. The Rottiak followed her.

She could see well in dim light, but the shop was pure black, so she set the illuminate function on her aPhone to the "ambient" level. Card-board boxes were stacked almost to the ceiling. She opened one and saw the biodegradable cup lids featuring Joocey Jooce's PLAY NICE! logo with its graphic of stick figures on a seesaw.

She opened other boxes at random. They also contained lids, and she found cartons of paper straws, too. She made her way between stacks to a corner of the shop that was set up with lab tables and chemistry equip-ment.

Shulky went to the side door and listened, which was very discreet since she enjoyed kicking her way into places. When she didn't hear any-thing, she opened the door to an office space. The industrial carpeting was grooved from where the space had once been partitioned, and two Steelcase desks and file cabinets were shoved to one side.

A simple wood crucifix hung on one wall, and another wall had an altar with oranges and incense to the Buddha. A small prayer carpet faced the north wall. There were floor-to-ceiling shelves on the final wall, and books filled every inch.

Shulky scanned the spines of religious texts in many languages and translations. There were books on philosophy, math, chemistry, physics, medicine, metaphysics, and veterinary care. Shulky opened drawers and file cabinets and found paper clips, legal notepads, and a pencil sharpener. Initial sketches of the PLAY NICE! logo filled the pages of one notebook.

"Weird, huh?" she asked the Rottiak, who was following her. "Someone's feeding and exercising you, right? Cuz you look fabulous."

She went back out to the shop and discovered an alcove with food and water bowls, a garbage bin filled with kibble, chew toys, and clean bedding.

She suspected that there were living quarters on the second floor, but she decided not to explore further, in case there were any alarms. Also, I was panicking that she'd been here too long, and I kept whining, "Let's go!" inside her head.

Shulky left the building safely, loped across the lot, and flipped over the fence, landing gracefully on her feet. She threw her arms in the air and whisper-shouted, "She-Hulk nails a perfect landing! Ten! The crowd goes wild!"

She was heading back to the car, thinking of where she'd like to go, when I shouted, "No, no, no! Let me out!"

"Chillax. No work tomorrow," she said as she took out her aPhone and began scrolling through Tweets. "Yes, dancing with Katy and Rihanna would totally be fun!"

I sat back and hoped she wouldn't get herself in the news again. Or wreck the car. Or hook up with a sleazebag. Or trash a hotel. Or decide to take a road trip to Tijuana for an X-rated tattoo. Any or all of the above. Again.

As she headed to ~~parts~~ parties unknown, I wondered about my PFLOML's tenant, Adam, a "heck of a nice guy" who read philosophy, studied religion, kept guard dogs, conducted chemistry experiments, and thought it was okay to pay rent in store coupons.

ASSUME

FEBRUARY 7

VALENTINE'S DAY RESOLUTION COUNTDOWN: 1 WEEK TO START

Everyone is calling to wish me luck! Amy called, my cousin called, and Holden left a message saying we should meet next week and "regroup." Ruth called and promised to route all situations to other superheroes unless absolutely necessary and said, "About Fashion Week . . ."

I felt Shulky brooding inside me, and I said, "Shulky understands why she was blacklisted after that fiasco with Mr. Lagerfeld." I smiled remembering how the small man had faced down Shulky and been mad or brave enough to call her wardrobe "vulgar," her behavior as deplorable as that of "a parlor maid who discovers the brandy," and her walk "graceless."

Ruth said, "I know how much she loves Fashion Week, but she probably shouldn't have suspended him from the rafters. Anyway, the AMAZING news is that she's been invited to be a celebrity guest at an interseasonal show in April, and I wanted to tell you to . . ."

"To placate her so she won't crash the main show. Duly noted. Thanks, Ruth."

"You know how I hate seeing her left out of things just because . . . she's so enthusiastic! The show's for a new mystery designer. Shulky's ensemble will be delivered with the invite for the show and the wrap party."

The invitation was enough to pacify Shulky, which was great since I don't want her to do anything that might leave a negative impression should I ever meet my imaginary gay boyfriend Tim Gunn.

Dahlia called me between appointments.

D: Knock 'em dead, Jen. But not literally since your hands are licensed weapons.

ME: I didn't take you literally.

D: Speaking of literature . . .

ME: We weren't.

D: Yes, we were. I'm sending you another poem from your rock star lover, circa several years ago.

ME: Don't! I want to be calm and collected when, I mean, *if* I happen to see him.

D: With his clothes on.

ME: Yes. No, not with his clothes on! I mean, don't—

D: Oops, Rodney just sent the link with his tiny little paws! He's so tech savvy.

ME: I'm not going to listen to it.

D: Sure, you are. He describes the perfection of your titties and how your lady bits are like—

ME: Dahlia!

D: A client just caught fire under the dryer. Gotta go!

I am not going to listen to the song. I am not going to listen to the song.

4:27 P.M.

Left a message for Dr. Alvarado and canceled my appointment because it conflicted with my job. "I'll be in touch to reschedule when I have some availability." Nevah!

Five minutes later he called me back, his voice all crushed blueberries and organic oatmeal sensitivity.

RA: Jennifer—

ME: Ms. Walters.

RA: Ms. Walters, your sessions are stipulated in the settlement. [blah blah blah]

ME: I will take your opinion under consideration, but my employment is a priority.

RA: You had time to go out dancing with celebrities!

ME: Not me, Shulky.

RA: When are you going to take responsibility for your behavior in your She-Hulk persona?

ME: Dr. Alvarado, I know it must seem very important to you to hear a patient's inner thoughts, but I'm working on a case in which children's *lives* are at stake. If you will examine the settlement agreement, you'll see that this exempts me from attending sessions for an indeterminate period.

RA: That wasn't in there.

ME: It's in the amendments.

RA: You wrote those!

ME: As I advise my clients, "A contract is a mutual agreement, and you should always negotiate for terms that are most beneficial to your side. It's perfectly legal to cross out or amend conditions." If you have any further questions, please submit them in writing for my review.

RA: This is for your sake, not mine. You are mentally ill, Jennifer!

ME: It's *Ms. Walters*, Rene, and have a nice day.

7:30 P.M.

Back from the gym. Azzan was glad that I can continue my private classes, but disappointed that poverty wouldn't force me into life as an international sexy times assassin. When I tried out a few "kapows!" he flipped me flat on my back, so I shut up and focused.

It's making me crazy thinking that Ellis might have sung about my breasts. I will only listen to a few seconds of "Gin Tsunami," the house party anthem, to assure myself that D is entirely wrong about the lyrics.

The tidal wave rolled over me
Her wavelength was longer
My reactions so much stronger
I rode the wave train and couldn't forecast
Destination or destruction,
Rising waters, deep induction
Because I was drunk with Gin
Caught in the riptide of Gin, sweet sweet sin.
Raise a toast to Gin, of Gin!
Swear to sin with Gin to the brim,
Slip and slide and ride the tide with Gin!

I stopped the song and thought, OMG, how much mental effort had I expended deluding myself that it was a drinking song when I knew the dirty, dirty truth?

FEBRUARY 8

VALENTINE'S DAY RESOLUTION COUNTDOWN: 6 DAYS TO START!

First real day at QUIRC!

- ☑ Suit neat and lint free
- ☑ Glasses cleaned, ponytail straight
- ☑ Extra panty hose and identical glasses in attaché
- ☑ Black pumps clean and polished
- ☑ Framed diplomas and photo of Mom and Dad
- ☑ Favorite UCLA pens
- ☑ Garment bag with extra suit just in case
- ☑ Lucky LAWYERS DO IT ON A TRIAL BASIS mug

When I went downstairs, Claude looked at me and tipped his cap. "Looking mighty sharp this morning, Counselor."

"Thanks, Claude. First day at the new job and I'm a little nervous."

He winked — but in a friendly ye-olde-fashioned way — and said, "Just be yourself and everyone will like you."

"Easier said than done." Planning to be myself was one thing; staying myself was a whole nuther thang.

Cabbed it to QUIRC. I arrived at the reception desk at precisely 8:20, ten minutes early, but the offices were already busy.

The receptionist said, "Good morning, Ms. Walters," and politely reminded me of her name (Penelope). "Your paralegal, Donna, is already here and will help you with anything you need."

I thanked her and went down the hall, glancing into open doors. Outside my office, a fortyish man who looked like a 1940s accountant was sitting at the assistant's desk with an old-fashioned typewriter on it. I introduced myself and asked him to point me to Donna.

"Donner. I'm Donner. Pleased to meet you . . ."

I said, "Call me Jennifer."

He stood to shake hands and I towered over him. He had dark brown skin, horn-rimmed glasses that made his hazel eyes look huge, and very short waved hair, and wore a bow tie and a herringbone tweed jacket.

He saw me peek at the typewriter and pointed to a screen behind it. He said, "It's wired to the system. I hope you don't mind."

"Not as long as the work gets done."

"The joke is that everyone at QUIRC has quirks." His hand went to his chest. "I didn't mean to imply that you have any!"

Rather than say, "It's okay," I smiled neutrally. As I always tell my clients, "A response may be seen as tacit agreement and used against you in litigation. If you are in doubt, simply look pleasant and remain silent."

A large arrangement of flowers was on my desk with a welcome note from Quinty and the senior partners. Donner brought me a frothy cappuccino and ran through basic company protocol. He asked me about my likes and dislikes. (Likes long evenings by a crackling fire reading case histories! Dislikes mean people delivering injunctions!)

"Got it," he said. "Any business contacts or special friends or family you'd like routed through quickly?"

"Client calls are my top priority. Everyone else knows to call me on my private line."

He smiled. "I know you did superhuman law for GLKH. I bet you have some stories."

"More than a few! But the truth is that New York State law is even more complex than superhuman law, because superhumans understand legal shortcuts like crashing a chair on someone's head to make your argument."

"We're a little quieter here. Guess it's time for you to meet the General."

I tried to recall anyone on the QUIRC roster with a military background as I followed Donner down the hall to an office with a handwritten sign hanging from a string that said, THE GENERAL IS IN!

Donner knocked and opened the door without waiting for a response.

We walked into a huge room that was filled from top to bottom and side to side with tables, books, file cabinets, and computers. Colored three-by-five cards covered a standing bulletin board. It took me a moment to see the pudgy middle-aged woman peering at us around a stack of legal texts.

"Morning, General," Donner said. "This is Jennifer Walters. She'll be lead on ReplaceMax."

I went forward to say hello, and the woman looked up at me with small, sharp gray eyes so light they were almost silver. She had freckled cheeks and a pretty rosebud mouth, which didn't smile. I held out my hand. "Good morning, General."

She puffed at a wisp of russet hair that was loose from a crooked ponytail and reached out to shake my hand. In a calm, sweet voice, she said, "That's not my real name. It's a joke. My name's Genoa Lewes, and I'm the associate assigned exclusively to your case."

"Pleased to meet you, Genoa," I said, as I noticed the numerous action figures posed on her desk and shelves. I automatically searched for Shulky or any of my friends, but all she had were dolls in Regency dress. "Who is this?" I said, picking up a brown-haired doll and using it to point to a yellow-headed one.

Her mouth set defensively. "You're holding Elinor Dashwood and the other one is her sister, Marianne, of *Sense and Sensibility*. I know most people follow the superheroes, but I prefer characters with rich emotional lives, even if they are fictional."

"You don't think Tony Stark has a rich emotional life?" Donner asked. "Wouldn't he look dashing in a cravat!"

Genoa blushed all the way to her forehead and reached for the Elinor doll.

I thought it was unusual for a paralegal to tease an associate, or maybe he was *pretending* to tease her in order to introduce the subject of Tony. I had managed to drag him to a few lawyer parties when we dated and everyone was all, "Tony Stark! May I kiss your fabulously firm and amazingly wealthy ass!"

I said, "Tony Stark's a genius. I wish I could invent something, but all I can do is admire how brilliant he is." He's extremely brilliant for a horse's ass.

Genoa gave me a grateful look and began talking about one of Tony's latest projects. She quickly got to a level of technical detail that I couldn't follow. "Oh, you've lost me! I think even a patent attorney would have trouble understanding that."

Donner smiled and said, "Now you know why we call her the General. She has a wider and deeper range of information than anyone else at QUIRC. She's the best."

"Glad to have you on my team, Genoa. You'll need to get me up to speed on organ-cloning technology, but in layman's terms. These high-tech cases are confusing enough to juries, and ReplaceMax will try to baffle them with science."

Genoa grabbed a thick binder from a stack nearby and handed it to me. "I've prepared preliminary information about the ReplaceMax process, and I can bring in experts to give you seminars."

"Thanks, General. Or do you prefer Genoa?"

"I like both," she said and ducked her head again.

I was taken to lunch by one of the junior partners, Fritz Durning, an intense man with a close-cropped brush of sandy hair, blue-gray eyes, and a hard, sleek physique. He was a typical type A, talking a mile a minute and ordering boneless, skinless chicken with a wedge of lemon and steamed veggies. He was attractive, but I suspected he'd had his teeth capped, and his nose was a little too perfect.

He tried to pry GLKH intel from me and became annoyed when I wouldn't tell him any backroom gossip. Before we were done with our first course, he was treating me like a prom date he wanted to dump so he could meet up with his cool friends.

And that's when I realized that I should have been scoping him out as a PFLOML just in case my budding relationship with Claude didn't work out. So I smiled and said, "Of course, Fritz, there are things I can tell you about GLKH that wouldn't violate confidentiality, but let's save that for another occasion when we have time to relax and talk!"

He looked pleased. And then I finally noticed the gold band on his ring finger, which was a bad omen for our future love life.

Another bad omen was my relief to get away from Fritz and spend the rest of the afternoon reading up on ReplaceMax and finding out:

- Our client, Dr. Sven Morigi, had approached ReplaceMax with a formulation for rapidly growing entire organs in a laboratory. Until then, they'd specialized in skin and bone grafts.
- When Dr. Morigi had reported problems with the lab-grown organs, he'd been shown the door despite holding the patent for the process.
- In addition to a higher than average rate of mortality for Replace-Max transplant cases, there were nearly two dozen of their patients in serious condition, all with malfunctioning replacement organs. The youngest was an eight-year-old girl who'd had four months of health before organ deterioration.
- Dr. Morigi still owned shares in the company, and he wanted the usual fines, the president's resignation, and to buy out the company.

I took the General's binder home, changed into my jammies, and spent the evening studying it and making notes. Before I knew it, the hours had flown by and I hadn't even checked my aPhone for chatter from Shulky's friends.

I wonder what Ellis is doing tonight. I am not going to revisit all his songs to look for clues about us. If there had ever been an opportunity, it was long gone and by his choice.

Moving on to the present and reality, I found out basic biographical info on Dr. Sven Morigi online, including his impressive credentials. Then I logged into the Mansion's network, which was not much good for celebrity gossip, but excellent for fact-checking. I found the same info, but no photos, which wasn't that odd. Scientists were often self-conscious about being in the public eye.

Not that I have any intention of dating him, even though he's single and successful. Sven Morigi. His name sounds like someone who holds his glasses together with a paper clip. Which I no longer do since Dahlia gave me an eyeglass repair kit with little screws. I would be more than willing to offer a screw to Dr. Morigi if he needed one.

Dahlia called and I told her about my first day at QUIRC, and she asked, "Did you have to face Amber Hammerhead?"

"That's tomorrow. I am kind of, sort of, totally dreading it."

"She probably knows you're the inspiration for 'Gin Spins Me Equatorially.'"

"I don't remember that one. You're making it up."

"It was only performed live on their final tour, Miss Gravity-rhymes-with-carnal-depravity."

"Oh, gawd! Don't say any more. Uh, I went to lunch with a buff hotshot attorney named Fritz today."

"Tell me all!" she said, and I was glad I'd successfully diverted her.

·9·

THIRD PARTY COMPLAINT

FEBRUARY 9

VALENTINE'S DAY RESOLUTION
COUNTDOWN: 5 DAYS!

Spent the morning panicking and drinking too many cappuccinos, so I was jittery and needed an intestinal sponge to soak up the caffeine. I ate one of the gourmet donuts (bacon, apple, cinnamon) that was in the breakroom. It was so good, I ate another (banana and pecan with maple glaze), and then another, the most scrumptious of them all, a peanut butter and blackberry jelly donut. As I bit into it, the jelly spurted out and onto the collar of my jacket.

I hurried to clean up the mess with paper towels, but the lint glommed onto the jam, making the smear worse. I glanced at the clock on the wall, and somehow it was time for my meeting with Amber. I rushed back to my office, planning to change into one of my extra jackets, but I was too late — the blond hammerhead was right ahead of me.

Donner's eyebrows went up behind his glasses and he said, "Ms. Walters, there's—"

As I went by him, I whispered, "I know! I saw her. Thanks!"

I yanked off my ponytail holder and shook out my hair so that it covered the splotch, and then I stepped into my office.

Amber was sitting at the round glass table by the window. I joined her and said the usual stuff, but I kept getting seriously eeped out thinking of the things Ellis could have told her about me. I remembered all the details because it had been a singular occasion for me.

Amber and I reviewed strategies for our case, but I could sense the hostility beneath her cool manner. Meanwhile, the donuts had kicked in, and I was fighting both a sugar and caffeine high and my ookometer was swinging wildly from side to side. My voice had a quaver in it, and every time I looked at Amber I thought of Ellis doing *those* things to her. It made me feel nauseated. Or it could have been the lethal breakfast combo of caffeine, sugar, and grease.

"I attended the initial meetings with Dr. Sven Morigi," she said, in a voice that was richer and sweeter than the delectable donuts. "Breach of contract is a given."

"What about wrongful termination?" I asked.

"He wasn't an employee of the company," she said, looking irked.

"I realize that, but his contract is structured more like an employment agreement than a consultant's, so let's look into it. I'll also go for patent infringement."

"*Obviously*," she said snippily, as if I was a clueless newbie. "Is there anything else?"

The fact that she routinely did the nasty with my fantasy man had thrown me off my game, but I said, "Yes, there is. Have you contacted anyone else involved in the case, even socially?"

"Do you mean, have I revealed anything to Ellis's colleagues at ReplaceMax? No."

"That's not what I was implying," I said. "I wondered if there was anything that hasn't been included in the preliminary report because it was assumed to be a known factor."

She put her left hand to her throat to show off her engagement ring. "Jennifer, it would be a waste of my time guessing what you might not know, but if you have any further questions, send an email. Your primary responsibility may be this case, but I have other clients."

I felt my shoulders creeping up with tension. "I'll do that and I would appreciate immediate responses. Mr. Quintal impressed upon me that we've got to get the case to trial before one of our witnesses dies."

Amber Hammerhead stood up and smoothed her skirt, which was already smooth. "I don't see what the rush is. There's nothing like a dead child to wring sympathy from the jury."

I stared at her appalled. Of all the women in the world, why was Ellis marrying this vile and heinous she-demon? What did that say about him as a human being?

"Now, if we're done . . ."

I knew I had to deal with the issue, so I said, "There is one final thing. I wanted you to know that my initial encounter with Ellis was an isolated, anomalous incident. He didn't even know my name properly, nor was there any subsequent contact."

"Yes, I'm aware of his history. I'm sure he didn't distinguish between all the Jennys, Ginnys, and Jillys, and he was long finished with drunken, love-struck groupies when he began pursuing me." Her nostrils widened as if she smelled something unpleasant. "Please try to be more present- able for client meetings."

I couldn't say anything because I was busy processing the flurry of insults. I really wanted to break something — preferably over her head or with her head — but I did my breathing exercises while she swept out of the room, and then I went out to see Donner.

"Sorry I was abrupt, Donner. I didn't want to keep Amber waiting."

He gave me an apologetic half smile and then held out a wet wipe packet. "You've got something," he said and touched his finger to his cheek.

I mimicked his gesture and felt something sticky. I know that evil hammerhead will smear to Ellis that I had blackberry jelly on my face for the entire meeting.

5:30 P.M.

Ruth called me from the Avengers Mansion to say that Shulky's Valentine's Day cards and gifts have been coming in by the truckload. She tried to lure me in with oatmeal-raisin cookies and hot chocolate, so that we could go through the packages together.

I try not to feel jealous that Shulky gets so much attention. I told Ruth to have one of the interns log the cards, messages, and gifts on a spreadsheet. She knows the drill—thank-you notes to fans, dispose of all organic matter (some okay and some seriously eww!), donate usable gifts to the women's shelter, and auction off valuables for the Avengers Charity Fund. "Ruth, if you see anything you like, please take it as a token of Shulky's appreciation for all you do."

"I did see a bath set — thanks, Jennifer!" Ruth said, "I think it's *amazing* how everyone still loves Shulky even if she's on a break from the main action. Don't you want any of the presents?"

"They're not really mine, are they? They're intended for Shulky. Oh, that reminds me, she's expecting an outfit from Christian Siriano, so keep that one."

"Will you or Shulky be going out on Valentine's Day?"

"I don't think so. She's supposed to stay out of trouble, and I've got a multibillion-dollar case to prepare."

10:55 P.M.

I'd just finished grinding through a kazillion mind-numbing pages on the ReplaceMax's clinical trials when my aPhone buzzed with a call from the night scheduler at the Mansion. He said, "We know you're taking a break, but we just got a call right near you in Tribeca. Someone is using a raygun — well, a moongun or something like that — and is carving up a bank. Sergeant Palmieri's already on the scene."

Once he gave me the location, I said I'd be there stat! (I really have to stop picking up Dahlia's vocabulary.) I stripped off my clothes. As I transformed, I felt the lingering humiliation from my day vanish, and by the time Shulky danced naked to her closet, my problems seemed inconsequential. She selected a slinky silver bodysuit with purple trim, matching boots, and armbands.

She preened in the mirror for only a moment, saying, "Who loves ya, baby?" before flipping back her hair, dashing into the elevator, and hitting the express subbasement button. It was exhilarating being in her body and getting that delicious surge of her energy that made me think, *Ellis who?*

She ran through the tunnels until she was only a few blocks from the crime scene, and then she slipped out to the street via a hidden door behind a brick wall. She saw the commotion ahead at National Amalgamated Savings & Loan. Gawkers were moving toward the bank, a blocky, squat building, and everyone was staring upward.

Directly across the street from National Amalgamated was a tall office building bordered on either side with narrow alleys. High atop this building was a structure with a huge reflecting lens and a mechanism that focused light from the full moon into a brilliant, intense beam that was aimed at the bank, searing through the thick granite walls.

Shulky deftly wove through the crowd — who now shouted, "She-Hulk! She-Hulk's here!" — and ran past a patrol car sliced lengthwise, each side tilting over to reveal the car's interior. A Joocey Jooce spilled from its cup onto the pavement.

She found Sergeant Patty standing at the end of the block with a dozen officers. The rawboned woman looked bulky in a down coat and flak jacket.

"Hi, Patty, what's shaking?"

"Thanks for coming, Shulky. Kickass outfit, by the way, and here I am looking like a goddamn Puerto Rican Michelin Man. Knock me over and I'll roll. Anyways, this miscreant set up a moonbeam raygun and sliced through my cruiser like a goddamn Ginsu knife. I didn't even get to finish my goddamn lime-papaya smoothie."

"That's a bitch — I'll have a friend send you some two-for-one coupons. Is the aforementioned asshole anyone we know?"

"I don't recognize him, and I can't figure what he wants," Patty said. "The bank is cut up through and through, but he hasn't made a move toward the vault. That office building has a freight elevator facing the alley. That's probably where the raygun gear was loaded in."

Shulky could see the lines crisscrossing the bank, like a series of Ts. "Someone capable of creating a moonbeam raygun is smart enough to think of a slicker way to rob a bank. You thinking what I'm thinking?"

Patty gazed upward to the top of the office building and said, "Same look-ma-no-hands, immature, attention-grabbing style as the water spheres hijinks. It would take a coordinated team of regular humans to assemble that goddamn moonbeam thingamajig on the roof, but there's no sign of anyone 'cept the aforementioned asshole."

"So either his crew is hiding out or he may have super strength. What's your team doing?"

Patty said that she'd sent for mirrors and hoped to reflect the moonbeam back to its source.

"Too dangerous," Shulky said. "One slip and you might flame out the entire building. Pattycake, create a distraction for me and I'll go up and destroy the mechanism. Can you get the access codes to the office building, and do you have any rappelling gear?"

"What kind of cop do you think I am? Of course I've got goddamn rappelling gear."

Two minutes later, Shulky was in the office building and keying in the code for the service elevator. The elevator hummed and began pulling her up through the dark empty floors. Even though I trusted her ~~completely most of the time~~ a lot, I always worried that an elevator wouldn't be able to hold her mass and we'd go plummeting to the ground.

Shulky felt her skin tingle with excitement and made a purring sound in the back of her throat. Normal women didn't do that. Maybe strippers did. I don't know, but once Tony asked me to "growl" for him and I'd firmly told him that I wasn't a dog. Tony always said that he didn't compare me to Shulky. Of course, I used to tell him that he was the sexiest man I'd ever met.

Shulky got out at the twentieth floor because she didn't want the elevator to announce her arrival. She tapped in the code to bypass the alarm on the emergency exit. When the light turned green, her favorite color, she murmured, "Green means go, baby, go," and opened a door to the shadowy exterior fire escape.

As she stepped onto the escape, the old iron creaked ominously. "Fine," she muttered. "I don't need youse anyway."

Seriously, *youse*? I think she thought she sounded amusing in an ironic way. I hoped she wouldn't start wearing a trucker's cap.

She swung the rappelling hook and threw it up to a ledge on the floor above. She would have liked to quickly scale up the building, but she thought a sneakier approach was needed. She kept to the shadows as she moved from ledge to ledge. The icy wind was refreshing over her skin. She relished it, thinking of the contrasting heat she'd feel when she went dancing later.

I tried to tell her, "No, we are not going dancing later! I have work tomorrow. No and no and no!" but she ignored me.

When Shulky was almost at the top of the building, she signaled down to Patty.

Patty scooted into a squad car and set off an ear-piercing siren. When she had the crowd's attention, she got out of the car with a bullhorn to announce, "You up there! Hey, I'm talking to you, jerkface! You are hereby ordered to cease and desist. Come down and give yourself up peacefully."

The moonbeam raygun swung around, scorching into the pavement near Patty, who jumped back.

This was the moment when Shulky threw the hook to the highest ledge and swiftly drew herself up. She stood in the shadows and spotted a man's back near the base of the raygun structure. He was wearing a hooded cape, but she could hear his childish laughter as he aimed the raygun back toward the bank.

She was moving toward him when a high-pitched *buzz-buzz-buzz* sounded, and she knew that she'd tripped an alarm.

The man turned around and shouted, "She-Hulk!" His face was hidden behind a blue mask.

She raised her chin, squared her amazing shoulders, and grinned, her lips curving upward. I knew that even in darkness, her eyes glittered like emeralds. "The sergeant asked youse nice to stop your mischief, and now I'm going to *tell* youse to stop, but not so nice."

Youse again!

She leapt toward him as he tried to target the moonbeam ray at her. The icy white beam swooped upward, cutting through the black sky.

Before he could gain control of the raygun, Shulky swung at him.

Any of her punches would have connected with a normal human. Heck, they would have blasted a normal human off his feet and across the street with a *kapow*! But the man ducked and wove away. He skipped agilely to the edge of the roof, and she could see his mischievous smile through the mask.

She stepped forward and teased him with "There's nowhere else to go, so just come here and accept the inevitable like a good loser."

"I'm not the loser today." He sidled along the ledge and then suddenly pulled out a small device. "Not while I have my moonbeam blaster junior."

"Nifty. I love travel-size versions, but you won't succeed with whatever it is you're trying to do."

"I already have," he said and giggled crazily. "I wanted you to come and here you are. I didn't get a good look at you last time. You really are a bigger-than-life green freak show! Goodbye, She-Hulk. See your tragic demise in my dreams."

He flipped a lever on the blaster jr., and there was a deafening whine as all the moon power from the massive parent mechanism was pulled into the handheld device in a beam of light so intense that she had to squint.

He pointed the blaster jr. at Shulky, and his arm shook as he strained to control the tremendous energy surging through the device. At the second when he steadied the blaster jr., she jumped away — and the beam cut through the roof that had been at her feet.

"You're fast," he said.

"Oh, now you're just flirting."

He giggled. "But are you fast enough?"

He turned and aimed the blaster jr. at the parent moonbeam's support structure. The ray cleanly bisected the metal framework.

At this great height, the wind was so powerful that it tipped the carefully balanced top half of the structure. The huge lens and its housing teetered for only a moment as the fierce gusts whipped around it.

And then the metal groaned as the contraption fell over, toward the crowd below.

Just as quickly, Shulky leapt to the edge of the roof and grabbed one of the moonbeam's support legs.

Gravity dragged her down and almost carried her over the ledge, but she threw her weight back. She braced her feet and lugged the hefty apparatus back onto the roof. The applause from the crowd below was loud enough to hear through the howl of the wind. She balanced her weight and hurled the contraption onto the center of the roof, making the huge lens shatter and the metal shriek.

She turned to the creep and stalked around the perimeter of the roof like a lioness circling her prey. "What are youse gonna do now without your moon power, twerp?"

He laughed his crazy laugh and said, "That was just for fun. The blaster jr. can harness enough power on its own for trivial tasks, and what's more trivial than a superhuman who's been kicked off the team because she's sooo obnoxious?"

"Why you—" she began, but he'd already pulled the lever. The blaster jr. sliced a chunk off the roof, and it fell away, taking Shulky — and me — plunging down into the space between the buildings.

It was one of those *Holy shit!* moments that made me want to pee my pants if Shulky had bothered to wear any, but it did not faze her one bit. She was only worried about pancaking anyone who might be below.

She threw out her arms, but her fingers barely grazed the narrow ledges that marked each floor, and she shouted, "Heads up!" I wished I could close her eyes so I couldn't see our impending death.

Two things happened so quickly that I could barely comprehend them. A window midway down the adjacent building shattered, and a giant lasso flew out and looped around Shulky, jerking tight. She grabbed onto the lasso and recognized what it was immediately: a length of emergency fire hose.

No mere human was strong enough to hold on to her deadfall weight, yet someone or something was not only holding on, but drawing her up toward the window.

Could Patty have brought a winch up here so fast? Shulky made it to the window, where a fire blanket had been placed over the broken shards of glass. Her legs were too long to swing them over, so she dived through the window, tucked into a roll, and stood up.

She saw a tall, slim man wearing dark jeans, a black hoodie, and a green ski mask. She liked him immediately.

He smiled and asked, "Are you okay, Miss She-Hulk?"

Shulky raised the fire hose lasso over her head and let it drop to the floor. "Always am, hon, but tonight it's thanks to youse!" She went to the window and peered out toward the roof of the neighboring building. The range of visibility was limited, but she couldn't see any more activity.

Patty called up with the bullhorn, saying, "All clear, She-Hulk! Come on down."

Shulky shouted, "Gimme a sec, Sarge!" She turned back to the guy in the hoodie. "It looks like the twerp perp got away. Thanks for the assist."

"Happy to help! Gotta run." He waved by holding up his hand and moving his forearm from side to side, the way a kid or a parade princess waves.

Shulky said, "Not so fast, stranger. Introduce yourself. My friends call me Shulky." She reached out to shake his hand, but he stepped back toward the door.

"Oh, I know who you are! I heard people talking about the moonbeam raygun and everyone said you'd show up to stop the criminal. I really wanted to meet you. You're awesome!" He ducked his head shyly. "And so beautiful."

"Thanks, sugar. I think you're pretty swell, too. You'll have to come with me to meet Sergeant Patty and then we're going to the Avengers Mansion. I have a lot of questions for you, and not fun questions like leather or lace — and, for the record, the answer is always leather with me. Reports have to be made." She thought for a second and said, "You can fill them out."

He shifted from foot to foot. She thought she could hear him breathing harder.

"It's too dangerous for me," he blurted. "Sorry, ma'am." And then he sprinted out of the room.

Shulky followed, but she lost a fraction of a second when her heel caught on the reel of fire hose in the doorway. Then she tore off after him. She ran so fast down the hall that she skidded into the wall. She yanked on the door to the staircase, but it didn't open, so she wrenched it back, ripping it off its hinges.

She catapulted herself over the stair railing and landed so hard that the landing collapsed under her feet and cement dust flew up. "Brand-new boots," she bitched. She kicked the rubble away and raced down the stairs.

When she reached the ground level, the door to the street was ajar. She yanked it open and stepped out. Her new friend was nowhere to be seen. "Ma'am!" she said, laughing, and made her way to Patty at the bisected squad car.

Patty saw her, shrugged, and reported, "The aforementioned asshole disappeared. My guys are searching for him."

"I don't think they'll find him. He's the same brat who trashed Broadway. I take it personal when someone endangers *Wicked*."

"Did you get any clues on who he is? And who threw out the rope to you?"

"It was a fire hose, necessity being the whatever of invention. They both wore masks and didn't identify themselves, but they must be superhuman," Shulky said. "The power in the creep's moonbeam blaster would have ripped the arm off a normal dude, and the other guy lifted me up easily and ran off with super speed."

Patty chewed her lower lip and said, "It bothers me when new ones show up on the radar without any warning."

"Tell me about it. The paperwork is horrible. I'll check in at the Mansion and see if anyone's heard anything."

"Didn't you think there was a Dr. Doom style to the moonbeam raygun?"

"There's a Doomish influence, but Victor von Doom's work is precise. There's an artistry to his madness and there's always a clear agenda. It could be a copycat."

Patty shook her head. "Tonight's bad enough without talking about goddamn von Doom. Oh, I almost forgot. One of my officers found this in the alley." She pulled a Swiss Army knife from her pocket. "It looks like the brat hacked the attachments. If you make anything of it, tell me."

One of the officers gave Shulky a lift to the Mansion, and they both laughed about Thor's complicated family before she went in through a side entrance.

She was about to shift back to make me do the paperwork, but then she realized that I wouldn't let her out to go dancing later. So she sat down and completed the superhuman incident forms.

1. Identity of superhuman if available.
   No name given. Hereafter referred to as Superbrat.

2. Please describe the physical appearance of the superhuman and detail **every** anomaly (i.e., did the superhuman possess an extra head, fins, prehensile toes, etc.?).
   Normal-size male with dipshit giggle hahahahaha.

[She scribbled a fairly accurate cartoon of the criminal, added giant ears poking out through the ski mask and wiggly "stink" lines, and titled it "Artist's Rendition."]

3. What powers did the superhuman exhibit? Circle all that apply: X-ray vision; fireball throwing and/or combustible abilities (please describe); elastic limbs and/or morphable body (please specify); sonic speed; command of wind, rain, rocks, or animals (please specify all); invisibility; magic and/or alchemy (please describe); ability to twin or replicate; other (please specify):
   Superhuman strength, agility, good but stooopid invention skilz.

4. Did the superhuman speak, and if so, what language and what dialect? List verbatim all comments made by the superhuman.
   Standard English, no accent, said "I dreamed of meeting you She-Hulk because you're so super hawt and fantastic and in real life you are even more sexy, geniusy, superfantastic, and incredulicious. I am in awe of your awesomeness! You are the most cooltastic greatest superhero of them all — way greater than Iron Man, who isn't hilarious or as gorgeous as you!!!"

5. What was the superhuman wearing? Did this outfit have any special features or emblems?
   Looked like a loozer barista with a blue mask. Stooopid cape like from a Halloween costume. Refer to Artist's Rendition above.

She-Hulk examined the knife, which seemed to have been taken apart and reassembled but not obviously altered. It had handy tools, though, so she slid it into her boot.

Shulky checked her aPhone and saw a message from Lindsay, who was in town hanging with Perez and Tweeted a direct message: "Shulky — Mtg Madge after her tour rehearsal tonight. Partay w/us?"

Which is how Shulky found herself doing the samba with a Brazilian footballer at 3:00 a.m. even though I was screaming, "Take me home!" On the plus side, he was an amazing dancer and his body was as muscled and sinuous as, well, a Brazilian footballer.

·*10*·

STRICT LIABILITY

FEBRUARY 10

I woke up feeling okay since Shulky was the one who'd gone to bed — by herself amazingly — which is a relief since Azzan is doing me a special with an early morning session. As I was going to the bathroom, I almost tripped on the silver boots Shulky had tossed on the floor. Then I saw this journal open on my desk.

She's responsible for all the additions to this entry: the picture of a dancing penis in the margin; the hammerhead shark in a suit; the obscenities. She's a remarkably good cartoonist, but her handwriting is so loopy and childlike. That's her note to "Send Pattycakes Joocey Jooce coupons," which is thoughtful of her, and "Tony is a such a DICK!!!" which is not, but she still resents him from the time he stole her powers. Okay, Tony *is* a dick.

She left something else between these pages. An ivory three-by-five card that read:

California-in-Manhattan Alumni Single
Professionals Meet-up!
Open to all *under 35* single alumni of UC system,
USC, Stanford, Cal Poly, etc.

Tuesday nights, 7–10
Register at website for event schedule and details.

Condoms and now this. Even Shulky feels like I need matchmaking help. I put the card in the frame of my dresser mirror. I can go this evening and, who knows, maybe I'll have an actual date for Valentine's Day! Or I could be on my way for my legitimately postponed VD.

9:40 A.M.

Fritz leaned into my doorway and asked if I was settled in. Since our uncomfortable lunch, he's become friendlier and given me recommendations for the closest and best sushi, the closest and best Russian bath, and the closest and best pharmacist. In return, I told him funny (though not confidential) details of my work at GLKH.

He grinned and said, "Feel free to use me as a sounding board for any questions about maritime law — don't laugh, because you never know when you'll have a case that deals with pirates."

If he wasn't a coworker and wasn't married, I'd practice my flirting with him.

10:45 A.M.

Had a break so I called Dahlia.

ME: I'm going to a singles meet-up for UC grads tonight. You should come.

D: I'm not single. I'm playing the field.

ME: Then expand your field.

D: That sounds too sixties expand-your-consciousnessish. If you want moral support I can go with you.

ME: I want moral support. Please come with me.

D: No, you have to learn to stand on your own two size-12 feet.

ME: Nine and a half. All I need is a wing-chick.

D: I have been to those alumni meet-ups. They're full of corporate snobs who act like I'm practically a hooker because I have a hair salon. Hair salon equals massage parlor equals streetwalker.

ME: Maybe you're right. Maybe I won't go.

D: Jen, you're a first-rate lawyer at an elite law firm. You're supposed to be one of the snobs. Go and intersnob with them. Snobnet. Whatever.

ME: I'm not very good at chitchat.

D: Oh, you poor naive snob-impaired geekette! Just mention QUIRC and GLKH and your superheroes affiliation, and let them do all the sucking up. Take your business cards. I expect updates at precise thirty-minute intervals.

ME: But if my workday is really busy . . . maybe next week . . .

D: I really don't see how the subject of Fringe Theory's "Stargazing" can be so shy—"Oh, baby, the way you extend my telescope and polish my lens smooth and wet with Gin/Pluto may not be a planet but Uranus—"

ME: Stop! Okay, I'll go!

D: Are you completely red with shame?

ME: No!

D: Pants on fire! Wear your hair down and tousled because it's sexier.

Called Nelson and asked where he went to college. He got his DDS from UCSF — score! Invited him to come with me tonight. He agreed to meet me in the lobby of the hotel near Times Square so we could strategize before going up to the penthouse bar. Yay! I told him not to wear any "provocative" shirts.

6:45 P.M.

Nelson waited for me at a table in an alcove off the lobby. He was sipping a drink through a straw. When I came in, he smiled and half-stood, bumping the table a bit.

"Want a ginger ale? It doesn't stain your teeth, but it's always best to drink through straws."

He wore a pale blue shirt, navy blazer, and khaki slacks. I noticed the bulky gold class ring on his neat hands, and I said, "You look nice. I should have worn some UCLA thing, I guess, but all I have is workout gear."

"I think it will be okay. It's different for girls. Short guys have to do more to look acceptable." He rubbed his head nervously and mussed his hair.

I reached over and smoothed it for him. "Nelson, just smile. You have a great smile."

"You, too. Do we have a strategy besides smiling?"

"I think we'll have to take turns being wingmen. I don't really know how to do it."

"Meeting girls makes me feel as if I'm shopping for a vintage car," he said. "The dealers are always so slick, and I walk away because I'm intimidated. I thought I'd learn something from Numinous's class, but he treats everything like a hostile takeover. I'm more interested in an amicable transaction?"

A lightbulb went off in my head. "Nelson, that's exactly it! What if we approached meeting people like a romantic mediation? I always advise my clients, 'When you go into a negotiation, be the first one to offer a number and psychologically set a value on the transaction. This will establish a starting point that favors you.'"

Nelson seemed interested and asked how that would work, and I told him, "We have to each present the other as valuable, worthwhile dates in clear, direct statements, and we need to repeat that information. It's a tactic for an item that is otherwise difficult to appraise. We establish an association with 'amazing date material' and that will stay in their minds."

"So I could say, this is Jennifer Walters, who graduated summa cum laude from UCLA, has practiced superhuman law with the universe's preeminent law firm, ran varsity cross-country track, et cetera. It's in your public bio. I hope that's not too stalkery."

I felt bad that I hadn't looked him up. "No, it's normal. What do you want me to say about you?"

His hand went to his head again, scrubbing at his hair. "I was the consultant for a cannibal movie once? To get the bite marks accurately?"

It took me ten minutes to pry more information out of him. I couldn't think of any way to tell him not to phrase everything as a question.

I saw some attractive career types heading toward the elevators. "I guess it's time," I said, and smoothed down his hair again. "We're going to do great!"

Nelson and I took the elevator upstairs to the penthouse bar. A bleached blonde at the reception table flipped back her hair and said, "Hi, I'm Wendy," I swear to God! I wished I could ask her to repeat it so I could sneak a video for Dahlia.

We took our name tags with our academic credentials listed in the lower left corner, and we looked nervously around the room.

"Let's get a drink and do reconnaissance," Nelson whispered.

"Okay," I said, but we stopped in our tracks when the event organizer tapped a mic and announced that it was time for speed introductions.

Nelson looked as if he'd been tossed out of a lifeboat when I was herded with the other girls to a long table with numbered plastic bags and handed four stickers.

The organizer said, "This is our lightning round and our sexy single girls have five minutes to sniff each T-shirt and mark the four — and four only — that get their engine revving. Happy sniffing!"

I frantically turned to the pretty brunette beside me. "What are we supposed to do? I didn't see anything on the website about T-shirts."

"It was announced last week. Every guy slept in a T-shirt for three nights. If we're attracted to their pheromones, it's a good indication that we'll like them," she said. "That's the theory, at least, but I predict some stinkiness and lots of cheating."

The organizer announced, "At the end of the lightning round, our sexy single girls will have five-minute chats with each of their four favorite musky males!" Which made me want to run out of the room, but I couldn't because the hostess said, "The clock starts NOW!" and I got swept up in the rush to the T-shirts.

It was outside my comfort zone, so I gathered my nerve and shuffled into the sniffing line. Shirt #1: pizza and sour sweat. Shirt #2: Bengay muscle rub. Shirt #3: fabric softener. Shirt #4: faint aftershave and something nice. Shirt #5 and #6: Calvin Klein Eternity for Women, which I guessed meant that two of these guys were sleeping with the same woman. Shirt #7: marijuana and chocolate, yum. Etc.

I put stickers on the least offensive ones, and then I caught sight of Nelson, looking uneasy in a corner.

The organizer rang a bell and said, "Sexy single girls, sit at the table indicated by the number on your name tag, and we'll start round two so you can meet your musky hunky selections!"

She really said that. I was trying to text Dahlia under the table, but my first choice came along, the guy whose shirt smelled of fabric softener and something nice, which was probably his skin.

His was about six-two, and trim and muscled under a narrow-fitting suit. He was nice-looking, with brown hair and gray eyes, and I thought that maybe there was something to this matchmaking.

We smiled, and he talked right away saying, "Hi, Jen, I'm Ryan. Thanks for picking my shirt. I'm a veterinarian and a vegetarian, basically v-things."

"I'm an attorney and a—"

"Attractive," he said. "Very. What kind of law do you practice?"

I hated sounding as if I was bragging, but this was part of the romantic arbitration. "I'm a specialist in superhuman law, and now I'm working on a complex biotech, intellectual property, and fraud case, so I really have to get up early to make it to the gym."

"Wow! So you know superheroes?" he said.

"And supervillians."

"What's your favorite workout?"

"I've been training in martial arts for a while," I said with a smile.

"Really? I'm on a volleyball team, indoors in the winter and beach volleyball in the summer, and I run daily with my Ridgebacks."

"I want to get a dog," I said, and I was thinking that Ryan was a really nice guy when the bell rang again.

He was my favorite of my four best-smellers, but the most popular smelling guy in the room was the pot-and-chocolate T-shirt dude, who was tubby and bearded. Women were clustered around him, trying to edge one another out.

I watched Ryan talking to other girls, who were laughing and touching his arms and shoulders. I was trying to steel myself to talk to him again, but when I looked for him after the round, he was nowhere to be seen.

I found Nelson and said, "Sorry about that. I didn't know they would be doing this."

He shrugged and said, "My T-shirt would probably smell like cinnamon mouthwash and Old Spice deodorant anyway. Did you meet anyone you liked?"

"Yes, but he vanished, so I guess he wasn't interested in me. Do you see anyone you want to talk to so I can wingman for you?"

"I'd rather wait. I learned that the next meet-up is an Italian cooking class, and I'm a pretty good cook."

While Nelson went to get our coats, I read flyers for upcoming events just to have something to do. That's when I felt someone's arm come from around my right shoulder to grab my left shoulder.

I acted instantly — grabbing the forearm with both hands, throwing my hips back out to unbalance my assailant, and bending forward quickly to flip him over my head and flat onto the reception table.

Ryan crashed down with a loud cry, and everything on the table smashed to the marble floor. A girl shrieked and the pot-and-chocolate guy said, "Dude!"

I said, "I'm sorry, Ryan! Oh, my god, I'm so sorry!"

A man rushed forward and said, "I'm a doctor! Don't move him," and someone else said, "You're a dermatologist."

I tried to help Ryan, but he was groaning and saying, "My back! Keep her away from me."

While I was hovering nearby, a man in a dark blue suit appeared with the event organizer. He looked as if he was there in an official capacity, and I said, "He surprised me . . ."

Nelson tried to help by saying, "It wasn't her fault. She's got multiple black belts and was only reacting!"

"I'm trained to subdue," I said quickly.

The man in the blue suit reached toward me, and Nelson added, "And also trained to kill!" and the man pulled back his hand.

His voice was low, but firm, and he said, "I'd like you to come down to our security office for a moment. You can give us your version of what happened there."

Nelson was nice enough to wait for me, and luckily a security camera had caught Ryan sneaking up on me with a flirty grin on his face. When the doctor (dermatologist) reported that Ryan was fine and Ryan himself confirmed that he wasn't going to press charges, I was escorted out of the office and told, "Ma'am, we do not tolerate violence and we ask that you not return."

Ma'am! Rubber chickened once again.

Nelson suggested a bistro right there on West 44th. I was skeptical that it could be any good and doubted that we'd get a table. The owner was Nelson's patient, though, and offered a small table in a corner. The mussels and sea bass were wonderful. As we shared a chocolate soufflé, I told Nelson about the allure of the pothead who smelled like chocolate, and he said he was going to put unwrapped Hershey's kisses and medicinal marijuana in his pockets the next time he tried to meet women.

As we parted ways, he said, "At least we tried going out and meeting people, and it wasn't as bad as the first time I met you."

"We'll have to iron out the bugs in our technique so that we're not harassing or assaulting potential dates. I'll see you at the Forestiers fight practice."

"I don't think you need any practice fighting, Jen."

"I need practice not to break someone's back. Do you have a game name yet?"

"The Gnashing Newt. I'm a spy who sneaks around and is always playing one side against the other, and is a talented strategist. I can slide in and out of places almost invisibly. Also, I love festivities and play the lute, which I actually do, almost. I'm teaching myself, but I play guitar. What about you?"

"I'm LadyGreene, whose lands have been stolen, but her family is cold-blooded, so she sides with the peasants. She has healing powers and is a fierce swordswoman, and she's always hiding out from her power-mad ex."

It wasn't until I was halfway home that I realized that Nelson hadn't spoken in questions, which was a good thing. Another good thing was that Ryan had come to flirt with me. Maybe my negotiation tactic worked!

The bad things: Blacklisted from yet another hotel. Unjustly ma'amed. Nearly killed a PFLOML.

FEBRUARY 11

VALENTINE'S DAY RESOLUTION COUNTDOWN: 3 DAYS!

I was already expecting to spend Valentine's Day alone when I went to Quinty's weekly meeting. After we'd given our case updates, Quinty cleared his throat, set his monocle in, and scrunched his eye to hold it in place. Why a monocle?

"We'll expect everyone to be here for our annual Valentine's Day party on Saturday," he said, and directed a smile to me. "I was so preoccupied starting this firm that I didn't realize our first official day of business was Valentine's Day until I got home and my wife reminded me — in no uncertain terms! Since then we've always celebrated QUIRC's anniversary on Valentine's Day so my wife is assured of a celebration. You're welcome to bring a plus-one."

Woohoo! Now I have something to do on Valentine's Day!

All I have to do is find a suitable office-party date. It won't have the heavy romantic implications of asking someone to dinner. What attorney wouldn't jump at the chance to network at QUIRC? This will be a piece of cake!

11:30 A.M.

I called an associate at GLKH, but he'd gotten engaged.

Subsequent invitations were declined for these reasons: out of the country, didn't remember me, had square dancing class that night, wanted to know if his mother could come, too. "Mom's lots of fun. You'll love her!"

I told him that I was sorry, but I was only allowed one guest.

Most of the guys at the Mansion were serious and accomplished, so I called Ruth to ask who was around. My phone call rolled over to the main switchboard and the operator said, "Hi, Ms. Walters. Ruth is busy helping decorate the ballroom for our big Valen — I mean, she's running errands. If this is urgent, I'm happy to help!"

"No, it's fine," I said. "Tell her that I'm, uhm, sending over some Joocey Jooce coupons to share with the volunteers."

Quinty said I *could* bring a plus-one, not that I *should* bring a plus-one. After all, he'd forgotten about Valentine's Day because he was engrossed in QUIRC.

Called Dahlia:

ME: Woohoo! The office is having a Valentine's Day slash Anniversary Party so technically I have a datish-thing for Valentine's Day, which was my goal.

D: Your goal was a *real* date, which I thought you postponed very bogusly.

ME: I believe my resolutions should abide by the spirit of the law, not the letter of the law. If I have a datish thing on Valentine's Day *and* I get a real date within my allotted time period, I have more than fulfilled the requirements of the goal.

D: Save it for the courtroom. Who are you taking as your plus-one?

ME: The only appropriate guys for this sort of thing are unavailable. I don't mind going solo.

D: Then Ellis Tesla will think you're a sad old spinster. Ginster, the spinster. Gin, the old maid, who once I did laid.

ME: If you think I need a date so much, you can come with me and pretend to be my sexy lesbian lover.

D: While I love being your wacky ethnic sidekick, I have a starring role in my own life. I've got several offers, but have yet to decide upon the lucky bastard. Be sure to look OMG! amazing so Ellis knows what he's missing. Come by the salon beforehand and we'll give you the works.

ME: One, I don't condone cheap ploys to manipulate men. Two, Ellis doesn't matter to me, Dahlia, rhymes with — whatever. And, three, is 5:30 okay?

FEBRUARY 13

VALENTINE'S DAY RESOLUTION
COUNTDOWN: 1 DAY!

I ordered a gourmet gift basket for Donner and a collection of cat-motif potholders and tea towels for Ruth. I also bought a KEEP HANGING IN THERE! mug for Nelson. I feel that I've got a firm grip on this usually knotty holiday. I'm a month ahead on points for my goals, and the QUIRC party will give me 50 more points. It would have been 100 with a date, but a date was only *part* of that specific goal.

Now that I've developed romantic mediation skills, I should have a real actual boyfriend very, very soon. Next up: finding a fantastic apartment!

PROMISSORY ESTOPPEL

FEBRUARY 14

Woke up thinking back to Valentine's Day when I was with Tony. He asked me what I wanted and I told him that I'd never been to Paris. He said he'd take me for the weekend, and I actually thought he would. However, with Tony it was always *Sorry, babe, I had to save the planet from imminent destruction and got sidetracked.* For some reason, petite bombshells were always critical to the world-saving process.

I am taking responsibility for my own fantastic Valentine's Day.

I left for work early enough to buy flowers for the HR manager and the receptionist. Bouquets and gift baskets covered their desks, and everything looked cheerful. As I walked by the conference rooms, I saw caterers already rearranging furniture and decorating for the party.

I was at my desk, studying ReplaceMax patient histories, when an enormous basket of flowers arrived with a bottle of champagne and a huge box of chocolates. The card inside said, "Happy Valentine's Day, your favorite cousin!" It was awful sweet of Bruce, so I sent him a thank-you message.

As people walked by my office, they glanced through the glass partition and noticed the big arrangement, and I worried that they might assume a boyfriend had sent them and that he'd be coming to the party.

I tried out one of Dr. Alvarado's stoopid affirmation exercises by whispering to myself, "I'm a successful attorney who has wonderful friends and was raised by loving, kind parents. I live in a beautiful loft in a fantastic city. I've dated brilliant men! I am Azzan's best student, and I have a fantastic wash-and-wear hairstyle! People care about me, Jennifer Susan Walters, and I care about them, too!"

After work, I hurried home and changed into my new dark scarlet dress. It hugged me in all the right places, and a verse from a Fringe Theory song, "Gin in Degrees," came to me:

> I don't suppose
> You would take off your clothes
> And throw those golden legs higher
> They are the protractor
> Measuring the precise angle
> Of my unyielding desire

I rushed to Dahlia's salon, and she arranged my hair in an updo and told me about her own plans for dinner, dancing, and nakedness with a waiter-actor-whatever. Another stylist applied my makeup and finished it with a spritz of what she called "makeup shellac. You can go out in a blizzard and still look perfect."

Dahlia stood back and looked at me. "My little girl is all growed up!" she said, and clasped her hands to her breast.

"Thanks, and you have a wonderful time, too, tonight. Be safe."

"I will. Besides, men don't mess with a girl who has a deep understanding of how to use razor-sharp tools," she said. "I still expect you to go out on an actual date within your bogus deadline."

We had started bickering re: the alleged bogusness of my deadline when I realized I had to leave, so I gave her a smooch good-bye.

I hadn't needed to rush, because I was one of the first to arrive. I left my coat and tote in my office before going to the conference room, which had been opened up to the adjoining room. Strings of twinkly pink lights and pretty flowers transformed the space. A long buffet had been set up, but, lesson learned, I didn't touch any of the delicious treats that might have gushy innards.

A cute waitress said, "Happy Valentine's Day!" and I said, "Same to you!" and she served me a glass of a sparkling pinot noir that was exactly the right pink for my datish night.

I stood near the window, staring out at the myriad lights. I thought this was the most heartbreakingly beautiful skyline I'd ever seen on any planet. When I looked out on it, I felt that everything was possible. I didn't know if the Parisian skyline was better. I remembered my ~~date liaison~~ hookup with Ellis and how we'd looked out at the night sky and he'd asked me if I spoke French.

"Why?" I'd asked.

"We're touring Europe and spending a week in Paris. Come with me. Take a few months off school. We'll have the time of our lives. Don't give me an answer now. Talk to your faculty advisor and tell me next month."

Now it seems utterly insane that I was seriously thinking about taking a leave of absence from UCLA Law School in order to be Ellis's on-the-road concubine. I should be totally grateful that he never called.

Then I heard voices in the hallway, and a moment later more guests arrived. The women wore lovely red and pink dresses and the men wore suits. I wished I could remember their names, but I smiled and said hi.

Quinty was the next to appear. He wore a navy pin-striped suit and his monocle was in place. "Hello, Jennifer! Why, don't you look pretty. My right to compliment women is grandfathered into my contract. It's called the Grandfather Clause."

"Good evening, sir."

As my coworkers began filling the room, he told me his wife was always late and asked if I'd brought a date.

I thought about my negotiating tactics and positioned myself as a high-value individual. I said, "I came on my own, sir, so that other employees might get to know me on a one-on-one basis."

"Didn't want to bore your boyfriend, eh? Can't say as I blame you. I think talking about QUIRC is endlessly fascinating, but my wife assures me that other people get tired of listening to me. Enjoy yourself before you sneak off for a romantic rendezvous!"

I smiled at him, a confident businesslike smile. "If you want to talk about QUIRC, I'm happy to listen endlessly."

He shook his head and said, "They all say that at first . . ." and then he strolled off.

I was feeling rather swell that I'd been so smooth about singlehood. And then Amber Hammerhead walked in with Ellis Tesla.

She wore the same suit she'd had on earlier. Ellis wore a black suit and his hair was brushed neatly. He seemed taller and more elegant than I remembered, but elegant in a manly way, as if his girlfriend had chosen his clothes because he was too macho to shop.

He had his hand on Amber's shoulder, and they looked like the ideal Manhattan couple, the sort who have magazine spreads about their vacations, renovations, and charities. They looked like the type of people who would have adorable, accomplished children and fantastic, impressive friends.

Then I remembered that *I* had a fantastic living space, did fantastic charitable work, and had fantastic friends. In fact, my friends were so fantastic that "fantastic" was right in their name. It's too bad that Shulky's antics have caused a rift in our relationships. I'm sure it's just temporary.

While I was mulling over my friends' fantasticness, I noticed that the women in colorful dresses were assistants and clerical staff. All of the female attorneys wore dark power suits. I saw Genoa across the room, and she was dutifully wearing a navy skirt and jacket. I waved to her and she smiled and waved back.

One of the partners' husbands introduced himself and said, "What a pretty dress! Are you Marie's temp — I know her assistant's out on maternity leave."

"No, I'm Jennifer—" I began, but he cut me off saying, "Very nice meeting you, Jenny. Now, don't let these lawyers intimidate you. I know I always tell Marie to remember that the administrative staff have lives outside the office. Where's your date?"

"I came on my own."

"Well, there are plenty of dating websites. Anyone can find a match!" he said. "Excuse me, I've got to see how the sitter is doing. Kids, huh?"

It went on like that, so I was actually grateful when Fritz Durning approached. In his narrow-fitting suit and buzz-cut hair, he looked almost aerodynamic. He said, "Hi, Jennifer. Rescue me from being harassed by all the couples. I think we're the only singles here."

I glanced down at his wedding band and said, "I didn't know you were single."

"I've been legally separated for three years. My wife lives in Connecticut with the kids. It works for our family. This place doesn't leave me much time for a relationship even if I wanted one." He looked a little abashed.

"Most people don't understand how all-consuming our jobs are. We can't just take the day off or meet up with friends at five . . ." I said.

"Or call in sick because we want to sleep in, or throw the case because we hate the client." He looked me up and down. "You look amazing. What do you do to keep in shape?"

I appreciated the compliment, probably more because he said it in a matter-of-fact jock-to-jock way. "I practice several martial arts, but please don't try to sneak up on me, because I have a tendency to react."

"You care to elaborate?"

I told him how I'd flipped Ryan over at the singles meet-up, and he laughed. "Actually, I knew about your martial arts, but I want to know more. I've got a home gym, and I compete in triathlons. I run the stairs here when I have breaks, and I'm on a basketball team with other lawyers, the Badgerers. There's a whole lot of trash talk."

He made me laugh, and I said, "I played basketball in high school. The assumption was that I'd be good because I was tall. I lasted all of one month."

"You ran cross-country, right? We should go running when the weather warms up."

"I'm always happy to have a running partner — if you can keep up." Hey, I was flirting!

That's when Fritz placed his hand on my back, low at the waist, and leaned close to whisper, "Not only can I keep up, but if you want something more — something to work off the energy without interfering in our careers, I'm your man and can provide a clean bill of health from my physician."

"I didn't mean . . ." I began and could feel my skin going pink.

"We're both serious, Jennifer, and our work here is our priority. If you would like a onetime test run to find out if we are compatible, we can schedule that. My primary goal is an intense cardio activity with a desirable outcome. I'm not seeking complications, but I do like companionship. There is no pressure and I won't take offense if you decide to decline."

Now, I always advise my clients, "When someone makes an unexpected offer, don't reject it out of hand. There may be benefits that you haven't considered, or you might be able to turn the offer to your advantage. Ask for time to explore the possibilities."

So I said, "That is an intriguing suggestion, Fritz, and I'll take it under advisement. Are you extending this exclusively to me and is there a time limit on it?"

It was at this moment that I saw Ellis looking at us. Naturally, I'd been ~~mildly somewhat~~ totally freaked out that he was in the room. He caught my eye, and I froze while Fritz said, "It's exclusive to you and any reasonable time limit — what about sixty days?"

I forced my gaze back to Fritz and smiled. "I will definitely have a decision to you within sixty days."

"Excellent! In the meanwhile, do you think you could teach me a few defensive moves?"

I casually glanced around, but Ellis was nowhere in sight. Amber was smeering at me from beside a table of heart-shaped pink macaroons and chocolates.

"Sure, Fritz, but not here."

So we went to my office. Because anyone could look in through the glass wall, I suggested my meditation room. I kicked off my heels and Fritz took off his shoes and jacket and loosened his tie. I started with straight punches to warm up and moved on to palm strikes. He had strength, but his core wasn't centered, so I bent over to position his legs properly, and he started laughing and grunting while he threw out his fists.

I wished I'd had a mat, because we fell over with a thud and laughter. I said, "That's enough for now," and we got up. I tugged down my hem and was glad my stockings hadn't run.

He was a good student, and I invited him to one of my sessions. We were jostling out of the meditation room, arranging our clothes, when I looked up to see Ellis standing by my desk. One of his eyebrows went up, and he said, "I didn't mean to interrupt. Excuse me," and he left.

This is what my brain was thinking: *Holy shit, holy shit, HOLY SHIT!*

Fritz just laughed again and said, "Okay, we've officially provided the gossip for the office party."

Then I spewed several OMGs, and Fritz tried to calm me down by saying, "Relax. We didn't do anything, and besides that was Ellis Quintal, who used to be Ellis Tesla. Do you remember him from Fringe Theory?"

"Yes, I met him already," I said, which was true.

"That band was out of control and he probably slept with a thousand girls. This is nothing to a guy like that." Then Fritz sighed. "One of their songs, 'Gin e-Motion,' was my slow jam in college. How did it go? 'She starts out slow as gin/acceleration then begins/my force, of course, meets hers and then/sexual commotion/explains my Gin devotion.' One of my girlfriends called it the white man's answer to Teddy Pendergrass."

I made a few *ers* and *ums* and smoothed my hair and said, "Let me go back first and you wait a few minutes before going in."

Fritz thought that was hilarious but said he would go first to protect my virtue. I waited about ten minutes, but then I thought I'd been gone too long, which was just as bad as showing up with Fritz. I was hurrying down the hallway, but I didn't hear the previous party chatter. Instead, one sweet pure voice pierced the silence. I slowed my steps as I approached the conference rooms.

Everyone had crowded at the front, where Amber was standing and singing "My Funny Valentine." She smiled as she sang and her phrasing and pitch were so perfect with the bittersweet lyrics that I felt my breath catch. Couples held hands and eyes glittered with tears. As she hit the last line, she looked right at Ellis and he looked directly at her, as if he was a sailor and she was a siren enticing him to the rocks.

Then the song ended and everyone clapped, breaking the spell. I made it to the buffet table and ate the neatest, safest canapés there (cheese on crackers). When I turned back to the room, I saw that Ellis was standing by the windows, hands shoved in his jacket pockets, at the periphery of a group. Amber was in the center, talking intently to a silver-haired woman, her back to me.

Face the fire, I told myself, so I walked right up to him and said, "Hello, Ellis. How nice of the company to put on a party."

"Hello, Jennifer. Yes, it's nice."

Was he being sarcastic? I looked into his dark eyes but couldn't tell.

He lifted his chin toward Fritz, who was chatting with a giggling young woman, and said, "I see you're making friends."

"Yes, Fritz is going to come to one of my Krav Maga classes, and I was showing him a few moves."

"Grab 'em Raw? Is that what the kids are calling it these days?" he said, and his eyes shone.

"*Krav Maga*. I train in the martial arts," I said, but he seemed to think that was funny, because his lips went up on one side, and I got so nervous remembering those lips that I said, "I would be happy to give you a demonstration of my favorite moves."

That's when he burst out laughing, loud enough to get Amber Hammerhead and the older woman's attention.

I tried to exert mind control, hoping that I'd suddenly developed it, so that Amber wouldn't come over, but she and the attractive older woman joined us.

The older woman said, "Ellis, won't you introduce me to your friend?"

"Mom, this is Jennifer Walters, who just joined the firm. Jennifer, this is my mother, Rosie Quintal."

Her expression changed a little and she said, "I thought I recognized you. I followed your case when you were representing Tony Stark — and dating him, too, I believe."

Ellis looked startled, but Amber didn't.

Now, I always advise my clients, "When someone introduces an unexpected element in a transaction, resist the urge to ignore or excuse it. Instead, immediately acknowledge it and position it to your advantage."

So I said, "Yes, I've been fortunate to know Tony both personally and professionally, having both sued him and won cases for him. Being around him is always intellectually invigorating."

"Yes, I bet it is *stimulating*," the blond hammerhead smeered.

Rosie Quintal said, "Inventors are so quixotic."

"Most, but Tony isn't tilting at windmills, since he's capable of achieving seemingly impossible goals. Because he's a genius." I saw Ellis's eyebrows go up, so I added, "And gorgeous, and a superhero," thereby establishing my value in that elevated realm. Not that I had to prove anything to any science teacher besides my cousin.

Rosie said, "Be sure to bring Mr. Stark to our next party! Where's your date tonight, dear?"

"She's with Fritz," Ellis said.

"No, I'm on my own. I find that work parties can be a little dull for those outside the field."

Rosie smiled slyly and said, "I refuse to respond to your comment on the grounds that, et cetera. If you'll excuse me, I must circulate. Delighted to finally meet you . . ." and here is where I needed a court stenographer because I could have sworn there was a very deliberate pause before she said, "Jen."

Amber stiffened and Ellis looked away, and I *erh*ed or *um*ed before I managed to say, "A pleasure meeting you."

Rosie hooked her arm through the hammerhead's and said, "Amber, do help me navigate the shoals."

I thought a siren would know a lot about navigating shoals. Amber didn't want to leave us, but she couldn't say no to her fiancé's mother.

I said to Ellis, "Amber's voice is very beautiful."

"She likes to be the best at anything she does."

"Well, er, your mother seems very nice."

"She is very nice," Ellis said. "I still can't get over seeing you again after all this time. I thought you'd vanished off the planet."

He was *so* bogus, and I returned the bogusity. "Ellis, it's nice seeing you, too. Now that I'm working with Amber, I imagine we'll encounter each other occasionally, and I would appreciate it if you didn't mention our previous association to anyone since I'm sure it would be detrimental to both of our public images."

"Your secrets are safe with me. Those secrets that I know." He had a sort of wild expression in his eyes, the same look he'd had when he threw out that flash paper at the concert.

"I don't have any secrets, Ellis, but I do respect private lives."

"Whatever you say, Gin. Jen. Jennifer."

I always tell my clients, "If you feel that you are losing control of a negotiation, don't hesitate to ask for a recess."

So I said, "Very nice seeing you again." I stepped away and walked right into a waiter, bumping him backward into one of the assistants, who stumbled into a woman in a pink dress. The woman's plate of prawns in ginger sauce flew up into the face of a guy in a pin-striped suit, who closed his eyes and walked smack into a bistro table with a soaring pyramid of puff pastries drizzled with caramel, which teetered precipitously before collapsing over and onto a partner.

The *bad* thing was that the domino effect continued in the crowded room: glasses crashed, plates clattered, expensive silks and cashmeres were ruined.

The *good* thing was that nothing splattered on me. When a chafing dish caught fire, I took it as a sign to leave. I glanced back into the mayhem of the conference room and saw Ellis leaning against a wall and laughing.

11:30 P.M.

The day isn't even over and I've already accumulated *lots* of points, which I will add up when I figure out how to get the spreadsheet program to work. My cogitating is being hampered by fixating on Ellis. What was he getting at? Was he getting at anything? He's a riddle, wrapped in a mystery, inside a hunky good-smelling but engaged enigma.

Thinking about him rattles my brain, which usually operates with the interplanetary precision of an Omega Galaxymaster. I made that observation to Dahlia after scoring perfect LSATs, and she said, "Yeah, you are a space cadet for sure." Anyway, I have occasionally advised my clients, "If you find yourself without any immediately pressing deadlines, take time off to relax. Not only will you feel better, but you'll perform better when you return to your task."

I went to the guest bedroom and opened the closet. Christian Siriano's wickedly fabulous anthracite leather jumpsuit with jet-black feather trim was hanging in the closet.

I took off my pretty scarlet dress and transformed. My confusion over Ellis and the hammerhead melted away.

Shulky, usually so happy to be naked, couldn't wait to pour herself into Siriano's sinuous garment. She posed in front of the mirror and purred, "I look fierce!" and snapped her fingers before heading out to parties.

IMPLIED CONTRACT

FEBRUARY 15

I am *not* looking at celebrity gossip about Shulky's Valentine's Day activities. It was a mistake to check on Twitter and see all the horrible Tweets about her with #superhasbeens.

I *am* looking at ads for apartments. I want to stay near enough to the Mansion to help out if they need Shulky or me, which limits my options. I called Ruth, told her about my apartment search, and said, "I'm going to miss the private elevator, and I really need a place that gives me easy sneaking-in-and-out access."

She promised to check around and said, "It's too bad that Shulky got you kicked out of the Mansion with all its amazing secret exits and entrances, but I'll try to find a place convenient to hidden routes."

"That would be great, Ruth. Thanks!"

I announced to Dahlia that I'm officially looking for a new place. We were at her pet-sit, a lavish condo whose owners had seemingly abandoned it to their horrible dog. Rodney was snorting and snuffling belly-up on a custom-made dog sofa. "D, why don't they just get rid of that awful animal so they can return home?"

"Jen, when did you become so coldhearted? You haven't told me anything about your interlude with your former loverrr." She made some disgusting kissing and sucking sounds as she dimmed the lights and opened the media armoire.

"He was inscrutable. I couldn't comprehend anything he said. I think he was just messing with me," I said. "Please mention to your clients that you have a friend who needs a new apartment. Two or three bedrooms because I need an office."

"You have one. It's at QUIRC. It sounds like Ellis was flirting with you."

"Wrong. His mother and Amber were right there. Are you really going to make me watch *When Harry Met Sally* again?"

She said yes, because "Sally Hershberger's subsequent cut for Meg Ryan revolutionized the shag. It literally dragged the shag from its dreadful 1970s prehistoric cave, where it was residing with the mullet, which should never again see the light of day, and the wedge, which is due for a comeback."

"One, that's not what 'literally' means," I said. "Two, I have limited tolerance for Billy Crystal's shameless mugging, and, three, okay, because Meg is supercute as Sally."

We watched the movie yet again, and after a few glasses of wine, D wanted to give me an updated shag, but I said no and really meant it.

FEBRUARY 18

My days and nights have been utterly consumed by prep for my meeting with our ReplaceMax client. Every minute with Amber is an exercise in patience. She's icy cool, very efficient, but too often I catch her watching me with a derisive lift to the corner of her mouth. Too bad being unjustifiably bitchy isn't actionable.

The tension is getting to me, so much so that I'm debating Fritz's offer. He's attractive, a good sport, and very fit. I could burn off energy and distract myself ~~from things from worries~~ from obsessing over Ellis.

UPSIDE OF SEXUAL RELATIONSHIP WITH FRITZ

- Will provide a certificate of health
- Attractive heterosexual male
- Can multitask by consulting on cases
- Enjoys strenuous aerobic workout with positive outcome (check to see if that includes *my* positive outcome)
- Conveniently located and knows my work schedule
- We have already established affable communications, which should promote pleasant exchanges in the bedroom

DOWNSIDE OF SEXUAL RELATIONSHIP WITH FRITZ

- No romantic component
- May develop uncomfortable/unbalanced/awkward romantic component
- Could result in negative workplace gossip
- Might hinder a relationship with legitimate PFLOML
- May be terrible at sex or a gross kisser
- Not especially enthusiastic about purely physical sex with anyone, inc. Fritz

Last night I woke at three in the morning in a cold sweat from an anxiety dream about the Joocey Jooce warehouse. I was being attacked by giant angry gamma-powered fruit that overpowered me. There were evil dancing bananas that looked suspiciously like Shulky's cartoons.

I didn't tell that to Dahlia because she'd insist there was a Freudian element based on her single human sexuality psych class.

The dream was still bothering me in the evening. I got back from QUIRC too late to talk to Claude, and Joocey Jooce's official corporate history is all crunchy goodness. There was no mention of trading electrical upgrades for a lease on a warehouse. In fact, according to the founder, operations had always been housed in New Jersey.

FEBRUARY 19

Claude was downstairs when I headed to work. I had to cut short his fascinating discussion of the (miserable, freezing) weather and say, "Have you thought about selling your property outright to Joocey Jooce? You don't want to deal with any problems in the future, and you could invest the money or set up a trust fund for your family."

He said, "The Joocey Jooce guy is a heck of a nice guy."

"Claude, if he was nice he would have paid his rent in a timely manner. Do you know why he even needs your warehouse? I think all their manufacturing is done in Jersey."

"I asked once and he told me he experimented with new flavors. It was a long time ago. He sent over more coupons. Take some." Claude opened the reception desk drawer and took out handfuls of coupons for free drinks.

I put them in my bag so I could send them to Sergeant Patty and Ruth. "Not everyone is as kindhearted as you. Please think about selling the building or at least getting a lease in writing. If Joocey Jooce backs the lease, your income will be assured."

Claude smiled and nodded, but I got the feeling he wasn't going to push the issue.

In the cab to work, I noticed the long lines outside Joocey Jooce and called Dahlia.

ME: D, what do you like best about Joocey Jooce?

D: Good morning to you, too, sunshine. I'm not even going to ask why you're asking. The smoothies are great and the people who work there are so nice. I always feel happier when I leave.

ME: "Play nice" is their motto. They have to be nice.

D: I don't think they're faking it.

ME: It's just weird for New Yorkers.

D: Oh, Jen, when did you get so cynical? Do you want to go out tonight?

ME: Only if you'll go apartment hunting with me.

D: Only online. No one's going to show you apartments on a Monday night.

ME: Okay, we can start online. So far all I know is that "cute" means "puny." That reminds me, don't bring Rodney tonight.

1:00 P.M.

First impressions count in business, and I set aside an hour to review my notes and organize my thoughts for my meeting with my first QUIRC client. Because I have to justify the meditation room, I went there and stretched out on the sofa. It was really very nice. Maybe I'll bring flowers in there, or something that wouldn't die from neglect.

At precisely 10:00 a.m., when Donner ushered Dr. Sven Morigi into my office, I was glad I'd taken the time to collect myself.

Sven Morigi was so stunning that I was speechless. He was tall and lean, his hair was jet-black and silky fine, and his eyes were deep blue like the interior of a glacier. He wore an elegant suit in a sleek cut. His lightly tanned complexion looked pore-less, his long, straight nose was just right for his angled cheekbones, and his square chin was exactly right for his face.

His only imperfection, if it was that, was his mouth: his lips were a bit *not* perfect. It was hard to say if they were too thin or too firm, because I kept getting drawn into those eyes.

"Hello, Dr. Morigi," I eventually said and made a spastic motion to the guest chair.

"Good morning, Ms. Walters. Do call me Sven," he said and smiled. He had a faint accent and his teeth were perfect.

I usually prefer formality with clients, but I found myself saying, "Please call me Jennifer," as I took my chair. "I'm so pleased to be representing you."

"You have a reputation as a formidable trial attorney, Miss Walters. I thought you would be terrifying in person."

Was this intended as a compliment? "Drama is required when one goes to trial. I've read over the notes from your meetings with our other attorneys, but I'd like to hear from you about your experience with ReplaceMax and your decision to bring legal action against them."

Sven told me that he'd approached Maxwell Kirsch of ReplaceMax with his process to rapidly replicate human organs. "Their own experiments were failing and limited to minor advances in skin grafts. Initially, Max Kirsch agreed to let me use a laboratory to continue my work."

I took notes so I didn't have to keep looking at him, because it was like looking at the sun: tempting, but I'd probably go blind, mad, turn to stone, or all of the aforementioned. The cadence of his speech stirred a memory within me. However, I knew I hadn't heard his mellifluous tones before. His voice was soothing — neither too light, nor macho deep.

"Why ReplaceMax and not a university medical center?" I asked.

"I abhor bureaucracy and academic politics," he said quietly. "ReplaceMax had state-of-the-art, highly secure facilities that provided everything I needed so I could focus on my research. In return, they had first option on investing in any of my discoveries. At the risk of sounding immodest, none of their scientists had comparable vision and abilities."

"Can you tell me more about your initial proposal?"

"Project Mimic," he said. "The problem with most organ transplants is rejection by the host. I was splicing the DNA of host cells with healthy cells to grow bioidentical healthy organs. In fact, these new organs could 'teach' other cells in the host to repair themselves."

"This sounds similar to the way cancer grows," I said.

He nodded. "We can learn many things from cancers, but while most cancers destroy and displace host cells, I wanted my bioidentical cells to be, in layman's terms, reformatted or upgraded. The program was initially so promising. An ailing body, one with a multitude of chronic conditions, could be rejuvenated with the transplant of a single new organ."

"You said that the research was *initially* promising — when did that change?"

"Once ReplaceMax saw the early results, they assigned their own scientists to Project Mimic. Very quickly, they started getting astounding outcomes. Although I believed in my project, I know the road to success is seldom so smooth," he said with a small frown. "I discovered that adverse results were being dismissed and hidden."

"What did you do then?"

"I immediately went to Max Kirsch and the company directors, and reported the problems. They said I'd used incomplete data. When I ran the numbers again, the results were subtly different in ReplaceMax's favor. I compared the studies and discovered that someone had altered the numbers."

"Could you have proceeded even with the less positive results?"

"Most certainly. Perfection is never instantaneous. It was always my intention to work until the cloned organs were free of any harmful defects. However, ReplaceMax was eager to push forward the products for their initial public offering."

"Did Max Kirsch ever mention the IPO to you?" I said as I figured out that the imperfection of his mouth was that his lips were tense, but it could have been the situation. Dahlia would have some theory about tense lips.

"He may have, but when I'm obsessed with my research, I pay little attention to anything else. I've been accused of being monomaniacal, but I prefer to think of myself as tenacious." When he smiled at me, I had to stop myself from giggling. "I believe Max and the directors thought they could resolve the problems before anyone realized they'd knowingly provided defective products in our clinical trials."

"Would you be more specific about the definition of 'products'?" I asked.

"That's what Max and the sales team called the livers, lungs, and hearts grown in our Project Mimic laboratory." Dr. Sven Stunning went on to tell me of his attempts to stop ReplaceMax from experimental use on critically ill patients.

That sounded really important . . . more important than the way his T-shirt would smell after three days. I bet it would smell like vanilla, coffee beans, and heaven.

He concluded, "Now you can see, Jennifer, why I need to bring this suit — because I believe the only thing ReplaceMax directors understand is money. If they suffer a severe financial punishment, others will be deterred from trying to sell defective organs for a quick profit."

I found myself staring into those intense blue eyes and felt a shiver run down my back. "Dr. Morigi . . . ," I began.

"Sven."

"Sven, I find your passion for justice inspiring," I said, which was true. Many parts of me were inspired. "But I've got to ask why you want to take control of a company that you feel is so fundamentally flawed."

"I won't abandon Project Mimic, and the ReplaceMax facilities are still among the finest available."

"I can't tell you how much I admire your willingness to go to court." I wished he'd stand up and turn around so I could admire 360 degrees of him. "Many others would quietly accept a deal and carry on their work elsewhere. I'll do absolutely everything possible to help you, Sven."

When he smiled, I felt ooky, but I think it was in the good way.

As he was leaving, Sven said, "Perhaps I'm being presumptuous, but would you like to join me tonight at the opening for Club Nice? I hope we might celebrate our new venture before you become embroiled in this suit."

I was trying to figure out if he'd said "embroiled" in a suggestive way. It sounded a little dirty, but maybe it was just me. Shulky had been invited to the club's opening, but she was invited to everything. This was *my* invitation.

I always advise my clients, "Take advantage of any opportunities to meet business associates off-site because they will often speak more openly and honestly in a relaxed setting."

I told Sven yes, but I knew I'd need a savvy wingman so I asked if I could bring a girlfriend. Sven said yes, and we arranged to meet at the club at nine. Shulky never went clubbing that early, but I wanted to talk to Sven before the place got raucous.

He shook my hand and his grip was firm and cool. "I know that this is the beginning of a wonderful association, Jennifer."

I nodded my head and watched him leave the room, the view of which was as impressive as anticipated, and then texted Dahlia.

Text to Dahlia:	Want to go to the opening of Club Nice 2night?
Text from Dahlia:	R U kidding? Yes yes yes yes yes!!!!! :-) OMG Amazing! How why? all the dirt?
Text to Dahlia:	Met PFLOML!!! who is my stunning client.
Text from Dahlia:	What about Ellis Tesla?
Text to Dahlia:	Wholis whatsla?

Admission: It is true that I hadn't felt the hot smexy fireworks with Dr. Stunning. However, I was overwhelmed by his beauty. My feelings weren't anything like they had been with Ellis, but I'd fallen for his music, then his images and his reputation, long before actually meeting him. I'd had a false impression of knowing him before our ~~passionate tryst~~ haphazard hookup. But I didn't know him. I still have no idea who he really is.

Tonight will count as a datish thing! I am giving myself 50 points — 25 work-related points and 25 social points!

JOINT LIABILITY

FEBRUARY 21

I spent too long trying to put in my contact lenses, which left me red-eyed and annoyed. I shifted to Shulky for fifteen minutes to get reenergized. She swilled a bottle of my best cabernet, watched wrestling on TV, sent new photos of her legs to the president of her fan club, called Ruth and caught up on superhero gossip, and ate a quart of Chunky Monkey before I could shove her back inside.

The trick worked, because I felt great and my eyes were clear.

Dahlia came to my place and helped me do my makeup, which meant she put on too much mascara and cat-eyed liner and said, "How did you swing an invite? I was maneuvering for weeks." She looked adorable in a tiny purple dress with layers of fringe that swung each time she moved. Her contacts were violet, and her crystal chandelier earrings brushed her smooth brown shoulders.

"My new client and future husband, Dr. Sven Morigi, aka Dr. Stunning, invited me. Wait until you see him. He looks like a movie star, but more stunning. Did I mention how stunning he is? Should I wear something beachy?"

"In February? Why?" she asked and messed with my hair.

"Because it's *Club Nice*, like *Nice* on the French Riviera."

"It's nice rhymes with mice, as in, 'It would be nice if you stopped moving your head while I'm trying to make you look glamorous.'"

"Ohhh," I said. "Accents always confuse me. I thought he might be saying 'nice,' but I wasn't sure, and he's so continental that I decided it must be '*Nice.*'"

"Your chronic problem understanding accents is exactly why you were so popular with sleazy foreign exchange students, like the guy you thought was asking you 'How do I get to San Fernando Valley?' but he was really saying 'How do I get some fellatio, baby?'"

"In my defense, lots of people need directions to the Valley."

Dahlia convinced me to wear a silver mini and said, "Your legs look OMG! amazing, but when are you going to stop taking big tote bags everywhere you go?"

"I need big bags because I have to take my work essentials with me since this is sort of work-related. Also, it's a requirement of being on call for the Mansion."

"If they need emergency legal advice, why don't they ask She-Hulk? Doesn't she have a papal dispensation to practice law everywhere? Are they paying you for lugging around a huge horse feed bag day and night?"

"D, if you like, I can write up the extensive details of She-Hulk's numerous law licenses and I won't even charge you."

"That's generous of you, Jen. I'm not going to bill you for just fixing your hair," she said, and I said, "I'm not going to bill you for that letter I wrote to your gym claiming that Rodney is a service dog," and she said, "I'm not going to bill you for that makeover I did on your witness so she didn't look like a psycho whore," and I said, "You *did* bill me for that and I have the documentation," and she said, "I didn't bill you nearly enough because, damn, that bitch was a psycho whore."

We did that for a while and then we cabbed it to Club Nice. At the outer edge of the Meatpacking District, I noticed a huge new mural of Shulky on the side of a brick building. She looked gorgeous and had a saucy grin on her face. "Larger than life," Dahlia said.

"She always is."

"Do you think she'll be at the opening? You can *finally* introduce me."

"If she shows up, I will, but she prefers making a fashionably late appearance."

The sidewalk in front of Club Nice was already packed with people trying to get in and those watching the arrivals. Photographers and cameramen stood and waited for celebrities and A-listers. A guy who'd covered one of my big court cases called out, "Jen, heard you're practicing terrestrial law again. How's everything?"

"Fine! Good to see you," I said.

"Are you meeting any of your superhero friends here tonight?" he asked. "Will Tony be here? Any tips you can give me?"

"Sorry! Attorney-superhero confidentiality," I said, and he went back to waiting for celebrities.

Dahlia took me by the hand and pulled me to the doorman. "Jennifer Walters Esquire and Lady Dahlia deFrootenloop," she said.

He didn't even look down at this clipboard, but gave a warm smile and said, "Welcome to Club Nice, Ms. Walters, Lady Frooten . . . err. Dr. Morigi is already here. Go on in."

We went into the crowded club, but no one was pushing or shoving. Everyone was acting nice. Most were drinking cocktails sponsored by Joocey Jooce — Jooceytinis and Jooceypolitans served in custom cocktail cups with lids and colorful straws. Neon signs blinked PLAY NICE! and smiling waiters and waitresses carried trays of appetizers.

Old playground structures had been repurposed into sculptures, railings, light fixtures, and seating and painted in cheerful colors. Peppy techno tunes pulsed through the club, but not so loud that people had to shout, which was unusual and surprisingly pleasant.

There was a tier above the first level with private areas, and another tier above that enclosed with mirrored glass.

D and I agreed it was really nice. The more we said the word, the odder it sounded, but I was also feeling anxious about seeing Sven.

A hostess guided us to him at a private table on the first tier. He'd seemed really handsome at the office, but now he was so ridiculously attractive all I could do was stare.

"I'm so glad you could make it," Sven said in a low voice, so that I had to bend my head close to his to hear him. He placed his fingertips on my arm as he spoke, and I almost shivered with nerves.

I introduced Dahlia, who tried to act cool, but I could see her eyes go wide with OMG! amazing! interest.

"I enjoy watching everyone from this level," he said, "but if you would like more privacy, we can go to the VIP room below, or to the upstairs gallery." He said privacy the British way, so it sounded more suggestive. At least I thought it did. I'd have to get Dahlia's opinion.

We wanted to people-watch, too, so we stayed where we were.

He had a bottle of champagne and we drank that. People stopped by to say hello to Sven, and he introduced us to entrepreneurs, restaurateurs, and socialites. Shulky was pals with half the people here, but they didn't notice me even when their eyes went to our table. Sven attracted all their attention. He was *that* handsome and self-possessed. If I'd brought another scientist here — say, my cousin Bruce — he would have been hunkered down in a dark corner and glowering.

When Dahlia left to hunt down a famous stylist who'd entered with a marvelously coiffed entourage, I went blank before saying, "Sven, thank you for inviting us. I appreciate the chance to know more about you."

"Ah, and I invited you here to learn more about *you*," he said with a charming smile. "Ladies first."

Dahlia had ordered me to find out if he was married, so I asked, "Is your family living here, or abroad?"

"I am quite alone in the world." His expression darkened slightly. "Perhaps that is why I invest so much time in my work."

"I'm sorry." I felt like confiding, so I said, "I lost my mother some years back and I always wonder how I'd be if she were still alive to, well, guide me."

He placed his cool hand atop mine and gave a light squeeze. "It seems to me that you are doing extraordinarily well, Jennifer."

I thought he was flirting, but maybe he was being friendly. I couldn't tell.

After a moment he removed his hand, refilled our flutes, and said, "How did someone who is in the highest echelon of the legal profession come to be friends with a . . . with your friend?"

His expression was warm, so I tried not to react too defensively. "I'm fortunate that Dahlia befriended me when we were college roommates. I was prelaw and she was a Western history major. She's one of the brightest, funniest, kindest people I've ever met. Everyone wanted to be friends with her, but she always took the time to draw me out, to make me laugh and feel . . . less lonely. She loves hairstyling as much as I love law."

He lifted his glass. "To your magnificent friend."

I smiled and toasted with him. I asked, "Were you always interested in biology?"

"Science and engineering have been my passions since childhood. Junkyards were my playgrounds, where I'd find broken machines and use the parts to create something new. I lived in my imagination, and my imagination was limitless."

I caught myself gazing at him and said, "Oh, gosh, forgive me for staring."

"No doubt you have caught me staring at you, too. You're a beautiful woman, Jennifer Walters," he said somberly.

Compliments make me uneasy. I decided to talk about a safe subject, so I said, "Interesting that Joocey Jooce has sponsored this event. Do you like their smoothies?"

Sven tilted his head quizzically, probably trying to figure out if I was really such an inept conversationalist. Luckily Dahlia returned to our table with one of her clients in tow and a second magnum of bubbly. When we'd all had another glass, Dahlia got to the point and said, "Sven, are you flying solo, or is someone waiting at home for you?"

"I'm quite available should I meet a woman who lives up to my standards, a woman who is as brilliant and kind as she is lovely," he told her as he looked at me, making me blush. "Of course, my standards are impossibly high because I'm an idealist. I always think I can achieve anything with enough effort."

Dahlia tennis-balled her eyes back and forth from me to Sven, and I was thinking this was going a little too fast, so I said, "Sven, so nice to see you before the case starts. I've got a busy day tomorrow and it's very late."

"Won't you stay just a little longer?" he said.

"I wish I could, but I would be neglecting my responsibilities to my top client, and he deserves the best representation I can offer," I said. "Dahlia, if you'd like to stay . . ."

"No, I'm coming with you. I'm *definitely* coming with you."

We said our good nights, and when we were out of Sven's hearing, Dahlia hooked her arm through mine and said, "I'm coming with you because, OMG, you *need* to tell me more about Sventastic! He looks like a model for German luxury cars, and he was totally giving you the hairy eyeball!"

"One, so I wasn't imagining that? Two, ugh, hairy eyeball sounds like something Rodney hacks up, so please refrain from saying that again about my future honey. And, three, do you think he was being a European fancyman on the make, or do you think he actually was into me as a human being?" I turned to her and was saying "I mean, was he *into* me *into* me," as I walked smack into a solid wall of something. A man-shaped wall of something. To be precise, an Ellis C. Quintal IV-shaped wall of something that was, in fact, Ellis C. Quintal IV.

Amber Hammerhead was beside him and she smeered, "Try to have a little decorum about drinking in public, Jennifer."

She caught me off-guard because I could feel a fizz of champagne and I had bashed into Ellis. He was looking at me with that crazy spark of mischief, so I said, "Excuse me. I wasn't looking."

"*Obviously,*" she said, and that is when I realized that she would always say this to me in the same nasty tone for the rest of eternity. I could see us both on the Supreme Court, me with a sensible gray bob and comfortable black muumuu and her with sleek golden locks and a tailored silk robe, and she'd be sniping "*Obviously,* Justice Jennifer!" and one of the men

Supremes would say "Meow!" with a clawing motion of his gnarled hand, and the rest of them would fall down in hysterics.

Dahlia studied Amber with the same disgusted fascination with which most people looked at Rodney. Then Dahlia saw Ellis and her expression turned flirty. "Hi," she said to Ellis. "Too bad we're just leaving. I know who you are and I'm Dahlia Arras. An easy way to remember is Dahlia Ar-ass, rhymes with bare-ass. I know you like rhymes!"

"Absolutely," he said with a smirk. "Some names rhyme better than others. Ellis doesn't rhyme with anything, and Amber rhymes with, hmm . . . nothing either."

"We're just leaving," I said. "Enjoy yourselves."

Once we were outside, feeling the cold air hit our warm skin, Dahlia said, "Was that the evil hammerhead!?"

"Yes, *obviously*."

"OMG, Jen, Ellis is still smoking hot! I think she must have brainwashed him. You'll have to kidnap him and have him deprogrammed. I've got handcuffs and do you know anyone who has a van?"

"I would rent one, but kidnapping would get me disbarred."

"So you have thought of it?"

"*Obviously!* But only as an act of hostility to the hammerhead. Need I remind you that Ellis never ever phoned me after our date — okay, our drunken hookup — and he broke my heart?"

"You are not as delicate emotionally as you think you are, Jen. You just need to be a little more confident," she said, about to launch into her empower-yourself speech, which I could recite verbatim.

Suddenly a phalanx of black Hummers roared down the street. Everyone watched, thinking that someone famous had arrived, and men began swarming out of the cars. They were dressed in black with black masks and heavy boots. I spotted two with Kalashnikovs, and others had sidearms.

"Holy—!" Dahlia said, but I'd already grabbed her hand and yanked her with me and around the back of the building, where one light fixture illuminated the kitchen door and trash bins. We could hear shouting and screams.

I turned her to face me, and I said, "Dahlia, I trust you completely, but I need to know right now if you want to deal with a life-or-death secret about me. I never wanted to burden you with it, and it's totally your choice. Say no and run away until you're far from here."

"No way am I going to leave you! I'll always have your back, Jen. No matter what horrible thing you've done. Give me the shovel and I'll help bury the body. Or bodies, whatever. I'm your girl."

"That's a good thing to know, but it's not *that* bad." I checked to make sure no one was around and then I peeled off my dress, revealing a fuchsia-and-gold bodysuit beneath, and kicked off my heels. I shoved my clothes and shoes in my tote bag and pulled out a pair of gold pumps while Dahlia watched wide-eyed.

I said, "Whatever you see, do not freak out. You're going to be safe, okay?"

She nodded, and I felt a deep sense of gratitude and affection for the marvelous and crazy little bitch.

And then I shifted.

The feeling was incredible. My ooky feelings dissolved as my body took on solid muscle mass and bodacious curves, and my skin bloomed vivid green.

Shulky shook out her luxurious green-black hair and slid her feet into the shoes. "Stay here, cupcake! I'll come back for you, but *stay* here," she said to my stunned friend, who crouched behind a trash can.

Shulky didn't have time for niceties, not that she ever saw the need for them. She tore open the heavy steel back door and stepped into the kitchen. Pots still simmered on the commercial range, and abandoned platters of food covered the counters. Since the catering staff hadn't run out the back door, Shulky thought they must be hiding downstairs in the VIP rooms. If the attackers trapped people down there, bad things could happen.

She strode into the dark club, where the music had stopped and nervous shrieks and cries filled the air. The attackers were shoving the crowd to one side of the room, and Shulky hoped they weren't planning execution-style slaughter. Everyone was so focused on the thugs that they didn't notice the six-foot-seven jade Amazon back by the kitchen doors.

One of them, the leader, shouted to the guests, "Dr. Sven Morigi — come out! You cannot hide from us."

Shulky spotted Sven trying to come forward, but Amber clung to him, holding him back, and clamping her hand over his mouth. He tried to free himself, but she held tight to her company's new asset.

Some guests cowered under tables, and more than a few men hid behind their female dates, which Shulky thought was not very gallant. Two armed intruders swung their weapons around to demonstrate just how much of the crowd they could take out in a burst of fire.

Shulky's M.O. was to dive directly into action, but she couldn't with so many bystanders.

The leader looked at the huddled guests and shouted, "Sven Morigi! Show yourself or we'll begin eliminating the obstacles!"

Then Ellis pushed people aside and shouted, "You can talk to me," and he caught sight of Shulky by the kitchen doors and lifted one brow in subtle acknowledgment.

The leader looked at Ellis, confused. "You're not Morigi."

The brawny man stepped into the center of the dance floor and said, "No, Morigi's over there!" He pointed away from the crowd and threw out something that burst into flames. The intruders were startled long enough for Shulky to vault to Ellis's side.

"Wanna dance with me, baby?" Shulky purred to him.

Ellis said, "Thought you'd never ask, gorgeous," just as the first assailant charged Shulky with a dagger.

Ellis ducked behind the assailant, and Shulky slapped the knife away and Three-Stooged him backward.

"Slowly I turn," Ellis shouted.

"Good idea!" In one of her signature moves, she yanked the thug up by his ankles and swung him around like a club, laughing as he knocked over his comrades, one after another.

As the thugs stumbled, Ellis seized their knives, clubs, and handguns. He ordered the club guests "Keep back!" but they were already rushing out the front door, adding to the chaos.

I didn't mind chaos because I'd learned that no one complained much about the damage Shulky caused when all hell broke loose.

A thug charged at Ellis's back, but Ellis flipped him onto a table, which split in two.

Shulky noticed a huge ice luge and said to a rushing attacker, "I'll take mine on the rocks, thank you very much!" She grabbed his forearms and squeezed them against his body. Then she lifted him and slammed him down the luge, sending him sliding to the floor with a shriek and a crash.

Ellis punched a thug in the nose. While the thug staggered back, Ellis clobbered him with a chair.

Shulky shrugged and said, "I'm guessing it's too late to hug it out," and then hurled the next attacker down the length of the long bar, laughing as he knocked over drinks and bottles. He flew off the end and smashed into the nearest wall.

The few remaining thugs scurried forward, but only to pick up their fallen comrades and carry them outside.

Shulky did a quick survey of the room to make sure all the guests were safe. She saw that Sven had freed himself from Amber's clutches and was trying to calm a hysterical bartender.

Shulky's eyes met Ellis's shining brown ones. He was breathing hard, and he gazed at her with wonder and excitement. She stared at him for long seconds, a smile playing on her lips.

Then she heard sirens wailing in the distance.

Shulky raced out of the club, and just as quickly as they arrived, the Hummers were speeding away. She wanted to chase them, but the club guests and all the onlookers and paparazzi clustered around her, grabbing at her and shouting, "She-Hulk! She-Hulk! She-Hulk!"

Cameras clicked and lights flashed.

Ellis joined her outside, with Amber trailing behind him. She looked small and had gotten grimy in the commotion.

But Ellis looked sexier than ever. Shulky ruffled his thick hair and said, "Thanks for the assist," in a throaty voice as she moved close to him.

"Anytime," he said in that gravelly voice.

"I'll take you up on that. I'll take you up on anything, playboy." She leaned toward him so that her nose was close to his neck, and she inhaled his scent. Nice — warm and manly. Ellis was so astonished he just stood there.

Shulky noticed Amber glaring at her. She gave the hammerhead a contemptuous look and said, "Beat it, pipsqueak. This is for grown-ups."

Shulky wrapped her arm around Ellis's waist and pulled him to her so that their hips crushed against each other, and I was thinking *OMG!*, and then she gave him a kiss that was so deep and long that it took all the air out of his lungs.

The fight and the sense of shared victory excited her, but She-Hulk and I both felt *something else* with Ellis. Maybe it was just my bittersweet memory of his taste, his scent, his touch, because she seemed almost melancholy as she broke from him. Amber grabbed his arm and pulled him away from the Jade Goddess.

I was ~~a little~~ a lot seriously FREAKED out. Because Ellis had kissed Shulky back, and I felt jealous in a hurt way. I was used to being envious of her, but this was different, as if she'd betrayed our friendship.

Then everyone began yelling as squad cars screeched to a stop outside the club, their lights turning everyone but Shulky red.

As she waited for Sergeant Patty to get out of the lead car, she glanced back and saw Dr. Sven Morigi in the doorway of the club, watching her with admiration. Shulky thought he was awfully pretty and she winked at him.

"Hey, Shulky," said Patty as she came forward with a frown. "What went down here?"

The women moved away from the crowd, and Shulky told Patty about the fight.

"Were you in the club when they invaded?" Patty asked.

"I was down the street and coming here when I saw the Hummers pull up. They were already inside when I entered through the kitchen," She-Hulk said. "You should talk to Dr. Sven Morigi, the Eurosexual eye candy by the door. They were calling for him and he might know who they were."

"Do you think they were goddamn regular humans?"

"They bounced off the walls like regular humans," Shulky said, with a grin. "It wasn't a real contest, but I had help from that big hunk o' man who's down the sidewalk with that nasty curdled-milk peewee."

Patty snickered. "Not everyone can have your stature, Shulky. Okay, I'll see what I can find out. Nice coincidence that you were here."

"Sugar, it's never a coincidence that I'm at a *partay*. Make sure Morigi gets protection. Those men weren't superhuman, but they're not amateurs either."

"I'll get on that right away. Just FYI, we haven't had any leads on Superbrat. Have you heard anything?"

"If I had, you'd know it. Till next time, Pattycakes."

People were now coming close and asking, "Shulky, are you staying?" and "Are you coming back inside?" and "You're so hot! Can I buy you a drink?" but she remembered that Dahlia was waiting and probably scared.

Shulky asked Patty to send a copy of her report to Ruth, and then she waved to everyone and said, "Go on inside and have fun!"

Once the crowd had hurried into Club Nice, assuming that Shulky would join them, she raced off into the night, making a series of turns to throw off anyone following her, before returning to the back entrance of the club.

11:30 P.M.

She-Hulk called softly, "It's me. You're safe and can come out now, sugarplum. They're gone." She leaned down to take Dahlia's small hand.

Dahlia was trembling and her eyes were wide.

"You're speechless. I have that effect." Shulky grinned. "Let me change into someone more uncomfortable." And I thought, *You're hilarious, Shulky,* and then she shifted into me.

I was standing in the skimpy bodysuit and huge shoes. I flapped my arms to warm them. "Wow, it's really cold."

Dahlia continued to stare with those wild violet contact lenses as she handed me my dress, shoes, and coat.

"Thanks, D." I quickly slipped on the clothes, changed shoes, and said, "Let's get out of here."

We'd gone two blocks and the only sound was our heels clattering on the pavement. Finally I said, "The silence is very peaceful, but I think I almost miss you talking. Almost."

She stopped and gripped my arm and then opened her mouth, shut it, opened it again, and said, "OMG, you're She-Hulk!"

"I'm me. She-Hulk is She-Hulk."

"A, how could you have kept this from me all this time? B, why didn't you tell me before? C, were you Shulky when we were roommates? And, D, OMG, I'm besties with a superhero!"

"One, it's been agony keeping my secret from you. Two, I didn't want you to know because I wanted to keep you safe from the villains who are part of Shulky's life. Three, I was contaminated by gamma radiation *after* law school and I'll tell you more in a warmer place. Four, there are things I can't tell you because they'll compromise others' privacy. Most of us aren't like Tony, public with our alternate identities." I couldn't tell her that I was given the contaminated blood by my cousin because he was really protective of his life as a chemistry teacher. "And, five, Shulky's best friend is whoever is around to party, but you are *my* best friend. Is that okay?"

"I think I can manage being BFFs with a famous attorney who's also a notorious groupie."

That made me happy because most people glom on to Shulky; maybe I'd always been afraid of losing Dahlia to her.

D was quiet again before saying, "I have so many questions that they've made a traffic jam of epic proportions in my brain."

"Let's grab a cab and go to your place. We'll make a pot of tea and I'll tell you and Rodney the general outline of my life, including what happened at the club tonight."

So that's what we did. I've never seen her as quiet and thoughtful as she was while I recited my story. She did ask, "Who gave you the gamma-radiated transfusion when you got hurt?"

"An associate who had it on hand. I'm not at liberty to say any more."

"It's horrible that the people who shot your mother almost killed you, too."

"Yes, it is."

"But you took your mother's murder with such . . . *maturity* isn't the right word and neither is *calmness*. You held it all in."

"Let's not get sidetracked by that." Two hours later, when we were discussing the night's events, she said, "Do you think that the attackers intended to keep Sven from testifying against ReplaceMax?"

"I always advise my clients, never jump to conclusions. The most apparent answer is not always the right one and you might miss the truth if you're only looking for reasons to support your thesis."

"So what you're saying is that yes, you think so." She poured the last of the tea, now cold, into our cups. "You macked on Ellis Tesla again after all these years."

"Shulky macked on him, but she's very affectionate," I said. "He still carries flash paper in his pocket."

"He's got a rocket in his pocket," she said with a grin. "He's still Ellis Tesla under the thin gloss of a civilized man. From now on, this date shall be known as the Night of the Smexy Men. I wish I could have seen you both fighting the baddies."

"I'm sure Ellis acted to protect Amber. I didn't fight, Shulky did."

"You keep making that distinction between you and She-Hulk."

"Because we *are* different people, or entities, or personas. When she takes over, I'm inside there, but only as an observer."

Dahlia suddenly laughed and said, "Well, that solves one mystery. I always thought that those sex vixen outfits you hide away were for a secret double life as a dominatrix. I was sad that you were not very good at it, because I didn't see any extra income."

I laughed, too. "D, if I was a dominatrix, I would dress more modestly than Shulky. Look, I have to call in a report to Ruth at the Mansion and then I've got to crash. Write down any questions you have about She-Hulk and me, and we'll have dinner and I'll answer as many as I can. Okay?"

"Just one last question! That kiss with Ellis — what did you feel?"

"Honestly? Confused. I don't feel her sensations as if they're my own, but she enjoyed it. The kiss isn't relevant about his feelings for Amber. When Shulky decides to kiss a man, he's always thrilled to reciprocate."

"Hon, you act like you've got nothing to offer. But Dr. Stunning's definitely interested, and Ellis wrote over a dozen songs about you. The Gin Cycle."

"He wrote over a dozen songs using Gin as a default name for groupies. I've been entirely over Ellis Tesla forever, except as a Fringe Theory fan. Besides, he thinks I'm a socially inept girl who has sex with coworkers in closets."

"What!"

"Add that to your list of questions," I said. "Good night and sweet dreams!"

· 14 ·

GRIEVANCE

FEBRUARY 22

I called the Mansion and reported the incident. Finally got to bed and couldn't sleep for thinking about everything that had happened.

THE GOOD

- Great time with Sven and got to go to cool club!
- Sven could be PFLOML, is single, and seems interested
- Shulky stopped assailants from kidnapping/hurting Sven and others
- Relieved to finally tell Dahlia the truth
- Ellis Tesla lives!
- Kiss was OMG! Amazing!

THE BAD

- ~~Maybe Probably~~ Have put Dahlia in danger by letting her in on secret
- Difficult to feel relaxed around Sven, and his client status forestalls any other relationship

- Why did Ellis kiss Shulky back if he's engaged to the hammer-head, and why do I even care?
- Sven still in danger since most assailants escaped

Ellis's flash paper made me remember the lyrics to Fringe Theory's "Game Theory."

I thought I was wise to game theory
I could see my lovers' schemes so clearly
A little heat with each girl and bounce to the next
A little fun, a few laughs, hey, it was just sex
It all balanced out, a zero-sum equation,
And I'm alone to blame for the conflagration

Cuz I threw Gin carelessly onto the embers
Not expecting ignition with my heart so inert
Thought I was a player, but I was just a jerk
I lost all equanimity and equilibrium
And I burn, I burn, I burn
To make love to her again

Why did he use my name — my alleged name — in all those songs? The lyrics couldn't be about me, because I am not a sex goddess or femme fatale. Because if he was singing about me, he would have called.

7:00 A.M.

Day 8 of New Resolutions!

Before work, I turned on the TV and checked online news sites. Headlines read NIGHTCLUB ATTACKERS NOT PLAYING NICE! and SHULKY RULES THE CLUB NICE PLAYGROUND. I turned off the show when the announcer said, "And now for our Cute-Clip-of-the-Day about a friendly furry-tailed rat that's delighting tourists at Rockefeller Plaza!"

I called Patty Palmieri to see what she'd learned. She wasn't in yet, but I talked to Detective Mike Washington, who told me that they'd apprehended the men in one of the Hummers.

He said, "They talked because they have nothing to tell. They were supposed to abduct Morigi unharmed, drive him toward JFK, and they'd receive further instructions en route. We traced their contact number to a Chechnya origin, but it was a burner and we lost the trail. You were with Dr. Morigi before the attack, right?"

I told him the essentials and said, "Mike, if the purpose was merely to intimidate Dr. Morigi, the thugs wouldn't have been instructed to take him to the airport. If the purpose was to silence him, they could have simply killed him."

He asked me if I had any theories, and I said that I didn't like to jump to conclusions, but it was possible that some individual or group wanted to use his genius for nefarious purposes.

Mike told me that Patty already suspected as much and that the Feds were consulting on the case.

When I mentioned that I was glad to have left the club before the invasion, Mike gave a warm *huh-huh-huh* laugh. "Counselor, for a lady who says she doesn't like danger, you sure seem to always get yourself in prickly situations."

"Prickly situations are all around," I said. "I guess that comes with living at the center of all superhuman activity in the known universe."

"Could be," he said. "Even if we don't find out any more about these mopes, we're glad to get them off the street. Me or Patty will give you a holler if we find out anything else."

As soon as I got to my office, I called Sven.

SR: Jennifer, you got out of the club just in time last night.
ME: I heard the news. Where are you now? Are you safe?
SR: My building is secure and I've employed round-the-clock bodyguards. I'll be fine.
ME: I'm so relieved that those criminals didn't harm you.

SR: I wanted to confront them, but your colleague Amber Tumbridge kept me from stepping forward. She-Hulk saved us all. She's really quite magnificent. I do wish she hadn't left so abruptly. I didn't have the opportunity to thank her for thwarting the abduction attempt. She's a friend of yours, isn't she?

ME: We've worked on cases together. Her legal prowess is as impressive as her physical strength. She can be reached via the Avengers Mansion.

SR: I'll send a thank-you note since we were not introduced. I am grateful to our superheroes, and you'll think me very dull, Jennifer, to be more intrigued with small miracles of biomedicine than the exotic mutations of superhumans.

When I hung up, I stared out the window at the gloomy day. I was glad that Sven seemed to prefer me to Shulky, but my thoughts kept getting diverted to Ellis fighting by her side. And the kiss. And that one weekend.

I continued obsessing about Ellis during my update with Amber. She went through a proposed list of depositions, and I thought I'd escaped without her talking about Club Nice, but as she gathered her notes, she said, "You neglected to take proper precautions with a high-priority client. Dr. Morigi was almost abducted last night. I had to hold him back because he intended to give himself up to the kidnappers to protect innocent bystanders. It's a wonder that he escaped unscathed."

"I spoke with Dr. Morigi this morning, and he said that She-Hulk quickly had everything under control."

"It was mere happenstance that her nightlife activities took her to Club Nice. The situation might have been resolved using diplomacy, but that trashy superhuman pole-dancer began destroying the room and assaulting people," Amber said, throwing her spin on things. "She wrecked any chance at negotiation."

"I don't think the attackers had any incentive to negotiate."

"How could you know, since you had already abandoned Dr. Morigi before they arrived? I assure you that there was ample opportunity to calm the situation." Amber stood and used her left hand to brush her hair back. If my conversations with her were seen as a poker game, her tell would be the way she showed her ring off when she was putting me down.

I counted to ten, because I didn't want my skin to take on a minty hue, and then told her that Sven had around-the-clock protection.

"It would have been better to avoid endangering him in the first place," she smeered and turned to leave the room. "*Obviously.*"

7:30 P.M.

I had to kick Dahlia out. She came here with Rodney, ugh, and a loooong list of questions that she wants me to answer, including:

Q: How does Shulky get those gorgeous on-trend Hollywood waves in her hair? Didn't she have a different style a few years back? What products does she use?

A: I don't know. She doesn't do anything — her hair just seems to change with current fashion.

Q: If you are aware of being inside Shulky, is she aware of being inside you?

A: She has limited consciousness inside of me, but I can't tell if it's because she's not really paying attention or because she's in a state similar to suspended animation — which feels really ooky by the way — until she's needed.

Q: Has Shulky ever fallen in love with the same man as you?

A: She falls in lust but doesn't fall in love. We have different tastes. She really likes muscle-bound dudes.

Q: Tell me the truth: is she your best friend?

A: Shulky is like a crazy sister. I love her and I'm stuck with her no matter what. You're my best friend.

Dahlia saw my muslin mock-up of my LadyGreene costume for the Forestiers May battle games, and she said, "I don't understand why you're playing this pretend game when you're already She-Hulk."

"I don't have control over Shulky, so it's entirely different. Besides, having a more balanced social life is one of my Valentine's Day Resolutions. I was fanatical about Robin Hood when I was a kid. My cousin and I would act out scenes in the backyard. I like the make-believe."

"Like my childhood connection to Barbie?"

"No, your relationship to Barbie is dark and twisted."

Dahlia rolled her chartreuse eyes, and I told her, "I wish you wouldn't do that with those contacts. You look totally possessed."

She repeated the crazy eye roll and said, "I bet that there's something dark and twisted in your fantasy sword-and-sorcery, too. Do you know that my autocorrect changes Shulky to Sulky every time? Does anyone ever call you Sulky? Because you act that way so often."

"I'm not sulky, and no one calls She-Hulk that more than once."

"You are so sulky. I've just thought of more questions for you."

"Save them. Nelson and I are going to a fight-scene workshop for LARPers."

"Like I said, dark and twisted," Dahlia said.

I ran to Johnny & Buggy's Diner, which wasn't far away, and people stared at me because I was carrying my shield and weapon. Nelson was waiting out front with a very convincing broadsword. He looked so much happier than the first time I'd met him.

I told him, "I think you'll like my friend Amy Stewart-Lee, whose sign-on is DamaskRose. We worked together in the district attorney's office, and she's one of the people I can always trust for thoughtful, smart advice. She said it was okay to tell you her real-life identity."

"I noticed her character profile. She's got a cute avatar."

"She is cute and sort of wry, I guess. She's serious but doesn't take herself too seriously."

"Is this a setup?"

"Only if you like each other. If not, we're all just making new friends."

When we went inside, Amy caught our attention by waving and calling, "Hail, fair lady and sir! Well met, and let us anon to the dungeon to commence our jousting pantomimes — but without our noble steeds."

Amy was dressed in camouflage cargos and a plum wool sweater with a crimson silk rose pinned to it. She wore her ink-black hair in cute braids. I introduced her to Nelson, and they smiled at each other in a promising way. He was about three inches taller than she was.

"You have a beautiful smile," Nelson told Amy, and she returned the compliment.

We headed downstairs to join the other LARPers, and she said, "I am hopeful that thee will forgiveth me for I am but a poor speaker of the Queen's English, but my goode intentions counteth more than actual preciseness or accuracy."

"Oh, DamaskRose, your words are as sweet as your personage is comely, and I beg that you will speak on."

Holy cow — Nelson had Medieval game!

The class leader gave us instructions in stage fighting and role-playing, and then we improvised. Halfway into the class, he took me aside. "LadyGreene, your talent at swordplay is admirable, but where's the drama? Think about your character and what you're feeling. Let your face and body language express your emotions and don't be afraid to be dramatic and vocalize."

"One of my coaches doesn't like it when I say *kapow!*" I admitted.

The teacher grinned and said, "You are in a safe zone for a well-timed *fie* or *huzzah!*"

"Excellent," I said. I even let myself be injured so I could enact a heartbreaking scene with Amy applying a poultice, and everyone clapped afterward. I didn't meet any candidates for PFLOML, but I'd had fun. Nelson and Amy stayed to have a drink in the bar, so all in all, the evening was a terrific success.

FEBRUARY 28

Two weeks into my resolutions and everything is going fantastic, including my new friendship with Fritz. I have forty-six days left to give him an answer about an uncomplicated sexual partnership. It really doesn't seem like that much time.

He met me at 7:00 a.m. for my Krav Maga class. He picked up basics very quickly for someone who has never done any martial arts. Azzan nodded and told him, "Good balance. Good reactions. Good instincts." He turned to me and said, "This one I like. Sign him up for my beginner class."

Fritz was beaming afterward, and I said, "Don't look so happy. He may try to recruit you as an international assassin."

He grinned and asked if I'd thought about his colleagues-with-benefits proposal.

"Actually, I've been really busy."

"Which is exactly why we'd be a good match activity-wise. I could be Kato to your Green Hornet, but once you pinned me down, we'd take off our clothes." He waggled his pale eyebrows, and I started laughing.

"You're sweetening the deal," I said.

"I can also throw in shiatsu massage."

"You know shiatsu massage?"

"No, but my masseuse does out calls. Let's get a Joocey Jooce." He pointed at the shop on the corner, with a line trailing out to the street.

"We have it at the office."

"It's not the same," Fritz said and shrugged one shoulder. "It's different in the paper cup with the logo."

He was right. There was something different about the bottled drink at QUIRC compared to the smoothies in the shops with their smiling counter clerks and customers. I told him to go on without me and headed into work on my own. I didn't need to confirm any gossip about us by showing up with him in the morning.

As I walked to the office, a man strode by me, carelessly dropping a crumpled newspaper on the pavement. Jerk. I picked it up, folded it neatly, and set it atop the trash bin in case someone else wanted to read it.

I met with the General to review medical fraud case histories. We waded through documents and photos of malformed babies and patients in wheelchairs. It was depressing. Tomorrow I'm going to the hospice to visit the little girl whose ReplaceMax heart is degrading.

At around seven, my vision blurred from straining to read thousands of tiny footnotes, and I knew I needed to go home. I'd put drops into my eyes, and they were watering as I went down to the lobby. I was looking at the freezing mess of darkness outside the building's entrance when I saw Ellis come through the doors.

I ~~graciously approached him~~ was about to run and hide, but he spotted me. I pulled off my glasses, wiped at my eyes, shoved my glasses back on, and went to say hello.

"Good evening, Ellis, how are you?" I kept thinking of the kiss, the solidity of his body, and the slip and slide of his tongue against Shulky's.

"Fine, thank you. Amber tells me you've been named lead on the case against ReplaceMax."

I saw the same spark in his eyes that Shulky had seen when they'd fought together. I wanted to reach into his jacket to see if he had flash paper. I wanted to reach into his pants and see if he had other things.

I said, "Yes, I am. I'm determined to see that Maxwell Kirsch and the ReplaceMax directors are called to account for their malfeasances." My arms seemed freakishly long, and the skin at the back of my neck prickled. I curled my fingers so he couldn't see the jagged edges of my bitten nails.

"You're wrong." His dark eyes met mine. "*You're wrong.* I told my father and I told Amber. Max Kirsch is a good man and ReplaceMax is doing vital medical research."

"I agree that Dr. Morigi was conducting important research when he was at ReplaceMax. I know that Max Kirsch is your friend—"

"He's not just a friend. I've consulted for ReplaceMax." Ellis took a step closer and my breath caught. He said in a quieter voice, "Don't you remember? Xam Archimedes. He was our drummer, Ginny."

Instead of correcting him, I said, "Max is the Xam Man?" The nickname came to me out of nowhere.

"One and the same. I'd trust him with my life. Drop the case."

Why hadn't QUIRC documents mentioned Ellis's consulting? Why hadn't Amber told me? "People look away from information that they don't want to know, especially when deniability can be profitable. Do you own shares in ReplaceMax, Ellis?"

His look turned stony. "Ms. Walters, when we met — the *second* time we met — you talked a good game about working for the public benefit — but I'm assuming you were merely reeling off your talking points. Just because your ethics can be compromised, if you ever had any, don't assume that everyone can be bought."

He walked away and I stood shell-shocked. *Stand up for yourself,* I thought, so I hurried to him quickly. I reached out for him, saying, "That's unjustified!" and my heel skittered on the polished marble floor, and I fell right into him.

He caught me.

For a moment, his hands gripped my arms. Our faces were an inch apart, I could feel the warmth of his breath on my cheek, and I remembered the taste of his mouth, the rumble of his laughter, the rough calluses on his fingers brushing my skin.

I became aware that I was clutching Ellis. I released my grip and pulled away. "I'm representing Dr. Morigi because I believe he's not only right, he's noble. He's saving people from being hurt by ReplaceMax at great cost, both personally and financially. The evidence will prove it." I heard my voice rising as I said, "If you think I've sold out, then you have no goddamn idea who I am!"

His expression was unreadable, and he continued to gaze into my eyes. After long seconds, he said, "No, I guess I don't." Then he turned and walked away.

My heart was pounding with the realization that Ellis hated me. I'd seen it in his eyes and my heart ached. It hurt even more than all those nights I'd waited for him to call and gone to bed in tears.

7:30 P.M.

When I arrived at Arrested Youth, Dahlia was reviewing the day's receipts with her manager. Horrible Rodney had a new streak of hot pink in his fur and was snuffling on a pillow.

I looked at magazines and experimented with products on the counter. I accidentally sprayed something in my eyes, which made them blur again.

Once we were alone, I swiveled in my chair toward Dahlia and told her about my encounter with Ellis. "It was awful. He loathes me. I can't believe he thinks I'm only out for money. And he thinks I have sex in the closet at work. And that I'm a floozie."

"Did you seriously say 'floozie'? He thinks that you're a fierce and brilliant attorney as well as a sex goddess," she said. "Men are crazy about you. I credit my OMG! amazing haircut. I cite as examples: Dr. Stunning, that Fritz dude, your smitten doorman, the guy you flipped over at the singles meet-up, Nelson, even though you're too tall for him. I'm sure there are legions."

Talking to D always made me feel better. "Did you just seriously say 'smitten'? Do you think so?"

"Fer sure. Let's talk syllogisms for a moment. If Ellis hates you because you are on the case against ReplaceMax, doesn't it follow that he'd also hate the evil hammerhead?"

"Maybe she's too perfect and sexually proficient to hate," I said. "Her voice sounds like the 'We appreciate your patience while you hold' music in heaven. No wonder Ellis is in love with her."

"Honey, Ellis already told us the truth—*Amber* doesn't rhyme with anything. Well, hammerhead. She doesn't inspire his fire of desire to go higher in a pyre . . ." She looked at the ceiling. "Okay, that's all I got. You get my drift. How do you feel about Cuban takeout and prank-calling Tony Stark?"

"Dahlia, there's nothing I'd rather do more."

"And then we can go dancing."

"It's a school night. I mean, work night."

"It's *Friday* night, and my date just canceled because he broke his foot or fell into a coma or something stupid. I'll become clinically depressed if I don't have anything to do."

"You have a kazillion friends you can call."

"But only you can get me into Club Nice, Sulky." Dahlia gave me a pitiful look, placing her hands palms together, prayer-like. *"Pulleeze, pulleeze!"*

"One, stop calling me that. Two, I don't like weekend scenes at clubs. And three, we couldn't get in."

"A, I'll stop calling you that when you stop being so mopey. B, we'll only go for the early part. And C, if you call the club as Shulky, we can get on the list," she said. *"Pulleeze*, for the love of all that is fluffy and sparkly, *pulleeze!"*

"Fine." I didn't want to shift just to do Shulky's voice, so I tried to imitate her throaty tone when I called. "Hello, darling! This is your favorite green glamazon."

"She-Hulk! This is Caleb, the manager. Thanks for kicking bad-guy ass the other night. Will we see you soon?"

"Absotootely, but not tonight. I'd like to have my friend Jennifer Walters stop by to observe things for me."

"The attorney with thoroughbred legs and gorgeous hair? She was here with Sven Morigi at the opening. I'll put her on the list."

"With a plus-one! Keep it hot for me, Caleb." I hung up and said to Dahlia, "You may be right about that haircut."

10:00 P.M.

D and I got to Club Nice before the crowd, and Caleb came right over and welcomed us with kisses. He was very cute, in a gawky trendy geek way, with oversize glasses, a shirt that was too small, and pants that were too short. He invited us to sit at his table, and a waitress quickly appeared with a bottle of champagne and glasses. After we'd chatted for a few minutes, I asked Caleb if he'd gotten any tips about the attack or the attackers.

"Nothing, but Sergeant Palmieri told me it's unlikely they'll come back since they were targeting Dr. Morigi," Caleb said. "It was incredible that She-Hulk saved us, but we did incur some damages."

"So I heard," I said.

He looked a little embarrassed and said, "I talked to our insurance company, but they said that She-Hulk's destruction falls under their 'random acts of the universe' provision."

"Don't worry, Caleb. Just send the bills to the Avengers Mansion, attention Ruth, with a note that I've authorized payment from She-Hulk's account."

"Thanks!"

I glanced around the club, and everyone was being so polite and happy. "I like the name of your club. Is Joocey Jooce more than a sponsor of your opening?"

I found out that the Joocey Jooce founders owned a small percentage of the club, mostly for bragging rights, and Caleb relayed the same story about the company's origins that I'd already learned: they'd built their first cart out of recycled parts and made their smoothies with organic fruit. All of Caleb's connections in the food service industry said the "Play nice" theme was part of their daily transactions.

A familiar throbbing song came on, and I heard Ellis's rough voice begin singing.

"Fringe Theory," Caleb said. "I thought I recognized Ellis Tesla at our opening. Now he's going by his real name, Ellis Quintal, the guy who helped She-Hulk fight the intruders. I think I must have listened to 'Flesh-Eating Bacteria Girl' a thousand times in high school. I asked the DJs to include the whole Gin Cycle on our playlists."

Dahlia scooted out of the banquette while yanking my hand and said, "Let's dance."

"But no one else is dancing yet!"

"So we can be the first and have the floor to ourselves."

I looked at Caleb, hoping that he'd want to continue talking, but he was singing along with the song.

"I hate being the first ones," I told D. "It's embarrassing."

"If you showed up at a reasonable time, like midnight, the dance floor would be jammed, so it's your own damn fault."

Ellis was singing "Love Dynamite," which threw me back to the summer I'd interned with the Los Angeles DA.

Nitroglycerin stops and starts my heart
Missing Gin is tearing me apart
Next time I'll be more careful and dilute my emotions
Next time I'll resist temptation
From the sort of girl
Who'll just explode my world.

By the beginning of the next song, other couples had joined us, then more people filled the dance floor, and I became lost in the music, back to that girl who was still hoping Ellis would call.

An hour turned into two. Dahlia said, "I've got to meet my Aveda rep early tomorrow. Let's go."

We waved good-bye to Caleb, and when we got out of the club, Dahlia asked why I'd wanted to know about Club Nice and Joocey Jooce.

"They just keep coming up."

"It's because they're part of the zeitgeist. I don't understand why you don't go dancing more often. You're so good and I can tell you love it. You didn't have to quit dancing just because you had a growth spurt."

"Yes, I did, because I couldn't walk without bashing into things. Jennifer Falters, ha ha, that's what the other girls called me. My ballet teacher used to pat me on my back with this look in her eyes like I'd accidentally run over her favorite cat."

"Who didn't have a horrible nickname?"

"I bet Amber didn't," I said.

"She does now, Amber Hammerhead. Tell that to Ellis the next time you see him," D said, and I told her I would take it under advisement.

INADMISSIBLE EVIDENCE

MARCH 6

I have now been following my resolutions for almost three weeks, and it is time to revisit my priorities:

1. ReplaceMax case

2. Find an apartment

3. Meet someone for postponed Valentine's Day date

4. Accept/Reject Fritz's Proposal Countdown: 40 Days

Work consumes my life. I feel like a tax preparer stuck in a time loop where every day is April 14. I get home too late most nights to do anything but eat cereal and turn on the TV to PBS, because that way I can score cultural education points. I count opera for quadruple points because I don't get it at all even when I read the subtitles. In fact, the subtitles make the stories even more confusing. Everyone has different agendas, too many secrets, and people don't talk to one another in a professional way, which would solve most of their dilemmas.

Maybe Fritz is right about taking a more businesslike approach to relationships. He doesn't pressure me for an answer, and when I ran into him at the gym, I asked, "Will you be upset if I say no?" and he grinned and said, "Jennifer, I have to beat girls off with a stick, so I think I'll survive." The more I know him, the more I like him, but still no sparks, or explosions.

On the apartment-hunting front, I've only seen a few places so far, but I've already learned the secret code:

Quaint = toilet in the kitchen (sure this must be illegal)
Cozy = can touch opposing bedroom walls with arms outstretched
Fantastic view = something somewhat recognizable is visible from roof
Exciting neighborhood = above a bar
Up-and-coming neighborhood = next to a methadone clinic
Executive living = gorgeous but have to sideline as international assassin to pay for amenities
Pets welcome = previous tenant was cat hoarder
Gracious living = duck motif on all tiled surfaces
Vintage charm = hot water only available between 11:00 a.m. and noon
Secure building = located in disputed gang turf
Open concept living = no closets or bathroom door

I met with a chic leasing agent who showed me two lavish apartments, both significantly over the price range I'd specified. She said, "Someone in your position should have a showplace to entertain clients and business associates. It's an investment in your reputation and career."

When I said the rents were too high, she showed me a squalid and depressing cramped one-bedroom with a view of the neighbor's dirty kitchen.

I always tell my clients, "When you are making a purchase, decide ahead of time what you can afford to pay and what you want to pay. Do not succumb to powers of persuasion or a desire to please the seller. Be willing to walk away."

So I broke off from the leasing agent, who said smugly, "You'll never find what you want at that price point, especially since a background check will show your *colorful* rental history. You'll be back."

I smiled and left, and then texted Ruth to please have the tech staff do another cleanup of my credit report.

At least my job is going well.

I like working with Genoa, who's as smart as a whip and pleasant, but in a calm way. After too many phone calls and messages back and forth, it made sense for me to work at one of the big tables in her office.

She has a bell on her desk, the kind they have at old shops to call for a clerk, and every time we finish a task, she rings it. "Interrogatory request for Daryne Cohen, chief lab technician, complete!" *RING!*

"Genoa, exactly what purpose does that serve?" I asked.

"Quinty gave it to me after I complained that I was getting nowhere on a case. I think he stole it from a deli. He said ringing it would make me more aware of achieving the small steps on the long journey. It's weird, but it works."

Quinty was right, because it was oddly rewarding to clang down on the bell every time I completed a task.

Genoa's windowless, book-filled office was really very cozy and warm. We drank tea, kvetched about missing and incomplete documents, and helped each other out.

I noticed that she'd kicked off her shoes, so I did the same, and we dug into our work.

9:00 P.M.

Spent an hour looking online for apartments. I tried to imagine them as places that would impress clients at swanky parties, where I would hold a martini in one hand and put the other to my throat as I threw back my gorgeous hair with a sultry laugh. I tried to figure out which apartment would be best for a romantic tryst with my PFLOML and I got sidetracked remembering Ellis naked. He looked good naked. Really good.

Then I imagined Amber naked with him — eew — and I wanted to get that image out of my brain, but all I could see on the insides of my eyeballs was Amber smeering while Ellis did perverse things to her. Ugh ugh ugh.

I went back to my apartment hunt, but the property descriptions blurred into one another. It made my brain hurt.

Called Nelson and told him to tell me if he heard of any openings in his building. He's going on a date with Amy tomorrow (hurray!), and they'll both be at the next Forestiers meet-up, when we're going to make medieval jewelry and accessories.

Emailed Dahlia and asked her for help with costume details because all I've come up with is a tunic over leggings.

I got a bottle of cranberry juice from the fridge, which made me think about Joocey Jooce. I felt like I was missing something.

- Joocey Jooce invested in Club Nice.
- Kidnappers attacked Club Nice looking for the Sven Morigi, who is suing ReplaceMax.
- A Joocey Jooce flavor inventor paid rent in coupons and has no last name.
- Their shops are ubiquitous and everyone likes everything about the company.

It didn't seem likely that there was a connection between Joocey Jooce and ReplaceMax, but I had an ooky sense. Sometimes you just had to see things for yourself. The Joocey Jooce plant was in New Jersey. I ran to the Mansion's garage, and the eager new attendant didn't make me sign a release. I really miss my old flying car. I chose a Cadillac with an invisibility shield, even though invisibility can be problematic.

I shifted on the shield as I approached the Joocey Jooce corporate campus. I parked across from the shipping entrance, beside the Play Nice sports fields. Trucks arrived and left the loading dock with fresh fruit and supplies. Everyone looked cheerful. One stock clerk whistled as he crossed the perfectly clean lot.

There was no barbed wire, no guard dogs, no eerie sense of abandonment. It was all very normal and my ookiness was unwarranted.

I'd only driven a few blocks from Joocey Jooce before I nearly got slammed by a big rig. Sometimes not being seen is more dangerous than being seen. I disengaged the car's invisibility shield and headed back to the Mansion.

MARCH 8

I had been calculating my postponed Valentine's Day by weeks and coming up with an incorrect date. February 14 is the forty-fifth day of the year, so my postponed VD should be no earlier than the ninetieth day of the year, which is the eve of April 1. I don't want any PFLOML to think a date the night before April 1 is a joke, so I am moving it to April 2.

MARCH 12

Another day of brain-scrambling paperwork with Genoa. One of the assistants brought in lunch and asked us what flavor of Joocey Jooce we wanted.

Genoa and I had just brewed up a pot of Earl Grey tea, so we said no thanks.

When the assistant had gone, Genoa added, "I don't drink Joocey Jooce on principle." She tugged at her ponytail, which is why it is always sideways.

"Why not?"

"I resent their motto. *Play nice.* I don't need some marketing person telling me how to behave. It's unnatural."

"No, it's completely organic."

"I mean their attitude. The niceness gives me the creeps. All those employees are too friendly. They're either being cattle-prodded or they've been lobotomized. It's not normal for New York."

"I thought that, too. But behavior can be changed."

"Only for five minutes, like with New Year's Resolutions — everyone starts out with great intentions, and two weeks later, they're completely forgotten. Actual change requires motivation, effort, and constant vigilance."

She picked up one of her action figures and walked it across her desk.

"Who's that?" I asked.

"Fanny Price from *Mansfield Park*. She's the poor, meek relation. She's always sick and in love with her wimpy cousin, but she stands by her principles. I know, a grown woman playing with dolls. Feel free to mock."

"Only if you mock back," I said. "I'm on a LARP team. Do you know what that is?"

"Terrestrial or extraterrestrial? Present-day or future?"

"Terrestrial and the Middle Ages."

"Do you have costumes and festivals?"

"I just joined this group and we're having battle games at the end of May. They'll be held near Woodstock. This job doesn't give me time to participate much."

Genoa danced the figure on her keyboard. "It's fun, isn't it, having an imaginary life with imaginary characters outside the tenseness of our jobs?" She smiled and said, "Donner suggested that I wear Regency-era dresses to work."

"Does he tease you often?"

"Constantly."

"I can talk to him about it if you like, or you can discuss it with HR."

Genoa stared at me with her clear gray eyes and then burst into laughter. When she was able to speak, she said, "I appreciate your offer, but I can tell my own husband to STFU whenever I want."

"Donner's your *husband*? He didn't mention it."

"It's company policy not to bring our personal business into the office. Amber's a good example. She never lets her relationship with Ellis the fourth — you do know about that, right? That doesn't influence her one bit as far as I can see. Amber is one hundred percent professional. She's the exception to the rule about resolutions. I bet she checks off every item on her New Year's List."

9:45 P.M.

Got home from work. Tried to microwave scrambled eggs for dinner. Bad idea. Tried to improve them with ketchup, a worse idea. Don't have the willpower to go to a singles meet-up. I will die alone surrounded by court dockets in an apartment that smells like cat urine from the previous tenant because I won't even have the time to hoard cats on my own.

Once I was a sexy flesh-eating bacteria girl and now I am a *ma'am*. I only hope that Fritz won't see the desperation on my face when I ask him out. Does that mean I have to sleep with him? He's probably good at sex. I probably thought Ellis was outstanding at sex only because I'd been so inexperienced. The bar was set so low that any guy who had a rudimentary grasp of female anatomy seemed gifted. To give credit where credit is due, Ellis's understanding of female anatomy was at the "class valedictorian," not "mandatory summer school," level.

DEMURRER

MARCH 16

I am one month and two days into my resolutions and halfway (thirty days) to my sixty-day deadline to give Fritz an answer to his colleagues-with-benefits proposal.

I just saw him walk down the hall and was gearing myself to go talk to him when Sven Morigi called, making me feel as if I was a death row prisoner getting the governor's reprieve. (I don't know why governors procrastinate until the last minute, because they could give timely reprieves and save everyone a truckload of anxiety.)

"Dr. Morigi, hello!" I said, sounding *way* too reprieve-relieved.

"Sven," he corrected. "I'm glad I caught you."

"Why? Do you have any more information about ReplaceMax's malfeasances?"

"Actually, yes. . . . Can we discuss it over dinner?"

I felt frazzled and grimy. "Or you can come in tomorrow and meet with me."

"I'm not available tomorrow. I'll pick you up in ten minutes in front of your building."

Dinner with Sven could definitely be classified as balancing work and life. I said, "I'll be there in fifteen minutes."

Dahlia had schooled me on fast makeover tips, and I twisted up my hair in a casual bun, blotted my shiny spots with powder tissues, and touched up my makeup.

I raided my armoire for an ivory silk shell with ruffle trim so I'd look more feminine. I pulled on heeled boots, willing to take the risk to be stylish. I glanced in the mirror and thought I looked good, not as if I was trying too hard.

I went downstairs exactly on time, just as a gleaming black Peugeot was pulling up. A large man in the front passenger seat jumped out to open the back door for me. I slid in beside Sven and noticed that the driver was also large. These men must be Sven's guards.

Sven was so beautiful that I went stiff with nerves when he gave me a kiss on each cheek, which might be the way Europeans conduct business. I have to check on their practices.

He said, "I'm so pleased that you could tear yourself away from work. I hope you enjoy Hungarian food."

I told him I'd never had it and asked if his family was from Hungary.

"We come from Central Europe and the borders changed frequently, but Hungarian is closest to our culture," he said. "My family was nomadic, moving from place to place looking for a safe haven."

"Have you found a safe haven here in New York?"

"I hope so, despite the Club Nice incident. Every time I see the Statue of Liberty, I remember my first visit here and how deeply moved I was at the sight. The skyscrapers and the streets teeming with life made me feel as if the entire city was a laboratory where I could conduct experiments that had never been imagined before." He smiled. "I am a scientist, and so I see through a scientist's eyes. I'm sure the experience was different for you."

"Yes, although I'm still dazzled by this city," I said. "Is everything going all right with your guards? Do you feel secure?"

"Indeed, and I look forward to a relaxing few hours with you, Jennifer."

The driver took us to MacDougal Street, and the other guard opened the back door for us. We got out in front of an old-time diner with boarded up windows. I looked around for the sort of fancy restaurant that someone like Sven would like, but he placed his hand on my elbow and guided me toward the closed diner.

"Here we are," he said. "I hope you don't mind, but I often miss food from my homeland, which is very difficult to find even in this metropolis. I keep this place for my dinners out."

One of the bodyguards opened the door for us.

As Sven and I stepped inside, I saw a small, inviting room with dark red damask wallpaper, shimmering crystal sconces, and oxblood leather seating. Delicious aromas wafted from the kitchen, and I could hear the faint clang of pots and pans. On a small platform, a man in a folk costume played the guitar and sang a melancholy tune in what I guessed was Hungarian. I liked it a whole lot better than opera, and I awarded myself twenty culture points.

A waiter greeted Sven and guided us to a table set with snowy linen, crystal, and silver. The old-fashioned luxury was very comfortable, and it was supercool to have the whole place to ourselves.

"Sven, this is lovely!"

"I'm glad it's to your liking. It's simpler than having the chef, Domonkos, come to my house, because he complains about the kitchen and argues with my housekeeper," he said with a smile. "Also, I like to dine out — it's different, isn't it, than having a meal at one's home?"

"It is. You've devised a wonderful solution."

Sven signaled to the waiter. I watched his face in the candlelight. He was so good-looking it was almost spooky. Wine would definitely help my nerves, and I was grateful when the waiter filled our glasses.

Sven looked me in the eyes, raised his glass, said *"Egészségedre!"* (which I have looked up to spell right). "It means to your health."

When I tried to repeat the word, he smiled and said, " 'Cheers' will do. The mispronunciation is rather rude."

I hated when that happened. "Cheers, then." I took a few quick sips of wine before trusting myself to ask him what important news he'd learned.

"Only that you're a most charming companion, Jennifer."

Whoa! Continental smoothie alert!

"I apologize for using a pretext to draw you away from work. I feared that if I asked you out to dinner, you would decline."

"You're my client, Dr. Morigi, so naturally I want to spend as much time with you as possible." That was a slick response, right?

"You're calling me Dr. Morigi again. I'm tremendously attracted to you, Jennifer."

"I, um, ah . . ." I was quickly reviewing my requirements for my boyfriend goal. Even though Sven didn't currently have a job, he was absolutely qualified. Okay, he hadn't been especially funny so far, but that contingency could be waived because he was so OMG! amazingly gorgeous!

"Surely this doesn't surprise you, Jennifer. Men must fall at your feet."

I couldn't say, "Only when I flip them over," so I just smiled and said, "Sven, I really want to focus on your very important case."

"As you wish," he said with a little nod of his head. "I wanted you to represent me because of your fine qualities as an attorney and an individual. I'm aware of all the charitable work you've done on behalf of the needy. The longer I live, the more I comprehend that kindness is a greater achievement than the acquisition of power. A court victory would mean nothing to me if I felt that my attorney didn't truly believe in justice."

Perhaps it was the wine, but I said, "Ellis Quintal the Fourth urged me not to take this case. He's friends with Max Kirsch and believes my only motive is financial."

Sven's expression altered slightly, but I couldn't tell what it meant. It was like when the optometrist asks me, "Which is clearer, A or B?" and the change is so imperceptible that I have no idea.

He said, "Ms. Tumbridge's engagement to Quintal Four was disclosed to me, and I'm assured that it will not interfere with her excellent work on my behalf. It goes without saying that you won't be swayed by his ignorant and hostile opinions."

If it went without saying, then why did Sven say it? "Certainly not. I'm fully committed to every client I represent. However, considering Ellis's attitude, I was surprised that he stepped in to defend you at Club Nice."

Sven tilted his head and looked at me quizzically. "How did you know that?"

"Um, I saw a video on the news when they managed to take time out of showing that Cute-Clip-of-the-Day about that frolicking rat." I focused on the sheep's cheese dip and said, "This cheese is delicious."

Sven's lips seemed tense as he said, "Ms. Tumbridge strikes me as more than capable of making important decisions, so I'm sure marrying Quintal is ideal for her — but I'm glad you're not the one engaged to him."

"Me? I don't even like him," I said too quickly. "I mean, I don't know him well enough to have an opinion of him one way or another."

Sven's eyebrows drew together. "He was raised in privilege, Jennifer. He really has no comprehension of what life is like for those who must earn their own way, people like us who succeed despite the odds."

It seemed a little unfair, so I said, "I would say that's true if Ellis had joined his father's firm, but science is a fiercely egalitarian field, and scientists are interested in results, not legacies. So far as I know, Ellis is well respected by his peers."

"Let's speak no longer of him. Tell me about yourself. I want to know everything — where you're living now and what led you into the law."

I told him the usual things, which seemed very dull when I edited out all the Shulky-related shenanigans. I desperately tried to think of something amusing. "One of my coworkers refuses to drink Joocey Jooce because she insists that something is wrong with the motto. She doesn't think New Yorkers should be so nice."

He laughed. "It's an interesting social experiment. However, most visitors to the city want to experience the New York attitude as much as see the sights. What inspired you to move to a city with such an aggressive character?"

"I was offered a great job, and I saw the opportunity to start fresh here."

"Are you speaking of the violent death of your mother?"

Even though news reports of Mom's death are easy to find, I felt a little ooky that he'd looked them up. "There was that memory, and I wanted to live in a more intense city."

"Do you find your life satisfying here?"

"Yes, especially right now as an attorney with a premier law firm, having dinner with my brilliant client, and about to embark on a truly challenging case."

"I'm so glad to hear that. You'll forgive me if I treat this as more than a business engagement."

"Sven, I don't date clients," I said. I didn't want him to think I was the kind of person who got involved with every client she defended, even though it had happened ~~once a few times~~ routinely, but only because it was the only way I ever met anyone.

He said, "I know you've made exceptions in the past. Make an exception for me."

"Personal complications can impede the case." For some reason I thought of Ellis accusing me of being bought.

"If you prefer that I withhold my feelings for you until the conclusion of the trial, I'll endeavor to do so. I make no promises, because I find your beauty and brilliance intoxicating."

I am not making this up. He actually said that. I had to dig my fingernails into my palms to stop my crazy urge to giggle. "I'm really very flattered, Sven."

"I only speak the truth."

I thought, *Woohoo! I've got a serious PFLOML candidate, flowers and candles on the table, music, wine, romantic conversation — yep, I just completed my Valentine's Day date goal! I'm totally back on schedule.*

As we ate yummy food (rich beef soup, chicken paprika, duck with fruit sauce, potatoes and onion, strudel and plum dumplings), Sven told me about the dishes and translated the lyrics of the folk songs. He was elegant and so relaxed that I began to relax. He was telling me a funny story about the donkey and cart he'd had as a child when my aPhone buzzed.

"I'm so sorry, Sven, but I need to take this call. Please excuse me."

I went to the hallway near the restrooms, where I could talk privately. "Jen here. What's up?"

"Hi, Jen. Ruth said Shulky was available for anything in the area," said the night dispatcher at the Mansion. "We've got a situation, and I know you don't want to bothered, but the scanner says that you're the closest to it."

He told me that an armed gunman had taken hostages on a tour bus and was demanding that his wife be moved up on an organ transplant list. The SWAT team didn't want to risk charging in because of casualties.

My first date datish thing in eons, I'm wearing sleek boots, and She-Hulk has an emergency! I asked, "How long do you think it will take?"

"The bus is over by Sullivan and Prince."

Shulky could take care of it, and I could still be back in time for dessert. I returned to the table, apologized for the interruption, and said, "Sven, I need to dash out for a brief but urgent errand. If you don't mind, I could be back soon."

"Not at all. It will give me the opportunity to have a glass of wine with Domokos. Would you like to take the car?"

"No, it's close by and I enjoy the night air. Back in a jiffy!"

As soon as I was away from the watchful eyes of Sven's guard on the street, I checked my aPhone for the closest passageway to the tunnel system. I hurried to the location and pressed my hand against a flat metal panel set into a brick wall. A hidden door slid open, and I ducked inside before it slid shut again.

I stepped into a changing cubby, stripped off my clothes, and hung them on hooks beside the sign that said, YOUR MOTHER DOESN'T LIVE HERE. CLEAN UP AFTER YOURSELF.

I sat on the bench and tugged off my boots, which took valuable extra seconds.

I preferred to shift slowly and enjoy the transition, but now I was in a rush. I felt the disconcerting jolt as my body stretched and grew dense.

Shulky didn't bother with shoes, but raced down a flight of steps to the tunnel system. Her bare feet pounded toward her destination. She used another hidden door to exit onto the street and then picked up speed.

Drivers on the street jammed on their brakes so they could stare. An

SUV crashed into a cab, and Shulky used the damaged vehicles as stepping stones to cross the street.

Ahead at an intersection, cops were pushing back a crowd of onlookers. A dozen cherry tops strobed in the night, and ambulances and fire engines idled nearby.

"Coming through," Shulky shouted, and she noticed that a big shiny tour bus had been parked at a crazy angle and was up on the curb with its front door open.

Everyone turned toward her. "She-Hulk! Shulky's here!"

She couldn't bask in their attention, because she was concerned by the police officers' tense body language. The cops pointed her to Sergeant Denny Tavert.

"She-Hulk! Thanks for coming."

"Denny, honey, we got to stop meeting like this. Where are the hostages?"

"Hey, I'll use any excuse to see you, sexy green mama. He's got them in there." Denny pointed across the street to a Joocey Jooce shop. The shop had its metal security gratings rolled down and blinds closed.

"Joocey Jooce again," She-Hulk said, and asked the sergeant for the details.

Denny said, "He's got about fifty hostages, plus the driver and a tour guide. His name is Burton Symonds, and he says he's keeping them until his wife Bonnie is taken into surgery and given a new kidney. He left her at Bellevue ER before coming here."

"What about a back door or basement entrance?"

Denny said, "It's locked down. There's a steel security door at the back, and the only entrance to the basement is through the shop. We're scouting out the roof, but we don't want to make Symonds panic and turn the place into a shooting gallery. It's got the standard Joocey Jooce layout."

"With so many hostages, he must be keeping them at the front of the shop. What's next door?"

"It's a jewelry store, and the owner unlocked the door for us, but it's got reinforced walls. Symonds would have lots of warning in the time it would take us to cut through them. He gave us an hour to give him an answer, and we've only got ten minutes left."

"That's enough. Can you push this crowd farther back and provide a diversion so I can go in?"

"Sure thing, She-Hulk. Do you want backup?"

"Thanks, I can handle this, but keep the ambulances running."

Shulky edged into the shadow between two fire trucks and waited out of view. In seconds, a line of cops herded the crowd away, and the pump truck let loose with a blast of water in the other direction. While the onlookers watched the action, Shulky raced into the jewelry store, shutting the door behind her.

She couldn't hear anything through the reinforced walls, so she gave up on her brief flirtation with subtlety and delivered a powerful kick to the wall.

The drywall shattered, beams splintered, and the steel caved. She swiftly punched out room for her head, and then barreled into the Joocey Jooce store so suddenly that the hostages gasped in unison.

The young man with the AK-47 didn't have time to aim before she'd plucked it up, momentarily suspending him from the weapon.

Then he dropped and rolled on the floor. He swiftly pulled a Glock from his jacket. He jumped up and waved the gun wildly.

She-Hulk leapt between the gunman and the terrified hostages, saying to them, "Everyone get out of here!"

"I'll shoot!" He pointed the gun at her, his arm shaking.

"You can, Burt, but you'll only piss me off. You *really* don't want to piss me off." She twisted her head and told the hostages, "I said, out!"

Someone said nervously, "Uh, the door's locked."

"Geez, just use the giant hole in the wall. Don't pinch any of the jewelry. Tell Sergeant Talbert to give me five minutes."

The hostages scrambled out through the broken wall, some of them sobbing with relief.

When they were gone, a look of hopelessness came over the gunman's face. She was just fast enough to flick the gun out of his hand as he lifted it to his mouth.

It skittered across the tile floor. He covered his face with his hands, and his knees buckled.

Shulky caught him as he fell.

She set him on one of the tangerine-colored benches and then sat beside him, stretching her shapely legs out front. "You can't do that, Burt, because Bonnie needs you."

"Why? What can I do for her?" he said. "She was on the ReplaceMax list, next in line, and they took her off."

"They had to shut down the list because the organs were defective. People were dying."

Burt looked up and said sorrowfully, "She's dying *now*. We had nothing to lose. I could have shot everyone in here, and then there would have been lots of available organs! An organ for everyone who needs one. That's what I should have done."

"So you kill lives to save lives? Would Bonnie want that?"

"What do you care, She-Hulk? Don't you have somewhere better to be, some party with billionaires and superheroes?"

"Billionaires are overrated, but superheroes always rock," she said, and was happy to see a flicker of a smile. "We better go out now. You'll be arrested and put under suicide watch. Do you have a lawyer?"

He gave a bitter laugh.

"It's okay," Shulky said. "I'll call one of my pals to meet you at the police station. We'll also get a social worker to make sure that Bonnie is getting good care."

Burt squeezed his eyes shut. "If only she'd stayed on the regular kidney list, she'd be at the top of it by now. But her doctor thought she was a great candidate for a ReplaceMax organ. He promised she'd be better than ever because the new organ was supposed to make all of her organs healthier."

"Project Mimic," Shulky said. "I'll ask that she be placed back on the regular list, prorated for the time she's already waited."

"I already asked and they said no," Burt said.

"I think planet Earth owes me a favor or two," Shulky said. "One last thing. Why did you bring the tour group in here? Was that always your plan?"

"I was going to make the driver take us to the hospital." Burt gazed around at the shop. "Then I saw the Joocey Jooce. Whenever I get a smoothie, people are always so nice, and I feel better for a few minutes. I thought that everything would be okay if I came here."

"Next time, play nice, Burt, and don't take hostages."

She led him to the front door and said, "Get behind me," and then shouted, "Sergeant Talvert, have your team stand down. We're coming out."

She nodded back at Burt, and then kicked, sending both the entrance door and the safety gate slamming down to the pavement. The crowd beyond the barricade was silent as she escorted Burt to the sergeant.

As Burt was cuffed and put in a police car, Shulky leaned in to gently squeeze his shoulder. "We'll look out for Bonnie for you." She shut the car door, and the crowd began cheering and chanting, "Shulky! Shulky! Shulky!"

She waved to them and took Denny aside. In two more minutes, she'd made arrangements for Burt and Bonnie. She would have liked to sign autographs and pose for pictures, but I was saying, "Come oooonnn already!" so she waved good-bye then raced away into the night, too swift for anyone to follow her.

As soon as she was back in the secret changing cubby, she shifted back into me. I rushed to put on my silk top, suit, wiggle into new panty hose, and yank my boots back on, before quickly sneaking back outside. I patted my hair and it seemed fine. I reached into my bag for my lip gloss and touched it up while I speed-walked back to Sven's restaurant.

The security guard opened the door for me, and as I walked in, I saw Sven coming through the kitchen door.

I smiled and took off my coat to hang it on the rack — and noticed that my ruffled shell was on inside out and backward, showing the HAND WASH COOL WATER label. I was already in forward momentum going to Sven.

I placed my hand flat over my chest and faked a cough. Then I pivoted my torso and grabbed a napkin from another table, shoving it into the collar of my top.

Sven looked puzzled, and I said, "I hope I'm not getting a cold."

He said he'd turn up the heat, and I claimed that only my chest was cold, which sounded ridiculous even to me, and he offered to send someone for a shawl, which made me feel very old ma'amish. I insisted that I was fine and said I hoped he hadn't had to wait long.

"No, and I've taken the liberty of ordering dessert for us." He signaled, and the waiter brought over an assortment of tiny pastries, each scrumptious.

Why didn't I eat scrumptious food all the time? Next year, when I make my resolutions, one of them will be to enjoy gracious dining, instead of eating whatever has the shortest prep time, like peanut butter on crackers and Count Chocula from the box. I will make a practice of having linen, candles, flowers, wine, as I banter cleverly with the impossibly handsome and attentive love of my life! And then we will tumble together, smooching madly, and make love on the hand-knotted silk rug in front of the fireplace of our deluxe loft/apartment/brownstone/etc.

I wanted to know more about Sven and all things Svenish, so I asked him about his interests. He described himself as a tinkerer and said, "I tinker with mechanics, and I suppose my organ cloning is also a form of tinkership. I'm driven to create and innovate."

"I wish I could do something creative. I'm more of a puzzler, at least in my profession."

He laid his fingertips on my wrist, sending off a shiver, and said, "Perhaps you have not explored your creative potential, Jennifer. Perhaps I can help unleash that force within you."

Was he talking about kinky sex? It's hard to tell with Europeans, but he may have been talking about taking a photography class, which is why I hate ambiguity. "Right now, my priority is winning this case. Thank you for this wonderful meal, Sven. I enjoyed myself."

"Can't I tempt you with a glass of Tokay and an espresso?"

When I declined, he offered his car and said he'd stay a little longer.

When he took my hand and lifted it to his lips, it brushed against the napkin still tucked in my top.

"May I return this to you later?" I asked Sven and coughed.

"Please keep it. Good night."

As his driver/guard took me home, I sunk back into the seat and thought that this Valentine's Day was definitely worth the wait even without passionate smooching, a detail I'd include in next year's resolutions.

I got home and arranged the napkin in the neck of an empty vase. If things worked out with Sven and I eventually revealed my secret, the napkin would be the hilarious story we'd tell our children. I can't wait to get over my nervousness around him! I know I'll feel all the exciting sparks once I get over being stunned by his looks.

· 17 ·

DIMINISHED CAPACITY

MARCH 20

RESOLUTION REVIEW

1. Get new job at top firm — COMPLETE! Buy business wardrobe that allows easy changing — COMPLETE!

2. Meet an actual human man who is considerate and romantic and establish an actual relationship — ALMOST COMPLETE!

3. Have a *real* date on [postponed] Valentine's Day — COMPLETE!

4. Seek balance in work environment and social life — EXCELLENT PROGRESS!

5. Stretch outside my comfort zone — EXCELLENT PROGRESS!

6. Find a new apartment— ~~IN PROGRESS~~ NEED TO DO ASAP!

If I had known how successful I would be completing resolutions set at a reasonable time, i.e., not January 1, I would have done this long ago. I could even write a how-to self-improvement book: *The Valentine's Day Total Life Makeover* by Dr. Jennifer S. Walters.

D always said, "People shouldn't call themselves doctors unless they're capable of performing an emergency appendectomy or giving me a pap smear that doesn't pinch." But readers might be reassured to know that I had professional credentials.

Writing a self-help book would be both creative and an outside-my-comfort-zone activity. It's possible that my book would be so incredibly popular that I would be invited as a guest on talk shows, or even asked to host my own talk show! *Dr. Jennifer's Lifestyle Makeover.* Or *Dr. Walters's Resolutions Done Right Show.* I should find an apartment that could do dual duty as a writer's haven.

As if he could read my mind, my former boss and current landlord called me. "Hi, Jen."

"Hi, Holden! So nice to hear your voice."

"The new associates don't think so, but I'm very stern with them and always comparing their work to yours," Holden said. "I'd like to take you up on that offer for a drink. How's tonight?"

Getting together with Holden is both work and fun, so more of those life-balance points!

7:30 P.M.

Holden wanted to meet at another dive bar, Juliet & Snickers, over on Second. Like the last time, he was there before me. The crowd was around my age, but casual in a way that made me feel ma'amish in my business suit. Holden, easily the oldest person in the bar, seemed perfectly comfortable in a booth with a glass of beer. As I came over, he signaled to the waitress for a round for both of us.

We greeted each other and I looked around. "Holden, why here? I'm sure everyone thinks I'm a narc trying to convince a prosperous crime lord to sell out one of his enemies."

"I certainly hope so! It's one-dollar beer night. Since you're treating, I thought I'd be a cheap drunk for you."

"That's very considerate," I said. "You like these sort of places."

"I like places where I can talk without any colleagues overhearing," he said slyly. "Also, there's always the chance of a brawl. You're a thing of beauty when you fight, Jen." He placed his hand on his heart and gave a sigh.

I said, "My Krav Maga coach says I'm getting sloppy because I spend too much time at the office and not enough training."

"How is the new job?"

"Exciting, but not *crazy* exciting. My associate is Genoa Lewes."

"The General? Lucky you. I'd hire her in a second," he said.

The cute waitress brought our drinks and I took a sip of beer. It tasted deliciously refreshing after my day. "I really like working with the General. She has a calm competence and never gets flustered."

"What about Amber Tumbridge? Isn't she second on the Replace-Max case?"

"That case isn't even filed yet, Holden," I said. "You know too much."

"I keep spies in all the popular legal watering holes." His blue eyes twinkled and he told me, "Amber's an iron maiden. Scares the living daylights out of most men. She's engaged to Quinty's son and probably put more strategic planning into that marital campaign than most nations put into a war, so QUIRC will soon be all in the family."

I tried to sound casual and said, "I think any man would be impressed with a woman like Amber."

"Impressed, yes, just like any man is impressed when my granddaughter lands a left hook on his jaw. God only knows what Amber will do with the firm when she gets control."

"Holden, you're trying to scare me back to you, aren't you?"

"Always, and bring the General with you, because I know you're not going to stay at QUIRC and watch Amber rise to senior partner," he said. "I give you two years tops before you need more thrills."

"I don't need more thrills. That's Shulky."

"You had enough trouble adjusting to life as a human practicing superhuman law with us. How are you going to manage as a human practicing normal human law?"

I mentioned the luxury of having a private meditation room. "Besides, the Avengers have defeated all the recent alien attacks just fine without Shulky. It seems that they prefer the Black Widow's detached efficiency to Shulky's more emotional and impetuous personality."

"Do I detect a little jealousy, Jen?" he said. "Black Widow is a wonderful asset, but she's not superhuman, and she could never replace Shulky's role in protecting the world. I can't speak for others, but I prefer Shulky's passion. She fights — and she lives — with heart and soul. When Victor von Doom returns, we'll need Shulky's help to defeat him."

"Have you heard anything about VvD?"

"No, but he never seems to stay away from you or her for very long. He's especially enraged every time she defeats him."

"Beaten by a girl," I said. "Men have issues with that."

"And what a girl!" Holden said. "Intelligence, beauty, strength. I'm talking about the both of you."

I blushed and said, "I know von Doom's evil, but I comprehend how he came to be that way — with his home, family, and people being vilified and destroyed. His genius rose out of nowhere, inspired to rescue his mother from Mephisto's grip. I wonder what he would have been like if his experiment hadn't gone wrong and he was never scarred hideously, making people fear him."

"Jen, you always want to see the good in others, but I assure you that von Doom would be the same evil bastard no matter what he looked like," he said. "I'd like to change my prediction for your stay at QUIRC to one year *max*, and we can discuss your napping — I mean, meditation — room. I need you on my team to fight the good fight."

"Which good fight in particular?"

"Totally confidential: my new branch will be dedicated to alternative human life form law."

"Wow!"

"Exactly. The other partners and I are setting the groundwork, and everything should be in place by the time you quit QUIRC or are asked to quietly get the hell out. The backlash against alternative life forms is coming. The fear and hatred always resurges one way or another."

"Like the laws to enforce a Superhuman Registry," I said. "Incite paranoia in the population and confuse the issues so that no one questions the real motivation: unnamed powers who want to identify every superhuman for eventual exploitation or extermination."

"This time we're going to be ready," he said. "How's the apartment hunt going?"

I told him that I'd been busy, and he mentioned that he'd heard about the recent superhuman incidents, but he didn't know who the two new superhumans could be.

"At least one of them was nice," I said. "*Nice*. It's coming up everywhere, just like Joocey Jooce is everywhere. Do you know anything about the owners?"

Holden looked at me like I'd lost my marbles. "Of a juice company? All I know is that their mango-apricot smoothie is my favorite. Now, about the loft . . ." He basically said that there was no hurry, but would I please leave soon.

We gossiped about the latest goings-on in superhuman law, and I told him a little about Sven Morigi. "I think he's spent all his life hiding in laboratories, because there's not much information about him otherwise. Well, that's how scientists are; they'd rather be looking through a microscope than be under one. I know Bruce hates being in the public eye."

"Morigi must be an extraordinary genius."

"Why do you say that?"

"If he was only an ordinary genius, he'd have Amber on first chair, because she's the obvious upper tier, golden girl choice. The fact that he appreciates your greater talent proves that he must be extraordinary."

"Holden, *you* appreciated my talent."

"Exactly. Point proven." Holden lifted an eyebrow and said, "Everyone talks about how good-looking he is. He's single, too."

"It's my policy never to date clients. Rarely to date them. I really try not to date them. Well, at least during a case. That's my intention, at least."

He was chuckling as I excused myself to go to the ladies' and crossed paths with the waitress.

"Are you and the silver fox staying for the show?" she asked.

"Only for drinks," I said, and then I noticed the small stage at the back.

"Too bad," she said. "Fractious Faraday is our new house band. They're killer. You should come back to see them. The lead singer — utterly panty-melting hot."

"I'll check them out," I said, just to be polite.

When I returned to the booth, Holden looked a little more serious and said, "Jen, I understand that you've stopped going to your therapy sessions. The Avengers have asked me to act as their representative in this matter."

"It's nice that they're suddenly interested in me, since they were fine with ditching me along with She-Hulk. The agreement allows me to suspend sessions if lives are at stake, and my ReplaceMax witnesses are terminally ill."

"Perhaps you need to review it again, particularly the condition that negates any loopholes you wrote for yourself."

"That condition isn't in the agreement," I said confidently.

Holden smirked. "You might not have noticed it because I had one of the time-manipulators set a delay function on it."

I drank the rest of my beer and said, "Holden, you're not only a silver fox, but a sly one. Okay, I'll make an appointment with Dr. Alvarado, not that anything is wrong with me."

MARCH 21

I started my morning with easy attack drills with one of Azzan's students, and when I got pinned to the mat for the second time, Azzan said,

"Jennifer, where is your eagle-sharp focus? Bang, bang, you are dead and your pretty neck is broken already."

"Sorry, I was thinking about work."

He flipped his hand and said, "Then go to work and do not come back until you are two hundred percent a sexy killing machine."

"Yes, sir." I felt bad that I hadn't even been 100 percent, but I couldn't stop angsting about the little girl I'd be meeting for my case. Sick kids have that effect on me, making me feel powerless.

When I arrived in the children's ward of the hospice, a nurse pointed me toward Mavis Bertoli's room. I walked into the cheery yellow room and saw a haggard woman dozing in a visitor's chair. Stuffed animals, picture books, and toys filled the counter below the window. Crayon drawings covered a bulletin board.

In the high bed, nestled among the white linens, was the tiny body of a girl. She was so shrunken, she looked much younger, and blue-veined eyelids were closed in her thin, pale face. Her brown hair had the dullness of illness. She was hooked to monitors that made a steady *beep-beep-beep*.

I cleared my throat and the woman's eyes opened. "Hello, Mrs. Bertoli. I'm Jennifer Walters from Quintal, Ulrich, Iverson, Ride, and Cooper. We spoke this week."

"Ms. Walters," she said. "Nice of you to come. Mavy, wake up."

The little girl's eyelids fluttered open. Her dark brown eyes looked too big in the tiny face, but I saw a spark of interest when she noticed me.

"Hello, Mavis, I'm Jenny," I said, using my childhood nickname.

"You're so tall, like a giant!" she said, and her mother said, "Mavy!"

"That's all right," I said. "Mavis, you're right. I'm very tall. If you need something off a top shelf, just say so. I can't climb a beanpole, though, because I'm afraid of heights. Don't tell anyone, because it's a secret."

When Mavis giggled, her narrow chest shuddered, and she coughed. I said, "How are you feeling?"

She looked at me hopefully and said, "I want to go outside and play."

I saw Mrs. Bertoli's panicked expression and said, "Mavis, it's sooo cold outside that my teeth chattered so hard I thought they would break into a million pieces." The girl laughed, and I added, "I'm a lawyer, Mavis. That means that I'm telling your story to a judge. I'm going to try to stop the people who gave you the bad heart, so they don't hurt any more children."

"Then can I play outside?"

I glanced at Mrs. Bertoli, who shook her head, and I said, "You'll have to ask your doctor. But I'll do whatever I can do to help you."

Mavis turned her head to the windows and looked out at the stormy day. She said, "That's what *everyone* says. All I want to do is go outside again."

"Mavis, I need to talk to your mom for a minute."

"Will you come back, Jenny?" she asked.

"Yes, sweetie, I'll come back and visit when I can. Is there anything you'd like?"

"I like story time. You can come and help read with Mr. Biggie. Then we play make-believe." Her eyes brightened for a moment, and she said, "I live in a castle. There's a magician and a big moat and a dragon that breathes fire! Mr. Biggie is a giant even bigger than you. He can be your giant husband!"

"How exciting! We can have giant babies and put them in giant cribs made from giant tree logs. I love stories with castles and dragons. You can tell me all about it at story time."

Mrs. Bertoli and I went into the hallway. She was probably close to my age, but her hair had gone gray and she had purple bags under her eyes.

"Mrs. Bertoli, I'd like to do a videotaped interview with Mavis for the trial. I'll keep it brief, because I don't want to wear her out."

"She'd like the company," Mrs. Bertoli said. "She gets bored staying in bed day after day."

"My paralegal, Donner Hightower, will schedule it. Can you tell me anything more about her situation?"

Mrs. Bertoli repeated the report: Mavis had had an operation to correct a minor congenital heart defect. In the hospital, she caught an infection that damaged her heart. ReplaceMax heard about her case and thought she'd be a perfect candidate for one of their cloned organs. They told the Bertoli family that Mavis would not have to endure any tissue rejection and promised her a happy childhood.

I asked if Mavis was eligible for another transplant, and Mrs. Bertoli told me that she wasn't strong enough to survive the operation.

Mrs. Bertoli said, "When she first got the ReplaceMax organ, it was like a miracle. She became healthy within a week, but it didn't last. It was a dirty trick giving us hope."

"Mrs. Bertoli, why haven't you retained a law firm to sue Replace-Max? I'm sure that QUIRC could take on your case."

She shook her head. "Ms. Walters, my husband had a breakdown and left us. My parents passed away. I've lost my job and can't pay my rent. Those things don't seem to matter because all I can think of is my baby. I get through each day for her, and when this is over, I'm going to leave the country, find somewhere warm where no one knows me, and try to go on. Fighting a court case, what good will it do me? Money won't save my Mavy."

My throat constricted and I nodded my head. "If you change your mind, please talk to me."

Mrs. Bertoli gripped my arm and looked me in the eye. "I don't want their money, but I want them to suffer, Ms. Walters. Make them suffer for what they've done to my baby. Make those bastards pay."

I asked if she'd considered applying for a suspended animation slot.

She gave me a look that could have fried bacon and said, "That's living death. Not for my child."

1:00 P.M.

Re: living death, I wished I could have been in suspended animation for the fifty minutes at lunchtime that I had to spend with Dr. Rene Alvarado.

He gave me a tofu-and-edamame-eating smile and said, "Jennifer, I'm glad you found the time to resume your mental health treatments."

"It's Ms. Walters, Rene."

"Dr. Alvarado," he said.

"You see how annoying it is when someone purposely uses a more casual address to diminish status in a relationship," I answered with a fake smile.

"It interests me that you consistently describe yourself as shy, yet you're always combative in our sessions."

"This is a meeting that serves no purpose," I said, and then he said blah blah blah, and I said "My life is excellent," and he said blah blah blah, and I looked at the time and said I had to attend to something important.

"Jennifer—*Ms.* Walters," he said, irked. "Your mental health is important, and you can't begin to resolve your rage issues and your bifurcated personality disorder until you first acknowledge that there is a problem."

"Rene—Dr. Alvarado, if I had half an hour to examine your life and your business, I would discover innumerable legal problems that I'd believe were urgent. If you met my salon-owning friend, she would tell you that you need critical hairstyle intervention, stat!" I was happy to see his hand go to his messy wavy mop. "The point is that everyone sees the need for his or her service. As I advise my clients, 'When you are offered an unsolicited service, ask yourself whether you would have ever sought the service on your own, and if it has any demonstrable positive outcomes.'"

I stood up. "There will be no charge for my legal advice, Dr. Alvarado."

"I didn't ask for your legal advice, Ms. Walters."

"Exactly. I'll call you to schedule an appointment when my calendar opens up."

As I was leaving, I heard him saying, "I'll have to report this to the Avengers Council!"

7:30 P.M.

Got home so late that I ate yogurt and filled the whirlpool bath. As I sunk into the hot water, I thought about Sven and how stunning and elegant he is. Dahlia called while I was pumicing my heels.

D: How are you? What are you doing tonight? Anything exciting?

ME: For me, yes. I'm soaking in the tub. I hardly ever get to do this, and I really need a mani/pedi.

D: Schedule an appointment, Sulky. Do She-Hulk's feet get hurt when she runs barefoot?

ME: Her skin is impervious to rough terrain and temperature extremes. I, on the other hand, wish I could wear boots in cold weather without worrying that she'll trash them in a transformation.

D: Although I find all of that strangely fascinating, it's Friday night again. You're not going to stay home by yourself, are you?

ME: I already went on a date this week, a major one. Not an official date, but a date-equivalent because Sven took me to his private restaurant and told me that he has feelings for me.

D: Feelings in his pants? Shut up!

ME: Gladly.

D: It's a sarcastic shut-up. Tell me everything in excruciating detail!

So I did, and afterward instead of screaming "OMG! amazing!" she said, "Hmmm."

ME: D, that sounded like a critical hmmm.

D: It's a curious hmmm, with several question marks at the end.

ME: So hmmm??? what?

D: Hmm, you talked about Sven's absurdly good looks, the pretty restaurant, the lovely music, the nummy food, your madcap mishap with your top, etc., and yet you did not mention any warm feelings in your pants for Sven, or urges to jump his bones, to ride that speeding locomotive, to make wild sweaty monkey love.

ME: D, in the immortal words of Jon Bon Jovi, you give love a bad name. Of course, I feel that way about him. I'm simply overwhelmed by his OMG! amazingness.

Dahlia hmmmed again.

ME: Could you please define the nature of that hmmm?

D: It was a skeptical hmmm, Sulky. I don't find your argument persuasive, Counselor. Can you offer any corroborating evidence, such as printouts of your sexting, cutesy photos together, or endearing nicknames such as Pink Bunnikins and Grizzly McSpanky?

ME: D, I wish you would stop smelling dye-stripper fumes, because those brain cells never grow back.

We bickered a little longer before she had to get ready for her date with someone she called a "musician slash performance artist slash pretentious pretty boy." I asked why she kept dating these guys, and she said, "He's very pretty *and* I plan to do a lot more than admire him with big moo cow eyes. Besides, you know I don't want a guy who interferes with my work, and these guys conveniently evaporate with the morning dew."

We said good-bye, and I was glad I could just baste in the water.

Dahlia is wrong. My feelings for Sven are developing at a mature Cary Grant/Kate Hepburn pace.

I slumped deeper into the tub, which was big enough for me to stretch my legs, and remembered Fringe Theory's "Love/EVOLution":

I'll crawl from the primordial sludge
For you.
I'll give up my gills and prehensile appendage
For you.
I'll invent the wheel, I'll discover fire,

Inspired by desire,
For you, for you.
I'll draw your pictograph on cave walls
I'll slay T. Rex with a sharp rock,
And all
To win your heart.

DISSENT TO DISAGREE

MARCH 26

Slept in until 7:30 and made it to my 8:00 a.m. class with Azzan. Afterward, I went to five different Joocey Jooces and gave each of the clerks a clean thermos.

They all said the same thing: "It costs more if you bring your own container."

I told them I was saving them money by providing my own container, and they said that they believed in spreading the PLAY NICE! logo.

Then all of the clerks offered — with a big smile — to pay the difference themselves. Which was too nice, so I paid the extra charge and left big tips.

I took the thermoses to the Mansion and was happy to discover that Ruth was there. "Ruth, what are you doing here on a Saturday?"

"Catching up on things, Jen. Don't worry, I'm taking Monday off. It's so great to see you! What do you have there?"

"They're fruit smoothies from Joocey Jooce, but something may be in them."

"Their smoothies are so terrific!" She opened one and smelled it. "Yum, raspberry. Sure, I'll have these checked by the lab. Any rush?"

"Within the week is fine. Thanks, Ruth."

"I'm glad that Shulky was able to handle the last situation," Ruth said. "We only got a few bills for the destruction of the front door and for the hole in the wall. She's becoming so OMG! diplomatic."

"She kind of is, isn't she?" I said. "You might want to mention that to Dr. Alvarado."

"Or you can, since you'll be seeing him soon," Ruth said. "I hope you don't mind, but he called yesterday and I scheduled an appointment. It's on your calendar for next Saturday morning right after Krav Maga."

"I'm very busy, Ruth . . ." I began, trying to think of a good excuse.

"Lots of doctors and psychiatrists have private entrances for confidentiality with patients. You can ask Dr. Alvarado if he knows of anyone giving up a place."

Instead of saying that I didn't want to live in a commune or an ashram, I thanked her. I'll cancel the session later.

MARCH 28

Drat. Ruth called and said that the Joocey Jooce samples don't show any traces of drugs or chemicals.

I advise my clients, "If it looks like a duck, walks like a duck, and quacks like a duck, you can make a preliminary determination that it may be a duck, but it's best to have an unbiased second opinion."

I called Amy Stewart-Lee. She only spent a few minutes catching me up on the latest cases at the DA's office before she told me that she was seeing Nelson again. She praised Nelson's kindness, his intelligence, and sweetness, and how he treated her like a lady. Then she asked me how I met him.

ME: Oh, we both went to watch *Game of Thrones* at a sports bar, but it was too loud and rowdy so we went somewhere quieter and talked and got to know each other.

ASL: I can't imagine him at a sports bar, because those guys always have such crude pickup lines. I'm glad you met him though!

ME: Me, too. Do you mind if I get your feedback on something?

ASL: At your service.

I described the ookiness I felt about Joocey Jooce and the many associations, including the recent hostage situation at a Joocey Jooce shop.

ME: Do you think I'm being too cynical?

ASL: Jennifer, if you were cynical, you wouldn't have dated men like Tony Stark.

ME: In my defense, Ironman is an interplanetary hero.

ASL: But Tony as a boyfriend? Not so heroic. Joocey Jooce is ubiquitous. It's inevitable that they'd show up in incidents in a way that appears disproportionate.

ME: One of my friends told me the same thing. So I'm overreacting?

ASL: I didn't say that, but your pals at the Mansion lab would have discovered any behavior-altering substances — not that I mind New Yorkers being more polite. In fact, if there *is* an altering agent, I'd like to dose my coworkers with it.

ME: Amy, I'm not an HR specialist, but I'm pretty sure there's a law against that.

ASL: There is, and now I deeply regret helping write it when I interned for the state legislature. I'll keep an ear out for anything about Joocey Jooce. Will you be at the next Forestiers workshop? We're making weapons.

My foam and PVC broadsword was falling apart and my shield was dinged up, so I told her I'd see her there.

MARCH 30

I blocked out two hours today to visit Mavis for story time. I'd dressed in jeans and flat shoes to be less giantish.

Mavis was sitting up, and her hair was neatly braided and tied with a red ribbon. "You came! You came!"

"I promised you I would, sweetie. How are you feeling today?" I snuck a look at Mrs. Bertoli, who smiled.

"Today she's good, and she really has fun at story time. You will, too."

"I like stories." I reached into my satchel and brought out a wrapped book. "This is for you, Mavis."

Mavis turned the gift until she found the tape. She carefully slid her finger beneath the ribbon and began wiggling it off. "The ribbon's pretty."

"We'll save that and the paper, too," her mother said.

When Mavis opened the book, she held it carefully.

"It's *The Island of the Blue Dolphins* and it was one of my favorite books when I was about your age. It's about a very brave girl who has to fight to survive. She's afraid and lonely, but she's a hero. It's all yours, Mavis, so if you spill something on it or bend a page, it's okay. It means the book has been read and loved."

She still didn't look very excited, so I rifled through my handbag and found a small spiral notepad that I'd planned to give to Ruth. "Here, this is for you, too. You can draw pictures in it."

She took the notepad and said, "It's got a kitten on it!"

"Kittens always make me happy. What about you?"

"I love kittens," she said with a big smile, and a volunteer came into the room and announced that story time was about to start.

Mrs. Bertoli seemed so tired that I offered to take Mavis. I also wanted to see the child away from her mom's anxiety and sorrow.

The volunteer showed me the proper way to lift Mavis into a wheelchair, and we went down the speckled blue linoleum hall, our shoes squeaking on the shiny surface. "Eek, eek, eek, I'm making mouse sounds," I said.

"You're a giant *and* a mouse," Mavis said.

"Maybe I'm a giant mouse."

A few other children were coming out of their rooms, and soon their high, clear voices filled the air.

I rolled Mavis's wheelchair into the community room, and she pointed me to a space at the front. "This is the best place," she said. "Here's Dr. Kate!"

A pretty pear-shaped young woman came into the room and sat on top of a table at the front. She was wearing a white lab coat with a huge DR. KATE name tag in the shape of a pinwheel lollipop. She had shining brown hair pulled back into a ponytail, rosy cheeks, and big hazel eyes. She seemed very familiar, and I wondered if I'd met her somewhere before.

She glanced at the clock and hopped off the table. Cupping her hands like a megaphone, she called, "Hellooo, children!"

The kids all called back, "Helloooo, Dr. Kate!"

"How many of you can read the clock?"

Several children raised their arms and said, "Me, me!"

"Ramon, what time is it?"

A boy said, "Five minutes after ten o'clock."

"That's right, so my brother, Mr. Biggie, is five whole minutes late. I see that Mavis has a guest today." Kate smiled toward me. "Would you like to help read our story?"

Mavis peered up at me. I didn't want to disappoint her, so I said, "Okay."

"And your name is?"

"I'm Jenny."

"Thanks for helping, Jenny. We're reading *The Once and Future King*, and we're on book one, *The Sword in the Stone*." Dr. Kate picked up a book from the desk, opened it at the bookmark, and handed it to me.

"I love this story!"

"So does my brother. Who is *supposed* to be here."

Mavis said to me, "He's the giant!"

"He probably had a giant emergency then. Maybe the shoelaces on his giant shoes broke and he needed to find a long rope to replace them," I said, and the kids laughed, which made me feel pretty swell. I've never thought of myself as funny, but maybe I've always had the wrong audience.

I opened the book, and the kids looked interested, except for a sullen older boy at the back, who was about thirteen. He had dull brown skin, no muscle tone, and no hair or eyebrows. I wondered how sick he was. I smiled when our eyes met, but he looked away.

I began reading, and the kids became so engrossed that I added a little more drama and gestures that I'd learned in my LARP class. I think I did an OMG! amazing Merlin, and my young Arthur was pretty good, too. Even the older boy started paying attention.

I got lost in the story and kept turning the pages. My throat became dry, and I reached for a bottle of water on the table and took a big swig. That's when I noticed that things had changed in the room. Big things, i.e., Ellis Tesla, who was standing at the back of the room beside Dr. Kate and watching me.

I spit out the water.

The kids burst into laughter and my face went hot. I swiped at the water dribbling down my shirt.

Kate came forward, saying, "Thank you so much, Jenny, for that wonderful reading! Kids, wasn't Jenny terrific?"

When the children clapped and cheered, I got that warm fuzzy feeling, which was muddled with my embarrassment. I realized that Mr. Biggie was Mr. Big E. Duh.

"Well, kids, that's our story time this week," Dr. Kate said. "Next week, I hope that Mr. Big E will be on time, because we're doing our art project." She shot a look at Ellis, and he smiled apologetically. He was wearing a navy-blue wool sweater under a brown corduroy jacket and jeans, which was totally sexy in a lumberjack professor way.

"We want Jenny, too!" a little girl chirped. "We like Jenny."

"Maybe Jenny can come back, and she and Mr. Big E can read together," Kate said.

Ellis's expression froze, and Kate grinned at him and said, "Yes, that would be best, for both of them to read and help us with our art project together. Right, kids?"

The children cheered again, and then the adults began taking them out of the community room. I went back to Mavis in her wheelchair.

She beamed at me. "You read real good, Jenny. Do you want to meet my friends?"

As Mavis introduced me to other children, I peeked and saw Ellis holding a toddler in his arms while talking to the older boy. Another child leaned happily against Ellis's legs.

Mavis sighed, and I saw her head drooping. "Time for you to get some rest, Mavis," I said.

Mrs. Bertoli came through the crowd and said, "I'll take her back, Ms. Walters. Thanks for spending so much time with her."

"Jenny, please. It was my pleasure."

"You promise to come to next story time, right, Jenny?" Mavis said.

"I'm absolutely positively going to try, but I have a lot of work to do."

"But it's our art project. We're making things from the story. Try, okay?"

I nodded and bent to kiss her cheek.

Before I could leave, Kate touched my arm. "You read wonderfully, Jenny, with so much excitement. You should meet my brother. Ellis! E, come here."

Ellis looked huge in the room with its child-size furniture, giving me some perspective on what She-Hulk would look like to these kids. He put his hand on the older boy's shoulder and said something to him — probably "Hide me!" — before coming forward and lifting his hand as a greeting.

I tried to smile, but my facial muscles seemed to spasm.

Kate said. "Ellis, this is Jenny. Thank her for saving your ass today with the kids."

"I had an emergency," he said.

"A flat tire is not an emergency," she said so sharply that he stood a little straighter. "Cardiac arrest is an emergency. Septic poisoning is an emergency. You haven't thanked Jenny or said hello."

"It's not necessary . . ." I began.

Ellis glanced at Kate and said, "We've met before. Jennifer is Dad's new hire at QUIRC. She's on the ReplaceMax suit."

"That's why I was here with Mavis," I told Kate. "I'm Jennifer Walters."

Ellis and I were quiet for only a second as his sister looked at us, and then an expression came on her face like that of someone figuring out a missing word in a crossword puzzle. "*You're* the new hire that Dad's been bragging about? The one who'll be working with Amber and . . . and you have *such amazing* green eyes."

Then she gave Ellis a satisfied look before saying to me, "How very very nice to meet you. Well, I've got rounds. Ellis, you still haven't thanked Jenny for *anything*. At least buy her a cup of coffee at the corner cafe, where it's better."

"Oh, I have to get back to the office," I said.

Kate glared at her brother. "See, you make terrible impressions on women. That's why they hate you."

"I don't hate him!" I said quickly.

"Kate is teasing, aren't you, sis?" Ellis said.

"Sure, why not? Little bro, I expect you to be on time next week. Jenny, the kids would love it if you came back." Kate's phone beeped, and she looked at it and said, "Really nice to meet you, Jenny!" and then she wove her way through the wheelchairs and out of the room.

I tried to leave, but there was a traffic jam at the doorway, and Ellis and I got stuck behind the kids and parents. Then we were alone in the room.

He glanced at me, and I tried not to stare at his face, his mouth, his wide shoulders, the line of his throat. He finally said, "You read the story very well."

"Do you mean, for a groupie who sells out for filthy lucre?" I snapped before I could stop myself. "Because your sister obviously knows who I am."

"I didn't tell her anything." He gave me a brief nod of the noggin and left the room.

I said, "Jackass," under my breath, and he paused, so I guess he heard me, and I was so turmoiled up that I didn't care, even though I never act that way.

I was fuming when I went to the elevator — where Ellis was standing. I tried to think of a reason for turning around and leaving, but the elevator *bing*ed and the doors slid open. A couple of staffers in scrubs got out, and Ellis stood aside to let me step in first. He got in and moved to the far side from me.

I always advise my clients, "If you're in a difficult dispute that has become personal, take a breath, regroup, and come back with a fresh attitude so that you can think clearly."

I said, "Ellis, pursuant to our discussion at the Valentine's Day party, I would like to propose that we dispense with the past and treat each other civilly."

He turned his dark eyes on me and asked, "That's what you want?"

"I think that would be best, unless you have any objections."

"We're not in court," he said. "Fine, if that's what *you* want."

"I didn't say it's what *I* wanted. Tell me what *you* want." This was the wrong move, because he got a strange look in his eye, opened his mouth . . . and then closed it again and nodded.

Another floor *ping*ed down and he stared ahead and said, "If you are going back to QUIRC, I can give you a lift."

"It isn't necessary."

"I'm going there to have lunch with my father."

I'd already lost too much time from work. "If you're going there anyway."

His car was parked in the basement garage. I sighed as I gazed at the Chevy Chevelle, painted in gleaming green with white racing stripes, and chrome so flawless that I could have used it as a mirror. "A sixty-six Super Sport?" I whispered.

"Yes, not only green on the outside, but I modified it so she runs clean and green, too. Hell, she practically flies. You know your rides."

"I like muscle cars." So did Shulky, and we always felt exhilarated getting behind the wheel of a Detroit beast and putting pedal to the metal. I walked around the car, opening and clenching my hands. The front fenders angled ahead as if the car was about to leap forward. "She's a beaut."

It was only when Ellis opened the passenger door for me that I realized I was standing expectantly on the driver's side. "You're shotgun," he said.

He got in and started the car, and the Clash blasted out of the sound system. I wondered if he was looking for trouble by offering the ride, or if I wanted it by accepting. Ellis switched off the music, and now I could hear the rumble of the engine.

I said, "I thought the car ran green."

"It does. I kept the rumble. I like a car that can roar," he said, with a glance at me.

I thought there might be subtext to his comments, but I couldn't figure out what it might be, so I just said, "Me, too" as he drove out onto the street.

"Um, who was that boy you were talking to?" I asked, sliding my hand along the side of the black bucket seat and wishing I was at the wheel. "The big kid."

"Jordy," Ellis said. "He hates being in the children's ward, but he's only fifteen, so pediatric medicine is the best place for him. Children's bodies are different than adult bodies and need specialty care."

"He seemed angry."

"He *is* angry." Ellis glanced me. "He's spent the last six years in and out of hospitals. He hasn't had a childhood and he's afraid he's not going to have an adulthood."

"What's wrong with him? . . . If it's not confidential."

"It's not. He has invasive cancer. His entire body is compromised, and his organs are on the verge of shutting down. Kate tells me that hope helps." Ellis negotiated a chaotic intersection. "Hope will keep him going while medicine looks for answers."

"He seemed to like the story. What else can be done to raise his mood?"

"I know one thing." Ellis didn't speak until we were stopped at a light. "He really wants to meet She-Hulk."

I kept my eyes straight ahead. "He told you that?"

"He saw a video of me with Shulky at Club Nice, and now he thinks I'm tight with her. I keep telling him that I don't even know how to contact her," he said. "She's a friend of yours, isn't she?"

Was he just using Jordy as an excuse to get to Shulky? "We're colleagues. You can leave a message at the Avengers Mansion."

"I suppose I can try. She probably gets thousands of messages a week."

"She does, but she has staff to sort through them, and you can mention that I referred you," I said. "Do you like her, She-Hulk?"

Ellis turned into the entrance of the office garage. "Jenny or Jennifer, what do you want me to call you? Inside every man is a teenage boy, and we're *all* crazy in love with Shulky."

This close, I could smell his aftershave again, or maybe it was his piney woods-scented sweat. Whatever it was smelled delicious, and I remembered it from long ago. I could see his strong wrists and large hands. I could make out the spot on his jaw that he'd missed shaving, which made me feel unexpectedly tender toward him, and see the variations of color in his thick hair.

I reminded myself that he'd never called me, but I couldn't help saying, "Ellis, I can understand your loyalty to Max Kirsch, but why are you singling me out as the villain in the scenario, when your father and Amber also support the case against ReplaceMax?"

He parked, shut off the powerful engine, and turned to me. "Amber brought Sven Morigi to QUIRC, and my father trusts her business acumen. She is a consummate pro and I admire that about her." His rough voice dropped, and he looked into my eyes and said, "But I thought you'd understand that sometimes you have to follow your instincts and swing from the rafters."

I had an intense desire for him to lurch over, mash me to the seat, and kiss me so hard that he bruised my lips. I wanted us to bang our elbows and our knees as we tried to maneuver to the backseat of a car that was a much bigger turn-on than a candlelit table at an elegant restaurant.

Could men tell when women were thinking the smexy thoughts about them? I didn't want to take a chance, so I opened the door, practically jumped out, and hurried to the elevator.

As we were riding up to QUIRC, I said, "You can call me Jen. Most people do."

"Jen, that's better than Jennifer. Jennifer seems like another person," Ellis said. "I'm sorry I got your name wrong . . . before. I feel pretty stupid. I called you Gin all weekend, didn't I?"

Then I met his eyes, and he sure didn't look sorry, but I said, "I thought that was just your way of pronouncing Jen. It was noisy when I told you."

The corner of his mouth rose, and he said, "I like noise. All kinds of noise."

If I'd had a court reporter with me, I could have asked that his last statement be read back to me and then asked for clarification. The words and implications jumbled in my brain, and I could feel my temperature rise.

We arrived at our floor and got out. "Thank you for the lift, Ellis."

"Next week at reading time we're making wizard hats and magic wands." He put his hand out as if he was going to touch me, drew it back, and said, "Kate's warned me that there may be glitter."

I nodded, and we both said, "Bye," at the same time, just as Amber, impeccable in a midnight-blue suit, came down the hall.

"Ellis, what are you doing here?"

"Hey, babe. I'm having lunch with my father."

"Please no endearments at the office. I heard he was out all day. Was he expecting you?" she said.

"I was nearby," he said.

"Doing what?" Amber didn't wait for his answer before giving me an up-and-down look. "It's not Casual Friday, Jennifer, and our Casual

Fridays are restricted to administrative and support staff. It's in the HR manual."

"I was visiting a client," I said.

Her Botox was good enough to allow her to lift her eyebrows just enough to show contempt. I glanced at Ellis, who'd shoved his hands in his pockets and was looking somewhere over Amber's head.

"Excuse me," I said, and as I was leaving, I heard Ellis say to Amber, "Who made you hallway monitor, pumkin?" It was enough to make me grin.

3:50 P.M.

Am trying to focus on cloning factoids, but I keep replaying everything Ellis said and did. Called D and told her about my Close Encounter of the Ellis Kind.

ME: So what do you think?

D: I think you should ask if those songs are about you. Of course, they are.

ME: If you're so sure, why do I have to ask?

D: Because you won't believe it until he tells you.

ME: What do you think he meant about swinging from the rafters? I think he meant that he wanted me to ignore evidence against Re-placeMax.

D: Probably, but I think he also meant that he wants to see you upside-down and naked on a trapeze.

ME: Right. I think he's just messing with my mind, because he knows that I was waiting desperately for his call for days and weeks and months.

D: You were a beautiful disaster then. You had a sort of Eastern European look, all luminous eyes and existential grief.

ME: That's nice, but you're not helping me suss out the E-situation. He's engaged, and even if he wasn't, I wouldn't be interested.

D: You've only told me about a kazillion times. You have insufficient data on the E-sit. You need to establish his statements and behavior in a wider range of situations. Go to the wand-making thingamajig.

ME: Maybe. After all, there could be glitter. I like glitter.

· *19* ·

COURT OF ORIGINAL
JURISDICTION

APRIL 2

My docs for the ReplaceMax suit were ready yesterday, but I didn't want anyone to think that the case was an April Fool's prank, so I held off the announcement. As I always tell my clients, "Be sure to check the calendar for national holidays and festivities that may conflict with scheduled events." I should have added, "And be sure not to schedule any kind of meeting with a party girl the day after her birthday because of the likelihood that she'll hurl on your beautiful new shoes."

Text to Holden:	Dear Holden, I just remembered that I was never reimbursed for the shoes your granddaughter ruined. Please remind accounts payable. Thank you.
Text from Holden:	Will request payment as soon as Im in receipt of payment for She-Hulk stomping on my prize double tulips prior to annual brunch.
Text to Holden:	She did save the world a lot the value of which is priceless.

Text from Holden:	Not priceless. My accounting staff can precisely calculate value of world.
Text to Holden:	You win.
Text from Holden:	Always do. Beer on me next time! Don't you have to go to court?
Text to Holden:	Yes! Beer will be my treat on $1/night.

Amber Hammerhead and I went to court to file *Sven Morigi, PhD, plaintiff v. Maxwell L. Kirsch, ReplaceMax Corp. et al.* with the court clerk. Quinty accompanied us, wearing that damn monocle. I keep expecting him to wear a top hat and spats, too, like Mr. Peanut. Then I made my plea for an expedited court date.

Even though the day was drizzling, several reporters and camera crews showed up, alerted by QUIRC's PR rep. I'd rehearsed my talking points until I could say them smoothly and confidently. Sven joined us so that people could see that the case was about people, not money. He wore a camel-hair coat over a navy suit. His black hair gleamed in the crystalline morning light, and he looked somber, yet seemed intelligent and compassionate.

The reporters practically swooned as he stood on the courthouse steps and talked about the importance of the legal system vis-à-vis medical advances.

I can't wait for the case to be over, so he can be my official PFLOML! I wonder if he has a smoking jacket with velvet lapels that he wears in the evenings. Does he ever dress casually? Would it be weird of me to ask him? I was thinking about this while Sven answered reporters' questions, and Amber stepped in to speak on behalf of QUIRC.

As the hammerhead was being interviewed, Sven came to me and said, "You're doing a marvelous job, Jennifer. Is it unreasonable for me to be jealous because my case takes up all your time?"

I repressed the urge to giggle because he gave me the jim-jams. "Amber's got everything under control. I've got to get back to the office. I'll call this week to update you."

"Till then. Adieu."

No shit, he actually said that, and I realized that an elegant accomplished man who said "adieu" was much more romantic than a confusing lumberjerk.

I returned to the office in Quinty's Town Car. My boss removed his monocle and said, "You did an excellent job framing the case. Replace-Max will immediately feel the pressure of public opinion, especially when Dr. Morigi's cause is so sympathetic."

"It's going to be a challenge, sir, letting them squirm before settling, because the victims are suffering and we don't need to add more stress to those on our witness list."

Quinty gave me a somber look. "I made a decision last night, Jennifer. We're not settling. I want to see ReplaceMax demolished in court."

My mouth dropped open in preparation to saying "Whoa!" but Quinty had anticipated my reaction, because he added, "I believe you've met my daughter Kate. She has a degree of fortitude that astonishes me. She bears her grueling days with a smile, but when she talks about the ReplaceMax victims, I can see her anguish. We need to demolish ReplaceMax in court to tell the world that there is no tolerance when the lives of children are at stake. Can I count on you, Jennifer?"

I always tell my clients, "Never automatically reject advice from someone who has far more experience, even when the advice runs counter to your initial reaction," so I said, "Yes, sir. I shall proceed with a jury trial as my desired outcome. However, I reserve the right to reassess my strategy if I feel that the health of the victims is being compromised by delaying a resolution."

Quinty said, "The ReplaceMax victims are already doomed, and our priority is to see that others don't suffer their fate."

"Sir, I am not willing to abandon hope for the current ReplaceMax victims in order to protect theoretical victims."

Quinty drew down his eyebrows and then said, "You can take the girl out of the public sector, but you can't take the pro bono spirit out of the girl."

"No, sir. Will that be a problem?" I asked as I felt my heart speed up. I was trying to decide whether it would still count as meeting my goal if I lost this job, but Quinty said, "No, it's not a problem."

The driver stopped the car and opened the doors for us.

I wanted to jump out and shout *"Kapow!"* It's really amazing when I can do the right thing *and* meet my goals.

My elation wore off by the time I returned to my office. I asked Donner to hold my calls, and then I went to my meditation room, locked the door, kicked off my shoes, took off my skirt, and sat cross-legged on the floor. I thought and thought, and this is all I came up with to help Mavis:

INFECT HER WITH GAMMA RADIATION

PROS: GR infection will cause her to be superstrong and will heal her damaged heart. She will also have great hair and an interesting fashion sense.

CONS: No child has ever been infected, and it's unknown whether she would survive. If survives, she may not ever grow up at normal human rate. Puberty as a hulk may endanger the planet.

PLACE HER IN SUSPENDED ANIMATION TO AWAIT MEDICAL BREAKTHROUGH

PROS: Painless way to pass time.

CONS: Must overcome mother's objections, religious or otherwise, and mother will age even as Mavis does not. Initial suspension process feels like a million ants are eating your body. No guarantee on when medical breakthrough will occur.

TRANSPORT HER TO PLANET WITH ATMOSPHERE THAT WON'T TAX BODY

PROS: Most kids dream about interplanetary travel. She'll be able to add cultural experience to her college applications. She may learn another language.

CONS: Mother may want to keep her on Earth and/or won't be willing to accompany her. Unless she's sent via a time/space fold, her body won't survive the travel.

TRANSFER HER CONSCIOUSNESS TO ANDROID BODY

PROS: Android body will be very low-maintenance and can come in terrific models.

CONS: She will have to undergo routine transfers to age-appropriate bodies. Mother may object to android body.

MAGIC HER TO GOOD HEALTH

PROS: Instant results, and she will be the same human girl but healthy.

CONS: Magic always has unintended consequences, usually deleterious. Mother may object due to religious and/or philosophical reasons.

All in all, magic seems like the best remedy despite the possible side effects. Sometimes I wish we had a truce with Dr. Doom, because he's skilled at magic, although he prefers scientific solutions, which have more predictable outcomes. He's also brilliant at creating androids, and they're phenomenal until they mutiny against him. Well, I can't say that I blame them.

As determined as I am to help Mavis, I'm not going to contemplate any deal with VvDoom, even if I knew how to find him. Really. There must be alternatives that don't involve bargaining with a verbose, paranoid, everyone-hates-me-guess-I'll-just-eat-worms-and-blow-up-a-planet villainous genius. I don't need to rush to a solution, since Mavis's condition seems stable.

APRIL 5

COLLEAGUES-WITH-BENEFITS COUNTDOWN: 50 of the 60 days have passed already. How am I going to have an answer for Fritz when I'm in the whirlwind of the work, etc.?

The ReplaceMax lawsuit had all the things the media liked: cute sick kids, heartbreaking stories, corruption, a stunning plaintiff for the prosecution, and a powerful and gorgeous team seeking a legal remedy. Okay, so maybe Amber Hammerhead is more gorgeous than I am. Gorgeouser. Whatever. Regardless, I looked very sharp in news footage with my stylish suits.

Our story got knocked out of the headlines by the infestation of weirdly fluffy frolicsome daytime rats that appeared near the Chrysler Building and were immediately exterminated. I found that a little disturbing, and the director of tourism said, "They're not only unhygienic, but they're freaking everyone out. Rats are like cyborgs: the only good ones are dead ones."

I called the mayor's office immediately to state my objections re: cyborg bigotry, but my logical mind still can't convince my girly mind that rats aren't gross and skeevy.

Sven is the ideal client. He and his media handler made the rounds of the major networks. He looks more like an actor playing a noble scientist than a noble scientist. He presents his case eloquently and effortlessly pivots a conversation to avoid traps set by the reporters. He's perfect in his somber suit. I'm so glad that I refrained from asking him to wear a white lab coat.

The ReplaceMax spokesperson's "No comment at this time" might as well have been an admission that they drown puppies and laugh *bwaa-ha-ha*.

Even with the media attention, I was still surprised when, in an unprecedented act of expediency, our case manager scheduled a May 1 court date.

Holy moley! We have only one month to prepare. How am I supposed to find an apartment now? I am reassessing my priorities, and the apartment has dropped down the list. Called Holden and left a message saying, "In light of the expedited blah blah blah, my apartment hunt is on hold, blah blah blah, and I appreciate your understanding, etc."

I called Mavis and told her I couldn't come to story time. All she said was "Okay" and then her mother was on the line. "I'm sorry, Ms. Walters, she's just disappointed. I'll explain that you're busy."

"I'll absolutely try to visit when I can." I tried to think of a way to ask her about alternatives for Mavis, but I didn't think saying "And what are your feelings about transferring human consciousness to a robotic body?" would be a good way to introduce the topic.

The only way I could prevent other children from being in Mavis's situation was to focus on the case. I told Dahlia over a dinner, "I don't know how I'm going to complete all the EBTs, interrogatories, and requests for admission in a month."

"Refresh my memory. What's an EBT?"

"It stands for examination before trial. It's a New York thing. Everyone else says deposition."

"Okay, what are requests for admission?"

"We send a document that basically says, 'Admit that you're a lying douchebag.'"

"Does anyone ever admit it?"

"No, either because they're *not* lying douchebags or because they are."

"Then why do you send them out?"

"Dahlia, do you ever ask clients if they've colored their own hair, and they deny it, but you can tell they're lying?"

"All the time. I ask so I won't be held responsible if their hair falls out like Rodney's the time he molted."

"Dogs aren't supposed to molt. And you wonder why I hate him."

"I thought you hated him because of his personality."

"That, too, as well as his frequent noxious emissions."

D plucked an orange slice off her plate and ate the entire thing, even the peel, before saying, "Rodney can be charming when he chooses to be charming," which made me laugh so hard that I choked on a mouthful of rigatoni.

After gulping down a glass of water, I said, "I'm deposing Maxwell Kirsch, who's the Max of ReplaceMax, aka Xam the Man."

"Xam the Man from Fringe Theory?" When I nodded, she said, "No shit! I heard he'd spontaneously combusted."

"A lot of drummers do, but not him. He finished his postgraduate work, went to Iceland for a few years to study Arctic biodiversity, and came back to the States and founded ReplaceMax."

She asked me if Max knew that I was the inspiration for the Gin Cycle, which I am not, and I said, "God, I hope not," and she told me to stop biting my fingernails.

APRIL 6

Valentine's Day Resolution efforts are on hold, which is fine since I'm way ahead on points and goals.

We deposed Maxwell Kirsch today. We were in the conference room where I'd been interviewed, which seems like a long time ago. I'd placed his seat so that the glare from the windows would be in his eyes. His water glass was slightly out of reach. His chair was uncomfortable and had a squeak. The idea was to throw him off his game.

As I sat staring at him, a reel ran though my brain of his younger self, Xam the Man. I'd seen him at the concert with his kit set up at the back of the stage, wearing a DO NOT OPERATE WHILE SLEEPING T-shirt, cargo shorts, and huge black-framed glasses. He'd been so skinny, I could practically count every rib through his thin T-shirt. Ellis had told me that I'd like Xam, that he was smart and funny.

He'd since filled out to fit his frame, and his olive skin had a sun-deprived sallowness. His hair was short and sparse across his scalp. He fidgeted uncomfortably in a tweed jacket, and he often referred to a spiral-bound pocket notebook. He seemed like a nice guy, but Shulky awoke inside me because she sensed the fury simmering behind his businesslike veneer.

Max answered our questions succinctly and with "yes" and "no" when he could. It's always astonishing when people actually follow their attorneys' instructions. They always say they will, but when it comes time to face opposing counsel, they pull out a freeze grenade or other weapon. Or, more typical with superhumans, they give *looong*, self-congratulatory speeches with way too much backstory, while I'm waving frantically for them to STFU.

I thought Max might know that I'd ~~dated~~ hooked up with Ellis, which made me feel ooky. Attorneys are used to knowing all the dirt about witnesses, not vice versa. But I couldn't ask, "Exactly what do you know about my missing pink panties, and when did you know it?" Nevertheless, I tried to maintain my composure as I went through my questions:

ME: What was your response when Dr. Sven Morigi told you of the disparity between his data and your clinical trial report?

MK: I told him that the report was accurate and he must have made an error in his calculation.

ME: How did you know the report was accurate?

MK: I had run the initial numbers myself — three consecutive times to verify them.

ME: What did you do when you were informed of the first organ malfunction, that of Patient A?

MK: Could you be more specific?

ME: When you were told that Patient A was in acute liver failure, did you suspend organ sales?

MK: No.

ME: Why not?

MK: I didn't suspend organ sales because those organs were biologically healthy and compatible, and because the subjects urgently required transplants.

ME: Dr. Kirsch, are a patient's chances of survival better if he has an initial transplant with a defective organ and a subsequent traditional transplant, or if he has only the traditional transplant?

Max looked at one of his attorneys, who drew his eyebrows down as a signal.

MK: Transplant surgery has advanced remarkably, but the recovery is still extremely difficult. Each transplant compromises the system.

ME: Yet you continued to offer your defective organs for transplant knowing that they would fail and require replacement.

MK: They *weren't* defective. Each organ was grown in stringent conditions for optimal health and tested repeatedly before being delivered. I would sooner lose everything I have than take even the smallest risk that an organ might be defective.

Max's attorney placed his hand on Max's arm and said, "I'd like to take a five-minute break." I used the opportunity to run to the ladies' room for a pre-emptive pee so I could be composed through the next several hours.

ME: On what date did you fire Dr. Sven Morigi?

MK: He was not an employee and I did not fire him.

ME: Let me rephrase. On what date did you sever your agreement with Dr. Sven Morigi and tell him that he could no longer use your laboratories?

MK: I believe it was March 12.

ME: What reason did you give for firing him? I'm sorry — I meant *severing* your agreement.

MK: I believed that Dr. Morigi was tampering with the trial results.

ME: So, less than two weeks after Dr. Morigi reported a problem with the organs to you — organs that subsequently failed — you fired him because you suspected he was tampering with trial results?

MK: Yes. (His lawyer cleared his throat.) I didn't fire him. I severed the contract.

ME: Did you follow the contract's requirement to go into arbitration before termination?

MK: No, because the contract could be severed due to criminal activity.

ME: (smiling genially) I'm sorry, but I don't have any record of you filing any reports or charges of criminal activity against Dr. Morigi.

MK: (looking at the table) I planned to take action once I found sufficient proof.

ME: Have you found any proof?

MK: I haven't found anything conclusive yet. I've been occupied with . . . other things.

ME: Other things? Do you mean dealing with patients undergoing the organ failures that Dr. Morigi warned you about?

MK: (looking at the table, nodding)

ME: Yes or no, Dr. Kirsch?

MK: Yes.

I kept my tone even and my face impassive the entire time. I'd had to practice that in the mirror for weeks, but now I can make my face completely inexpressive in my sleep. After a few hours, the questions began to wear Max down. He leaned from side to side in the uncomfortable chair, and he looked frequently at the out-of-reach water glass as his voice grew hoarse. He had to half-stand awkwardly to get the glass.

Finally, his brow furrowed and I knew that he was doubting himself. I was pleased that I'd been successful, but it wasn't a happy pleased. It was more of an *I've filed my tax returns* sense of completion. When the questioning was concluded, we stood and exchanged chilly good-byes. As we left the conference room, Max met my eyes, leaned close, and whispered, "So this is what became of Gin."

It sounded like something on a tombstone. I glanced around, but no one had noticed him speaking to me. He walked into the hallway before I had a chance to respond.

Not that I had a clever response.

Went home, yanked off clothes, and crawled into bed. After ten minutes, I called Dahlia and told her what had happened.

ME: How come I never have any devastating retorts?

D: Because you waste all your energy on torts, not retorts. Why is your voice so muffled? I told you never to call me when you've got a blanket over your head.

ME: (pulling the comforter down to my waist and sitting up against the pillows) My voice isn't muffled.

D: Not now. Stop sulking, Sulky, and meet us at Society Billiards. The salon team is going well-coiffed head-to-head with other salons in a tourney.

ME: No, I've had a hellish day. Max, aka Xam, knows about me.

D: A, you are the whiniest superhero I've ever met, and, B, I need your mad skilz on the eight-ball table to help us humiliate Fabulous Follicles.

ME: One, I'm not a superhero — Shulky is — and let me assure you that most of them whine and complain incessantly about what a burden it is being superheroes. Two, the last time I played for your team, you forgot to tell me that you were betting and pocketing the winnings, and, three, I have earned a sulk.

D: A, I refuse to accept your spurious hearsay vis-à-vis superwhininess. B, I didn't want to taint your innocent joy at the delicate sport of princes by making it seem like a cheap moneymaking venture. C, you know every cent I have goes into the salon, where, D, you get free cuts and use of products. Also, E, you need a trim.

She failed to lure me out, though, and I pulled the blanket over my head and went to sleep.

·20·

NO-FAULT PROCEEDINGS

APRIL 7

I woke suddenly. My brain was spinning and I was starving. I grabbed Shulky's most revealing purple shorty-shorts, black leather bikini top, silver fingerless gloves, and purple boots from the closet. I didn't have a clear plan in mind, but I transformed with a satisfying shiver and She-Hulk took the elevator down to the private entrance.

She used the tunnels to get to her favorite all-night food truck, then ran as fast as she could to the children's hospice. The amazed night nurse let her in and gave her directions to Jordy's room.

Shulky tapped on the door before slipping inside, and delicious aromas wafted from the paper bag she carried.

Jordy's bed was on the far side of the room, by the windows. She pulled the privacy curtain around it and sat on a visitor's chair, crossing one divinely long leg over the other.

"Jordy!" she whispered. "Jordy!"

The teen opened his eyes. He took a second to focus on her.

"God, please don't let me wake up from this dream!" he said.

She took a cardboard box out of the bag, flipped open the cover, and picked out a French fry. Then she chomped it down and said, "Yummy!

I'm both a dream of a girl and real, all six-feet-seven-inches. Are you hungry?" She reached over to stroke his forehead. His skin was feverishly warm.

He clutched her hand. "Shulky, you're really here! How did you . . ."

"Big E passed a message to my friend, Jenny Walters. She was here the other day for story time."

"That weird geeky girl?"

"Yeah, that's the one." Shulky grinned. "Do you want some nacho fries? They're like nachos, but with French fries instead of chips, and Filipino barbecue beef."

He frowned. "I had my dinner like hours ago."

"Then you must be hungry again. It's the most genius meal in this part of the galaxy, and quite possibly the entire universe." She passed a cardboard container to him.

He took a bite of the cheesy fries, and his face lit up. "Oh, my god!"

"Right?" she said. "I hope whoever invented this doesn't use his powers for evil instead of for good, because I'd be helpless."

As they noshed, he said, "Will you tell me some stories?"

"Jordy, I bet you've heard all my stories. Tell me some of yours. Tell me what you're going do when you break out of this place."

His expression became serious. "I don't think that's gonna happen. When I pretend I'm sleeping, I hear the docs talking about me. They only give me six months to live, tops."

Shulky twirled a French fry and grinned wickedly. "You want to know how many times I've been told I'm going to die? *All the frickin' time.* Dr. Doom says it to me every time he sees me." She opened and closed her hand, mimicking a mouth. "'She-Hulk, the time has come for you to bid farewell to your reckless and vulgar existence, yadda yadda yadda!'"

Jordy laughed. "Dr. Doom didn't really say yadda yadda yadda!"

"Maybe not, but I kind of zone out when he talks because he keeps *going on* about how he's going to kill me and how my resistance is futile against his greater will and intelligence. The thing about Victor von Dumb is that he's toxically bitter and he desperately needs to vent, so he describes in boring detail his scheme to control the world that done him wrong just because his face is hideous. And I'm like, 'Dude, seriously?' Meanwhile, I'm figuring out a way to smash his stupid head in and foil his sinister plot. He never learns, and he always comes back for another beat-down, which I am pleased to give his whiney ass."

"Maybe he's got a crush on you," Jordy said, and started laughing so hard he coughed.

Shulky handed him a glass of water. "We're talking about me again. Tell me what *you* want to do when you get better."

"Computer stuff. Not ruling-the-world computer stuff, but hacking for our government, keeping us safe."

"The Avengers always need good hackers. It's a continual game of one-upmanship, trying to create unbreakable encryptions and also trying to crack them."

"That's what I like to do! I like puzzling them out and making twistier puzzles," he said. "I wouldn't be a dweeb or anything. I'd have slick suits and travel everywhere and be cool, like Big E."

In a show of loyalty, Shulky said, "There are different kinds of cool, a whole spectrum of it. My friend Jennifer's totally cool, but in a quiet, nerdy, charmingly awkward way. Where would you like to go?"

Jordy mentioned exotic locations and international hot spots. She'd been to some of them, so she gave him tips on her favorite beaches, favorite ski slopes, favorite active volcanos, and favorite gelato stands. He reached to the shelf for his laptop and said, "Can I interview you about your adventures?"

"Sure," she said. "Get set up and I'll tell you about the time I was standing in for the Thing with the Fantastic Four and got stuck on an artificial planet."

They talked and laughed, and when she heard the night nurse down the hall, Shulky said, "Say, Jordy, have you ever thought about suspended animation?"

"You mean like until a cure gets found for my condition?"

She nodded. "Yeah, like that."

"No way. I hear that it feels horrible, like ants taking apart every cell of your body and trying to put them together again, and what if someone forgot to wake me up? Or woke me up a hundred years from now and everyone I know is dead and the world is ruled by evil unicorns or something."

"The last evil unicorns left Earth during Prohibition. They're major boozers and mean drunks. Okay, so suspended animation is out. What about a cyborg body?"

He shook his head. "Nah, I want to feel things. I don't care what people say about cyborg synapses; they're not at the same level as a human's, and don't ask me if I want a brain transplant. I don't want *any* body but my body, except healthy."

She grinned and said, "Thought I'd run a few things by you, but I see you've considered them."

"I have — but I know you're a brainiac, so it's good to have you thinking, too. We'll figure something out, right?"

"Right!"

The nurse tapped on the door and said, "Time for Jordan to get some rest, Miss She-Hulk."

"May I hug Jordy good-bye?" Shulky asked.

"Only if you don't crush him. Let me remove his IV."

Shulky lifted the teen from his bed very gently and twirled around with him in her arms.

"Can we go up on the roof?" he asked, and Shulky said, "If it's okay."

The nurse nodded, and Shulky bundled a blanket around the boy and carried him up onto the roof. She was aware of the frailness of the arms circling her neck.

"I want to go out there," Jordy said, looking up into the night sky. "I want to see a new planet — even an artificial one — at least once."

"Jordy, you hold tight to that dream. The astral plane where spirits live is beautiful, but there's no need for you to rush there," she said. "The one thing I've learned is that life isn't simple and linear. You never know where it bends, folds, or gets in a tangle, so I always keep my balance and try to ride out the waves, dude."

He repeated the phrase, and then she said, "Time for me to say good night."

She carried him back to his room, set him on the bed, and then kissed his cheek.

"I'm not ever gonna forget this night, Shulky."

"I won't forget you either, Jordy. Sweet dreams."

It was times like these that I forgave her for every crazy exasperating thing she did, which is why I didn't complain when she decided to toilet paper Karl Lagerfeld's penthouse and use shaving cream to write "More is More is More!" on all of his windows. While he had guests inside. At least Nicole thought it was funny, but Aussies always got Shulky's humor.

APRIL 9

The Fritz Colleagues-with-Benefits countdown looms. I have six days to give him my decision. On one hand, I like him and he's got a trim, firm, athlete's body. On the other hand, still no *zings!* If I had a third hand, like some of my clients, there's also the fact it has been a very long time since I've ~~dated~~ ~~had romantic relations~~ had sex. The reason friends-with-benefits doesn't work is because someone always wants more time together. But Fritz and I spent our days together already. Efficiency is a strong selling point.

Ellis's sister called me at the office and said, "Hi, Jenny, I know you're terribly busy, but the kids have been asking if you'll be here tomorrow."

"Hi, Kate. I *am* terribly busy . . ." I said, which was usually enough for most people, but she was undeterred.

"I know you're caught up in the ReplaceMax case," she said. "It's just that the kids don't understand adult deadlines. They live for the moment, and the moment is all many of them have. If you can spare an hour . . . Oh, and Jordan, the older boy, really wants to see you again. He wants to thank you for telling She-Hulk about him. He said that was a really cool thing to do."

"She enjoyed meeting him." I looked at my crowded calendar and saw a break between depos. "I'm sure Ellis will do a great job with the kids."

"He will, but they liked you. I know things were a little awkward before, when he showed up so late, but he's usually very responsible. Maybe you weren't aware of that. I mean, if that was what's keeping you from coming back."

"No, of course not. I'll try to make it."

"That's great! See you tomorrow."

Here's how my brain translated that conversation:

KQ: Hi, Jenny, I'm aware of your obligations, but I think you should come to story time.

ME: I cannot ignore my obligations for your whims even if your brother wasn't going to be at story time.

KQ: You can endure some time with Ellis for the kids' sake, and what did you expect when you had a drunken hookup with a rocker?

ME: Although it meant nothing to him, it was a significant and meaningful encounter for me. Also, he's as weirded out to be around me as I am to be around him. It's weirdness squared.

KQ: You're paranoid. He's no longer an irresponsible player, and he has a deep and unshakeable relationship with Amber, who is perfect and sings like a choir of angels and was editor of the *Yale Law Review*, as well as being America's most accomplished toddler. You should grow up.

ME: I am so over your stoopid brother, and I will prove it by going to story time.

KQ: I'm overjoyed that you have succumbed to my cheap manipulation and I'll see you then!

I stared at the phone as if it had been an accomplice in betraying me.

After settling into my paperwork, I had almost quelled my Ellis anxiety when I heard an ominous *tap-tap-tap*, like Poe's raven, on the glass wall of my office. I looked up with a sense of foreboding and saw Ellis standing there, looking exactly like a guy who'd perfected the art of steamy sexual congress in the tight confines of muscle cars.

He'd seen me, so it was too late to hide under my desk. I raked through my hair with my fingers, wishing I'd had a trim, and waved him in.

He entered and closed the door behind him, and I became terrified that he would proposition me. Because I didn't know if I could resist his overwhelming virile allure.

"Hi . . . [significant pause] Jennifer."

"Hello, Ellis. Nice to see you again." I tried to sound clipped and efficient. I was a renowned attorney! I ~~never very rarely~~ only occasionally had carnal relations with men at the office. And I never ever have carnal relations with engaged men.

I could see Donner at his station, with his typewriter/computer, pretending not to watch.

"I was in the building . . ." Significant pause with a meaningful look that made me want to confess to kidnapping the Lindbergh baby, committing the Black Dahlia murder, and shoplifting a grape-flavored Chapstick from a gas station minimart when I was ten. "Actually, I wasn't in the building. I came here to thank you for asking She-Hulk to visit Jordy. He's been on cloud nine all week."

I fought the urge to throw myself at his feet and plead for mercy from his overwhelming hunkiness. "Shulky likes kids. Well, she likes most kids in theory, but she said she liked Jordy in person." Why had I used "theory"? Would he think I was referring to the band? Was my subconscious creating its own subtext? Agh! He shrugged his big hunky shoulders. Or brawny. He had that old-timey kind of manly build, that *let me carry that for you little lady* appeal. He said, "I didn't think you'd do a favor for a jackass."

My face went hot, and other parts of me did other things. "The favor was for Jordy, not for you."

"Good point," he said, and the corner of his mouth lifted. "Since She-Hulk visited, Jordy's interacting more. He laughs and talks. He's hopeful."

"Thank you for telling me."

Instead of leaving, Ellis dropped into the visitor's chair, and my anxiety, already on ten, cranked up to eleven. He looked around the room. "Nice office."

"It isn't my artwork. I think I'm supposed to order some, but I really can't tell what's good and what's not."

"Amber collects postmodern pieces. She has a very discerning eye. You can ask her for advice."

"This is fine." I sat up, and I inhaled deeply, needing oxygen. I saw his glance travel down to my bosom. That shows how anxious I was — I was thinking with my grandmother's vocabulary. Did he think I was trying to show off my boobs? "Um, artwork doesn't really matter to me."

"Really? [Significant pause.] So many people move here because of the arts."

"What I meant to say is that I'm more interested in the performing arts. I follow opera and theater," I said, thinking of the Three Tenors and *Wicked.* "Also, literature. It was wonderful reading *The Once and Future King* to the kids. I must have read it half a dozen times when I was young."

"I always thought of it as a boys' story."

"Girls are interested in magic and sword fights, too."

"I didn't mean it as a criticism. I'm just trying to [significant pause] figure you out."

We stared at each other. My throat became dry, and I had that panicky feeling I get sometimes right before Shulky emerges. But I didn't feel her anywhere inside. I said, "Sorry, most men assume that all we want is to be the fairy princess."

"Lots of girls *do* want to be the fairy princess. [Pause.] But I never took you for that type. [Excruciating pause.] I'm sorry. I'm presuming to know you better than I . . . do. You, of course, know me from my songs, right?"

Which songs did he mean — the songs I knew before I met him, the Gin Cycle songs, or his entire discography? I had to swallow in order to speak clearly. "Ellis, I feel that we have not effectively established a mutually satisfactory association. Is it possible we can be, um, cordial to each other the way we would be if we had just met and you were my coworker's fiancé and I was your father's top attorney?"

He grinned in a way that made me all woogly inside and said, "*Top* attorney, huh? I won't tell Amber you said that."

We shared a smile and then he said, "I hope you can make it tomorrow. Kate and the kids thought you were great." He stood, seeming to take a long time to get to his full height. "Good-bye [long pause], Jen."

"Bye, Ellis."

He nodded and left the room, and I realized that he hadn't answered my question about starting fresh.

BILL OF PARTICULARS

APRIL 10

It is eight weeks since I began my Valentine's Day Resolutions. I had intended to create an Excel spreadsheet to track my goals with a complex system to tally points. However, I always advise my clients, "If you find yourself doing busywork — tasks that serve no real purpose — feel no obligation to continue them. Aim for efficiency." So I'm giving up the tallies and nitpicky updates.

I have hit a roadblock that is shaped a lot like Ellis Tesla. I am *supposed* to be looking for an apartment. I am *supposed* to be attending cultural events. I am *supposed* to be focusing on Sven Morigi, the ridiculously good-looking future love of my life. I am *supposed* to give Fritz an answer about the sex thing.

I am *not* supposed to be hiding in my work again (even though it's super-important) and listening to every Fringe Theory song looking for secret meanings in the lyrics that I never found all the other times I obsessively listened to their songs, especially the perplexing "Forged in Fire."

I asked, you gave
You asked, I craved

We melded hot and fluid
Like metals in a scorching furnace
An amalgam strong and burnished
By our grasps and grabs, pushes and tugs.
But it was the Arctic freezing
And then the mischief pulling
That shattered us into a thousand shards.
I didn't know love could be so hard.

I've read dozens of reviews of that song, many with scientific analyses that said it was a commentary on a possible shift of magnetic polarities, but I always thought it meant something else. I have no idea what, although that isn't the reason I took a little more time to get ready to go to the hospice. I took more time because I thought I should look nice for the kids.

I arrived at the hospice's community room just as Ellis finished reading a chapter. When he saw me, he looked surprised, and then he smiled.

"Look who's here, kids — it's Jenny, and she's going to help us with our art projects, right, Jenny?"

"I sure am," I said, and went to the front of the room. I hoped that children weren't like dogs and couldn't sense fear.

Jordy waved to me from his wheelchair. "Hi, Jenny!" he said, and the kids called out to me, too.

"Jenny, do you have any project ideas?" Ellis asked.

"What about magic wands and truncheons?"

"Brilliant, and I'll do the fairy princess crowns."

He was different when he was with the kids, which is good because smoldering and/or irate were not approved qualities in a child caregiver. We spread out crafts things, and Ellis put Jordy in charge of a table of younger kids.

I helped Mavis make a magic wand. A boy said, "We did wands last week. Only superheroes have magic."

"No, anyone can find magic," I said. "Magic is often right in front of us. We don't see it because it's invisible or disguised as something else. Anyone can be magical."

"Even Big E?"

I looked at Ellis, who was trying to cut cardboard with children's round-tipped scissors. "Yes, even Ellis."

The hour whizzed by and soon we were packing up the art supplies. As I picked up scraps of construction paper, Ellis said, "Stay still." He touched my cheek and brought his finger away. "Glitter. You can't go back to the office looking like you've been to a kindergartner's party."

"Or a rave."

We smiled and then he said, "I'll see you next week."

"I can't make it then."

"I meant at my EBT. It's scheduled for Monday."

"Oh, I thought . . ." I began. "I'm sorry, Ellis."

"If you were really sorry, you wouldn't go forward with the lawsuit."

"I'm sorry that you're caught up on the opposing side."

"I'm not. It's the right side, and I should know because I wrote the ethical guidelines for ReplaceMax." His jaw tightened. It was such a nice jaw, too.

"It is inappropriate for us to discuss this here and now."

"But you will tear me apart under oath, won't you?"

I wanted to tear him apart in all kinds of ways, but I said, "All I ask is that you tell the truth."

We were silent and then he turned and walked away from me.

Called D and told her all the pertinent facts.

D: I'm not interested in the pertinent facts. Tell me the impertinent ones.

ME: You know them.

D: I think it's ridiculous that you don't ask him straight out about the songs and if he's still in love with you.

ME: I think it's ridiculous that you even think there's a chance that he ever felt anything about me. Allow me to repeat: he did not call me and didn't even remember my name.

D: Then why the sparks?

ME: He's sparky on his own, which is, I believe, in his job description as geek rock sex god.

D: Speaking of sex, how was sex with Ellis compared to sex with the person whose name rhymes with Stony Lark?

ME: Not going to say.

D: That incredibly good? Or is Money Quark bad in bed?

ME: That incredibly good, and Crony Dork is OMG! amazing, but he's always more interested in the real-time hologram display over his bed than in his lovely partner. Back to Ellis, he's disarming me with his utter smexiness now. However, once I'm questioning him under oath, I'll go into killer-attorney mode, and afterward he'll really, really hate me. They *always* hate me afterward. I mean, it's one thing if Dr. Doom hates me because I'm always thwarting his diabolical plans — and even then it's more of a professional animosity . . .

D: Like how Wile E. Coyote and that sheepdog go out for a beer after they clock out?

ME: Yes, except for the going out for a drink part. Victor von Doom and I won't be chatting and laughing over martinis anytime soon. Anyway, I am not comfortable when ex-boyfriends hate me.

D: You've got a very generous definition of "boyfriend." It is absolutely normal for exes to despise each other. You really need to see a psychiatrist about your issues.

ME: I do see a psychiatrist, but not about that.

So I told her all about Dr. Rene Alvarado, we both laughed a lot, and then she said, "You should go to your sessions."

ME: Why? You don't see a shrink and you have all kinds of issues.

D: I don't need to go to a shrink because I have Rodney. Rodney is my therapist.

ME: What kind of advice can that horrible little rat-thing give you?

D: Brilliant advice like never try to hump something that's going to turn around and bite you.

ME: I am not trying to hump anyone.

D: Then stop sniffing at his man parts. Gotta run!

10:45 P.M.

Woohoo! I get more boyfriend and socializing points — not that I have to keep track of them anymore.

I was still stewing at the office about my close encounter of the Ellis kind, when Dr. Stunning returned a call. I went over a list of questions I had for him, and after he answered, I said, "Thank you so much for your time, Sven. I know litigation is so stressful, and you've been doing a marvelous job in your public appearances. If you ever need to vent, I'm here."

He chuckled on the other end of the line, one of those worldly, elegant chuckles, and said, "You are too kind, Counselor. Now I have kept you late at your office. Allow me to make up for it. Won't you join me for dinner at my home? We can discuss whatever you like, even if it's the case."

"I don't want to put you to any trouble," I began.

"My meal is already being prepared, but I'll enjoy it more with your company."

My PFLOML was so gracious! I envisioned a life together where we had amazing careers, went to fancy places, and lounged in our luxurious canopied bed discussing opera as a prelude to sophisticated, worldly sex, which I hoped wasn't too pervy.

I always tell my clients, "If you are offered a job that exceeds your experience, simply request a trial period in which you perform a small task to see if you are comfortable with the larger assignment." I would restrict pervyness to dressing up and pretending that I was new in town. I had no idea what I'd do if he suggested spanking. I could try giving him a smack on his bottom, but I knew that Shulky wouldn't tolerate anyone spanking me, even Dr. Stunning.

I gussied up (why had Ellis inspired Gramma's vocabulary?) and wore a scarf to be consistent with my claim that my neck sometimes got cold. Keeping up falsehoods took so much effort that I didn't know why people lied without a compelling reason.

Sven's driver picked me up and took me to his house on East 91st. *House* is not the right word. House is a three-bedroom ranch with a Weber grill on the flagstone patio, like my family's old place. This was a frickin' old-school magnate's mansion of white limestone, red brick, arches, balustrades, and even a garden surrounding it. I'd always assumed this building belonged to the Smithsonian.

A butler opened the door and told me that Dr. Stunning was waiting for me in the conservatory. Jeeves or Alfred or whoever led the way down a hall and to a magnificent indoor garden with a leaded glass dome overhead. Exotic plants grew lush and tall, and vivid tropical flowers scented the air.

Sven was standing by an enormous telescope, and Dahlia would have commented on the symbolism. The telescope wasn't like anything I'd ever seen, and it had extra mechanisms that buzzed and hummed softly.

"Jennifer, I'm so pleased you could come," he said, coming forward and taking my hands in his. He gave me a kiss on each cheek, and I felt as if we were well on our way to serious discussions in our luxury canopied bed.

"Your house is so beautiful," I said, and I noticed that an intimate table was set for two beside brilliant red ginger plants. "It seems familiar."

"Like the surrounding buildings, this was a home before it became a museum, and now I have returned it to its rightful state."

My mind was whirring away, trying to figure out what this would have cost, when Sven said, "One of my patents provided me with the ability to finance what must seem like an extravagance for a single man.

However, restoring beauty is a passion of mine, and this building is exquisite."

He went to a drinks cart and poured wine for us. Handing me the glass, he looked at me intently and said, "What we interpret as beauty is actually nature in symmetry and balance, and balance is, of course, the guiding principle of all sciences."

"I'd never considered that correlation." I sipped my drink. "I've known scientists, but some assume that I intuitively understand their motivations, and others think no one else is capable of comprehending them."

"Yes, I know about your client Tony Stark," Sven said with a sardonic smile. "A most remarkable fellow with such excellent hair!"

I laughed. "Dahlia, whom you met at Club Nice, thinks so. Joking aside, Tony's creative mind is astounding. But you're an inventor, too. Is your lab here?"

"I require advanced facilities for bioscience experiments, but I keep a workshop here for tinkering. This device," he said, pointing to the telescope, "is an innovation of mine."

He kept looking at me, making me feel jittery, and I glanced around. "You're a stargazer?"

"I've always been fascinated by the worlds beyond our own, Jennifer, but my Timescope does more than a standard telescope. Come see." We went to the instrument, and he made a few adjustments and then said, "Look now!"

I peered into the eyepiece and saw a star that flared intensely and then went black. "What is that?"

"You have just witnessed the last seconds of a dying star. Perhaps you are the only one who has seen it in all the galaxy."

It brought back a memory. "You're trying to make me feel special, but light takes so long to travel to us. The star died out long ago."

His smile was unnerving, or maybe I was already unnerved. "The image was transmitted through a fissure in the space-time continuum, and that star died the very moment you saw it die. I wanted to give you an exceptional experience because you are an exceptional lady."

Just then a servant came in with a rolling cart, and Sven and I sat down for a delicious French seafood dinner. I would have enjoyed it more if I hadn't been thinking about the night that Ellis Tesla and I had stared out at the sky and talked about the stars. Ellis hadn't talked about stars dying. As my mind wandered, I became aware of the rhythm of Sven's speech.

He had a singular, melodious voice, yet there was something in it that bothered me slightly — like a scratchy tag on a shirt collar that once noticed couldn't be *unnoticed*. I found myself trying to figure out why it seemed both familiar and wrong — like waking up in an alternate universe where the sun gave off a different kind of light. No matter how often that happened, it was always ooky.

Dr. Alvarado would ask me to ask myself why I was being overcritical of a stunning, available, brilliant man who'd just gifted me with a unique experience. That's why people are always eager to lawyer-up and not shrink-up. When my clients hire me, they get not only expert answers to specific inquiries, but also useful advice.

When Sven and I finished our after-dinner brandies, I hoped he'd offer a tour of his lab, but he didn't. Maybe he was saving it for another date. He took my hand and kissed it, which is super-elegant! I am going to buy a book on manners and practice my etiquette, which will count toward culture points.

Once home, I found Crane's note cards that a GLKH guest had left in the loft, and I wrote out:

Dear Sven,
Thank you for the

That's where I stopped because I was still his attorney and I didn't want to sound too datey. I could thank him for the delicious meal. Or should I thank him for his time? Or both, or maybe for showing me the purported last seconds of a star?

I spent fifteen minutes writing cards and used them all up except the last, where I wrote:

Dear Sven,

Thank you for having me to your lovely home for a delicious dinner. I enjoyed seeing your Timescope and I especially enjoyed our bracing discussion of the finer points of intellectual property law.

Best,

Jennifer Walters

That sounded right — not too flirty, but warm and businesslike. When Dr. Stunning and I are a couple and I have a real address, I will order engraved stationery in whatever style the etiquette experts say is best for a top professional lady. "Lady" sounds old, like "ma'am," but Sven called me an "exceptional lady." Hmm, it sounded better when he said it with his suave accent.

Ellis used the word "lady," too, but in an entirely different way.

Lady Green Eyes
Her sweet moans and sighs
Are my sexual lullaby
Let me rock you, baby,
Rock you till morning dawns
And your cries of pleasure end in yawns
As you sink deep
Into soul-satisfied sleep.

I remembered when Ellis pulled the curtain back from the window and we gazed out at the stars. He said, "What are you thinking?" and I said, "I wonder if any of them has already died and we're only seeing the light now."

"Ah, you're a star's-half-burnt kind of girl. I'm a star's-half-blazing sort of guy."

I settled back into his arms. "Nothing goes away. It transforms and changes."

"I thought you said you didn't like science, but you're schooling me on physics and [significant pause] biology."

"I'm not teaching you anything you didn't know," I laughed. "I never cared about science until I heard your band. I listened to 'High School Chem-Mystery' about a kazillion times while studying for my SATs. I wanted to understand all your allusions and analogies because you made it sound so exciting."

"It is so exciting." He was quiet for a minute and then said, "It's so vast and overwhelming."

"I want to see it all. I want to get out of LA and see this world and other worlds. I want my experiences to transform me into . . . into . . ."

He said, "You're already naked, so don't be shy. Into what?"

"Into someone who has the power to make a difference."

"You've already made a difference with me, babe."

I wiggled happily against him. "You know what I mean — the reason I want to be a lawyer is not the money or prestige, but to advocate for people who need someone to defend them. Except . . ."

"Except?"

I felt safe enough to confess my insecurities. "How do you do it? How do you get in front of an audience when you know they're all looking at you and will see any flaw or mistake?"

"Because they really want to be entertained and I really want to entertain them. So it's not all about me, but about doing everything to give them an awesome experience. There's that moment when everything connects, and it doesn't matter if I trip on the equipment or change up lyrics, because it's all part of the show. It's what makes that performance different and special. Find your own connection in the courtroom." He brushed back my hair and said, "You're not there for yourself, but for those who don't have your legal knowledge or abilities, so you have to be big and bold and badass to defend them."

Despite the warmth of the evening, I shivered because his words resonated with something within me, with the years of play-acting in the fields as a warrior on the side of good.

"What about you?" I asked. "What do you want — besides the band, which is amazing."

"That gets complicated by what others expect of me — to be a certain type of person and fit in their lives a certain way, to join the family business."

"I can't imagine you in any family business, unless your family sails under the Jolly Roger. You're Ellis Tesla. You're cataclysmic! You're supposed to make music, and you're supposed to make people realize how thrilling and explosive science is. You bring the wonder of it into lives. It's what you do — and it's why I . . . I . . ." I stopped because I knew better than to tell him that I loved him when we'd only just met.

And he'd pushed me back onto the mattress and murmured, "Tell me with your body, green-eyed girl."

· 22 ·

ASSUMPTION OF RISK

APRIL 14

My deadline to respond to Fritz's offer is tomorrow. Since he hasn't said anything, I feel no need to rush to a decision.

Finally, other people are noticing the disturbing trend of niceness! A *New York Times* feature got picked up by cable news, and someone in the Department of Tourism leaked a report that tourism has declined because visitors are confused and disappointed. One sweet old matron from Cedar Rapids sobbed, "I asked the man how to get to Jerry Seinfeld's coffee shop, and he politely wrote down directions instead of saying 'Fuck you, Gramma.' I'm never coming back!"

The city is eerily quiet without the constant honking of taxi horns.

I called Sergeant Patty to see if she had any idea what was going on, but she said, "I can't stand this goddamn niceness; it's as unnatural as a leftover chicken wing after a football game at my house. At least no one's seen those freakazoid rats anymore, and criminals are behaving better."

"Has violent crime decreased?"

"Nah, but murderers are turning themselves in at a higher rate. When we ask them why, they say, 'It seems like the right thing to do.' What kind of bullshit is that?"

I agreed that something was wrong. "One last thing, Patty. I thought that Joocey Jooce might be involved with this terrible epidemic, but tests show no additives in the product. You drink their smoothies. Do you feel any nicer lately?"

After a long pause, she said, "I haven't been hanging up on my god-damn crazy sister so fast. So I might be infected?"

"I don't know, but you might want to keep away from the smoothies, just in case."

The city might be nicer, but apartment hunting isn't. I frequently advise my clients, "Before you begin any negotiation, decide on your ideal outcome, an acceptable outcome, and nonnegotiables. Start from your ideal result and be willing to make reasonable compromises."

But I can't start from my ideal, because it doesn't exist in my price range. I set up appointments for tours of "acceptable" places during my lunch hour and after work.

This is what I have seen:

- An overpriced luxury pad with a stripper's pole in the master bedroom. I'm sure there's icky biological material soaked into every surface.
- A spacious flat with a sewage stench and rot on the window frames. When I commented on the smell, the leasing agent said it was like the "historic neighborhoods of European cities."
- A duplex with walls covered in dusty fake fur. It would be like living inside of Sasquatch, except that Sas keeps his soft fur impeccably clean and shiny.
- A reasonably priced, cozy, immaculate, updated two-bedroom with a rainwater shower, views from every window, and even an office space. However, every entrance and exit from the building is too public for Shulky.

The leasing agents all say (nicely, ugh!), "You'll have to make some compromises," which I already knew. Needing to talk to someone who I knew wouldn't be spookily nice, I called my cousin.

ME: Hey, Bruce, I thought of you when I went to the shooting range. Used my old Smith & Wesson, but it's not the same as being in a wide open field with the whole day free.

B: You were the one who liked to shoot. I was more interested in the velocity and trajectory of the bullets.

ME: And in your homemade rockets. You were always burning off your eyebrows. In all our family photos, you look very surprised.

B: You're welcome to Photoshop eyebrows in for me. How's everything?

ME: On the job front, excellent. QUIRC is way less stressful than working for Holden. I've even been able to go out occasionally and have a social life.

B: I've always thought having a social life was overrated.

ME: I know you have, but I'm not as solitary as you. I was balancing my work and social life wonderfully, until Holden told me that I have to leave the GLKH loft soon. Finding a place that fits my needs is impossible.

B: Did I just hear Jennifer Susan Walters say that something was impossible? That loud thud you hear is me falling to the floor in shock.

ME: Very funny, Bruce. I'm not giving up, by any means. Also, I think I may have a boyfriend. I'm not officially dating him yet because he's a client. Have you heard of Dr. Sven Morigi?

B: Do you mean that slick pretty boy who was on *Good Morning America*? Didn't seem like your type.

ME: What do you mean?

B: He looked like he wears an ascot and has a love child with his teenage housekeeper. Douchebag alert, Will Robinson, douchebag alert!

ME: You're so off-base. Sven's a brilliant scientist and we have a lot in common.

B: Like what?

ME: Um, like an interest in astronomy, international cuisine, and we both like opera and the arts.

B: [laughing until he coughed]

ME: I live in one of the most cosmopolitan cities of the world, and I don't know why you think it's so hilarious that I've developed more sophisticated tastes.

B: [trying not to cough] Because you've always preferred a bar band to an Italian tenor, because the only show you've ever liked onstage is *Wicked* — which you've seen how many times now? — and because your favorite *international* cuisines are French fries and nachos.

ME: That was the way I used to be before I set important self-improvement goals, one of which is to find a serious relationship with a worthwhile man, and Dr. Sven Morigi is very interested in me. I think he could be an ideal boyfriend.

B: Yeah, that's why you sound so excited about him.

ME: Bruce, I've had my hopes crushed before, so I'm trying to be more practical this time. I'm glad I've met someone with no observable major issues.

B: Little cousin, he's hired a powerful and expensive law firm to sue his former boss over defective organs that are killing kids. I'd call that a marker for a major issue. However, if you need to make changes in your life to be happy, I understand that. How's Shulky doing?

ME: She'll never admit it, but I think she's really bummed that she's gone from saving the world to handling local crime. She has run into a few new superhumans, though.

B: Yes, I read that in the *Avengers Advocate*. Have either of you heard anything about Doom lately?

ME: Nope, zip, nothing, *nada*. It's as weird as polite cabbies.

B: I might not have a Spidey-sense, but I am getting a feeling that something's not right.

ME: I get that ookiness, too, that something's off-balance. You know, nature seeks balance in all things.

B: Did your Krav Maga coach tell you that?

242 · MARTA ACOSTA

ME: No, Azzan tells me to duck into tighter rolls to protect my torso from knife attacks. A scientist told me that.

B: I think you should listen to Azzan. I hope you're not being influenced to become nicer.

ME: I've been keeping a journal of my behavior. I haven't noticed any disturbing increase in niceness.

B: That's good. You're already too nice. You've let the supers roll all over you.

ME: Easy for you to say — they accept you in that boy's club, but I had to completely agree to their terms if I wanted to preserve any of Shulky's Mansion privileges.

B: And by "completely agree," you mean that you managed to amend them in your favor. Speaking of Shulky, if she's patient — and I know that's not one of her strong points — I think the other Avengers will reevaluate teaming with her again.

ME: And we can go back to living at the Mansion? Because it would be great to have immediate access to the cars and all my weapons!

B: Let's not get ahead of ourselves.

APRIL 16

Yesterday's deadline for answering Fritz passed without comment. He knows I'm consumed by this case. I really really wish that we didn't have to depose Ellis, but my responsibility to my client supersedes my personal reluctance.

Amber Hammerhead smeered when I told her that I didn't think it was appropriate that I question him. "Although Sven signed with QUIRC knowing the personal complications, I'm very uncomfortable bringing Ellis in."

"The EBT for Ellis is restricted to the ethics guidelines he drew up for ReplaceMax, which are public information," she said coldly. "Even if he had remembered your name, it doesn't make any difference to him who questions him. If you think it makes a difference to our client, you should call Sven and explain why."

"That's unnecessary, because as first chair I've made the decision to ask Genoa to conduct the examination."

"Fine, whatever."

Shulky woke inside me, like a grizzly who'd been hibernating in a cave, annoyed at being disturbed. I snapped, "Fine, whatever," back at Amber and ended the conversation before my jade girlfriend decided it was time to come out and play tetherball with Amber's noggin.

I was anxious about seeing Ellis in this context, and it didn't help that he and I arrived at the QUIRC conference room doorway at the same time.

He gave me a stony look and said, "So you're going through with this?"

"Of course, QUIRC is going through with this. Was there ever any question?"

"I thought there might be."

"Not for me." Glancing into the conference room, I saw the General and Amber already seated. "Where's your attorney?"

"I told him not to bother coming."

"You're the son of a lawyer and engaged to a lawyer, and you didn't bring any representation?" I heard my voice rising. "What is *wrong* with you, Ellis? Never mind. I don't care."

"Are you sure you don't [meaningful pause], Jen?"

The others were watching us, so I went into the room and took the chair farthest from Ellis. A moment later, I'd regained my composure and sat impassive as the General smoothly ran through our series of questions. Ellis told us what we already knew: he and Max were friends and colleagues, and he believed that Max would never knowingly sell defective products. I knew Genoa liked Ellis, and I could tell that he respected her by his calm, complete answers. He never treated me that way.

Ellis explained each ethical principle, and I found myself admiring his sound reasoning. I struggled to maintain my astute professional observation instead of gazing dreamily at him. Occasionally, I looked at Amber to see if she had additional questions. She took notes, now and then lifting her eyes to Ellis. I couldn't read her expression for the life of me.

The examination ended, and Genoa excused herself, but Ellis stayed behind and came to me. "You're making a mistake and destroying a good man."

"The facts are irrefutable. ReplaceMax organs failed. People died and are dying."

He gave me a hard stare before he left.

Amber came over and said, "Don't mind Ellis. He thinks that no one is as principled as he is."

I could have been wrong, but I thought I heard bitterness under the dulcet tones of her voice.

· 23 ·

ALTERNATIVE DISPUTE
RESOLUTION

APRIL 17

My level of stress at work has ratcheted up since Ellis's EBT. I changed into running shoes and took a circuitous route home, walking briskly enough to burn off my tension. On Franklin Street, I recognized an annoying hipster who always dropped candy wrappers and flicked cigarette butts on the sidewalk. Then I saw him move toward a trash bin and toss a Joocey Jooce cup inside.

I tapped his shoulder and said, "Excuse me."

"Yes?" He smiled at me.

"Would you please tell me why you threw that cup in the trash?"

"That's where it belongs, right?" His expression was pleasant but puzzled.

"I've seen you around the neighborhood, and you always littered before. Why are you throwing garbage away now?"

He shrugged. "I don't know. I want to be nicer, I think. If you don't mind, I don't want to be late. I'm meeting a friend. Have a good evening!"

"You, too," I said. "Thank you for cleaning up."

It was all very perplexing, and I walked to Dahlia's salon. She was showing the last client out, and she let me in and locked the door after me.

I clicked off the main salon lights for her and said, "This case is making me so tense my skin is crawling. I need a drink, and don't suggest Joocey Jooce!"

"You need to change out of your work clothes *and* change out of your work brain. Let's have a bite and beer. I'm in the mood for a grilled cheese with bacon and jalapeños, which I believe covers all the major groups on the new food pyramid."

"Is that a new food truck special?"

"No, it's my own special. Take Rodney for a walk while I finish closing up, and we can go to my place."

I glared at Rodney, and he made a hideous snorting sound. He didn't like me walking him and kept dropping his butt to the ground, making me pick him up and carry him most of the way. When a woman looked at us and said, "Cute dog!" I knew that niceness had gotten completely out of control.

However, the food and the beer helped, and Dahlia let me rant on about Ellis's hostility, Amber's bitchiness, how I would never find an apartment and was now stagnating on my Valentine's Day goals.

Dahlia ranted about problematic clients, a stylist diva, and her lack of a sexual partner who didn't interfere with her job. "I hate it when they fall in love with me."

"You're infuriatingly lovable," I said. "However, I fail to comprehend why you don't fall in love back."

"Because they are not worth taking time from Arrested Youth, which, as you know, is my life's dream."

"When I met you, your life's dream was anthropology. You wanted to go to Egypt."

"Ancient Egypt had revolutionary hairstyles, and if you ever time-travel back to the land of Pharaohs, I expect you to take me. As I was saying, I'd like to find someone who is both worthy of my time and yet doesn't intrude."

"I want a real boyfriend and an intellectually collaborative relationship. I think Sven and I could have a wonderful life together."

"You haven't even had sex with him."

"Plenty of people don't have sex before they get married."

"Oh, please, poodle, be serious. You wouldn't buy a car without test-driving it."

"Are you implying that I'm a car or a driver?"

"Both. What you need is a She-Hulk adventure, and I will accompany you."

"I don't want to go dancing tonight. I'm too arghed and ooked out!"

"Are you arghed enough to turn into She-Hulk?" Dahlia asked excitedly.

"No, but if you want to come on one of *my* adventures, you can. I'd like to visit the 'heck of a nice guy' who rents from Claude, the doorman."

"Claude, the former potential future love of your life?"

"Yes. I don't know if his 'heck of a nice guy' tenant will be in. Claude doesn't have his phone number."

"You said the welding shop was in Jamaica Heights. I'm not taking public transportation all the way out there. You should have a car. It's weird that you don't since you've always been such a car fanatic."

"I am not a fanatic. I have a sensible appreciation for well-made machines," I said, which set off a round of crazy eye-rolling.

It didn't take long for me to borrow a ride from the Mansion's fleet and return to pick up Dahlia. She wasn't impressed when I pulled up in the beat-up Buick LeSabre, but her expression changed when she got in the car and saw the glowing lights and gauges on the dashboard.

"OMG, Jen, this looks like the control panel for a spaceship! What does this do?" she said, reaching for a switch.

I batted her hand away. "Rocket launcher. *Do not touch anything,* because I always get blamed anytime something gets wrecked, even when it's totally not my fault, or incidental to hero stuff."

"I thought you'd be more fun as a superhero, and don't tell me that you're not a superhero."

"Okay, here's something fun for you. Hang on tight!" I flipped on the stealth glide and said, "Now they see us, and now they don't!" and the car shuddered as it became invisible.

In a matter of seconds, I shifted to PeakSpeed, and we were swiftly weaving in and out of the stream of heavy traffic.

"We're going too fast!" D said, and grabbed the dashboard as we sharply swung between a big rig and a careening van.

Suddenly the car veered into the next lane and the tight space between two speeding cars, and D said, "Holy shit!"

The car ahead slammed on its brakes, and we swerved into the narrow space between the lanes, with less than an inch of clearance on either side.

Dahlia screamed and stared from side to side in horror, saying, "Shit, shit, shit, shit!"

"It's all automatic." I lifted my hands from the steering wheel, but D was jamming down on an imaginary brake and frequently shrieked during the ride.

She was pale and shaky when we approached our destination. I switched off the PeakSpeed, and when we were clear of traffic, I flipped off the stealth glide and took control of the steering again.

When Dahlia pried her fingers off the dashboard, I said, "You *told* me you wanted an adventure."

"But I didn't want to be terrified!"

"If you're not scared, it's not a real adventure." I parked by the old welding shop and said, "Come on," as we got out.

She turned her attention to a new worry. "There's no one around, but I feel like we're being watched."

"Probably. You can either come with me or stand here by yourself."

She hurried to my side. We neared the fenced yard, and the dogs bounded out, snarling and snapping. Dahlia skipped back and said, "Yikes!" and then I heard a *yip yip* noise and her tote bag bulged on one side.

"D, did you bring that horrible rat-thing with you!"

"Don't be churlish *and* sulky. I didn't know how long we'd be gone."

"Great. Now they'll try to tear him to shreds. I'll do my best to keep them back." I put my palm flat on the fence, and the big Rottie sniffed it and began waggling his rear. "Hey, bowser, how's it going?" The other dogs quit barking and came to the fence to say hello. They sniffed toward Dahlia's tote, but they didn't growl.

Light edged out from behind the blinds on a second-floor window, and I said, "I think Heck-of-a-nice-guy may be in there." I buzzed the bell at the gate.

We waited, and after a minute, the blinds on the upstairs window moved. Then the buzzer at the gate sounded. I pushed at it and said to Dahlia, "Follow right behind me. If anything happens, take cover and let me handle it."

As we entered the lot, the dogs circled us, sniffing and wagging. A few nudged at D's bag, and she twisted away from them as a growl came from within.

"Don't hold me responsible if this pack eats that horrible hairball," I said.

"Rodney can defend himself."

"You're delusional." We walked to the door marked ADMINISTRATION, and the security camera swiveled toward us. I looked into the camera and tried to keep my expression neutral to defuse any suspicion.

After a moment, the door opened. A man in a hoodie stood there, his face angled into shadow.

"Hello," I said, holding out my hand, "I'm Jennifer Walters, your landlord Claude's attorney."

"You're the one who wanted me to pay rent in money not coupons," he said in a gentle, deliberate voice. "I apologize for that confusion. I'm Adam."

He took my hand tentatively and shook it, keeping his face ducked down.

"This is my friend Dahlia. May we come in and talk?"

He nodded, his hood throwing his face into more darkness. We went into the room, which only had one low-wattage desk light on.

"Do you mind turning on a light? It's very dark."

He hesitated and then said, "I have a facial disfigurement. I didn't want to frighten you."

I couldn't help but think of Victor von Doom and the scary mask that he wore to cover his scarred face. "Thank you for telling us, but there was no need to worry."

Then Adam switched on the overhead and I saw what he'd been hiding. The top left of his face was a mass of new scar tissue, still viciously red and rough.

"You're horrified," he said.

Dahlia stepped toward him and said, "Yes, because you've got a horrible cut."

"It's a burn," he said, shyly.

"No, I mean your haircut. Your hair is really fabulous — great texture, and are those natural highlights? But the style is an absolute crime!"

"You're making a joke." His smile was so radiant that he was instantly attractive, and I realized that he was quite young. "Most people don't get to notice my hair."

"All Dahlia *ever* notices is hair," I said. "It's one of the many reasons she's special."

"Well, I have a gift. You've been self-cutting, haven't you?" She leaned forward, pushed his hood back, and ran her fingers through his hair just as she always did with me when I was a little down. "There will be no more of that."

"Did you come to talk to me about hairstyles?" he said, and he lifted his blue eyes to Dahlia's crazy turquoise ones. I saw her hide a smile as she looked around the room, with its bookshelves and religious icons.

"Adam, I wanted to introduce myself and learn exactly what you're doing here in this shop," I said, keeping my tone both friendly and businesslike.

"Am I doing something wrong?" he asked earnestly.

"I don't know until you tell me what you're doing to the Joocey Jooce cups. It's something that makes people nicer."

He dipped his head downward into shadow, and I realized where I'd seen the same gesture on someone exactly the same size and build. "You're the one who helped She-Hulk with the moonbeam raygun!"

He looked up quickly. "How did you know?"

"There was a surveillance camera in the office building," I said quickly. "She-Hulk showed me the video. We often consult with each other on legal matters."

"Everyone knows that Jennifer is Shulky's dear friend and associate," Dahlia offered. "I'm also friends with the jade goddess. Isn't her hair amazing?"

"Let's talk about Joocey Jooce," I said. "What exactly are you doing with the company?"

Adam said, "Please have a seat," and indicated the floor.

After we all sat cross-legged on the old industrial carpet, he said, "When I first came to New York, I met the Joocey Jooce founders, Joe and Anat, at their cart in the park. They always gave me free smoothies and fruit because I didn't have any money. They were so nice. I wished everyone would be that nice."

"New Yorkers aren't supposed to be nice," Dahlia said.

"They let me do errands and even let me sleep on their sofa. Joe loaned me his library card, and I spent my free time there, learning about lots of things, including business. I gave them ideas on production and marketing."

"Did they pay you?"

"They gave me part of the company, and I guess they set up a bank account for me, but all I want is a place to do my experiments and keep my pets," he said. "I thought about using the cups to help people be nicer."

"How did you do it?" I asked.

"I was fascinated by the idea that graphics could be used for messaging on a more intuitive level. There are certain symbols and shapes that recur in civilizations throughout history. Humans respond to them. I experimented with designs until I came up with one that had a pacifying, cheering effect."

"The PLAY NICE! image," I said.

"It's an extremely precise graphic. One percentage point of difference and the logo is merely a line drawing."

"What's the other part? Drugs?"

"Gosh, no! I use a blend of chamomile, a touch of rosemary, lemongrass, and other traditional herbal medicines. The flavors, which are in the covers and straws, are mildly pleasing on an almost subliminal level. The scent has aromatherapy qualities that induce a sense of well-being. It took a lot of experimentation, but the effect both soothes and stimulates the mind and senses."

"Would you provide me with covers and straws so I can have them tested?"

"Of course," he said. "Joocey Jooce is completely organic."

"And tasty," Dahlia said, and just then an awful yipping-snorting-snuffling sound came from her tote. She smiled and said, "That's Rodney." She unsnapped the flap cover, and the dreadful little dog's head popped out.

As we were both shouting "No!" Adam reached over and picked up the dog. I waited for the puny beast to bare his pointy needle teeth and begin his speedo biting. To my astonishment, Rodney licked Adam's face and nestled happily in his hands.

I have seen many fantastical things in my life, and this was one of them. Dahlia and I exchanged *OMG!* glances.

"What a nice little puppy, or is it a rat-dog hybrid?" Adam smiled and scratched Rodney's belly.

"Rat," I said while D said, "Dog."

"I like both," Adam said. "The Joocey Jooce motto is only a motto, but a gentle reminder has a cumulative effect, especially since everyone wants to be nice."

"Most people, but there are dangerous exceptions," I said. "You witnessed a miscreant destroying a bank and trying to kill She-Hulk."

He smiled disarmingly. "I also saw She-Hulk and the NYPD helping others at the risk of their own lives."

I asked him how he'd come to be at the moonbeam raygun attack, and he told us that he'd just dropped off Joocey Jooce coupons for Claude and he heard the commotion. "Everyone said that She-Hulk would come to stop it, so I ran to the bank, hoping to meet her. I entered the adjacent office building intending to go to the roof and see if I could help from there, because I hoped maybe she could help me in return."

"But you didn't ask for her help," I said.

He looked embarrassed. "I'm just no one and she's She-Hulk."

"Adam," I said carefully, remembering his superhuman power and speed. "Where do you come from?"

He frowned. "I don't know."

"You must come from somewhere," Dahlia said gently. "I come from El Paso, which is just as bad as everyone says it is." She reached over and squeezed his arm, which was muscular for a guy interested in aroma-therapy, but common for a superhuman.

"Tell us how you thought She-Hulk could help you, Adam," I said.

He spread out his hands and I saw the scars all over his fingers. "The first thing I remember is a fire. I was in the flames and in agony. I crawled out, yanking off my burning shirt and pants. I was in an almost empty room with a cement floor and cement walls. I grabbed a large vacuum canister from a counter because I knew it was important, but I didn't know why. I ran outside and kept running as fast as I could for hours. I had no concept of time or distance. I stopped when I saw trees and shrubs. I hid there, because I knew someone had tried to kill me."

"Why?"

"I don't know. I didn't even know how to speak yet. Some of the home-less people gave me clothes and watched out for me," he said. "I crouched in the shrubs and listened to conversations, and language came to me — not just English, but all the languages I heard — Japanese, German, Croa-tian, Dutch, Hindi — the words made sense. I'd eat whatever I found in the trash bin near the Joocey Jooce cart. Joe and Anat began leaving food for me. I was afraid at first, but they were patient. They brought me shoes, a sleeping bag, and other things."

"When was this?" I asked.

"A few years ago, I think. I'm not sure because time was different to me," he said. "My friends helped me find this place, and Claude was so nice he let me stay in exchange for work. He's a very nice man."

"He thinks you're very nice, too," I said. "Adam, have you learned or do you remember anything else about who you are or who tried to kill you?"

"No. There's no missing person report on me." He waved toward all the philosophy and science books on the shelves. "Who I am is not as interesting as *why* I'm here. I think I must be here to do good things for people. I just don't know what exactly."

"You did good by helping She-Hulk," I said. "Adam, I believe you're a superhuman."

Dahlia gasped and said, "OMG, really?" and Adam looked a little confused.

"It would explain your strength, speed, and ability to learn so rapidly. It would also explain why someone tried to kill you. For every good-hearted superhuman, there's one who is bent on destruction."

"Am I an alien?" He pinched his arm. "What does an alien feel like?"

"You look like an Earth human to me. I can't say if your super traits are inherited or acquired. Would you like me to ask She-Hulk to see if she can discover more about you?"

He agreed, so I took photos of him, and then I quizzed him about his other abilities.

"I can solve a Rubik's Cube."

"So can I," Dahlia said.

"With your eyes shut and with your toes?"

Dahlia looked at me. "Are flexible toes a super ability?"

"No, but sensing without seeing is. Adam, you mentioned a vacuum canister. What was in it?"

"I don't know. I still have it in the refrigerator. I've run rudimentary tests on the contents with my limited equipment. All I've discovered is that it's not radioactive, explosive, or poisonous."

"Keep it secure. When we find out more about you, we may find out more about the contents. I'd like you to keep a low profile. Whoever tried to kill you is still out there."

I stood, and Dahlia stood more reluctantly.

"Thank you for visiting, Jennifer." He gazed at D and handed her back Rodney, who whined. "Dahlia, it was very nice meeting you and Rodney. If Rodney would like to come back to play with any of my pets, he's always welcome."

"We're available anytime you want to talk," she said sweetly, cramming the dog back in her tote, "or to show us any other interesting abilities."

I suddenly wondered what else this odd young man had been doing with his genius, and said, "Adam, are any of your other pets rats?"

He smiled in wonder. "Yes, they are, Jennifer! They're upstairs if you want to meet them."

"No, thank you. Have you been altering rats through gene splicing or mutations?"

"How did you know! It seemed so sad to me that such an intelligent animal should not be living in better harmony with personkind. It's the tail, you know, the hairless tail that bothers people, as well as their nocturnal behavior. I thought that people would like them if they could see how cute and smart they are."

"That was you!" Dahlia said, excitedly. "I must have watched that fluffy rat video a dozen times."

"Your intentions were wonderful, Adam," I said, "but happy, frolicsome daytime rats freak people out. It's unnatural."

Dahlia gave him a sympathetic look. "When I was a girl, I had a pet rat named Oscar and he was the best pet ever. But you can't change attitudes overnight."

I advised Adam not to release any more of his pets/biological experiments, and we said good night.

When we'd left the lot, Dahlia murmured, "I wonder what else he's good at in the dark."

"I *knew* you were wondering that."

"So do superhuman men have superhuman, you know . . ."

I was glad she couldn't see me blush. "Some of them. But trust me when I tell you that a nice guy without superhuman, uh, accessories is a better boyfriend in every way than a superhuman who's a jerk."

"You're ruining all my fantasies, poodle. How often do superhumans go missing?"

"Frequently. Do you remember that time I said I was transferred to France? I was stuck on another planet," I said. "I *still* haven't been to Paris."

"You sent me postcards!"

"Ruth sent you postcards."

"Well that explains the kittens in berets." She opened the rear door of the car and got into the backseat. "I'm going to lie down here and close my eyes while you drive back. A little adventure goes a long way."

11:00 P.M.

I sent Adam's photo to Ruth with a message asking her to check the Missing Superhumans Database and cross-reference it with any reports of a fire in the US or Canada. Adam could have run hundreds of miles.

What were the chances that my former PFLOML's tenant was a superhuman amnesiac? In this city, a lot.

QUESTIONS TO ANSWER

- What is Adam's real identity?
- What is the cause of his superhuman abilities?
- Is he connected to Superbrat?
- Who tried to kill Adam and why?
- What is in the insulated canister and why is it important?
- Should I include warehouse rentals as housing possibilities, and does my visit to Adam count as a social activity? I think it probably should.

Dahlia instantly crushed on Adam. She liked his smile, his muscles, and especially his appreciation of Rodney. Why don't I feel that way about Sven, who is stunning, brilliant, successful, cultured, and interested in me? I really, really don't want to talk to Dr. Rene Alvarado about my love life, but maybe he can help.

That's just how desperately clueless I am about romance: I am actually hoping that a trippy hippie brain shrinker can give me advice.

HARMLESS ERROR

APRIL 19

Went to see Dr. Rene Alvarado today. He was very happy that I'd come. I know because he told me so and because he kept tugging at his scruffy beard as if he couldn't believe his good fortune. Nelson would say that he has an engaging smile, but I feel that there's a fine line between "engaging" and "smarmy." This is how our conversation went:

RA: Jennifer, I'm so glad you've taken this important step toward becoming more balanced.

ME: Ms. Walters. As I always tell my clients, "Once you sign an agreement, you are required not only by law, but also by societal ethics to adhere to the conditions, Rene."

RA: Dr. Alvarado. Is there anything you'd like to discuss today?

ME: Not particularly. As a top-tier attorney, I am very involved in my current case, so my mind is on that.

RA: You're very invested in your identity as a lawyer.

ME: You say invested. I say dedicated.

RA: Let's discuss your involvement in the ReplaceMax case. I saw your client, Sven Morigi, on *The Daily Show*. He's strikingly good-looking.

ME: Since you brought up Dr. Morigi, I should probably mention that he's expressed interest in me romantically.

RA: I know that you've been involved with several of your clients in the past.

ME: Not several. One or two. A few. Definitely less than ten. I often spend so much time with clients that it seems to be a natural progression; however, I have informed Dr. Morigi that I cannot date him until the case is resolved.

RA: Hmm (annoying pen tapping on teeth). Why do you think you were eager to have physical relations with your other clients, yet are withholding it from Dr. Morigi?

ME: You are assuming facts not in evidence. I have *never* expressed that I was eager to have physical relations with my clients.

RA: Were you reluctant to have physical relations? Did you feel pressured or required to offer yourself sexually?

ME: I never said that either. I had a normal amount of desire for a few men who happened to be my clients.

RA: And now you have an abnormal amount, or lack, of desire for Dr. Morigi (teeth tapping). Why do you think that is? He's extraordinarily good-looking.

ME: You said that before. I enjoy his company very much and look forward to developing a mature and responsible relationship with him when it will not conflict with my professional obligations. I believe we are intellectually compatible, and I enjoy his insights on astronomy, folk music, and international cuisine.

RA: (sighing and slumping) That sounds awful. What about passion? What about romance?

ME: The most I've learned about romance was at a weekend divorce law seminar. Here's a tip: transfer all your assets to private accounts before you tell your partner that you'd like a divorce. Aren't you supposed to be nonjudgmental?

RA: I'm allowed to use some discretion, Jennifer, and you're talking about dating Dr. Morigi like you're scheduled for a root canal. Romance should be impetuous, unpredictable, exhilarating. It should

260 · MARTA ACOSTA

sweep you up and consume you (pausing to think) with the un-
stoppable, irresistible momentum of a flesh-eating bacterium, like
in that song. You remember, (singing) "My heart, my soul, my life,
I can't protect—"

ME: That was only a song! It doesn't mean *anything*. Real love isn't just
infatuation; it takes time to build . . . doesn't it?

RA: (shrugging) We Alvarados have always believed in love at first
sight. But maybe it will be different for you.

ME: I used to believe in that, too, but it hasn't worked out for me, Rene.
Sven is quite possibly the most handsome man I've ever seen, brilliant, and attentive, so why am I holding back? Why aren't I thinking of excuses to justify making out with him or touching him? Is it
because he's *too* perfect?

RA: That's an interesting possibility, Jennifer, and your subconscious
knows whether you would find perfection threatening or sexually
discouraging. There may be another reason, something as simple
as a lack of response to his pheromones, or as complex as your
earliest sexual feelings and experiences. There's even the chance
that your rational mind has become even more dominant than
your emotional mind, and that would be a cause for concern in
light of your personality disorders. But I see that your time is up, so
we'll explore that at your next appointment.

It was the first time that he'd been the one to end our session. When
I said good-bye to him, his smile seemed genuine, and I think mine was,
too.

I don't know if this is a good development, or the first step of complete
mental disintegration.

APRIL 20

Shulky's alert inside me, pleased that she's going out tonight for the interseason runway show by a mysterious new designer. Everyone will be at

Lincoln Center tonight, and Designer X, as he's calling himself, has sent out beautiful, tasteful gowns and ensembles to all the VIP guests, including Shulky.

Ruth had called and said, "This dress is OMG! amazing, and I love it, but it's not quite Shulky's style."

"Is it tight?"

"Most people would consider it a snug fit, but it's a little . . . well, you'll see. It's so fantastic that she has clothes designed especially for her. I'm sure she'll be the center of attention!"

"That's how she likes it."

"I'll have it delivered and left inside your place."

I worked at warp speed all day and by five-thirty, I was out the door and rushing back to my loft. Somehow I'd missed the onset of spring, but it was here and people on the street were cheerful. Everyone seems to be adjusting to the eerie niceness, which has leveled off enough so that tourists still have a fifty-fifty chance at getting cussed out when they ask for directions.

Once home, I unzipped the garment bag that Ruth had sent. The floor-length dress inside was a soft ivory shade and made of a fabric that slipped between my fingers like satin but had a subtle pearly luster. It had been cut on the bias and would move with Shulky. I thought it was one of the most elegant dresses I'd ever seen.

I undressed, breathed out, and then let Shulky take charge. Her strength flowed through me and her good humor washed away my stress. She did a little bump and grind, singing *da-da-da, ta-da-da-da* to a burlesque tune she'd learned from Kat von D.

Then she picked up the pretty custom gown between her thumb and forefinger and said, "Booorring!" and dropped it on the floor. She opened her closet door, grabbed the wicked black Siriano catsuit, and held it in front of her body before wiggling into it. She didn't care that she was expected to wear Designer X's gown to the show. She only cared that the catsuit clung to every curve of her body with the zeal of a drowning man to a lifesaver.

She strapped on violet snakeskin stilettos and posed in front of the mirror. She fluffed the iridescent ebony feather trim at her collar and wrists and said, "Shulky like!"

She was going to do it again, going to cause a disruption at a high-profile event. It wasn't enough that she was superpersona non grata at Fashion Week. There was nothing I could do now but settle in for a night of bad behavior.

She took the elevator down to the subbasement and used the tunnels to run to the Mansion. She didn't bother going into the administrative offices, but stood in the shadows near the garage. When one of the night-time volunteers arrived for his shift at the entrance on an Indian Chief Classic, she stepped forward and said, "Sweet ride! Hey, let me park that for you!"

"She-Hulk!" the biker said in admiration. "Sure, uhm, sure."

"Maybe I'll take it out for a spin first if it's okay with you."

"Well, uh . . ." he began, but she'd already straddled the bike, revved the engine, and said, "Thanks!" And she took off, screaming through a turn, and tearing into the street.

Traffic was backed up, so she jumped the curb and roared down the sidewalk. Pedestrians scattered before her and shouted, "She-Hulk!"

She did a wheelie and waved to her fans, before spotting a moving truck's open loading ramp. Sometimes I wished I could lie down in a backseat like Dahlia and close my eyes, but I watched as Shulky sped up the short ramp. At the very last millisecond, she veered off it and went soaring into the air above a long line of taxis.

She landed on one, its roof caving inward with a loud thunk, and she jumped the bike onto the taxi in front, and another and another, leaving a trail of dented roofs, stunned cabbies, and onlookers who shouted and cheered.

Klieg lights cut through the sky from Lincoln Center, and limos pulled up to the red carpet as fans and reporters watched svelte celebrities arrive, all dressed in ivory gowns and suits provided by Designer X. The crowd parted as Shulky skidded to a stop in front of the TMZ crew.

They rushed forward with their mics and cameras, shouting, "Shulky! Why aren't you wearing Designer X's clothes? Is it true that you've been backbenched by the superheroes and you're now a Superhasbeen and a She-zero?"

She dismounted, tossed back her luxurious hair, and laughed. "As for my ensemble, I don't do discreet, baby. I'd rather be a tasty babe than a tasteful one," she said, chucking the cutest guy under the chin. "Now, do you really think I'm a has-been?"

She stared down at him with her sparkling emerald eyes, and he stuttered, "No, uh, no, of course not!"

"Damn straight. I'm still in the world-saving game, but sometimes a girl wants to take time off and just have some fun."

She posed for the cameras and answered questions about her own ensemble, in no rush because she knew that these shows never started on time. An event coordinator came forward, saying, "Miss Hulk, we're so honored to have you! Didn't you receive your gown? I thought you would be joining Designer X on the runway at the end of the show."

"Tell him thanks for the dress, but it didn't work for me." She looked around at the sea of fashionistas entering the building in their cream clothes. "I don't like to blend in with the herd, moo!"

"We understand, Miss Hulk; however, if you would you reconsider — why not just try on something? I'm sure we can find a, um, shorts and a top that you would like."

"You are assuming facts not in evidence. Now, run along and make sure I have a good seat, preferably next to Karl, if he's here. We have so much to catch up on."

After signing autographs and chatting with Nicki, who was wearing a gold wig, Shulky gave an interview to Melissa and Joan, who asked if she was proud to be at the forefront of the nippleage trend ("Absolutely — it pays to advertise!"), and had a green-eyed smizing competition with Tyra that came down to a draw. When she finally got around to going into the show, the doors were closing, and the gray-suited attendants locked them after her.

Shulky stood in the dark recesses at the back of the hall, still calculating the best seat to get the most attention. She was looking for a spot nearest the only other guest not wearing cream — Karl's black suit was in striking contrast to his magnificent white mane. There was some last-minute seat-changing and Gwyneth sat in the place Shulky had been eying. Then the houselights dropped completely.

Spotlights swirled and then focused on a man coming down the runway. He was dressed in an ivory suit, ivory shirt, and ivory gloves, with a wrestler's face mask, and he was holding a hand mic. He lifted it to his mouth and said, "Welcome to my very first runway show! I'm Designer X, and you'll soon see how my line will radically change the profile of New York fashion! Let's begin the show."

His voice seemed familiar, but Shulky couldn't place him in the fashion world. Then techno began thumping, and she turned her attention to the first tall, thin model, who strode down the runway in fluid cream palazzo pants and a tight matador jacket. She was followed by other high-cheekboned, rail-thin girls wearing streamlined resort wear, street chic, and evening clothes, all in Designer X's signature silky cream fabric. She-Hulk thought they were all as fragile and colorless as cabbage moths.

Finally, a girl in a bride's dress glided down the raised platform, and everyone clapped, except for Shulky, who subscribed to the theory that monochromaticism wasn't style. She turned her attention back to the snowy white head of hair in the front row and was just about to surprise Karl when the entire cast of models came out clapping.

Concluding the procession was Designer X, holding hands with the girl in the bride's gown. But Designer X stopped midway on the runway. He brought a mic to his mouth and shouted, "And now, let the real fat-shion show begin!" and the techno cranked up another decibel.

People looked around expectantly — and then a model screamed as her thighs began expanding within her clothes.

Other models shrieked as their stomachs filled out to giant bellies, and their tiny asses grew to enormous dimensions. The VIP guests, all in their cream clothes, joined in the madness, watching their narrow bodies bloat within the confines of the cream clothes.

The clothes! Everyone who was wearing Designer X's fashions was swelling.

Shulky bounded down the aisle. "It's the clothes! Take off those clothes."

Designer X jeered, "She-Hulk! Working the Ho's-R-Us look as usual. But it's too late. My fat-shions have already transformed all the beautiful people of the fashion industry into jiggly, blubbery beasts! The economy of the state will soon collapse, leaving New York in shambles. And there's nothing you can do about it. In ten minutes, the hideous anatomical changes will be irreversible, and these fashion elites will forever be assumed to want to supersize their greasy fries with that shake. *Sayonara*, you big tacky, Slutsky!"

It was Superbrat again!

She-Hulk roared, "Don't you ever talk trash about French fries!" and leapt over a mass of screaming guests, who plucked helplessly at their cream garments.

When she lunged for Designer X, he giggled maniacally, pressed a button on his jacket, and was jettisoned upward on invisible wires. A panel in the ceiling parted and he flew through it, and then the panel slammed shut.

"Get those clothes off!" Shulky ordered the models and VIPs, who whimpered and cried in their efforts to undress.

The gray-uniformed attendants, fearful of fatfection, struggled to get out of the doors, but they'd been bolted shut.

Anna W. tipped over and rolled down the aisle. She was almost trampled by howling, lumbering models whose tears poured down their plump cheeks. Then Karl, impeccable in his narrow, high-collared shirt and black suit, came forward and said brusquely to Shulky, "The fabric is made using superhuman technology. It's too strong for any of these lovely undernourished girls to rent asunder."

"How strong are you?" she asked.

"Strong enough to wield these Adamantium shears," he said, as he brought out a gleaming pair of scissors and held them aloft in his beringed hand.

"Let's get the clothes off before the fat permanentizes!" Shulky grabbed the closest model by the thin straps of her gown. Shulky flexed her massive shoulders and pulled. The cream fabric resisted for a moment, then ripped. The nearly naked girl looked with horror at her rotund body — and then it deflated like someone letting the air out of a balloon.

The floor shook as other colossal models stampeded toward She-Hulk. Karl snipped away at the cream-colored clothes with disdainful efficiency and sneered, "Synthetic fabrics. I would never dress Claudia in this."

The minutes flew by and Shulky shouted, "Time!" and someone shouted back, "Twenty seconds, nineteen, eighteen . . ."

As the last seconds ticked down, Shulky found a catatonic and roly-poly Victoria wedged between two rows of seats and said, "Tell me what you really, really want," as she ripped off her pantsuit. The style icon shriveled back to her former emaciated frame, opened her eyes, and put her hands on her skeletal rib cage. Then she rose to her knees, saying, "Thank you, thank you!"

Grateful fashionistas clung to Shulky as she strode to the doors and ripped them open. The camera crews outside went hysterical at the sight of half-naked models and celebrities. Shulky left Karl to talk to the reporters, trusting that his comments would be sufficiently eccentric for the both of them.

She turned down a dozen invitations, posed for a few more photos, and got back on the borrowed motorcycle. She returned to the Mansion and filled out a superhuman crime report. In the "additional comments" section, she wrote, "Who is Superbrat and what is his overarching goal? Why did he invite me to this event when he knew the likelihood that I'd foil his evil plan?"

She had just filed the report when she heard voices and laughter coming from the Avengers' living quarters. It sounded like a party and she hesitated in the hallway, wanting to join her old friends and hear about really important battles and intrigue. She wanted to wrestle with superheroes, toss back drinks, and play a round of jetpack lacrosse. She wanted to talk about old times, gossip, and flirt. Suddenly her adventure at the runway show seemed frivolous and inconsequential.

"Time to go home, sweetie," I told her, and instead of fighting me, she nodded and left the Mansion.

11:45 P.M.

Dahlia called and said, "Tell me everything, Miss Thing, and start with Nicki's hairstyle! Fabulous wigs are due for a comeback. Did Shulky get a swag bag?" I felt better by the time we said good night.

APRIL 23

I clicked off the TV this morning when I saw the scrolling newsreel reading, "Has She-Hulk tumbled off the superhero catwalk? Does interseason mean out of style for city's rowdy emerald party girl?" How quickly the media turn on you. One minute, they're encouraging crazy shenanigans and the next they're tut-tutting them.

I was gathering my things for work when I noticed a goldenrod sheet slipped into this journal. I flipped open to Shulky's bookmark and grinned at the cartoon panels of her and Karl battling together at the fatshion show. I liked her version of events, especially when she used Karl's shears to cut off Superbrat's mask, with the caption ". . . only to reveal . . . coming soon!"

I unfolded the goldenrod sheet. It was a flyer from Juliet & Snickers for shows by Fractious Faraday. Bruce is right: I do love a good bar band more than opera. That will change as I become more cultured. I'm sure Sven can teach me to appreciate the finer points of the arts, and I can teach him things, too, once I learn more about his interests. I'll have to figure out a way to introduce knife-throwing into the conversation, because it's loads of fun once you get the hang of it.

My optimistic mood changed as I walked into my office and saw my desk covered in files. Sometimes I wish we'd go back to the days when sending a letter meant making a carbon copy on a typewriter, because then people would think twice before writing a memo.

Genoa and I have been cross-checking and fact-checking every statement and every report on or by ReplaceMax. Donner runs back and forth from the copy room bringing us stacks of printouts and coordinating exhibits.

Every few hours, we take a ten-minute break with the General's Regency-era dolls. I don't know any of the social rules of those times, so she explains them to me. For example, I didn't know that when a property was "entitled," it could only go to a male heir, which meant that a second cousin might inherit an estate and throw out the girls who'd lived there.

"That's fascinating!" I said. "I had no idea these stories were about property law and inheritance. Everyone just talks about the romance."

"The romance is directly tied into property and status," Genoa said. "I've always wished there was a romance novel theme park where visitors could participate by arguing legal cases using chronologically accurate legal principles."

"That's a brilliant idea, Genoa! What lawyer *wouldn't* want to go there on her vacations? I'd book myself into a medieval love story, because medieval law was wonderfully arcane and superstitious. Did you know that medieval courts could arraign bugs for crop devastation? Of course, handing out punishments was not especially effective."

We spent a few minutes discussing names for our imaginary theme park (Tender Discoveries is our top choice!) and features, like a gift shop and carriage rides.

"Excellent! As soon as the case is over, we can work up a prospectus for the park." I picked up a male doll in a checked suit. "I've decided that this guy is a lecherous gambler who has arrived in town planning to poison his sweet rich aunt." In my best English accent, I said, "Ahoy, there, my good lad! Can you fetch my carbuncle from atop the barouche? I will be stopping at this, er, fine stopping place for nuncheon, and I heard you concoct an excellent liver-and-squid pie."

I flounced my doll's coat while waiting for Genoa to respond, but she was looking at something over my shoulder. I turned and saw Amber standing in the doorway with Quinty, who was fiddling with his monocle and trying not to smile.

"I hope I'm not interrupting anything important," the hammerhead said coolly.

Genoa didn't bat an eye. "We were taking a well-deserved break from the avalanche of paperwork."

Quinty looked up. "If I see a Saint Bernard with a barrel of whiskey, I'll steer him your way. How are things progressing?"

"Everything's on track, sir," I said. "We're receiving the expected delay tactics, but we're persistent."

"Very good. Tell me, Jennifer, what's the most important lesson you learned in your legal career?"

"The person with the biggest pile of paper wins."

"Indeed! Enjoy your break."

"Yes, sir."

He walked off, and Amber paused to give us a contemptuous look, then left.

Genoa immediately returned to her doll

"Aren't you intimidated by her?" I asked.

"I'm only intimidated by people I admire, and I don't admire her."

"I heard her singing at the Valentine's Day party. Her voice is so lovely."

"Hmm," Genoa hmmed. "I think that's probably how she got Ellis. I remember her singing at our annual picnic when he was there. But her voice is just technique with no honest emotion. I'd say she's a cyborg, but many cyborgs have soul and heart."

If Ellis liked singing, I never stood a chance with him. I said, "One of my favorite pals at GLKH is an android, and he's terrific. When I was there, the hot topic of discussion was cyborg rights. Holden Holliway, who founded the superhuman division, believes that android, cyborg, and bot identity law will be the single biggest issue of the next century."

"I'm always wondering what makes us human — not biologically human, but human in feeling and thought. How can we justify treating clones as property?"

"Good question. Personally, I don't think it's right to create clones that go into systemic failure and die before they grow out of their toddler years."

"Someone will solve the regeneration problems, and then clone rights won't be a merely theoretical issue," she said. "I've been going to a lecture series on artificial intelligence and alternative personhood."

Donner tapped on the open door and walked in. "That's one of her many obsessions, isn't it, General?"

Genoa blushed and said, "Don't you have work to do?"

"Yes, but I actually have a reason to be here," Donner said and then told me that Sven had asked me to call, but it wasn't urgent.

I returned to my office and called Sven. He picked up on the third ring — not too soon and not too late.

"Hello, Sven, how are you?"

"I only wanted to say that I appreciate all you're doing. I look forward to this being over, when I can return to my research — and also see you on a personal basis."

"Me, too!" I'm sure that after a few more sessions with Rene, I'll fall madly in love with Sven.

"I'm so glad to hear that, Jennifer," he said. "I wondered if you've spoken to your friend She-Hulk recently. I heard about the incident last night with the suspected superhuman. What are they calling him? Superbrat. She's frequently in the proximity of dangerous situations, and I wonder if this could be at all connected with the foiled abduction at Club Nice."

He was sort of making it all about himself, but it was understandable since he'd been the target of the kidnapping attempt. "The NYPD has not made a connection between those incidents, Sven. The trail's gone cold for the nightclub assault — but at least there hasn't been another. As for Superbrat, I think he's an inventive crackpot. Last night's situation was more of a prank. You still have your security team protecting you, right?"

"Of course, just as you advised. I listen very carefully to everything you say, Jennifer. Your opinion is important to me."

My ooky radar began swinging around, probably because I wasn't comfortable with effusive compliments. "Thank you, Sven. I'll be in touch."

MALICIOUS PROSECUTION

APRIL 25

I go to sleep thinking of the case. I dream of the case. I wake up thinking about it. I desperately needed a break from the legal world, and so I took Saturday off and went to a Forestiers fight practice session held in an old ballroom dance studio.

When I arrived, a dozen little girls in leotards were pulling on their tiny jackets and tiny warm-up pants. At that age, my classmates and I always went out with our dance togs on, wanting everyone to see that we were ballerinas. Shooting up six inches in one year had slapped the attitude and coordination right out of me.

The little girls stared at the adults with our Nerf swords, balsa wood shields, and lacrosse helmets decorated with silver foil.

Nelson and Amy were already there, wearing matching vestments made from striped beach towels with crests pinned to their chests.

"You guys look so cute together!" I said. "I hope I'm not embarrassing you."

Amy reached up to tug at my ponytail. "Jen, if wearing a towel poncho doesn't embarrass me, nothing will."

One of the little girls said to her friends, "What a bunch of nerds!"

My friends and I looked at one another and burst out laughing. Nelson said, "Scorn even from the youngest. I'll remember that the next time a kid begs me not to tell his mother that he hasn't been brushing."

We had a fantastic workout. I got to practice several different kinds of injuries and was given great direction for more dramatic stealth attack scenes.

"You've just been smote with a two-headed ax, so we need you to *emote*, Jennifer!"

"I'm emoting smoting! I'm emoting smoting!"

I was having so much fun that I didn't realize our session was over until our leader clapped and thanked us for coming.

I was trying to straighten out my muslin tunic, which had twisted over my coarse cotton leggings, when I heard someone say, "Jennifer?"

I looked up and saw Fritz Durning, holding hands with a darling little girl with white-blond hair who was squinting at me. "Oh, hi, Fritz."

"Jennifer, this is my daughter Maisie. She's staying with me this week."

"Hi, Maisie."

She scrunched her face and said, "You're not a ballerina. Daddy. You said this was a ballet class!"

"I *am* bringing you to ballet." Fritz looked around at the motley crew of mostly young adults in faux medieval garb. "What is this?"

"It's a sword-fighting class for a live action role-playing group."

"You were on the floor," the little girl said. "It's all dirty."

"It's okay for girls to get dirty," Amy said.

"I think so," Fritz replied. "Maisie, go on and say hello to the other girls."

I introduced Fritz to Amy and Nelson, and they did that New York thing of finding out what friends they had in common. Then Amy and Nelson said good-bye, and I was alone with Fritz.

He smiled and said, "You continually surprise me, Jennifer Walters. I wouldn't take you for a LARPer."

"You know about LARPing?"

He laughed and said, "I wasn't always the polished metrosexual you see before you. I still miss those games."

"You can join our team."

"No, you already lured me into Krav Maga, and Azzan thinks I need to practice more. You know, we have some unfinished business."

"Are my sixty days up already?"

"You know they are," Fritz said. "Actually, my ex and I are trying to work out a way to be together."

"So you're rescinding your offer?"

"If I thought you were interested, I'd extend it," he said with a wink. "So who is he, Jennifer — the guy you're hiding?"

"I don't know what you're talking about. I'm not dating anyone."

Fritz held out his arms to display his body and said, "Hon, if you weren't interested in anyone else, you wouldn't pass on all this!"

I started laughing and was saved from a serious response by Maisie, who skipped back with a new friend.

Question 1: Does everyone assume I'm dating someone? Question 2: Whom do they think I'm dating?

2:00 P.M.

Rene has office hours every other Saturday, so I came in, bringing a Joocey Jooce for him and a double latte for me. He sat in his big armchair, looking like a nice hippie grampa, and said, "You handled the situation at Lincoln Center very efficiently. Well, except for stealing the motorcycle, breaking dozens of traffic laws, and damaging all those taxis."

"Thanks, Rene, but that was Shulky, not me."

"Okay, we'll keep working on merging your bifurcated personality," he said. "But Shulky didn't go out afterward and cause a ruckus, and that's a huge improvement. She also collaborated with a former antagonist."

"Thanks, I guess, but I think she's feeling a little down at being left out of things with the other superheroes. She finally goes out to have some innocent fun—"

"Which involved vehicular theft and damage."

"Innocent fun — the bike was a loan — only to have her evening interrupted by Superbrat, who seems to have it in for her. Once again, she saved the city from devastating economic and emotional collapse, and all the media says is that she's a superloser and a She-Hasbeen."

"That hurts your feelings?"

"Yes . . . because I care about her. She's cheerful and brave, and her primary desire in life is to defend the vulnerable."

"I see," he said, sipping thoughtfully on his Joocey Jooce. "Are you ready to talk about your mother's death yet?"

I shook my head. "No."

"Later then, but you have to face the source of your rage or else you'll — Shulky, I mean — will keep acting out inappropriately."

"I will face it, but not just yet." I hoped the calming herbs had worked on him already. "There's something else I'd like to talk about, but you have to promise not to tell anyone."

He looked affronted. "Jennifer, everything you say here as yourself or as She-Hulk is strictly confidential."

"Just confirming that. Okay, you know how you were talking about passion and you brought up 'Flesh-Eating Bacteria Girl'?"

"The Fringe Theory song? It's one of my favorites."

I took a breath and got up my nerve. "Rene, I'm the flesh-eating bacteria girl."

He choked on his smoothie and went into a coughing fit. I got up to pat him on the back until he caught his breath. He gazed up into my face and said, "Holy moley! Seriously? Your green eyes, your long legs, your pert — Of course, you are."

So I told him about meeting Ellis Tesla and having the most passionate weekend of my life, waiting desperately for Ellis to call me, and eventually giving up on him. "Every time I heard one of his songs from the Gin Cycle, it was like a knife turning in my back. I knew it was just a lie because he hadn't called me."

"He might have had a good reason for not calling, and you could have gone to him, Gin. I mean, Jennifer."

"Right, I could have showed up at a concert and hoped he'd pick me out of the crowd again. But what if he didn't? What if he picked out some other girl and told me, 'Hey, it's only rock 'n' roll'?"

"You'll never know, though, because you gave up after leaving one message."

"Everyone gives up after leaving one message," I said, and then I saw him smile. "Except you, Rene. You kept trying to get me to come back here."

"I like a challenge, and you're a challenge," he said warmly. "You overcome resistance in your career, yet you relent so easily in your emotional life. How does She-Hulk feel about Ellis Tesla? Didn't she kiss him at the Club Nice incident?"

"She thinks he's sexy and dynamic."

"*You* think he's sexy and dynamic, Jen."

"It's different because he was interested in her, too. All men are interested in her. Even Victor von Doom has a sick fascination with her," I said. "It's more complicated anyway. Ellis is engaged to my heinous colleague, Amber Hammerhead. I don't stand a chance."

Rene stared at me for a long time while he tugged at his beard and then fiddled with his wooden prayer beads. There was a tapping at his door. "I think we're getting more to the meat of the matter, and we need to continue this discussion, Jennifer, okay?"

"Next time." And I don't know why, but I hugged the crunchy little man before I left.

5:00 P.M.

I went for a run in favorite neighborhoods to look for moving trucks and people vacating apartments. Saturdays are for couples, and that's all I saw — couples holding hands, having drinks at window tables, pushing baby strollers together, carrying groceries . . . While I was looking into a flower shop window, an attractive couple bumped into me as they ran by in their matching gear.

They didn't even say sorry, which meant that things were a little more normal in the city, but I was annoyed. I picked up my pace and passed them easily. I could hear their footsteps behind me, trying to catch up to me, and I turned and ran backward. I smiled and waved at them before leaving them in the dust.

I'm usually not so petty and show-offy, but I feel like I've hit a wall with my resolutions. The prospect of an OMG! amazing boyfriend is not the same as the actuality of one on a Saturday night when everyone else is going out. Even amnesiac superhumans had better social lives than me. I know because Dahlia called to ask me if I thought it was okay for her to have dinner with Adam.

"Absolutely, but go somewhere low-key. He's still got an enemy out there."

"I'm going to his place and he's cooking. Evidently that's one of his talents."

"Be careful, Dahlia, and you can always call me if there's any problem."

"What are you going to do tonight?"

"Work."

"But it's Saturday night."

"I already took the afternoon off and had lots of fun."

"Yes, because you're a sparkling goddess of whimsy. What did you really do?"

"I went to an amazing salon and got a brand-new cut and went blond."

"You didn't! You couldn't! How could you!"

"Kidding! Bye, and be careful, D."

I will enjoy a worthwhile evening of important self-improvement tasks!

- ☑ Filed even my ragged fingernails
- ☑ Folded my towels so the edges all face the same way
- ☑ Threw out all the mini-containers of condiments from takeout meals
- ☑ Ordered recordings of the Three Tenors to be delivered to Bruce

- ☑ Cut up old sheets so I can make cute dish towels from the material
- ☑ Ordered sewing books from Amazon
- ☑ Bid on a sewing machine at eBay
- ☑ Bid on an autographed cast photo of *Wicked*
- ☑ Bid on Fringe Theory's rare *Grilled & Melted* LP

9:00 P.M.

Yippee! Just got a call from Ruth, and I thought it was because I was the only one available for a Saturday night crisis because everyone else was out either saving the world or on a date or both. But she said, "Hi, Jen! Are you still looking for a new place?"

"Yes, I was looking today. Have you heard of something?"

"I have — so long as you don't mind that there's not a lot of natural light. Actually, there's no natural light, but it's totally bombproof. It's huge, completely updated, with high ceilings, two full master suites, an office, a guest bedroom, and an additional bath. The best part is that it's got OMG! amazing secret access to the entire city."

"It sounds too good to be true. What's the rent?"

"Take a seat because this is OMG! amazing! The cost is *nothing*! The apartment is in one of the old subway tunnels and it's available only to superheroes. You can live there for a month or for years. It's completely up to you."

I was standing up and clutching the phone. "How come I haven't heard of it before?"

"Hawkeye built it one of the times the Mansion was wrecked, and you know how he and Shulky are always at each other's throats. It's a fantastic place, fully furnished. I'm sending you pics now."

Her photos showed a luxurious space with an expansive wall of windows and a skyline view. "It's marvelous," I said. "But I'm looking at a panoramic view."

"The windows display time-accurate scenes with artificial sun so you can keep a sense of the day. The space can function as an emergency bunker, and there's a fully equipped personal gym. You can throw bodies around and no one will hear you."

That cinched the deal.

"There's just one thing," Ruth said. "You've got to promise that Shulky won't demolish it."

"That's no problem, because She-Hulk has turned a corner and matured. She's got her wild personality completely under control."

"That's amazing, Jen! I knew you would work things out."

I left a message for Holden that I'd be out of the loft by the end of the month.

I wished that South American soccer announcer could yell, "Goooooooooal!" for me, because I've completed another resolution. As I was writing this, I saw the goldenrod flyer about the bar band at Juliet & Snickers. I suddenly feel energized, and I still have time to score more culture and outside-comfort-zone points.

10:30 PM.

Arrived at Juliet & Snickers wearing new jeans, demi-boots that I can kick off if necessary, a tight black T, and a sixties cropped leather jacket. I'd used Dahlia's four tips to achieve big hair, which actually require fourteen steps and three products, and applied extra mascara and dark liner so my eyes would look sexy behind my glasses.

A homemade poster announcing FRACTIOUS FARADAY LIVE! was in the window. The crowd filled the sidewalk, no one bothering to stand in line. I edged forward, inextricably drawn by the band, even though the sound was muddled on the street.

The bouncer waved at me, saying, "Squeeze yourself in, stretch."

Once I was inside the jam-packed bar, the noise coalesced into music, which I recognized yet didn't recognize. Because Ellis Tesla was at the front of the small stage looking as if he'd stepped right out of my fantasies and memories, with his thick brown hair mussed up, wearing a vintage Laika and the Cosmonauts T-shirt and beat-up jeans.

He said, "This is a new one. It's about how we delude ourselves about the one that got away. It's called 'Incomplete Data,'" and then the lead guitarist let loose with a surf rock intro, and Ellis began to sing in that tequila-and-gravel voice that made all my girly parts thrum.

> *An individual incident*
> *Is not a valid set of information*
> *But I extrapolated*
> *Arriving at the wrong destination*

And when he sang the next line, the crowd roared as they recognized who he was.

> *That green-eyed bacteria girl*
> *Threw me into confusion*
> *When I lost her, I thought I'd lost a dream*
> *But she was only my delusion*
> *Because she isn't what she seemed*
> *Because she's hard and cold and mean*
> *Because I wasted all that time*
> *Singing Gin with every rhyme*
> *Because infection wrecked my brain*
> *I didn't even know her name.*
> *I don't care, don't care, won't care*
> *Anymore 'bout that green-eyed girl.*

It was at that moment that he stood at the edge of the stage, leaning out over the first row of the audience. He looked around and he saw me and jerked back as if he'd been struck. There was a second when we were caught in each other's gaze. And then he sang directly to me, about me, and I felt a deep, overwhelming ache as my heart broke all over again, just as it had when I'd realized he was never going to call me.

Don't care, don't care, won't care
Anymore.
A woman who is real's worth far more
Than someone who never was what I thought
Shouldn't have extrapolated
With insufficient data because
That green-eyed girl was only a brief, wild ride
And I've got a long journey ahead.
Don't care, don't care, won't care
Anymore about her.

There was a moment of silence, and then the crowd started clapping and hooting, and I turned and pushed my way out of the club, shoving people aside as I said, "Sorry, sorry, sorry!"

I broke through the cluster crowding the door and I was out on the sidewalk. I rushed forward, trying to breathe, but it felt as if my throat had closed up and my lungs had collapsed. I blinked to stop the tears and told myself, *Don't cry, don't cry!* Because I never ever cried in public. I never ever showed my pain or loneliness, but now tears blinded me.

I swiped at them and bumped into someone, who said, "Watch it, ma'am!"

I began running. I ran until my muscles burned and a heel broke off on cracked pavement. I ran thinking of how Ellis had once gazed into my eyes and told me he loved me and how I'd told him, "I love you, Ellis Tesla, and I always will," and then he'd kissed me all over and I'd tried to show him with my body how much I cared for him, how he was everything to me.

But he'd never answered my message.

I stood at the edge of the curb and slammed my good heel against it until it broke off, and then I turned toward home. My entire body prickled with Shulky inside, her soul raging and furious like a caged animal, but this time I wouldn't let her out. This time I would endure my misery until I overcame it . . . and overcame misplaced, undeserved feelings for an Ellis Tesla who had only existed in my imagination.

Because the real Ellis only used me as fodder for his songs.

Because Ellis Tesla is as false as his name.

11:50 P.M.

In bed with the blanket over my head. I am cried out, having gone through a box of tissues, and now at least able to breathe regularly again. It's just a song. It doesn't mean anything. I don't care, don't care, won't care anymore for Ellis Tesla. There is only Ellis Quintal IV, and he's a cold-blooded bastard.

I'd rather face down Dr. Doom, because VvD is always honest about his desire to exploit others.

MITIGATING
CIRCUMSTANCES

APRIL 26

VALENTINE'S DAY RESOLUTIONS
STATUS

On track to accomplish every goal. All it took was proper planning to dramatically improve the quality of my life.

I have successfully not fixated on Ellis. In fact, I go for extended periods of time without looking for Fractious Faraday videos, reading their fan page, or checking on my eBay bid for Fringe Theory's LP.

I'm glad I saw him on the same day that I found out about my new living space because now I can move on both physically and metaphorically. I'm sure Rene will be impressed when I tell him. I wish I had time for a session because we've got so much to talk about.

I've moved enough to know that it always takes longer than you think, requires more cardboard boxes than you have, needs more trips than you first calculated, and no matter how careful you are, you'll lose and forget possessions. However, after the last calamity at the Mansion, I hadn't acquired much besides my clothes and Shulky's more extensive wardrobe. Ruth sent over a van to collect my boxes at 7:30 a.m.

At 8:00 a.m., I met Ruth on Fifth, a block away from the Mansion, with my last duffel bag of gear.

She was wearing pink pleated khakis and a sherbet-yellow polo and looking a little more nervous than usual as she led me to a plain steel door between two buildings.

"I thought I knew all the secret doors in the city," I said.

"No one knows all of them — well, except Tony, but he's a genius!" When Ruth opened the door, I saw a room with trash bins and other debris. She closed the door, flicked a switch, and the entire room began descending.

"You will love this place, Jen! It's super special."

"I'm glad to be able to move before my next case goes to court, because it takes up every second," I said. "Is everything okay?"

"Sure, absolutely! Here we are!" She opened the door and we stepped onto a brick walkway that ran alongside two sets of rails.

Antique gas lanterns were fitted up with modern lights, so I could see the roughness of the stone-block walls. I knew about the ancient tunnels, which ran beneath the modern subway, but I hadn't been in them before. I took a sniff. "The air smells fresh."

"The ventilation is modern. It's this way."

I followed her, and the tunnel opened up to an old station platform where a compact, shiny single-car train was parked. Ruth explained that the train ran on perpetual energy and hovered just above the rails. "You can use the Solomobile in any tunnel because it's synched into the system to prevent collisions. Once it's running, the invisibility shield engages."

I looked around and saw that the station platform was walled off with opaque glass that shimmered as a thin sheet of water fell down over it.

"Oh, I should have mentioned the waterfall wall!" Ruth said. "Isn't it pretty?"

"It's lovely — but where's the apartment?"

"Right behind it. The wall isn't really glass. You could drive a tank through it, but it's better if Shulky doesn't try, okay?" She went to a post set into the platform and entered a code on its panel. Then she placed her hand against a bio reader on the wall. "You know what a security nut Hawkeye is. He's very protective of this space."

The waterfall parted, and a section of the wall slid open to reveal an open concept space that looked like the presidential suite of a fancy hotel.

Ruth told me the code and said, "Your handprint and Shulky's will unlock the door. Oh, you'll be so close to the Mansion! We can see each other all the time."

I dropped the duffle bag on a fifteen-foot-long sofa. All the furniture was elegant but sturdy looking, and there weren't any easy breakables, like glass knickknacks, or any easy ruinables, like white carpets. It was the sort of place where I wouldn't have to worry about accidentally trashing anything. "Ruth, you're amazing. This place is terrific!"

"I know you'll never want to leave," she bubbled.

"It's the most perfect apartment ever for me!" I said, as I sank into a leather armchair that was deep enough to be comfortable for my long legs.

6:30 P.M.

Dahlia helped me give the GLKH loft a final going over, and she was excited about my new place, which she insisted on calling "your underground lair" in a deep voice. She was wearing bright pink contact lenses, and I kept staring at them and looking away because they made her look a little inhuman.

I told her, "I'll have you over to my fab new bachelorette pad soon. I can take you down in a private elevator, and I'm going to cook an international gourmet dinner, which isn't one of my resolutions, but I'm going to add cooking to my goals since I'm accomplishing so much already. I'm also going to learn how to sew so that I can upcycle clothes that Shulky rips. I'm trying to be more green. I mean, you know what I mean."

"Please, poodle, don't worry about becoming a Holly Homemaker for me. Experiment on another victim first. Where were you last night? Adam and I wanted to meet up with you."

"Well, um."

"Shut up! Did you do the sideways Viennese waltz with Dr. Stunning?"

I looked at her. "D, that's the first time you've ever made sex sound less dirty than it is."

She looked as confused as I felt. "That's weird, isn't it? Well, you're not giving me any repressed urges to riff on. Or maybe I don't have any repressed urges to riff on."

"Maybe you're not repressed because Adam has released your repression — and please don't tell me anything explicit or graphic."

"Oh, Jen, he's the sweetest, smartest, most wonderful man I've ever met! I don't even care if he self-cuts his hair, *that's* how much I like him. Rodney loves him, too. He's becoming part of Adam's pack."

"I'm so happy for you, D," I said and ruffled her hair, which was fuchsia to match her freaky eyes. "But be careful. Humans who hang around superhumans often get caught in the crossfire or used as hostages in criminal enterprises."

"I've been around you since frosh year and nothing bad has ever happened to me."

"Not yet, and I hope it won't. Just be careful, hon."

Although I'd liked living in this executive loft, I'd held back from settling in because it wasn't really mine. We went from room to room, opening every cupboard and drawer to make sure I hadn't missed anything. I found an old piece of dry fruitcake on a high shelf in She-Hulk's closet, with a man's banana hammock thong. D and I both said, "Eww, gross!" and I threw them away and washed my hands with lots of soap and hot water.

D said, "How did Claude, your former potential future love of your life, take the news that you're leaving?"

"He said I'm his nicest tenant and that he'll miss me and my statuesque green girlfriend. And I thought I was being so sly. He said he won't forget me."

"Speaking of forgetting, you didn't tell me where you went last night."

"Erm, I was packing."

She caught me in her mesmerizing pink gaze, and against my will, I told her about going to the bar and discovering Ellis and his new band. She emitted a lot of OMGs and shut-ups, and she wanted me to call him and demand to know what it all meant, and I told her it meant that he hated me and his songs were full of shit, and that I'd wasted years fantasizing about someone who was a jackass. A really, really, smoldering hot jackass.

Maybe I associate jackassedness with hotness, e.g., Tony, which is why I'm not burning with desire for Dr. Stunning — who's a gentleman and a scholar.

I really need to see Rene and talk about this stuff.

Bruce called to congratulate me on my new place.

B: It's got a great gym.

ME: Does everyone know about Hawkeye's secret pad except for me?

B: Don't make this all about you, Jen. I give you six months max before She-Hulk destroys it.

ME: Ha-ha. It's indestructible.

B: Don't underestimate her, because I don't. Make it four months.

ME: You ought to get together with Holden Holliway. He likes to make bets about how long it will take me to go back to superhuman law at GLKH. Guess what? I located one of the new superhumans! He's a really nice guy, but he can't remember who he is or what happened to him. He already helped Shulky out, though, with that moonbeam raygun.

B: Watch out. He might get his memory back and discover he's a murderous maniac.

ME: I really hate when that happens, but I got a very sweet vibe from him.

B: You and your vibes, California girl. What kind of vibe do you get from your new boyfriend, Dr. Douchebag?

ME: Oh, I wanted to mention that I'm going to learn how to sew. You can give me all your wrecked clothes and I'll make quilts out of them or something.

MAY 1

I can't believe how quickly time has flown by. This morning our QUIRC team — Amber, Genoa, Quinty, and I — marched up the steps to the courthouse. Sven and his security guards arrived by separate car.

Reporters were waiting for us and shouting at me, "Jennifer! Jennifer! Will She-Hulk come to cheer you on or give you legal advice?"

"No, she reserves her appearances for cases of superhuman law."

"Jennifer! Do you have any clues about the identity of the superhuman who built the moonbeam raygun, shot the water spheres cannon, or created the fatshions?"

"The NYPD and investigators at the Mansion are still looking into the incidents, and you can address your questions to them."

"Do you think Dr. Doom is involved?"

The hammerhead had paused on the steps, and now she glared at me as if I was responsible for getting all the attention. I said, "While these do resemble Doom scenarios, Victor von Doom's work has a mad genius's skillfulness and catastrophic results. It's never this amateurish."

Amber moved to step in front of me, flipping her blond hair in my face. "Now, if there are no more questions about the ReplaceMax case . . ." she said, and her honeyed tone soothed the frenzied reporters.

I followed her into the courthouse and resisted the urge to wrap her hair in my hand, lift her up, and wring her out like a wet towel in a locker room. Because I am a mature professional.

We selected a jury, which is both tedious and terribly important because we needed people who could grasp the basics of cloning and bioengineering. I excused anyone who was interested in celebrity. Max Kirsch's lead attorney, Melissa Christoph, and I were both looking for jurors who were sympathetic to organ transplants — that was the easy part because most people knew of someone who needed or might need an organ.

I ran into Melissa in the ladies' room during a break, and we caught up on news about friends and family.

"It's going to get ugly. I'm going to go after you like a junkyard dog after a T-bone," Melissa said. "I've told my tween not to watch the news, so she doesn't hate me more than she already does."

"Give me what you got, because I'm gonna make you roast like a drunk arsonist with a can of gasoline and a lumberyard," I said. "I'm glad I don't have to deal with angry kids, Missy, but I have acquaintances who aren't happy I took the case."

"It could be worse. We could be going against She-Hulk in court. I'm too old and slow to duck flying furniture."

We both laughed until we got to the door, and then we put on somber, serious attorney faces.

9:00 P.M.

I avoided my phone by working out on the punching bag in my awesome new gym. It's not the same as Azzan scolding me, but Fritz has become his new favorite student, so at least Azzan isn't lonely. I groaned when my phone buzzed again, but then I saw that the call was from Holden.

"Holden, hi!"

"Hi, Jen. Congratulations on getting Hawkeye's place. I've been to a lot of great poker games there."

"Am I the only one who didn't . . . ?" I began, but it was obvious everyone else knew about the underground lair. "I'll have a housewarming when this case is over."

"How's Missy?"

"Her son is going to be Scrooge in his school's *A Christmas Carol*, so she's got a personal incentive to wrap up things by December."

"Tell her hi for me. Are you tired of human law yet?"

"No."

"Just thought I'd check!"

Spent the rest of the night practicing my opening statement in the mirror, until I knew it by heart.

Resisted looking up the Fractious Faraday schedule. Songs are make-believe and I have to deal with real life.

MAY 2

The first actual day of trial was exhausting. I felt energy buzzing through me as I gave my opening statement. It's different than the energy I get transforming, but it's still a sweet high, marred only by the fact that Ellis Quintal was sitting in the courtroom glowering at me.

He was so tall that the bailiff asked him to move to the back row. He'd grown his hair longer and had a beard, which made him look even more like his piratical lumberjacky self and threw me off my game just enough to miss a few beats.

"The jury will be shown how Matthew, I mean, *Maxwell* Kirsch brazenly rejected Dr. Sven Morigi's warnings that the organs were detected. *Defective*. The organs were defective." I took a breath to calm myself. I kept my gaze away from Ellis and hit my stride, letting my statements build upon one another until the entire courtroom was transfixed by me.

As I sat down at the plaintiff's table, Amber met my eyes for a second and turned away, but Sven gave me an encouraging smile.

When I looked around, I saw that Ellis was gone.

The emotional high faded once I left the courtroom. I took a long walk before heading down to my subterranean lair. It was really fun to watch the waterfall part and the door slide open to my awesome new pad. After I'd flopped onto the couch, I checked my phone.

Jordy had texted me. "I need yr help. Not important cept 2 me. Bring burgers fries shakes."

I was happy that Jordy wanted burgers, because that meant he was feeling well, and I was complimented that he'd ask me, Jennifer Walters, for help when I knew he idolized Shulky. Maybe he'd decided to go into suspended animation and wanted me to draw up the paperwork. Or maybe he needed advice about transferring his brain into an android body.

I changed into running pants, a sports bra, and a hoodie, and I called in a to-go order for burgers. I used my aPhone's locator to guide me through the old tunnels and climbed a ladder to go to the surface. I picked up our food and was soon in Jordy's room.

So was Ellis. He was leaning against the wall of windows strumming a ukulele, and when he saw me, he said, "What are you—"

Jordy sat up in bed. "Hi, Jenny. Thanks for coming. Big E, I asked her here because you can't help me."

"I can help you with whatever you want, Jordy," Ellis grumbled. "You haven't asked me to help you with anything."

"Okay, teach me how to dance," Jordy asked Ellis. "We've got a dance here on Saturday, and one of the candy stripers asked me. Tanya." Jordy looked at me and said, "I need to know how to old-people dance." He saw the bag in my hand. "Big E hasn't eaten yet."

I handed the bag to Ellis, who held it as if it contained poisonous snakes. "Go ahead. They're the most delicious burgers in the city according to my best friend."

"Yeah, go ahead, Big E," Jordy said. "We had mac and cheese tonight and I had seconds, but I'll take a shake, chocolate if you got it."

I handed him a drink.

Ellis opened the bag and unwrapped a burger as if it was his final meal. We ate in silence, until Jordy said, "So, Jenny, can you teach me? I have a slow jam mix." He held up a player and a portable speaker.

"Let me finish my burger and I'll teach you to two-step. It's really easy."

"I already got an okay from my doc," Jordy said, and buzzed for the nurse. "Jenny, I've been investigating that strange pretty dude you're representing, Slime Mold Rug Guy."

I shot a look at Ellis, who shrugged and said, "His nickname, not mine."

292 · MARTA ACOSTA

"Dr. Sven Morigi," I said to Jordy.

"That's what I said: Dirtbag Slime Mold Rug Guy." Jordy exchanged a grin with Ellis. "Something's not legit with him."

"I appreciate your concern, but he's a very well-respected bio engineer."

"Yeah, that's what the internets say, but they're whack, like they say there's no Sasquatch, when he lives just outside Duluth."

I didn't disagree, because I'd spent a really nice Thanksgiving at Sas's wonderful lakefront home.

Jordy tossed his paper cup into a trash bin and said, "If you lift the top layer off Slime Mold Rug Guy and look beneath, it's all wonky."

"Jordy," I said. "Please don't tell me that Ellis has you hacking into sites to discredit my client. Dr. Morigi's credentials are unassailable."

"I haven't done a thing," Ellis said. "Jordy acted on his own."

"Like I believe that," I said, trying to smeer.

"Big E didn't ask me to check, Jenny, and you're right that this stuff is unsailable — it would sink like a bag of rocks. You gotta watch your back with Dirtbag Slime Mold Rug Guy."

I glared at Ellis, then moved out of the way for the nurse, who was the same guy who'd let Shulky take Jordy to the roof.

The nurse skillfully removed Jordy's IV and said, "He's doing great this week. You can use the community room. No one's there now."

Jordy wanted to walk, but Ellis said, "Save your energy for the ladies, dude," and helped him into a wheelchair.

As we made our way down the hall, Jordy said, "Tanya's into smart guys. She dated a guy at Columbia so she could sit in on his classes. She wants to be an astrophysicist and she made me cupcakes for Valentine's Day. She's pretty and she likes to laugh."

"She sounds great," I said.

The community room had one low light on. The windows outside showed the sparkling skyline. I loved the Manhattan skyline even better when it was real and not a projected image in my underground bunker.

Ellis said, "Okay, I'll see you later, Jordy."

"E, you said you'd teach me to dance, and I need you to help me back to my room later."

"I thought Jenny was going to teach you. Just don't count on her to show for follow-up lessons."

I stared so hard at the side of Ellis's head that I thought he should feel my anger burrowing like a weevil through his brain. "I'm extremely reliable, Jordy. I can provide references. But someone has to actually be interested enough to call me, or I won't know that he, um, needs a dance lesson."

Ellis's rough voice was cold. "What if someone wanted a dance lesson but was unable to call? A concerned teacher would try to find out why a student was absent."

Jordy made a face. "Why do adults always talk in code? Yo, dying kid here! Am I going to have to call the Make-A-Wish Foundation because you two have issues?"

Ellis and I broke off our staring contest and looked at Jordy, who said, "You guys have to show me how it's done, so, Big E, slow-dance with Jenny so I can watch your feet and stuff."

"I'm sure she doesn't want to dance with me," Ellis said flatly.

"Why not? You're acting like a complete dick, but I know you're not a douche."

I started laughing, and Ellis slowly smiled and said, "Jenny might disagree."

He'd called me Jenny again!

Jordy was scrolling through his playlist. "I'm finding the right song. My uncle gave me this playlist of old-school stuff. Go ahead."

Ellis breathed out loudly through his nose, an exasperated sound, and held out his arms. I stepped to him and put my hand in his large one, sending a current through me. My heart thumped faster when he placed his other hand on my back.

Jordy clicked on the music, and we heard the tinkly intro of a cover to "The Closer I Get to You." I felt like I was in a motel lounge.

Ellis took a step to one side and I followed him, robotically.

My voice was pitched too high when I said, "The basic two-step is very easy, Jordy. Step together, step." I could feel the heat from Ellis's hand on my back. I smelled his woodsy aftershave. I saw his dark eyes shining in the dim room.

Then I heard a squeaking sound and began to turn, but Ellis kept hold of me.

The nurse was taking Jordy out of the room in his wheelchair. "Sorry, the doctor dropped by for his rounds and wants to check Jordy's vitals. I'll bring him right back."

Ellis took another few steps and I followed him. "Jenny, I think we've been conned by a teenager."

"Why?"

"He doesn't like Amber and thinks I should be with someone taller."

We kept dancing awkwardly, and I said, "Why doesn't he like Amber?"

"She's not exactly cuddly [significant pause] *obviously*. Why don't you like her?"

"You're assuming that I don't. Do you think he's coming back?"

"No idea. This song is awful."

"The song you sang the other day was awful," I said and felt the tension in his body. And that's when the music player made a clicking sound, and then we heard the plaintive notes of an oboe.

I yanked back, but Ellis held on tight and pulled me close. "He's not coming back," I said, panicked.

"It doesn't matter," Ellis said as the music swelled and Karen Carpenter's pure contralto sang out the words that I'd cried to for months: "*I fell in love with you before the second show . . .*"

I hid my face against his shoulder so he wouldn't see my anguish.

"You said you loved me, Gin."

"You never called me!" My voice was muffled by his shirt. "We promised to call each other, and I called you and left a message, but you *never* called me. I waited and you never ever called." I tried to stop the tears, but the music took me straight back to those lonely nights.

"Oh, babe," he murmured. "I didn't know you'd called and I didn't have your number. The guys pranked me by stealing my phone, dunking it in liquid nitrogen, and then using it to skeet shoot."

A puzzle piece fell into place. "That's what 'Forged by Fire' meant about mischief pulling."

He laid his head against mine, and his arms wrapped around me, pulling me close. "Yes. I wrote all those songs for you because it was the only way I knew to find you. I looked for you at every show. I trolled fan sites hoping to see your name, and I checked the band's mail compulsively. I roamed the halls of USC's law school asking people if they knew Genevieve, until campus security told me not to come back."

"UCLA. Jennifer."

"You should have corrected me then."

"I thought it was your East Coast accent, and most of the time you didn't say my name. You said . . . other things."

"Why didn't you get in touch when you heard the songs, *your* songs?"

"I thought they were just songs. I thought Gin was anyone, any girl."

He pulled back to look me in my face. My glasses were steamed up and smeared from my tears, and he took them off and set them on a ledge. "But, Gin, songs are *everything*. You weren't any girl. You were *the* girl. You were everything."

"I didn't know. . . . I thought I was a weekend hookup."

"No, you were the one who told me I was cataclysmic. You were the one who told me that I made others understand the excitement of science. It's because of you that I didn't go into high-tech law and started Manic Quantum Mechanics. You were the one who inspired my music. You're the one, Gin, you're the one."

"You said you didn't care anymore."

"I lied. I care. I can't stop caring." He pulled me close again. "And now it's too late."

"Because you're engaged to Amber."

"Yes. I gave up hoping for you," he said, and his hand dropped lower on my back and he pulled me tighter to him.

296 • MARTA ACOSTA

My sexual brain was thinking: *I want to bang him harder than the porch door.*

My logical brain was thinking: *Why is he telling me this at the very time that I'm leading the lawsuit against his pal and former drummer?*

My ethical brain was thinking: *It's entirely wrong to rub up against an engaged man.*

Logic won out, and I stepped away just as the song ended. "Ellis, I find it reprehensible that you're using our past to manipulate me on the ReplaceMax case." I grabbed my smeared glasses and put them on, which made everything blurrier, a metaphor for my situation.

"Are you that cynical?" he said angrily. "Of course you are. I can't believe I was falling for your sweet lost nerd act again. Because if Quinty put you as lead on the case, it means you're even harder and tougher than Amber, but at least Amber takes ownership of her ambition."

"That sounds like love to me!" It didn't make any sense, but I wasn't in a courtroom, so it didn't have to. "I hope you two have a wonderful life together in your stupid brownstone with your perfect kids, Tripper and Emily! Oh, and if you need a rhyme, I've got one for you that goes with bad luck! And my name is *Jen*. It's always been Jen, and you might hear more clearly if your head wasn't stuck so far up your ass."

My anger and pain impelled me forward, and I ran for miles before descending to the tunnels of the subway. I couldn't remember ever yelling at anyone like that. I couldn't remember ever being that angry and not shifting into She-Hulk.

I really need to have some sessions with Rene, if only because I need to tell someone how much I hate hate hate Ellis Tesla.

WORDS AND PHRASES
LEGALLY DEFINED

MAY 9

I've gone over the next day, May 3, a kazillion times. I'd spent the night tossing and turning, and resisting the urge to transform into She-Hulk, find Ellis, and beat him to a pulp. But I always tell clients, "Impulsive action is motivated by emotion, not reason, and the momentary satisfaction soon wears off, while more judicious behavior will have long-term benefits." I kickboxed the punching bag until my arms and legs were shaking, which made me tired, but no less angry.

I fell into bed and had finally gone to sleep when my alarm went off.

My limbs felt heavy as I showered, dressed, and brushed my hair. I had dark shadows under my eyes, which reminded me of how Mavis's eyes looked when I first met her. I should have visited Mavis last night instead of being ensnared in drama with horrible hateful Ellis.

I had a few spare minutes before I had to go to the courthouse, so I called the hospice. "Mavis Bertoli's room, please."

I heard the other end of the line *click-click*, and then a woman said dully, "This is Bobbie Bertoli."

"Hi, Mrs. Bertoli. This is Jennifer Walters. I wanted to say hello to Mavis because I won't be able to come to story time today."

I heard a deep intake of air. A few seconds later, she said, "Mavis slipped into a coma a few hours ago. She's not going to make it out." Then there was another intake of air and a sob. "My poor baby's battle is almost over."

Then she hung up.

I bent over and gasped. I heard myself say, "I thought I had time."

I don't remember going to the courthouse. I just remember standing at the front of the witness box, and Max Kirsch was on the stand. That's how insanely confident he and Ellis were that I had no chance of winning the case — there was no way Missy Christoph would have let him take the stand if he hadn't insisted — and I wanted to wipe the self-righteous expression right off Max's face. I would prove to Ellis that he was wrong . . . about everything.

I remember holding up an eight-by-ten of Mavis playing by a duck pond and asking: "Mr. Kirsch, were you aware that Mavis Bertoli, an eight-year-old recipient of a ReplaceMax heart, went into a coma this morning and is not expected to survive?" I remember the silence in the room, and how I felt hot tears running down my face and how I didn't care that everyone saw me weeping.

My blood rushed through my veins, and Shulky raged inside me, wanted to get out and break things, hurt people, but I pressed her back down, and attacked the defendant with questions and facts, spitting them out so fast he didn't have time to answer, reciting dates, test results, analysis from the AMA, doctors' reports . . .

I was aware of Max dropping his head in his hands and sobbing, "I'm sorry, I'm so sorry!" and then the judge slammed his hammer down and said, "I'm calling a recess. Counsel, chambers please," and Genoa came to me and took me by the arm. I tasted the salt of my tears on my lips. My glasses were fogged and shapes moved in front of me and conversation sounded as if I was overhearing it through a wall and I was really all by myself in a room, alone and unable to help anyone, let alone Mavis.

I remember feeling numb as I watched Missy confer with Max and then come forward and say, "My client would like to settle for the full amount of your suit."

I remember the blinding lights of cameras, and reporters shouting questions. I moved through them without speaking. I stepped away from Sven, who tried to embrace me before he was pulled away by Amber and back toward the reporters.

I remember walking by Ellis. Our eyes met, and I thought for one second that he understood my deep sorrow, but I also saw the fury in his expression.

I walked to the closest secret passageway and descended into my underground lair.

I routed my calls to Ruth and put my aPhone under a sofa cushion so I wouldn't see it. I didn't turn on the television or my computer. Food tasted like sawdust, and the artificial light in the room hurt my eyes. I changed the setting to dusk and let it remain there.

At some point, I called Quinty and asked for a leave of absence.

"Of course. You've earned it, Jennifer. Take a week or even two, and come back refreshed. I know this has been difficult for you."

Eventually, I checked my messages. Bruce had called, so I sent him a text saying I'd contact him soon. Dahlia had left a dozen messages and told me she'd come whenever I needed her. Holden's message said, "Congratulations, Jen, and I'm sorry about your little friend. Call me when you're ready."

I spent a day in bed with the blanket over my head. I spent the next several days working out. One night I shifted into Shulky, and she ran through the tunnels, pounding on the walls, and shouting her inchoate grief. She didn't want to go to any parties.

I always tell my clients, "Think of your long-term plans. Don't let one failure deter you from achieving your ultimate goals." So I got up, took a shower, and got dressed. My ultimate goal was to help people, and I wouldn't accomplish that by hiding in the dark.

When I walked into the QUIRC lobby, the receptionist grabbed the phone. Within seconds, all of the attorneys and staff were standing around and clapping. I gave one of those fake smiles that I used to use on Rene. Note to self: return Rene's calls.

As I passed Fritz's office, he said, "Great win, Jennifer!" and patted my back.

Fresh flowers were in my office. Donner was dressed in a wide-lapel suit with high-waisted bell-bottoms and an orange polyester shirt with a wide collar. His hair was picked out into a short Afro, and he was four inches taller in platform shoes. A sky-blue IBM Selectric typewriter had replaced the older one hooked to the computer.

He brought me a latte and asked, "Are you all right?"

I nodded. "Yes, I'll be fine." Curiosity overcame my ennui, and I said, "Okay, I have to ask. Why did you skip ahead thirty years?"

He smiled slyly. "I keep slips of paper in a fish bowl at home. Every six months, I pick out one. Last week the paper said 1977. Genoa and I do the Hustle under a disco ball after dinner every night."

Laughing felt great, as if a tight band around my lungs had been loosened.

I began going through my backlogged work. Dr. Stunning had called several times, and I was ready to call him back. Now I could appreciate him truly, because he wasn't a major jackass, nor was he a douche, nor had he lied to me or tried to manipulate me.

"Sven, hi, this is Jennifer. I apologize for being out of touch."

"Don't concern yourself. Quinty explained that you were taking a respite. I'm delighted you called, though. I'd really like you to accompany me to the International Bioethicists Gala tonight."

"Oh." I had somehow forgotten that we were celebrating a win.

"My dear, I think it will do you good to spend time with men and women who can comprehend the difficulty of upholding ethical standards in medicine. I know they would like to meet the woman who set an example for all bioengineering companies that greed at the expense of humanity will never be tolerated. Please say you'll come."

"Of course, I'll come. I'll meet you there. Tell me when and where."

"Tamborlaine Towers at seven p.m., in the penthouse ballroom."

A gala meant dressing up. Even though Sven had told me he came from humble beginnings, he seemed like the kind of cultured man who dated ladies who wore tiaras to soirees and jodhpurs to ride to hounds. I didn't own any tiaras, but I did have access to a follicular genius.

After work, I went straight to Arrested Youth and looked through the front window at D chatting to a client as she removed the foil from a strand of hair and set her back under a dryer.

When I went in, Dahlia saw my reflection in her mirror, whirled around, and shrieked, "Jen!"

She hugged me so tight I said, "Let go — you're going to squish the insides out of me like a Twinkie."

"OMG, I was beginning to think I'd have to file a missing persons report!" She asked her manager to finish with the client and dragged me to the break room. "What is going on with you? Why have you gone AWOL and MIA?"

"I couldn't cope with Mavis, the little girl's, situation so I stayed in my underground lair, worked out, and ate cereal for every meal."

"Did you watch sappy movies?"

"No, I watched a few shows with irate judges. No one was giving very good legal advice, but I really liked the way cases were wrapped up in twenty-minute segments. Also, I liked the *dum-ta-dum* music, which I wish we had in real trials."

"I feel selfish because while you were miserable, I was with Adam. He makes the best buttermilk waffles I've ever tasted. He can do the crossword puzzle in less than five minutes in pen. Well, so can I, but he doesn't make up words. He is training his dogs for search-and-rescue work and he has taken up art. He's sculpting a life-size statue of me in marble."

"That's ambitious for a beginner."

"He's incredible."

"Speaking of incredible, I need to look that way. Can you help me with my hair and makeup? I'm going to a gala with Dr. Stunning tonight, and in a matter of weeks, we'll be madly in love and I can cross that boyfriend resolution off my list."

Dahlia grinned and gave me one of her affectionate hip bumps. "OMG, soon we'll both be madly in love with fantastic men!"

EVENING

Since Sven hadn't seen my dark crimson dress, I wore that. I upended my tote on the table and threw things into an oversize velvet clutch: walking slippers, my aPhone, money and a credit card, mints, lipstick. I found the three-pack of condoms that Shulky had left for me and tossed those in, too.

I spotted the Swiss Army knife that Patty Palmieri discovered at Superbrat's crime scene, and added it to the bag. I might need the scissors to snip a loose thread, or the file to smooth out a nail, or maybe Sven and I would steal away with a bottle of wine and need the corkscrew attachment.

I'd only tried out the Solomobile once, but I didn't want to ruin my heels on the stone surface of the subway, so I got in the car and logged in my destination. The car lifted gently and then swiftly carried me through the tunnels toward Tamborlaine Tower. After a minute, a hidden wall opened and the train moved up to a newer section of rail. The invisibility shield kept anyone from seeing us, and I saw commuters' confusion when they felt the rush of wind as we went by. The train dropped back down to an older section of tunnel and stopped at an ancient station.

I went to a shiny new door, ID'd myself with a palm print, and an elevator opened and took me to the street level. I walked out between two buildings, and the door shut behind me.

The Tower was only half a block away, and I could see limos and classic Town Cars waiting to drop off guests. I was relieved that this was not a tiaras and jodhpurs crowd, but a geeky glasses and happy nerd group.

I went up to the penthouse, which was filled with cheerful, chatting scientists.

A woman with permed gray hair noticed me and said, "You're Jennifer Walters! You just won the lawsuit against ReplaceMax."

Others heard her and came to say hello. I was so busy answering their questions that I couldn't get to Sven, but he came forward and said, "You must excuse me, but I would like to welcome my marvelous date to this wonderful event."

He was wearing a black suit that fit perfectly. When he came to hug me, I touched the jacket, which was cashmere soft. "Hello, Sven," I said, but I could hear Jordy's voice inside my brain sneering *Dirtbag Slime Mold Rug Guy.*

"You look very lovely, my dear. Come, let's have some champagne, and tell me how you've been."

He took two glasses from a passing waiter, raised his, and said, "To the most radiant and accomplished attorney in all of New York."

"The city or the state?" asked a familiar voice.

Amber Tumbridge was standing nearby, and I don't think I'd ever seen an angrier smeer. Ellis stood behind her, looking away, as if he thought he was too good to associate with us.

Sven put his hands on Amber's toned golden shoulders. "I should have said, to *one* of the two most radiant and accomplished attorneys on planet Earth. How exquisite you look tonight, Amber."

She was perfection in a simple black sheath dress. Diamonds glittered on her ears, on her ring finger, and on a bracelet around her slim wrist. She saw me notice the bracelet and said, "My Valentine's Day gift from Ellis. Jennifer, that's *obviously* your favorite dress — you wear it everywhere."

Ellis glanced over and said impassively, "Morigi. Ms. Walters."

"Quintal," Sven said, chilly. "Amber, I do hope we'll all have the opportunity to talk later." He took my arm and guided me away.

"I have a gift for you, Jennifer, a belated Valentine's Day present, since I knew you wouldn't accept it earlier."

"You didn't have to, Sven." I followed him to the terrace. A kazillion lights twinkled and glowed, and I saw the Statue of Liberty beyond. It was so lovely it made me want to cry.

Sven reached into his pocket and took out a long black velvet box. "This is for you, my dear."

When I opened it, I saw a necklace made of linked gold medallions that were set with large topazes and rubies. "Sven, it's too much."

"Jennifer, you've given me back my dream, and that is priceless. Wear this for me tonight at least."

Holden always says that nothing is priceless, and his GLKH accountants could put a current value on Sven's dream, but I merely smiled and stood still while Dr. Stunning brushed my hair back and latched the necklace.

He stood back and gazed at me. "You are my ideal, Jennifer."

"Sven, I am as flawed as anyone. More than most."

"I doubt that, but I won't argue the point when we should be celebrating our victory and the beginning of this new stage of our relationship."

I found myself wondering if Rene would say, "Where's the passion?"

We returned to the hall and mingled, which is easy at business gatherings, because I can ask about people's jobs and smile while they go on in too much detail; my brain was free to hate hate hate Ellis and Amber and their perfect coupleness. I wondered if they sang duets. Probably.

Sven and I were seated at a front table with several prominent bioethicists. Sven was a featured speaker, and he told the audience, "I am going to resurrect ReplaceMax like Lazarus from the grave, and we will see a revolutionary new era of cloned organs." He angled his exquisite face for the news cameras, and his glacier blue eyes blazed like ice and fire. "No longer will we fear the assassination of a beloved leader, which could cause a nation's upheaval, or the loss of a child, which would cause a family's misery."

I looked down at the table. I got an ooky feeling from his use of "beloved leader" and mention of a child's death. I was being too sensitive.

Later, after Sven had finished his speech and was chatting with colleagues, I went outside to the terrace to be alone. I breathed in the cool air, which carried spring scents from planters of freesia and tulips.

"Jennifer."

I turned and saw Ellis.

"Hello, Ellis."

"I wanted to apologize." His brow furrowed and he let out an exasperated huff. "I keep saying the wrong things to you. I wish I knew the right things to say, but I feel as if I've said so much to you already."

"In your songs."

"Yes. That was then, and this is now. You're Amber's colleague and my father's favorite, so it's best if we try to get along."

"I'm your dad's favorite? Really!"

"My dad's favorite is always the one who's won the biggest case most recently," Ellis said.

He ran a hand through his thick dark brown hair. His beard was neatly trimmed, and I wished he was wearing a gold hoop through his ear and an eye patch.

"What?" he asked.

"Nothing. Yes, let's try again to get along."

"Except that I want to tell you that you were wrong."

I contemplated pushing him over the railing and into traffic, but because I'm a mature adult woman, I said, "Oh, for fuck's sake, Ellis, stop telling me I shouldn't have represented Sven in court! It's over. I kicked ass and I won."

His mouth tightened. "I meant you were wrong that I was trying to manipulate you the other night. I care for you more than I've ever cared for any woman." He came close to me and ran his fingers down my cheek. His voice was low and rough, and just the sound of it wrapped around me, tugging me toward him. "My gorgeous green-eyed flesh-eating bacteria girl."

"Well, isn't that too, too sweet?"

Ellis and I jumped away from each other and saw that both Sven and Amber had come out to the terrace, shutting the glass doors to the ballroom.

Amber looked at Sven and said, "How many times have I said that we don't need them in our lives?"

"Amber?" Ellis asked. "What are you talking about?"

"Shut up, Ellis." Amber looked at me. "Jennifer, what an annoying, stupid, clumsy giraffe you are. If I never see you again, it will be too soon."

She was a bitch and she was going to marry the man I loved and I hated hated hated her. "Amber, for the record, I am trained in several martial arts and could kill you with my bare hands, but I don't want to ruin my manicure." I tucked my clutch under my arm and walked to the double doors. I pulled at one. It remained shut. I pulled at the other.

"It's no use, Jennifer," Sven said. "They're locked. Don't try breaking them. The glass was replaced by an impenetrable soundproof polymer. You'll find your phones useless here, too."

"What the hell do you mean by this, Morigi?" Ellis said, grabbing Sven by the arm.

Sven threw him off as easily as throwing off a kitten. Ellis flew into the wall bounding the terrace and lay motionless where he fell. I saw the glint of silver — a pin — in Sven's hand, and I ran to Ellis. His eyes sought mine, but his body was immobile.

"You'll be okay." As I dragged Ellis into a safe corner, I slipped my hand into his inside jacket pocket and found the sheet of paper I knew would be there. I kept it hidden in my hand.

I turned to Sven, trying to see him again, *really* see him below the surface of Dirtbag Slime Mold Rug Guy. He was smiling coolly at me, because he knew that I knew he wasn't what his official bio said. No mere human was that strong.

"What did you do to him, Sven?"

"It's only an immobilizer. It lasts a few hours and I can give him a memory wipe," Sven said. "Then he and Amber can go on as if this never happened. She will handle legal logistics for my takeover of vital corporations, and the Quintal fortune will fund our start-up."

"That was *your* plan, Sven," she said. "I don't even want him. He's still mooning after this stupid slutty groupie, and I hate his beard, his stupid science school, and his stupid new band. Why should I get second best? Why should *you* get second best when you could have me? I was editor of the *Yale Law Review*!"

Shulky was awake inside me, and I was assessing the situation and wondering why this crap happened every single time I got dressed up for a party. I circled away from Sven, who gave Amber a scathing, super smeer, a smeer that made her own look like amateur hour at Camp Condescension.

"Amber, I'll forget that you insulted science education, because I'm feeling magnanimous today. However, compared to Jennifer Susan Walters, you are cheap gilt finish over pot metal. Do you want to know why I wanted her to be lead on my case? Because she is good and she *believes*. When she spoke about the dying girl, the jurors heard her authenticity. The only things authentic about you are your avarice and ambition."

"Cheap! We had a deal," she snarled. "You told me you wanted to be with me, that we would stay young and strong forever, that I would be beautiful forever."

"You're deluded, Amber," I said. "Haven't you learned anything from the ReplaceMax tragedy?"

"You stupid bitch," she shouted, her lovely voice cracking into a shriek. "Those organs were flawless! Sven took Max Kirsch's initial rapid skin-growing technique and used his facilities to perfect Project Mimic. We can clone anything, and the cloned organ will make the entire body healthier and stronger. But having incorruptible Max in control wouldn't do us any good, *obviously*. So after the organs passed inspection, Sven introduced a modification that set off a scheduled malfunction. Thanks to your legal skills, we now have complete control of ReplaceMax and Project Mimic."

I froze and looked at Sven's beautiful face, *impossibly* beautiful. "Victor von Doom!" I said to my nemesis, shocked that I hadn't known the man I'd fought so many times.

"I know you'll agree that there are advantages to alternate identities, my dear. Rearrange the letters in *Doctor Sven Morigi* and you get *Victor Doom reigns*! I dropped the von, which had seemed right at the time but now is a little much, don't you think? Like using punctuation for a name. Glad I never did that!" He came toward me. "I'm not Victor

Doom anymore. He was hideously mutilated. I'm Sven Morigi now. I will eliminate all other bioethical authorities, and I alone will decide who benefits from Project Mimic. The world's leaders will come begging to have a liver, or a kidney — most don't need hearts." He didn't bother to hide his true *bwaa-ha-ha* laugh.

I needed to keep him talking yadda-yadda-yadda while I thought of a plan. "How did you make this transformation? Why is your voice different? Why do people remember you as Sven?"

"My voice was an easy adjustment to my vocal cords, setting a pitch that is as intoxicating as my glorious visage. As for my history, I established a fabricated biography with a mesmerizing code."

That's what Jordy meant about Sven's bio being wonky. "You arranged your own kidnapping attempt at the Club Nice opening and invited me to witness it."

"It was an efficient method of establishing ReplaceMax as the villain, and I enjoyed the theatrical touch," he said. "Your sympathy always goes to the victims, Jennifer. If you hadn't been able to fight them off in either of your personas, I would have engineered an escape."

I glanced over at Ellis and saw confusion in his eyes. I was confused, too. "Sven or Doom, whatever, why did you bring me here tonight? What's the point of this whole charade?"

Amber fumed and said, "Sven, would you just kill her already?"

He gave her a scathing look. "Don't interrupt when I'm talking to my girlfriend."

Girlfriend!

He saw my stunned expression and said, "People believed that brilliant and beautiful Sven Morigi exists. I *am* brilliant and beautiful, and finally we can consummate the relationship that has been building between us for so very long. The world loves me now, just as you do."

"I don't love you." Did it count as having a boyfriend if a madman thought he was dating me?

"Not yet, but you will, Jennifer. We've already had marvelous evenings together, and it was so funny when you were wearing your blouse inside out and saying your neck was cold! We'll laugh about that in the coming years and develop a deep intellectual connection as well as a rewarding physical one. You know what they say — happy wife, happy life, so we will marry and have the most brilliant, beautiful, and inventive children in the galaxy. We will be the perfect family. I'd like to get a golden retriever; and we'll have stunning family photos from our ski vacations on our Christmas cards."

Amber grabbed his arm. "What about me?"

Sven gazed coldly at her hand. "Amber, I would sooner trust a rabid honey badger to raise my children than you. A mother should be loving, noble, and brave, as my own mother was, and as Jennifer is. Ugliness made me a monster. You have no justification."

She tried to claw his face, and he used another pin to immobilize her. She slumped to the ground, her blue eyes wide and manic.

It was time for Shulky to handle her nemesis, and I relaxed so she could come out. I felt her struggling — but nothing! I wasn't changing.

Sven smiled calmly and said, "Jennifer, we can leave here after the bomb clears the ballroom in exactly twenty minutes. The timing mechanism is on a loop. If you try to dismantle it, *boom!* I'd rather use a more creative weapon, but I can pass conventional weapons off as a terrorist attack. It will be quite a tragedy, and we will be at the center of media attention, allowing us to frame the narrative. Would you like to go over our talking points?"

I paced and flexed, trying to release Shulky, but she couldn't get out.

Sven said, "The necklace is made of an alloy that you can't break, and it blocks your morphing ability. As much as we care for each other, Jennifer, I think there may be a period of adjustment for She-Hulk to embrace our destiny together. You'll see that this is what you truly desire, what She-Hulk desires, to rule over inferiors without having to submit to the petty house rules set by the other holier-than-thou superhumans. I'd like at least four children. What about you?"

"I'll *never* love you and I'll *never* have your children!"

I heard a creepily familiar high-pitched giggle, and a voice said, "She better not, because I'm your favorite!" Superbrat's head appeared over the terrace railing, showing straight dark hair and mischievous dark eyes, disappeared, and then reappeared.

"Tonio!" Sven said. "What are you doing here?"

Superbrat bounced onto the terrace. He laughed and pointed to his feet. "It's my new invention — skyhopper shoes. I did what you said, put the bomb under the ice sculpture. What do you mean about her having children? I'm your favorite."

"You're my favorite genetically modified *clone*," Sven said. He looked at me. "I added a little Genghis Khan as well as the great military strategist Sun Tzu. I started alphabetically with A for Adam, B for Bertram, C for Curtis, etc. One has many failures before a success. I had to incinerate the others because of irreparable defects of personality or aptitude. Only Tonio showed my genius for invention as well as an extraordinary propensity for creative destruction. When he is matured, he will be one of my greatest creations."

If I couldn't call on Shulky to vanquish Sven, maybe another superhuman could defeat him. "Tonio," I said. "The man you think of as your father will replace you just like he replaced his other clones from A to S. He's an obsessive perfectionist, and when he finds fault with you, as he soon will, he'll develop other clones, U for Ulysses and Z for Zeus and he'll make them more powerful and dangerous than you."

"Don't listen to her," Sven said. "Trust me."

I spoke to Superbrat with the same sincerity that I used each time I gave a consultation. "Tonio, I always advise my clients to investigate an associate's reputation before entering into a contract. Someone who has a record of mendaciousness and broken agreements is also lying when he says that he is trustworthy."

Tonio's eyebrows knit together, and I added, "I am on record as believing in and supporting the rights and liberties of all human variants, including bots, droids, borgs, and clones. Ask Sven how he implanted chips in his Doombots so they won't challenge him. He doesn't believe that cyborgs or clones are entitled to the same basic rights as humans. He doesn't believe you're a person, and he'll never treat you as his equal."

Superbrat looked from me to Sven and back again as the seconds ticked by. Finally he said, "That makes sense. Thanks for telling me, ma'am." Superbrat reached into his pocket and pulled out a weapon.

I tried not to fixate on the "ma'am," which no one else seems to find outrageous.

Sven said, "Tonio, what is that?"

Superbrat waved the device (which I would have to add to his M.O. in my report: "excessive waving of destructive devices"). "It's my new Discombobulator. It discombobulates molecules and arranges them in another place and time. I've got it set to 'Random.' First, let's get rid of your talky girlfriend, because I don't need any siblings."

He pointed the Discombobulator at me, but I flung out my arm saying, "Look!" as I threw the flash paper to the side. It ignited in flames, catching Superbrat's attention long enough for Sven to lunge at the Discombobulator, and for me to do a tuck and roll to the other side of the terrace.

Sven gripped the device and squeezed but not before his clone had pulled the trigger. I watched in fascinated horror as a wavy kaleidoscopic cloud encompassed them and then — poof! — they vanished.

I tried my aPhone, but it was still blocked. Twelve minutes had passed. I needed Shulky to break into the ballroom, evacuate the guests, and take the bomb to a place where it could be detonated safely. I strained again at the necklace and felt it dig into my skin. I stepped over Amber, ran to the doors, and pounded on them, but no one in the room beyond the vestibule could hear me.

I needed to use both fists, so I dropped my clutch — it opened on impact, and Superbrat's Swiss Army knife tumbled out. Why would a mad inventor take apart a knife and put it back together?

I flicked open the attachments until I came to the tiny scissors. "Please work. Please don't kill me." I slid one little blade under a link of my necklace and then I pressed the little handles together. I heard a *bzzzzz*, and the metal around my neck vibrated and grew so hot that I felt blisters rise on my skin. And then there was a snap and a clink as the link snapped, and the necklace fell onto the tiles below.

I went to Ellis and said, "I have to get rid of the bomb. I'll send help, but you're safest here. I love you, Ellis Tesla. I've always loved you and I'm sorry that I didn't believe your songs."

His brown eyes met mine with such emotion that I wanted to hold him and stay with him until the immobilizer wore off. But now I had to put on my BeDazzled super big girl thong and save hundreds. I tore off my crimson dress, kicked off my shoes, and called on Shulky.

I morphed so fast that my muscles burned, and then she was here, as big and bold and badass as she wanted to be.

Shulky stuck her foot in Amber's face, wiggled her toes, and said, "Smell you later, bi-atch!"

And then she winked at Ellis, shouted "Kapow!" and gave a round-house kick to the terrace doors. They resisted, but she kicked again. The panes were impenetrable, but the metal frames groaned as they warped and bent.

The doors collapsed inward and fell with a solid thud.

The crowd of scientists noticed the spectacular giantess running toward them. "She-Hulk!"

"Hiya, Poindexters," she called as she ran to the cart with the ice sculpture. She knocked over the sculpture and ripped off the linen cloth covering the cart. A bomb rested in a box beneath, ticking away. She had six minutes left.

She picked up the box and ran out of the room. The elevator would take too long, so she went to the stairs, leaping down them one flight at a time. Every time she landed, the floor shuddered. She ran out and down the block to the nearest secret passage door.

The elevator was there, and she hit the express button, sending the elevator plummeting down into the ancient subway tunnels. She ran out of the elevator and onto the Solomobile, then switched on the turbo drive, and the train hurtled forward. If the bomb went off early, she'd destroy the entire network of tunnels, shutting down the city's critical transportation system.

"Come on! Come on!" she shouted, and then the train slammed to a stop at our home station. She had twenty seconds left as she ran off the train. She input the code on the security post, pressed her palm against the I.D. scanner, and said, "Hurry, hurry!" with seven seconds left.

The waterfall parted, and the wall section slid open. She admired the luxurious living space one last time and sighed. She tossed the bomb inside and pressed her hand to the biopanel again. The wall section closed and the waterfall merged again, with one second remaining.

Then the ground beneath her feet shook as if there had been a minor tremor, the sort that people in LA barely pause to acknowledge before continuing their conversations.

The movement was so slight that Shulky wondered if the charge had been smaller than she'd assumed. After all, Dr. Doom's expertise was with weapons of mass destruction, not minor explosives. She did several jumping jacks and then a hundred one-handed push-ups to give things time to cool down before she opened the door to her lair.

Black smoke billowed out. Everything was burned and soaked, as overhead sprinklers showered the debris.

Shulky ambled along the tracks, went to street level, and walked somberly to the Mansion. Ruth was on the phone, and Shulky sat down in the wonderful massage chair. She took a box of tissues from a table and swiped at sooty smears on her fabulous legs.

Ruth hung up and said, "Shulky! I just heard about the Bioethicists Gala."

"Hi, Ruth. There's good news and there's bad news. The good news is that I saved the world from being taken over by Victor von Doom."

"OMG, that's amazing! And the bad news?"

"I kind of blew up Hawkeye's apartment. Sorry."

"It's okay. We all sort of expected it."

"You're a good sport, Ruth. I'm going to explain everything to you, and I'd like you to fill out the reports for me, because I'm tired of paperwork.

We've got a lot to do tonight, and then I'd like a plane to take me to LA. I think I'll stay in my family's old cabin and recoup."

"You mean Jennifer's family's cabin."

"Yes, our family's cabin. I'm her and she's me, and we may as well stop treating one another like annoying roommates. I'd like to soak up the sun and shoot cans off fence posts and not listen to any more goddamn opera."

MUTUAL ASSENT

MAY 20

Officially, I'm on a leave of absence from QUIRC. The partners are still dealing with the repercussions of winning a case on behalf of one of the world's greatest villains. I think they'd like to fire me, but they're aware that they solicited Sven's case and allowed him to insist on hiring me. If I was a litigious person, I could sue them for all sorts of things.

I've been filling my days clearing the scrub brush around the cabin and hiking to a murky shallow pond and splashing around in the cool water. I occasionally open this journal at random and read it — it was spared from destruction because I'd hidden it under a pile of weights in case Dahlia came by and snooped. I spend hours in the fields with my Winchester practicing trick shots, and I sing Fringe Theory songs and contemplate the lyrics from my new perspective. I should have trusted that Ellis's songs were for me. I should have gone to another concert or called him again.

I'm sooo relieved that I didn't actually have sex with Sven, eww. If I'm being fiercely honest, I ~~might probably would~~ definitely would have had sex with him if I hadn't seen Ellis first — because once I saw Ellis, I didn't want anyone else. Ruth tells me that no one knows where the

316 · MARTA ACOSTA

Discombobulator relocated Doom and Superbrat. In the chaos of the gala, everyone assumed that Amber was a victim. Once the immobility injection wore off, she slipped away and no one has seen her since.

When a team from the Mansion raided the lavish home where I'd had dinner with the man I thought was Sven Morigi, all they found were empty rooms. He must have rigged the contents to vanish or teleport elsewhere.

Victor Doom will show up again, with or without the *von*, because he always does. An alert has been sent out for any other Doom clones who may have survived destruction in the incinerator.

Adam took the news that he's a clone with equanimity. He said, "But I'm not an alien clone, am I?"

I told him that no, Victor von Doom was originally a regular human. The other superheroes are mentoring Adam, but warily, because there's the chance that he may eventually exhibit VvD's madness. Dahlia doesn't believe he will. She believes in his essential goodness. Before I left New York, I sat her down in a salon chair, twirled it around to face me. She wasn't wearing colored contacts and it seemed strange, yet comforting to look into her chocolate brown eyes. Then I told her the truth about Adam.

"He's a Victor von Doom designer clone, D, conceived in a laboratory and grown at rapid speed. He didn't have a childhood or teenage years. He never had a mother's love or skinned his knee skateboarding. He didn't share secrets with his best buddy, and he didn't get a crush on the girl next door. The personality you see has developed in virtual isolation, and we have no idea what he'll be like after more human interaction. As a clone, he has no rights — including the right to marry, parental rights, or property rights. In fact, under current law, Adam is Dr. Doom's personal property to do with as he pleases, including using him for spare organs or terminating him."

"He's a real person!" Dahlia held Rodney a little closer, but she didn't freak out. "I *knew* he was special, and he is, but I'm glad he's not alien, because I didn't want Interplanetary Immigration grabbing him and throwing him off Earth."

"D, it's possible that Doom's *real* time bomb was not the explosive he left at the gala."

"Are you saying . . ." she began.

"Yes, Adam could be a time bomb. Doom could have programmed him to turn evil after we've all taken him in and trusted him with our secrets. The rest of the world might be relaxing, but the superheroes know never to underestimate VvD."

"I *know* that Adam's good. I feel it to the very core of my being."

"Believing something about someone — we all make mistakes in judgment. I think Adam's good now, but he may not stay good, D."

"Jen, you weren't brave enough to follow your heart. I am."

"This isn't about Ellis!"

She took Rodney's leg and raised it toward me. "Talk to the paw!"

I am not one of the galaxy's top attorneys for nothing, though, and eventually I convinced her that Adam could have been programmed to transform into an international menace. She promised to tell me if she saw any warning signs.

I made public and private apologies to Max Kirsch. He was swell about everything and said, "Your intentions were good. I was trying to heal patients, and you were trying to protect them from harm." Quinty and the other partners held a press conference where they ripped up the settlement papers and paid Max for damages to him and ReplaceMax.

There was some great news: the liquid in Adam's vacuum canister was the last sample of Dr. Doom's Project Mimic solution. Max, back in charge of ReplaceMax, was able to use that tiny amount to grow bioidentical skin grafts for all the victims of the sabotaged products. People forget that skin is our largest organ, and the grafted skin taught all the other organs to repair themselves. A week after the grafts, the patients were completely healthy. Mavis came out of her coma and was discharged from the hospice.

Genoa is working pro bono to get charges reduced against Burt Symonds based on temporary insanity. His wife, Bonnie, visits him every day at the detention center.

I asked Max to grow a graft for someone who hadn't been in the Re-placeMax program: Jordy. Because his cancer was so invasive, his recovery is taking a little longer, but he called to tell me that he'll be well enough to attend a late-summer session at Manic Quantum Mechanics, and he'll be going to high school in the fall.

Mavis calls me every day and tells me all the things she's been doing. "Jenny, we have sticks and we're playing sword fights! When will you be back?"

"I don't know, sweetie, but when I come to New York, I'll be sure to visit you. I'll take you to the park and we'll play."

Someone whose name rhymes with Macaroni Bark left a message for me:

"Jen, you did a terrific job saving planet Earth from the evil machinations of Doom. Too bad about Hawkeye's underground lair. It was a great place for our pop-up sushi restaurant.

"The next time Shulky's in town, have her set up a lunch meeting with me. Would enjoy seeing that sexy sassy bitch and talking about ways she can work with our team again. I'd be happy to have a naked wresting match in oil with her to negotiate details.

"Also, please tell Claudette that I think Hasselhoff Stark is an *awesome* name for our kid."

Rene and I have long phone conversations as I try to sort out my thoughts. I told him that I could have cleared everything up with Ellis years ago when I heard the songs.

He told me, "But then your entire life's path would be different. Ellis, too, could have listened more closely and not confused Jen with Gin and USC with UCLA, *go Bruins!* If you had been with Ellis, you wouldn't have been in the situation where you were infected with gamma radiation. If you were less shy, you wouldn't have manifested as She-Hulk. The world needs all manifestations of you. It was meant to be."

"I thought psychiatrists believed in self-determination, not fate."

I could hear his hippie beads clinking against the phone. "We have some discretion. We Alvarados like to think there's a greater force of good at work in all universes."

"And passion."

"Yes, we believe in passion. You'll have to deal with Ellis sometime, Jen. You love him."

"I nearly got him killed. I destroyed his friend's reputation and life's work. I made his father's firm a tool of Doom's world domination scheme. I accused him of trying to tamper with the trial. I callously ignored a dozen love songs over the years."

"Callously? I thought you cried yourself to sleep with a picture of him on your pillow and wrote his name with little hearts over the i's."

"Are you getting snarky on me, Rene?"

"We have some discretion about that, too," he said, and chuckled. "We'll discuss these things in our next session. Keep writing in your journal and try to see recent incidents in the larger perspective of your life."

"The pages in my journal are almost filled up. I guess I'll have to buy another KEEP HANGING IN THERE! kitten notebook." I sighed. "I keep hanging on."

He didn't answer right away, and I listened to the calming *click-click* of him fiddling with his beads. Finally he said, "Jen, has it occurred to you that you're taking the wrong message from the kitten? You told me that Ruth said she admired fluffy kittens for a reason."

I thought back to the beginning of the year. "She said that kittens have an internal gyroscope so that when they fall, they can twist into the right position to land on their feet."

"Why is the kitten hanging on?" he said.

"Because it's terrified of being hurt. It's hoping that someone will come and rescue it."

"Do you need rescuing, Jen?"

I thought about the wide eyes of the panicked kitten. "No, I always land on my feet."

"Then stop being afraid," he said. "Let go."

MAY 27

I've been trying to make bread, which really shouldn't be that much harder than winning cases on other planets, but it is. I'd thrown out yet another inedible loaf when I got a call from Dahlia.

"Watcha doing, poodle?"

"Baking nummy homemade bread, except for the nummy part. More like mummy bread that should be put into a tomb and forgotten for a thousand years."

"Are we back to talking about ancient pharaohs again, or are you going to audition for a reality show as a sister-wife? They have awful hairstyles. I've finished decorating your Medieval tunic, and Nelson and Amy have made your weaponry."

"I have no idea what you're talking about."

"Jen, our relationship has been one of support and mutual admiration. You admire my fabulous style, and I support your right to be you, which means that I endured your unreasonable hatred of Rodney and your obsessive ranting about Tony Stark."

"You liked to gossip about Tony, and hating Rodney is reasonable!"

"Adam doesn't think so. He thinks Rodney is delightful, and Rodney is now the alpha dog in his pack. My point is, you've had your sabbatical, and now it's time to return to civilization before you bleach your hair blond and start auditioning for detergent commercials as 'Young Suburban Mom.' The Forestiers are expecting you to show up and fight battles for their team."

"A, since when do you care about my LARP team, and, B, I don't feel like it."

"One, if you come back, I'll treat you to Filipino nacho fries. I hear on good authority that they are the most genius food in the galaxy. Two, I wasn't asking you to come back; I was telling you. And three, you have moped after Ellis Tesla for years too long. If you don't want me to call you Sulky, stop acting like a lovesick teenager. Come home."

MAY 28

I stayed at Dahlia's condo the night before the Mayfest weekend. I tried on the costume she'd made and said, "It's too bad my sewing machine got destroyed in the explosion. I was going to learn to sew."

"Please, Jen, kindly stop talking shit about homemaking skills. You're a superhero and a top-level attorney. Focus on that."

I stood in front of the mirror wearing my forest-green tunic, tights, leather and velvet slippers, breastplate, and cape.

D adjusted my gold-braid headband and said, "I've got something for you." She went to a drawer and pulled out something wrapped in tissue. "Close your eyes and sit down."

I did what I was told because she was in a bossy mood. She brushed my hair, lifted it, and pinned and arranged it for several minutes.

"Okay, look in the mirror," she said.

She'd added long pieces to my hair, so that glossy waves flowed below my waist.

"Oh, D! It's so pretty."

"You're so pretty."

I took off my glasses. "Ladies didn't wear glasses in the Middle Ages. Should I try my contacts again?"

"You're not the only one who gives advice to clients, Jen. I always tell mine, 'Find a signature look and stick with it.'"

MAY 29

Amy and Nelson gave me a lift to the Mayfest battle games outside Woodstock. They sat in the front of the car and kept holding hands and smiling at each other. I was glad things had worked out for them. If I hadn't been trying to follow one Valentine's Day Resolution — find a boyfriend — I wouldn't have met Nelson and made a new friend. So things worked out for me, too.

A series of narrow lanes and turns led us to a sprawling farm property with a red-and-blue satin banner reading, WELCOME, MAYFEST CELE-BRANTS! We all signed in at the registration table, and then Nelson and Amy went off giggling to the B&B where they were staying.

I asked, "Is anyone else from my team here?"

The man in a gray roughcloth-and-leather yeoman's costume said, "A new member of your folk is working on the castle battlements." He pointed on the map. "You're in the Marigold Coop, which is here." He indicated squares on the map.

"I'm in a co-op? But I reserved a private space."

He smiled. "Not co-op. Coop. The cottages are renovated chicken coops, but they're very comfortable and pretty, so the maids say."

I followed the map and found a small white structure with a porch. The walls inside were painted yellow, and the bed had a white coverlet. The only other furniture was a table with two wooden chairs. If I hulked out here, the whole place would come down.

I changed into my costume and walked through the verdant fields. I could hear birds singing and the rush of a creek nearby. Ahead was a stand of trees, and as I walked toward it, I saw a team in black-and-red costumes practicing a jousting scenario. A little farther along, I ran across teenagers dressed as minstrels who were swinging across a gully on a rope.

When one fell into the muddy water, his team laughed in a good-natured way, and I applauded his awesome emoting. Everyone looked magical and wonderful.

"Fair lady, where art thee headed?" asked a woman dressed as a farm-er's wife.

"I am to Lyncolnewoode to meet with my good fellows."

"Oh, they hath a most valiant knight, who now prepares the castle against the king's forces, which will arrive tomorrow. You will find him yonder, past the largest oak. God keep us in these perilous times."

"I thank you, kind mistress. Fare thee well."

I slowed down as I walked through the shrubberies, wishing that I had some carpentry skills so I could help. For my next Valentine's Day

Resolutions, I would add practical skills, and by the year's end I would be able to fix a sink, make a pot roast, and build a coffee table.

A tall man with broad shoulders was reinforcing a balcony column with a wooden brace. His dark hair was long and curled at his nape. He wore a silver tunic on which was a gray hawk against a black background, and his tights and shirt were green — the green of the forest, the green of She-Hulk, the green of those who risked their lives to defend the powerless.

He looked really hunky and brawny, really capable even from behind. Speaking of which, what a fantastic behind!

"Sir Knight!" I called.

He turned around and we both froze as our eyes met.

"Lady Greene," he said, and we each took a step closer.

"Yes, I am she," I said, though I could barely speak, or believe that I was meeting him here. I did a small curtsy.

His dark beard made his smile rakish and seductive, and his longer hair made him look wild and woodsy. "Do not be so formal, good lady, for you know how I feel. Verily, I have proclaimed my love for you so many times." He took another step toward me. "I have proclaimed my love in every way you have come to me — when you are Gin or Jen, or Jenny, or She-Hulk."

He reached and took my hand in his. He kissed it. "You must have a sorceress's blood, my lady, because you always bewitched and bewildered me. I did not comprehend how my love could be so diffuse. It was as if I was trapped in a hall of mirrors. Each aspect of you captured my heart, and I was misled into thinking that I loved many women, when it was always you."

"Good dear Sir Knight, I thought 'twas you who had magics, for I loved you first as cataclysmic Ellis Tesla, then as amiable, affectionate Big E, and as angsty, smoldering Ellis. Do you still have feelings for me?"

"Indeed, my lady, and I have always carried your favor," he said, reaching into his tunic and pulling out a scrap of lace-edged pink silk.

My stolen panties!

I blushed over my entire body. "Oh! Ellis, do we have to keep talking like this?"

"Let's not talk. Let your body tell me how you feel." He returned the panties to his pocket and took me in his strong arms, and he smelled the way I remembered. Then his mouth came to mine, and his lips were as eager as I remembered. And our lips parted, and his mouth tasted the way I remembered.

And the rest of the world fell away.

MAY 31

Ellis had rented a house nearby, which was good because Shulky — I mean *I* could cause a ruckus when I was in my superhuman form. I am proud to say that I banged that big man harder than a porch door.

Dahlia had plotted everything with Nelson and Amy. D was an excellent plotter, and she and Adam showed up after Saturday's skirmishes, when there was a bonfire and entertainments. On Sunday, while in the heat of battle with the king's forces, Ellis and I clambered up the ladder to the castle parapets. We cried havoc and fought side by side.

We decided to stay another day. After all, he was his own boss and I didn't have a job.

We were walking out in the night, looking at the starry sky, and he said, "What do you want me to call you?"

"Call me whatever you like."

"You're still Gin in my heart."

"Then call me that."

"Good, because it rhymes well and I plan to write more songs," he said. "Amber hated the band. I need to tell you some things."

"That's probably a good idea. First, of all the women in the world, why Amber Tumbridge?"

"Did you hear about the incident with the pumpkins and the tank in Oslo? Well, my father had to use diplomatic connections to keep us out of jail. One of the conditions was that we would break up the band, agree to effectively disappear, and become productive members of society. I didn't think I'd ever see you again, and no other woman made me feel the way you did, and I decided to accept that I'd lost my one chance. So when Amber pounced on me, I considered myself lucky enough. She was pretty, smart, and really nice at first. She kept mentioning how happy my father would be if his company stayed in the family. Her voice was so beautiful that I thought I could listen to it forever. All I heard was the sound of it, not her selfishness, coldness."

"Her voice is beautiful," I said. "Amber Hammerhead."

"That's a good rhyme. She had our life planned out — the houses, vacations, clubs, careers, all of it. She wanted me to franchise Manic Quantum Mechanics and change the curriculum to something that wouldn't get us sued every time a cannonball accidentally crashed through an abandoned grain silo," he said, brushing my hair back. "But I don't want to live carefully, and I don't want a showplace instead of a home. I want a comfortable house where you don't have to worry if you knock something over with a football. I like couches that are long enough to stretch out on, and I have old LPs and instruments everywhere. My original artwork is by my brother's children. Amber wanted me to buy art as an investment."

"Ellis, you seem to have the delusion that women only want to marry you for your money."

"You dated Tony Stark, so I thought you might have expectations."

"One, I dated Tony because he can be really funny and because I loved to watch him invent things. I didn't have to hide who I was with him; in fact he often urged me to come out as a superhuman. We were always working together, and it seemed like a natural component of that relationship." I realized that I'd often tried colleagues with benefits before. Maybe the fact that I hadn't gone for Fritz's offer was a sign of my maturity. "Also, Tony loves fast cars."

"*I* have a fast car."

I grinned. "I know, and we'll be taking that baby out for a spin . . . and more . . . later. Back to the subject. Two, I'm more comfortable in jeans than designer gowns. Three, when I have a job, I'm an extremely highly paid attorney. Four, I own a collection of swords and weaponry so priceless that even GLKH accountants couldn't put a value on it."

I pulled him close and shifted. His hands gripped my growing form as my summer dress shredded to reveal my spectacular green body. "And, five, you are my most precious possession, Ellis Tesla."

Later, when he was naked, sweaty, and gasping on the ground, I changed back and nestled in his arms. When his breathing normalized, I said, "Ellis, tomorrow we've got to go back to the city. What's next?"

He wove his fingers in mine. "Because my wedding was canceled on short notice, I wasn't able to get the refund for the wedding hall. I have the hall and the caterer . . ."

"I love you, but I'm not going to marry you so soon!"

"And I've loved you since I saw you dancing by the stage, but my proposal will be more romantic," he said. "I thought we could use the hall for a banquet and games event. We can have sword fights and an archery contest. Jordy and I have been drawing up designs for a trebuchet that launches casaba melons with a high degree of accuracy. I think it's time for a reunion of Fringe Theory. We can mix up a batch of Rocket Fuel."

"That sounds genius. Genoa and Donner would love it, and Mavis could come for the day events. I'll invite Ruth from the Mansion, and my friend Rene and his wife love your band — how big is the hall?"

"It holds four hundred. Less with jousting, flying melons, and a mosh pit. Let's say one hundred and fifty comfortably, and I'll invite some of the kids who've gone through my school," he said, "After that, well, I'd scheduled two weeks off for a honeymoon."

Jealousy blazed through me. "You want me to go on *Amber's* honeymoon?"

He smiled. "*I* didn't even want to go on Amber Hammerhead's honeymoon. She had us booked at a resort in Latveria, and now I know it was because of Dirtbag Slime Mold Rug Guy."

"So what are you thinking?"

"I'm thinking that you never came with me to Paris when I asked. Gin, will you go with me to Paris?"

"It depends. Say something dirty to me in French and I'll take it under advisement."

JUNE 14

It has been six months since I began my Valentine's Day Resolutions. As the General said, real change requires continual effort. Here is my status report:

- COMPLETE! Got a job as my human self at one of my top dream law firms.
- COMPLETE! Develop friendships and participate in normal activities. Genoa and I are great pals and we are currently drawing up a proposal for Tender Discoveries Legal Historical Theme Park. Fritz, Amy, and Nelson are excited to help with our project. Medieval barbers and pirates!
- REJECTED: Avoid shifting unless urgently required. I pay the dues of being a superhuman, so I'm going to enjoy the perks.
- COMPLETE! Find a boyfriend. He's sexy, employed, makes me laugh, and I love love love him because he's OMG! amazing!
- IN PROGRESS! Seek balance in work environment, i.e., have fun and learn how to speak up for myself. I'm confident I'll get there.
- IN PROGRESS! Find another apartment. Sadly, my record as a tenant has not improved. When Ellis learned how many places I'd destroyed, he suggested that I keep a separate place when I need to get my ya-yas out as She-Hulk, but stay with him when I'm Jen and Gin and Jennifer. When I went to the subterranean lair to shovel out the debris, I discovered that the guest bedroom suite had survived because paranoid Hawkeye had built it as a bomb shelter within a bomb shelter. It's not ideal, but I'd already been prepared to compromise for a living space. I brought in a mini-fridge and a microwave. I couldn't ask for better access to the

tunnels and secret passageways, giving me an easy escape
whenever I need to get to a party or rescue the world.

Next week, Ellis and I are hosting our first big weekend party, with the
reunion of the Fringe Theory. He's writing new songs. There will be jousting, sword fights, and, yes, catapults and trebuchets launching various types
of melons and squash. Food trucks will provide snacks around the clock.
Bruce accepted my invitation when he learned that things will explode, *ka-
bam!* Then we're going on to Paris, a goal that I was planning to put on
next year's Valentine's Day Resolution list, so I'm already ahead!

Karl will be hosting a party for Shulky at his château and doing a
photo shoot with her. With me. With us. Rene says I need serious work on
my bifurcated personality, but I'm in no hurry. There are some things you
can't put a timeline on.

QUIRC has decided that they want me back, but Holden is trying to
lure me away to head his new division of Alternative Life Form Law, which
will represent clones, cyborgs, androids, and robots. It's extremely tempting, but as I tell my clients, "Consider all your options rather than rushing
to make an important decision." Because life offers more possibilities than
you can imagine.

Marta Acosta is the author of the comic Casa Dracula series, *Nancy's Theory of Style*, and *Dark Companion*, a young adult gothic. She has a degree in creative writing and English and American literature from Stanford University and was a frequent contributor to the *San Francisco Chronicle* and the *Contra Costa Times*. She lives in the San Francisco Bay area with her family and rescued dogs.

www.martaacosta.com

THIS SUMMER, TWO CLASSIC MARVEL HEROINES COME TO LIFE IN AN ALL NEW FORM

In Marta Acosta's *The She-Hulk Diaries*, readers will meet Jennifer Walters. She thinks like Bridget Jones, but fights like, well, The Hulk, or in this case The She-Hulk, the Marvel heroine who's thrilled fans for decades and shares her cousin Bruce Banner's ability to morph into an all-powerful, crime-fighting creature.

"AN ABSOLUTE DELIGHT. Those who are unfamiliar with Bruce Banner's wayward cousin are in for a treat... Whether you like She-Hulk straight up, comedic, or a combination of both, *The She-Hulk Diaries* is the She-Hulk endeavor for you."

— Peter David, long-time writer of *The Incredible Hulk, She-Hulk,* and *X-Factor* and author of *Pulling Up Stakes*

With Christine Woodward's *Rogue Touch*, Anna Marie, later known as Rogue is seen through the lens of a young twenty year old, just coming to grips with her devastating powers, and just coming to grips with her first love.

"A lost chapter from Rogue's past, told with elegance and conviction and attention to detail. **REALLY ENTERTAINING."**

— Mike Carey, author of the Felix Castor novels and writer of *X-Men: Legacy*

HYPERION

TWO GREAT HEROINES. TWO NEW FULL-LENGTH NOVELS.

NOW AVAILABLE AS TRADE PAPERBACKS OR HYPERION EBOOKS WHEREVER BOOKS ARE SOLD